Also By Dorothy Clarke Wilson

Hilary: The Brave World of Hilary Pole

Jezebel, Wicked Woman of the Bible (formerly: Jezebel)

Lady Washington

Lone Woman Doctor (formerly: Lone Woman: The Story of Elizabeth Blackwell, The First Woman Doctor)

Moses, The Prince of Egypt (formerly: Prince of Egypt)

Palace of Healing (formerly: Palace of Healing: The Story of Dr. Clara Swain, The First Woman Missionary Doctor)

Queen Dolley (formerly: Queen Dolley: The Life and Times of Dolley Madison)

The Brothers: James and Jesus (formerly: The Brother)

Wheel Chair Doctor (formerly: Take My Hands: The Remarkable Story of Dr. Mary Verghese)

Woman of Mercy (formerly: Stranger and Traveler: The Story of Dorothea Dix, American Reformer)

The Awakening of Jesus

Dorothy Clarke Wilson

This book is a publication of StoryWorkz, L.P.
http://www.StoryWorkz.com
Email: publisher@StoryWorkz.com

Dorothy Clarke Wilson's Website
http://www.DorothyClarkeWilson.com

UNITED STATES OF AMERICA

First StoryWorkz, L.P. Edition 2012
Copyright 1957, 1985 by Dorothy Clarke Wilson as the *Gifts*

Library of Congress Cataloging - in - Publication Data is available
ISBN: 978-1-938659-08-9

In order to be as true as possible to the
historical background of The Awakening of Jesus,
the author has chosen to use the Hebrew names
Jeshua, Miriam, Jacob, and *Johanan*
in place of their more familiar forms—
Jesus, Mary, James, and *John*—which have
come down to us through the Greek New Testament

GOLD

ALTHOUGH the Boy had seen the objects at least a half dozen times before, on the morning of each birthday since early childhood, his eyes were as bright with wonderment as a clear night with stars.

"Tell me again, Mother, please!" he begged. "What were the three strangers like?"

Two tiny lines threaded the woman's smooth forehead as she tried to remember. "They were—like kings, I think," she said slowly, "though I have never seen a king. Their robes were of the fine stuffs that traders from Damascus carry in their saddlebags, and the trappings of their camels shone in the sun like Mount Hermon when the dawn first touches it."

"Not their clothes, Mother! What were *they* like?"

The woman considered. Her eyes were large and luminous and, like her son's, the color of warm earth drenched with sunlight. "One of them," she remembered, "was tall and young and eager. He was the first one down from his camel, the first to offer his gift. His eyes were golden, as if he had been looking at a sunset."

Thoughtfully the Boy lifted the small leather bag, reached inside, and let some of the yellow coins slip through his fingers. "Gold," he murmured, "like the gift he brought. Go on, Mother."

"The second, the one who brought the frankincense—" She paused. "I can't remember how he looked, but after the other's sunlight he seemed like a quiet shadow. He stood waiting a long time, looking at us, and then he moved very slowly. There was light in his face, too, but it came from inside—deep—like a flame burning in a still place."

The Boy slipped curious fingers around the slender vessel of finely wrought silver and, raising its cover, sniffed vainly at its sealed contents.

"What would it smell like," he wondered aloud, "if we should burn it?"

"Like the temple incense, I suppose," she replied. "But you've never smelled that, have you? Well, perhaps a little like the fragrance of balsam when the wind comes from the south."

Reluctantly the Boy relinquished the vessel, turned to the remaining object. "And the other," he prompted, "who brought the little wooden box?"

"The myrrh" Her hand hovered for a moment over the sandalwood surface and the outspread wings of the dove carved on its lid. "He was very old," she continued thoughtfully. "It took him a long time to get down from his camel, but he seemed in no hurry. It was as if he had lived so long that time did not matter. His hair was the color of goat's milk, and his face wrinkled as the wilderness lands about the Sea of Death. But his eyes were two pools, deep and untroubled."

The Boy was silent for a time, his finger tracing the outlines of the blunt beak, the graceful wings. Then, "Mother?"

"Yes, my son?"

"Why should men like that have brought gifts to *me*?"

The woman's eyes darkened. "Why, indeed?"

"Are you sure they didn't make a mistake—didn't mean them for somebody else?"

"*They* were sure." She looked away, remembering. "They were looking for a—a king, they said, him that was to be born king of the Jews."

The Boy laughed merrily. "They must have made a mistake. I'm only a carpenter's son!"

"David," returned the woman softly, a little breathlessly, "was only a shepherd."

The Boy laughed again. "You're just like all the other boys' mothers," he teased. "They all think their sons are going to be Davids."

"Do they?"

"Anyway," he continued practically, "I wouldn't have time to be a king, even if I could. I'm going to be too busy."

With sudden eagerness the woman leaned forward, gripping his slender shoulders with both hands. "Doing what, my son?"

He stirred uneasily, as if frightened by her intensity. "I don't know," he evaded, "it just seems as if there must be something, not just carpentering." His gaze cleared the stone wall of the courtyard, climbed swiftly to the tip of a slender cypress, focused on the blue sky and racing clouds beyond it. "I—I've felt it up on the Hilltop sometimes. Or in a big crowd on a feast day. I—I can't explain it. It's as if—as if a Voice—"

"Yes?" The woman barely whispered the word.

Slipping out of her grasp, he turned toward the objects lying on the bench. "Let's put them away, Mother, shall we?"

Her breath caught in a little sigh of disappointment. Then she smiled. "Yes, dear. Here are the linen cloths. Wrap them carefully, won't you? Then put them back in the corner of the big chest, deep down under the summer garments—you know, where you always find them."

He did as he was bidden, wrapping each object separately—the small leather bag, the silver vessel of incense, the little sandalwood box—then winding another length of cloth about all three. Suddenly he stopped.

"Are they really mine," he asked soberly, "to do with just as I please?"

"Why—" The woman's first startled uncertainty changed to sudden purpose. Now was a good time, as good as any, to tell him. Then her eyes flew to the street entrance of the courtyard. A stocky, broad-shouldered man was just stooping to enter, the turban which crowned his curling gray locks barely missing the low wooden door frame. In spite of her preoccupation she smiled with tender indulgence. Poor Joseph, it was so hard for him to bend his proud neck, even to pass through a doorway—especially this early in the morning after his visit to the synagogue! Sometime, with his eyes closed like that and the tips of his blunt fingers, fresh from the *mezuzah*, laid to reverent lips, he would surely bump his head.

Swiftly she scanned the deeply lined features, still aglow with stern ecstasy, and the purpose faded from her eyes. No, this was not the time to tell the Boy their plans for his future. This was his birthday, his twelfth, his last before she would lose him forever to the world of manhood. Let it be untroubled by any hint of change—above all, by the slightest ripple of disagreement!

She turned quickly, smiling into the Boy's solemn eyes. "Why, yes, dear," she said hastily. "Of course."

2

BECAUSE IT WAS his birthday, he did not wait when school was over to help his teacher, Rabbi Ben Arza, wrap the leather scrolls in their thick linen cloths and replace them in the little niche behind the heavily embroidered curtain.

He was out of the building almost as quickly as the scampering six-year-olds, exulting in the fresh warmth of sunlight after winter rain, gazing eagerly up the terraced housetops toward the crest of the hill far above.

But the children surrounded him before he had gone a dozen steps.

"Play with us, Jeshua!"

"Let's play sheep, and you be our shepherd!"

"I'd rather have a story…"

"Yes, a story!"

"Not today." He laughed good-naturedly, hiding his impatience. I have to go straight home to help my father." Deftly he eluded the small arms and eager, clutching fingers, then paused at sight of the disappointed faces. "But you don't need me—you can play a fine game all by yourselves."

The faces lighted. "What? Tell us what to play, Jeshua!"

His gaze swept the circle of eager faces, rested on one a little apart from the rest. I know! Why don't you play merchantman?"

The faces were still eager, but puzzled. "How, Jeshua?"

"Pretend Benjamin there is a rich merchant going to a far country to seek treasure, with all the rest of you for his caravan."

"Benjamin! *Him*—a merchant!" Their young eyes were scornful. That babyface? He can't even throw a stone straight!"

"You don't need to throw stones straight if you're a merchant."

"What you need is a quick eye, like Benjamin's, and long fingers for feeling silks and jewels."

He watched the little procession weave its way down one of the stony lanes, the puny figure of Benjamin strutting importantly in front of a straggling line of miniature camels. His lips broke into a smile.

"Oho! Playing with babies again, carpenter's son? Is that why you were in such a hurry to get out of the synagogue?"

He turned, his smile fading. The boys of his own age were coming now, among them Abel, the son of Jered, chief elder of Nazareth. A handsome youth he was, as unusually tall for his age as the Boy himself, though stockier,

"Play you a game of slingshot!" he challenged eagerly, pulling a strip of shiny new leather from his embroidered girdle. "I know an old tree where there's always a flock of crows."

The Boy shook his head. "Sorry. I must go straight home and help my father in the shop."

There was genuine regret in his voice. Perhaps if he could find time to do more things with Abel, there would not always be this tension between them. He watched the eagerness in the restless eyes change to hostility.

"Sure it's not because you're afraid of getting beaten? Or because you're too much of a coward to kill a bird?" As the Boy flushed, the son of Jered grinned derisively, "Didn't know I saw you that day, did you? Finding that sparrow I hit and putting a splint on its broken wing and taking it home—!" He gestured scornfully as if no words could describe such unmanly conduct.

A sudden commotion among the others diverted Abel's attention. The Boy's eyes followed the boldly confident and expensively attired young back with a mingling of discomfiture and relief. At least he was spared further taunting for the moment. But—was he really a weakling and a coward, as the son of Jered always managed to imply? Was it less manly to want to feed birds than to kill them?

He was starting slowly homeward when a sound came to his ears, a voice neither human nor animal, yet a composite of both. Something—somebody—trying desperately, without the proper tools of speech, to make itself understood.

The Boy's heart sank. It was Gad, of course, the son of Old Simon the shepherd, who long ago committed such a terrible sin that he had been excommunicated from the Nazareth congregation. Gad, with his hunched back and dragging foot, his twisted lip and cleft palate which could not shape words plainly! The boys were making sport of him. They always did if he gave them a chance. Why, then, if his father had sent him to town on an errand in the market place, did the cripple persist in making this long detour past the synagogue, certain at this time of day to invite trouble?

The Boy's steps lagged. It was not his responsibility, certainly, to protect Gad, and especially not today, when he was anxious to get home and finish his work so that he might have some time for himself! Just because Old Simon had once helped him find Bunty, the family goat, and because since then the shepherd and his unfortunate son had become his friends... He turned and walked slowly toward the open space in front of the synagogue, where a group of his schoolmates clustered in excited glee about their victim.

"*Ay yah!* Talk some more, son of the evildoer. What language is it? Dog or Latin?"

"Sounds as if he had a mouthful of dirt!"

"What's that thing on your back, Gad? An extra head?"

"What did your father do that was so bad, son of Simon, to make you like that? Did he really curse God, the way people say?"

Backed against a low wall of loosely piled stones, the cripple faced his hecklers helplessly, the child-face on the stooped man-body a conflict of distress and bewilderment. A simple face it was, but not stupid, and far cleaner than some of those around him. The tunic of coarse homespun under the rough sheepskin coat was also spotless. But only to the Boy's ears, accustomed to such attempts at speech, was the torrent of words pouring from the twisted lips partially intelligible.

"Bad boys, don't hurt Gad. Gad just want see—place God is, find out God still angry. Boys not say Gad's father bad. Say it again, Gad hurt."

The Boy stood watching, distressed and silent. To intervene at this point would but increase the cripple's troubles. Abel's appetite for excitement, sharpened by excessive leisure, would be further whetted by the challenge. The son of Jered, intoxicated by a sense of leadership, seized on the last jibe with gleeful enthusiasm.

"*Ay yah!* Tell us what your father did, Gad, to get put out of the synagogue. Is it true he can't even wash his face or cut his hair? Phew! No wonder everybody keeps four cubits from him! And if he isn't allowed to wash, then how can you keep so clean? Come, boys! By our father Abraham, we can't let the son of the evildoer go home with a tunic as clean as that!"

Darting into an angle of the wall where water still stood from the recent rain, the son of Jered scooped up a handful of mud and flung it with unerring aim, spattering the spotless tunic from girdle to hem. But before he could gather a second handful, Gad was standing over him. His child-face was distorted by anger, his man-body tensed with passion, one of the loose stones from the wall held high in powerful hands. Trapped, Abel screamed and cowered, his ruddy cheeks turned a pasty white.

"Don't you dare!" he gibbered, "I'll tell my father—he'll have you killed!"

The Boy felt rooted to the ground. He knew Gad's strength even better than Abel. He had seen those powerful hands take a thick acacia trunk and break it in two. Would the son of Simon recognize him as a friend, remember the sound of his voice? It took all the courage he could muster to move forward.

"No, Gad!" In spite of the tightness in his throat his voice sounded firm and confident. "Don't do that. Put the rock down, Gad. See! It's Jeshua. Your friend, Jeshua."

As the Boy came steadily nearer, the tensed body turned on him with even more violence, its lips bared over clenched teeth, arms drawn back in readiness to throw. The knot of boys dissolved in sudden terror, leaving the son of Joseph to face his would-be assailant alone.

"No, Gad," he repeated evenly, moving resolutely forward. "Don't throw. Look! Don't you know me? I'm your friend, Jeshua!"

Slowly the distorted features smoothed, assumed again the placidity of childish innocence. The twisted lips stretched in a grotesque smile and emitted a burst of delight.

"Yenh whunh!"

"That's right. Jeshua." Gently the Boy removed the rock from the uplifted hands and put it back on the wall. It was almost heavier than he could lift. The powerful arms dropped beside the bent and ill-developed body, reaching almost to the ground. The Boy slipped his arm through one of them. "Come, Gad. It's time to go home. I'll go with you as far as the edge of town, where the path begins."

His schoolmates trooped after them a little way, voicing their admiration from a safe distance.

"*Ah hah!* He might have killed you, Jeshua!"

"How did you ever dare—!"

"It was just because he knew me," the Boy explained simply. "He really meant no harm. If you don't make him angry, he's as gentle as a lamb."

"Ha! What would some of the elders say if they knew another elder's son had been making friends with an outcast?" It was Abel's voice, loud but shaky, coming from well in the rear of the procession. "Maybe I'd better tell them!"

Leaving Gad to follow the familiar path home, the Boy returned alone, making his way through narrow winding lanes to the Street of the Carpenters. He moved slowly, not with the eager buoyancy he had when he left the synagogue, and his wide eyes, instead of traveling eagerly from one object to another, remained focused on the ground.

3

THE WOMAN, standing in the doorway of their courtyard nimbly spinning a thread of wool from distaff to spindle, watched him coming, and her fingers became still. As if a sudden cloud had obscured the winter sun, she shivered. Had something tarnished the gold of this, his long-awaited day? But then he raised his head, saw her, and again the day burst into sunshine.

"Mother! Have you seen what a wonderful day? Have you heard the voices?"

"What voices, child?" Though her eyes were fixed on his glowing face, her sure fingers were moving again in rhythm with the rapidly spinning whorl.

"All of them. Birds, wind in the cypress trees, even the singing of your spindle. All wishing me a happy birthday!"

"I did hear the crows cawing about something," she admitted teasingly.

Her glance enfolded his slim figure like a caress, exulting in the straight limbs, the sturdily square shoulders already on a level with her own. And, though her fingers itched to smooth bade the two wings of wind-blown hair and adjust the goat's-hair rings of his headcloth, she kept them pulling and twirling steadily between distaff and spindle. As well try to keep that inquisitive head covered as to lure a skylark into a trap!

His face lifted now to the windy sunshine, sending the wings of hair soaring and the headcloth tumbling to the ground.

"Just look, Mother! The sun shining and the world washed clean with rain! I can't wait to find out what other surprises my Father has for me."

"Surprises?" The woman looked bewildered. "But—how did you know—Oh!" Her fingers suddenly stopped. Strained by the momentum of the still whirling spindle, the thread snapped. "You don't mean—"

The wide brown eyes were anxious. "Did I say something I shouldn't have? You are frowning, and your thread broke!"

Her fingers fumbled. "It's just that your father thinks it isn't right—isn't reverent—your talking so about the Most Holy One, as if—as if you actually *knew* him!"

He continued to regard her anxiously. "And do you think so, Mother?"

She spread her arms helplessly, the two threads dangling. "I—oh, I don't know, my son. All I know is, I want you to be happy on your birthday. I don't want anything to happen to spoil it—*anything*!"

"Then you must be happy too." Swiftly he leaned toward her and, making a V of his index fingers, smoothed the flesh above her brows, wiping away the frown; then, seizing the broken threads, deftly twisted them into a single tight strand. "*Ay yah!* The frown is all gone and the thread mended." He waved his arms in a pretense of magic. "There you are, lady. Any other devils you would like me to dispose of? That's my business, you know, getting rid of devils."

It was a kind of game they often played. "Oh, is that so, sir? I thought you were a carpenter."

"And so I am, lady. But there are devils in wood, didn't you know that? If you don't believe it, cut a branch of that olive tree hanging over your courtyard, and try to tame it with an adze. So bad an old devil is in it he'll likely snap the wood in two!"

The woman looked dutifully astonished. "And you mean, sir," she marveled, "you can really drive out a wicked old devil like that?"

He snapped his fingers. "Pooh! It's nothing. Like most devils he's just a big bluff!"

"What's this I hear?" broke in a man's voice, full of shocked amazement. "My own wife and son trifling with sacred things?"

The woman's relaxed fingers tightened, her smile vanished. "Oh, Joseph! We—we didn't see you—"

"And is that any excuse for irreverence? Must a man watch to keep his family out of mischief as a herdsman does his goats?"

"But, Father," though the Boys lips quivered, his sturdy legs beneath the short homespun tunic spread more widely apart, "we didn't mean to be irreverent. We—we weren't even talking about the Most Holy One. We were talking about devils. And," the dark eyes dared a mischievous gleam, "surely there isn't any connection between the two!"

The stocky figure in the long striped coat and leather carpenter's apron loomed bulkily in the doorway of the stone house. The tight lips belied the natural gentleness in the deeply lined face and kindly, nearsighted eyes. Yet for all his tense anxiety, Joseph looked more bewildered than angry.

"You were talking about casting them out," he returned accusingly, "and only the Most High can do that."

"Of course. But we have to help him, don't we? In fact"—the gleam was a bit bolder now—"I've seen you do it almost all by yourself."

"I!" The blunt fingers tightened about the wooden hammer.

"Yes, Father. Remember how you said there must be a demon in unseasoned olive wood? And then when you put it away for seven years, wasn't the demon gone? Didn't you make of it something beautiful and—and holy, like the carved vine for the doorpost of the synagogue?"

The man's face suddenly crinkled into deeper grooves. "So I did, son, so I did. But"—he shook his head stubbornly—I still say it's a dangerous thing to jest about driving out devils."

"You just did it yourself," the Boy laughed delightedly, "drove out a devil by jesting! He was there a minute ago, inside you, the devil of anger! And now, because you laughed—poof! He's gone!"

Helplessly the man threw up his hands, hammer and all, and with a half groan, half chuckle, disappeared into the courtyard. The Boy touched reverent fingers to the Holy Name on the bit of parchment fastened to the doorpost, raised them to his lips, and followed.

The woman looked after them fondly. Tucking her spindle under her arm with the distaff, she stooped and, retrieving the Boy's fallen headcloth, shook it clean. Then she carefully folded it into diminishing triangles, smoothing and stroking each one as tenderly as if it had been a child's flesh.

"He liked the cedar box you made him, Joseph."

"No better than he liked your gift. It's a fine prayer shawl. Now when he becomes initiated as a Son of the Law, he'll be dressed as befits a descendant of King David."

"You and your dreams of royalty!" chided the woman lightly. She gave the spindle a few quick twirls and pulled a fluffy wad of wool from the mass on her distaff.

The square of matting on which Joseph squatted assumed the dignity of a throne. Reaching for a plow and anchoring its curved handle firmly between his toes, he vigorously rubbed the already smooth surface with a bit of sandstone.

"It's time," he said abruptly but with his usual measured slowness of speech, "that we told the Boy our plans for his future."

Speaking of him to each other, they had never called him by his name, Jeshua. At first, to distinguish him from Joseph's sons and daughters by an earlier marriage, it had always been the Little One. Later, when the other children had grown up and gone away, he had become in both thought and speech the Boy.

The spindle jerked unevenly. "*Our* plans, Joseph?"

The gray beard lifted to a prouder angle. "You know what I mean. The boy is destined for something more important than carpentry. We must prepare him for the time when he takes his proper place in the world."

"His proper place." Her voice was intentionally low, so that it would not carry beyond the courtyard. "And what is his proper place, Joseph?"

The sandstone grated against the iron share. "You, a daughter of Israel and a descendant of the royal house, need to ask that? *Ay yah!* It was you who were so certain from the first that he was destined to be a leader! You said you'd seen visions and heard voices—even quoted words—"

The woman's eyes darkened, and her hands became still.

" 'He will be great,' " she repeated softly, her voice rising and falling rhythmically,
" 'and will be called a son of the Most High. And Jehovah will give to him the throne of his father David.' "

"*Ay yah!*" The beard elevated itself to a new height. "You see? And what else would be the proper place for a good son of Jehovah and a descendant of David than on the royal throne—"

"Joseph!"

At her startled cry he glanced toward the outer door and lowered his voice. "Oh, I'm not saying he should be another Maccabeus. No, nor even another Judas of Galilee, rising in rebellion against the accursed Roman interloper. There are other ways of restoring the glory of Israel than by winning her independence. What we need in these days—"

"Hush! He's coming, Joseph."

With a patter of bare feet, the Boy came dashing into the courtyard.

"When did you make it for me, Father? It's the most beautiful cedar box I've ever seen!" Dropping to his knees on the mat, he stroked the smooth surface lovingly. "Like the skin of a baby goat. And look, Father! See how the gifts of the three strangers fit inside!"

"So they do, so—What's that you say?" The note of gratified pleasure sharpened into disapproval. "You'd better put those back where they belong, son, in the big chest, where they'll be safe!"

"But they fit so perfectly, as if it had been made to hold them!"

"And so it was." The woman moved quickly between them. "Remember, Joseph, how you said it was to hold his most precious possessions?"

"But I didn't mean—"

"And didn't you make a lock for it, so it's really a safer hiding place than the old chest? Have you tried the bolt, son, to see if it fits?"

With keen delight the Boy thrust the miniature wooden bolt into its carefully grooved counterpart, laughing aloud when he heard the tiny iron pins fall into their matching holes.

"It's just like the one on our door!" he exclaimed. "How did you make it so small, Father? And with a key no longer than my little finger!"

"Amen. So be it." The man's consent was grudging. "Let the gifts stay in the box. And—" he extended a broad calloused palm— I'll keep the key."

But it was the woman's swift fingers which enclosed the thin strip of wood. "It's so small," she said gaily, "you'd be losing it in no time, Joseph, like your lump of sandstone. See? You've lost it now! I'll braid him a chain of yarn, and he shall wear the key about his neck. Now run and put the box away, my son."

The Boy jumped up eagerly. "I know! I'll put it in my secret hiding place behind the loose stone in the wall just over Graylegs' manger."

Before the slow-motioned Joseph, fumbling for his rubbing stone among the shavings, could protest, the Boy was gone, and the woman's deft fingers were unrolling long threads of wool, knotting them into strands, braiding them.

"Why did you do that? He's only a boy. He can't possibly realize the value—"

He's a man now, Joseph," answered the woman composedly, "about to become a Son of the Law. You just said so yourself."

"But his whole future depends on those treasures you're letting him handle like—like mere baubles!"

"*His* treasures, Joseph, not ours. We must remember that."

"His! Of course they're his." Attempting to rise, the man caught his foot in the long folds of his coat and stumbled to his knees. "His one chance of coming into his rightful heritage as a son of David! And you let him cache them away behind a loose stone in a donkey's stall!"

Though the woman's lips remained dutifully solemn, her eyes gleamed with fond amusement. How those proud bones still yearned for royal purple even after nigh a thousand years of homespun! He would rather fall flat on his face than tuck his coat in his girdle like an ordinary peasant.

"Surely they're as safe there as in the chest," she replied.

In one awkward motion the man regained both dignity and upright posture. "You're sure the Boy has never told anyone about the—the Gifts?"

"Very sure. He's not a lad to boast. Why—" her voice rippled with amusement—"remember the time he didn't want to wear his new coat to school for fear it might make the other boys envious?" *Ah hah!* she thought. *I shouldn't have mentioned that. It might remind him.*

It did. "Yes, and the first time he wore it he came home without it, because he had given it to a beggar!" Unable to adjust the folds of his disordered coat to his satisfaction, Joseph loosed his girdle and folded it determinedly. "It's time we told him, Miriam."

Her slender body tensed. "Not yet. Please, Joseph! We've been so happy together except once in a while, just lately. I can't bear to think of anything happening to—to change things."

He looked bewildered. "But—I thought you wanted him to go..."

"Oh, I do, I do! Only—I want to be sure it's what he wants too."

"What *he* wants!" Laying the tightly woven square of wool across his knee, the man punctuated each vigorous folding motion with a smack of his hard palm. "And why shouldn't he want it? He loves the Law. He's the best scholar in school. Ben Arza says so himself, in spite of the time he wastes asking foolish questions. Then why in heaven's name—"

"I know, I know." The lengthening braid of yarn tightened. "It's surely what he'll want to do. Only—let's not hurry him, please!"

The man threw up his hands, girdle and all, the neat folds falling again into confusion. "Woman! How can a man know what to do to please you! Here you've insisted from the beginning your son was born to perform some—some holy task in Israel, yet when the time comes for him to make ready—"

"It fits, Father!" The Boy's voice preceded him into the courtyard. "I took all my other treasures out, the stones and shells and the toy plow you carved for me. And you needn't worry about its not being safe, because the loose stone is away down under the hay in Graylegs' manger."

At sight of him the woman's eagerness changed to startled apprehension. But the Boy did not notice.

"Look, Mother! I like your surprise too. It's the most beautiful prayer shawl I've ever seen." He pirouetted gaily for inspection, stroking the white wool with its purple and red and blue stripes, counting the eight threads in each of the four hyacinth-blue tassels. "When I wear this to the synagogue, I'll look as fine as a roller bird or a hoopoe up early to sing his morning prayers!"

"No, no!" Joseph stared at the slim bright figure in unbelieving horror. "Take it off! Must I stand here and see my own son besmirch with unclean fingers the garment of holiness?"

Silently, stung to the quick, the Boy removed the shawl, careful even in his distress that the precious tassels suffered no contact with the ground.

"I—I took care, Father, when I put it on to repeat the prayer just as you taught me. 'Blessed art Thou, O Lord, our God, King—' "

"Stop!" The man lifted unsteady hands to cover his ears. "Isn't it enough to handle a sacred *tallith* like a common *simlah*? Will you also make a mockery of holy words given by the divine to be spoken only by solemn lips and on designated occasions?"

"But I'm not making a mockery of them, truly I'm not, Father. I meant every word, even just now, when I was repeating them."

Though the Boy's lips quivered, the clear eyes lifted to his father's shocked face were steady. "And God doesn't mind if we talk to him at other times of day than the three when we're supposed to pray. He likes us to. I'm sure he does, Father. Why, I've talked to him dozens of times today already!"

"Enough!" Convulsively, Joseph gripped the square of cloth, lifting it with that instinctive horrified gesture of a devout Jew about to rend his garments. "Talking of the Most Holy One as if he were one of your peasant playmates! A little more, and I'll be hearing my own son speak blasphemy!"

The girdle strained under his tightening fingers until it seemed it must be torn in two, but in his harassed eyes there was still more of bewilderment than of anger. When the stout cloth refused to give, his hands became limp, his fingers suddenly trembled.

"Why does he say such things?" he muttered, fumbling helplessly with the untidy folds. "He used to be so—so obedient."

"I'm sorry, Father." Puzzled and unhappy, the Boy shifted his weight from one brown bare foot to the other. "I always mean to obey you."

"Here, let me do it." The woman deftly folded the cloth diagonally into a long narrow strip and, lapping one edge of her husband's coat over the other, belted it neatly about his waist. Then she turned to the Boy with determined gaiety. "Your father has a birthday surprise for you, son. Tell him, Joseph."

"You tell him, Miriam."

Glad of the change of subject, Joseph returned to his mat. One hand reached for the plow handle; the other groped in the pile of shavings.

"Here it is, Father. You dropped it when—when you were folding your girdle." Relinquishing the bit of sandstone, the Boy's fingers caressed the curling grain of the wood. "What a fine plow! Isn't it almost finished?"

"Almost," agreed Joseph, adeptly clamping the curving base into viselike rigidity between his toes. "It had better be. Jonathan, the son of that sluggard Benjamin, is coming for it soon." He added grimly, "And there'll be nothing to pay for it even when the harvest comes, that I'll wager."

"But you're making it just as carefully," observed the Boy thoughtfully, "as if it were for the rich landowner Jered."

Joseph attacked the handle vigorously with his rubbing stone. "If a son of David must be nothing but a carpenter," he replied succinctly, "at least he can be a good one."

"*Ay yah!*" Marveling, the Boy rubbed the shining curve with the tip of his finger. "It's already as smooth as Jered's silk coat! Shall I help you with the plow, Father, or work on something else? I know!" He sprang up eagerly. "Why don't I do some more planing on the wedding chest for Lilah, Jonathan's betrothed?"

"Not today," interposed the woman gaily. "That's your surprise, son. You're to have all the rest of the day free, to spend exactly as you wish. I have a lunch packed for you—fresh loaves and ripe olives and some of your favorite fig cakes."

At sight of his face her heart soared. Though the day had been tarnished a bit, she had succeeded in rubbing it bright again. She fastened the leather pouch containing his lunch to his girdle, made sure his headcloth was in place with the goat's-hair rings pulled down firmly over his forehead. Then, with a glance over her shoulder to see that Joseph was not watching, she slipped over his head the chain of braided yarn, tied it in a secure knot at the nape of his neck, and tucked the wooden key beneath the rounded neckline of his tunic.

4

A WHOLE DOWNWARD SPAN of the sun for his own, to spend just as he wished! Not since he had been old enough to sweep up shavings with a tiny broom of twigs did he remember possessing such wealth of time. Six hours! At least six, for the sun was still short of the zenith, and, though it sank early these winter days, there would remain still that breathless interval akin to the weekly lighting of the Sabbath lamp, when the world tiptoed about on hushed feet, waiting for the kindling of the stars.

He knew even now what he would do with his six hours—most of them, that is. Oh, a few minutes, perhaps, in the market place, or passing the time of day on the steps of the synagogue with Rabbi Ben Arza, or stopping at Deborah's place to see if he could run any errands for her and her blind son Joel. But most of his treasure would be hoarded, along with the fragrant loaves in his scrip, for the Hilltop.

Incredible good fortune, all these precious hours to spend in his favorite trysting place! And today, of all days, on the birthday which would mark his solemn initiation into manhood! Today surely he would be able to look farther, see more clearly, perhaps even hear faintly the Voice for which all his life, it seemed, he had been listening.

Oh, it was a good world, a beautiful world, a happy world, this which his Father had made!

"I'll go with you to the market place," he said cheerfully to Jonathan, who arrived at the carpenter shop just as he started to leave. Balancing the new plow on his shoulder, he adjusted his step to the tall young farmer's measured stride. "The plow is too much for you to carry with that other heavy burden."

Jonathan muttered his thanks. Always frugal of speech, today the son of Benjamin seemed to have encased himself in morose silence. He had accepted the plow without his usual appreciative smile, saying merely, "Sorry. The olive crop already is spent. You get pay with barley—I hope." Even the sight of Lilah's wedding chest, beautiful with its grained top of rippling gold, failed to kindle pleasure in the square, honest features.

Glancing sidewise, the Boy noticed the fist clamped about the loose ends of the bundle, and the bare reddened forearm above it.

"Aren't you cold, Jonathan," he inquired anxiously, "without your *simlah*? Even though the sun is warm for winter, the south wind has a coldness on his breath."

Jonathan might not have heard, so unbroken was the moody rhythm of his heavy sandals. The Boy smiled to himself. He knew the magic word which would dispel the dark cloud.

"Lilah is going to like the chest," he chattered. "Can't you imagine how her pretty face will light up when she sees it? She's going to be such a beautiful bride, Jonathan! And it's only a few more weeks to your wedding!"

One of the big sandals twisted on a loose stone and missed its rhythm. "Going to be no wedding," blurted the young farmer miserably.

"No wedding!" The Boy's shocked gaze lifted to his friend's grim features. Jonathan without Lilah! He had worshiped her since the days when, a tongue-tied youth no older than Jeshua, he had hung about the workshop of her father, the jolly but indigent Abner. His rapt gaze had neglected the fascination of the potter's wheel for that of a twirling skirt and copper anklets.

A fool he had been, explained Jonathan bitterly, to expect he could ever pay the settlement agreed on at the time of betrothal. Always, when it seemed there might be a chance of breaking even, something happened. Like this olive harvest. As if it weren't enough their losing half their trees to Jered by mortgage foreclosure, the hailstorm had come and destroyed most of what little crop they had left. He was going now to beg of Jered enough barley seed for the planting. With his father Benjamin not—Jonathan flushed—well, not so active as he might be and nine mouths to feed...

The Boy could not leave him to face Jered alone. When he laid down the plow and turned away, it was as if his friend reached out a groping hand to detain him. Reluctantly he lowered his eyes from tile rim of hills in which the little town lay nestled. He took up the plow again and swung it over his shoulder.

Jered, the town's foremost businessman as well as its chief elder, conducted his affairs in a commodious booth erected on the edge of the market place. His features were as boldly handsome as his son Abel's yet without the latter's sullen restiveness, for Jered, who had assembled his riches out of dire poverty, had had time for neither leisure nor boredom. If he had let himself become overlarge and a bit soft, it was to compensate for those early years of leanness. And if his stern ardor for religion was but another garment in the many layers required to cover the memory of rags, at least he wore it with distinction.

He welcomed Jonathan with genial effusiveness.

"Ah! *Shalom*, son of my dear friend Benjamin! Now indeed is the promise of this day fulfilled. All that I have is yours, my friend." His expansive gesture included the brimming baskets and bulging leather sacks filling the thickly carpeted platform and overflowing into the dim lower spaces on each side where a scribe and two ill-clad servants were squatting.

Jonathan was not deceived. Taking care that his headcloth of coarse homespun maintained a respectful distance from the multiple overgarments of fine and costly weave, he all but prostrated himself. Let the elder's cup of goodness be overflowing, he murmured abjectly, in proportion with his generosity. He would not ask much of his good friend's largesse, only a little barley that his father Benjamin might have seed to plant his fields.

Shedding his cloak of geniality, Jered gestured abruptly to his scribe.

"What's this? Benjamin asking another loan? But already I have listed all his fields and orchards as security for previous loans! Is it not so?"

There was a rustle of papyrus down among the shadows. "It is so, master."

"But if we are ever to repay the loans," Jonathan protested more boldly, "we must have seed to plant our fields."

"*Your* fields?"

The young man flushed. "Ours, at least," he maintained doggedly, "until you—until the most merciful of creditors forecloses."

Curling one of the seven oiled and perfumed strands of his beard about a well-groomed finger, Jered surveyed the young suppliant with meditative eyes. Too vivid a reminder of his own sordid past, this son of a Nazareth ne'er-do-well who soon would not own enough earth to shake off his sandals! No creditor had shown mercy to his father when he had gone groveling like this Jonathan. As for himself, he had never groveled. Even when smarting hotly under his fellow townsboys' contempt (including that of this same Benjamin) he had remained as unbending as the slim reed of a boy regarding him steadily over the humbly lowered turban.

"Your brother?" he inquired of Jonathan curiously.

"No, sir." It was the Boy himself who replied. "I am Jeshua, the son of Joseph, the carpenter."

"Ah!" The eyes warmed. "A good man Joseph. Poor, but not a borrower. And a good servant of the Law." One of the few also, he might have added, who had not made sport of a ragged child whose father had been the butt of town jokes. "And what are you thinking about behind those bright eyes, Jeshua, son of Joseph?"

"About your beard," replied the Boy with prompt candor. "It's like the seven-branched candlestick which sits before the sacred niche in the synagogue."

Jered looked pleased. "You noticed that? An apt tongue as well as a discerning eye. Continue to use both, and you'll be no poor man like your father. I'll wager by this same beard you're already scheming how you can some day be sitting here in the seat of chief elder, surrounded by all this wealth!"

"No, sir." The denial was respectful but firm. "It's written in the Law, 'You shall not covet.' "

Jered clapped his hands. "Well spoken, son of Joseph. A true son of the Law and of your father. You will never come sniveling to a moneylender, begging favors for which you can give no security."

But he had brought security, Jonathan protested with dignity. He untied the four corners of his bundle. Jered appraised the pathetic array of objects with a sharp but contemptuous eye: a few crude farming implements, an earthenware jar with a crack in its lip, a carefully rolled *simlah*. Lifting the latter and shaking out its folds, he examined critically the heavy striped woolen cloak for evidence of wear or moth holes.

"It will do." He nodded, then issued a brief command to one of his servants. "You shall have the seed, son of Benjamin. And the cloak will be yours again when you return the loan after the harvest, with double the amount for interest."

The Boy watched, perplexity and distress mounting, while the measured grain was poured into the now empty square of cloth, the *simlah* rerolled and surrendered with the other objects to the shadowy recesses behind the platform. He could not believe his eyes. Jered, the chief elder, who often read from the Law in the Sabbath service! His pulses began to pound. He could not say anything, of course. Jered was a man, an important man, and he was only a boy. And yet—

"It is told in Nazareth," he said suddenly, "how the great Jered is one of the *Haberim*, those who are faithful to all the Jewish laws."

The dark eyes kindled like tapers surmounting the seven-branched candlestick. "The son of Joseph also has sharp ears," commended the elder approvingly. "His father and I are among the few comrades in this heathen Galilee who are devout keepers of the Law."

"Then," returned the Boy quietly, "you can't keep Jonathan's coat, can you?"

The tapers were as suddenly extinguished. "Why not?"

"Because," the boyish gaze was straight and unabashed, "he is cold without it. And he needs it to wrap himself in at night. Doesn't the Law say, 'If the man to whom you are making a loan is a poor man, you must not sleep in the mantle he pledges. Return it to him at sunset, that he may sleep in his own mantle and bless you'?"

Jered looked long and hard at the Boy before his lips curled into a smile and his head nodded approval.

"So it does, so it does. Ben Arza has taught you well. I remembered that old law, of course. Indeed, I was about to urge the son of my dear friend Benjamin to return and reclaim his pledge when the sun goes down." Slowly Jered began coiling one of the black strands of his beard tighter and tighter about his finger. "You have bold lips also, son of Joseph."

5

"YOU SHOULDN'T have said that," worried Jonathan as they plunged into the bedlam of the market place. "Jered does not forget. Better that I should have no coat to cover me at night than that you, my friend, should for my sake incur the displeasure of the chief elder."

"I just told him the truth," replied the Boy soberly.

The plow over his shoulder, eyes moodily downcast and unseeing, Jonathan strode through the confusion of open-front stalls, street vendors, haggling bargainers, and scuttling animals and children. Not so his companion. The Boy loved the market place. His nostrils quivered with the exciting scents of far-off places, of Arabian spices and pungent hides and saddlebags, of balsam and Lebanon cedar and Indian sandalwood. His eager glance darted from booth to booth, reveling in the pinks and saffrons and corals of heaped grain baskets, the rainbow hues of Damascus brocades and Tyrian purples...then suddenly froze. He hastened his steps, hoping his companion would continue to keep his eyes on the ground.

A treble of laughter tinkled in the chill air. Jonathan swung toward it. "Lilah!" he muttered, his somber features brightening.

She was leaning against the carved wooden booth where Jason, the Syrian-Greek, had arranged a tempting display of cloths and jewels. Her generous, perfectly proportioned body was rhythmically graceful even in repose—the heavy folds of her coarse woolen garment could not hide its lissomeness. The shining brass water pot poised on her shoulder seemed but a reflection of her golden skin.

Engrossed in the merchandise, she was completely unaware of them and of everyone else. Jason also appeared engrossed, but not wholly in the merchandise. His dark narrow face, as generous of lip as it was sharp of eye, was so close to her ear that he had barely to murmur the blandishments he lavished on all female customers.

Lifting a length of gold-brocaded silk to her shoulder, his fingers managed casually to brush the smooth flesh beneath the flaring sleeve. Jonathan's knuckles whitened on the plow handle and his features turned an angry crimson, but he remained motionless. His free hand reached out and grasped the Boy's shoulder.

Startled by some intuitive fear she scarcely understood, the girl shied away from Jason, but her dark eyes yearned over the shining fabric. Indifferently the merchant tossed the glistening coil to one side of the booth, where it lay in an untidy heap, its golden threads shimmering in the sunlight. Then, apparently forgetting both it and Lilah, he spoke sharply to an urchin reaching timidly over the edge of the platform to stroke the soft nap of the carpet.

"Off of there, bastard! Take your dirty hands away!" Producing a strip of leather kept handy for the purpose, he whipped it warningly across the child's knuckles.

The Boy saw that it was Danny, the small son of the woman Mulcah, who lived in the dilapidated stone cottage on the terrace just above the inn. The child uttered no complaint, merely crouched deeper into the shadows beside the booth, lifting his smarting fingers to his lips.

Unable to resist the temptation, Lilah slipped back to finger the shining fabric, lifted it, and let it fall again in a shimmering cascade; then, setting down her water pot, she draped the cloth about her body, laughing delightedly to see how well its gleaming threads matched the gold of her skin.

"How do I look?" she demanded, pirouetting as gaily and unselfconsciously as a child.

Though startled as always that the voice issuing from such beauty should be so high-pitched and sharp, the Boy stared in sheer delight. Jonathan's fingers dug with painful sharpness into the hollows of his shoulder.

"Ravishing!" complimented Jason, still fingering the strip of leather. "Like Aphrodite, the goddess of love or, better yet, like the lovely Helen whom Paris persuaded to flee away with him."

With a sudden hoarse exclamation, Jonathan strode forward and laid a hard brown hand on her shoulder. "Lilah! What are you doing here?"

She spun toward him. "Jonathan!" After their first startled narrowing her eyes widened in innocent pleasure. "I was just wishing you would come. I—I was on my way to the well."

"The well!" His scowl deepened. "By way of the marketplace?"

"Of course. I always come this way when I have time. It's the only chance I have to get away from that dirty, smoky little house. And you know how I love beautiful things. Surely you wouldn't begrudge me the pleasure of just looking!" Feeling his tense fingers relax, she slipped nimbly from his grasp. "Look, Jonathan, isn't it becoming? Isn't this how you would like your betrothed to look?"

He gazed at her wretchedly, torn between jealousy and adoration of her beauty. "No! We can have no part of such things. I'm only a farmer, and you're the daughter of a poor potter. Take it off, I tell you!"

Again he reached toward her to pull the gleaming stuff from her shoulders, but she eluded him. Her full red lips, habitually parted to reveal small, milk-white teeth, managed to smile and pout at the same time.

"Jason doesn't mind. He likes to see how things look on me. He says it helps to attract customers. Besides—" her dark eyes were accusing—"you know it's for you I want to look beautiful, Jonathan. And if you can't afford to buy such things for me—"

Yielding to the misery in his gaze, she unwound the shimmering drape and replaced it reluctantly on Jason's piles of merchandise. "I'm sorry," she said, honestly contrite. "You know I didn't mean to hurt you. Only I do so love beautiful things."

"I know," the young farmer returned unhappily.

Jason traced the gold lotus design in the brocade with his long pointed finger. "Would the son of the peasant Benjamin like to be able to purchase for his betrothed the clothes and jewels worthy of her beauty?"

Jonathan groaned. "Would the slave like to be rid of his chains!" he retorted bitterly.

"Then come with me." The merchant's voice was brusquely practical. "I need an apprentice, one with strong fists and shoulders like yours to protect my goods from thieves and one honest enough not to rob me himself. You'll do. I'll pay you in both money and goods. With those blunt fingers you haven't the making of a good judge of fine cloths and jewels, but you have other assets." His eye flicked toward the girl. "With a wife who would look like Hera in an emerald tiara and like Aphrodite in a veil of Sidonian gossamer—"

"You mean," Lilah's voice soared to shrillness, "I could come too?"

The merchant winced at the sound. "Naturally. That's the condition under which I make the offer. Only—suppose we make your partnership a silent one."

Lilah flew to Jonathan and, seizing his coat, punctuated each excited phrase with a tug of her fingers. "Did you hear, Jonathan? Think what it would mean! All the things I want most—no more poverty—nothing but happiness—and each other!"

While Jonathan's left hand enclosed her small fingers with hungry possessiveness, his right clung doggedly to the plow handle. His square features revealed bewilderment, caution, and, like the slow breaking of sun through thick clouds, an incredulous hope.

"You mean—you really want me to do this? Leave everything—my plowing, planting, my—my home and family?"

"Yes, oh, yes! We can be married then, can't you see? Not some time years from now when you've saved enough to pay the marriage settlement, but soon—now!"

The Boy watched, tense with excitement, as oblivious as his friend of the curious stares of idlers attracted by the unusual. Some of these, quickly sensing the situation, ventured to offer advice.

"Lucky Jonathan! What man of us wouldn't rather handle pearls than barley?"

"I'll wager you'll plant more seed as a merchant than as a farmer!"

"Is it a pair of stout hands Jason wants or a pair of pretty shoulders?"

The proposition made, Jason himself appeared uninterested in the result. He refolded the brocade, drew a silver toothpick from his girdle, and leisurely explored his molars. Then he suddenly roused himself at sight of the same childish fingers timidly reaching over the edge of the platform to finger a jeweled necklace. Reaching again for the leather, he roared indignantly.

"You again! Didn't I tell you to begone, boy? Want me to wind a real chain about that spindly neck of yours—tight?"

He lashed out with the makeshift whip, this time eliciting a faint squeal of pain. But the Boy was too busy watching Jonathan to notice. His friend looked as if the heavens had opened to reveal a glimpse of paradise. Marriage to his beloved assured! No more worrying about paying off family debts! Except for one thing...The Boy's throat ached with sympathy.

"No." The light went out of the young farmer's face. "You know I can't do it. They're depending on me, my brothers and sisters and—and my father."

"Your father!" The girl's shrill protest was ugly with disappointment. "He's nothing but a sluggard, and you know it. He—"

"Hush!" Jonathan's quiet sternness was more effective than a shout. "Isn't it written in the Law, 'Honor your father and your mother?' It doesn't say, 'if he's prosperous or—or energetic.' It says, 'Honor him.' I'm his son, and I'm responsible for the family." With strong fingers he unloosed her clinging grasp and gently set her hands free. "Come now, beloved. I'll take you home."

She started to follow him, weeping, then, remembering her brass water pot, returned to Jason's booth.

The merchant shrugged his shoulders. "A pity," he murmured. "But what can you expect, my dear, with a stiff-necked Jew for a prospective husband? It's the Greeks who know how to enjoy life."

The girl made no reply, only hid her tearful face in her veil as she lifted the vessel to her head. "When you become tired of scraping an empty grain pit," he called after her in a loud voice, "remember my offer, pretty one. I'd as soon have a female apprentice as a male any day."

Jonathan wheeled and, dark features ablaze, strode back, pushing aside the onlookers as if they had been stacks of straw. Before the chuckle had died in Jason's throat, the farmer was towering above him, muscles knotted around the plow handle, its iron share poised high and ready to descend. The merchant squealed in terror.

"Jonathan!" the Boy cried out in panic. "Think! What are you doing!"

Slowly lowering the plow, Jonathan stood for a moment trembling. Then, stepping forward, he gave Jason a mighty shove which sent him sprawling back into the booth among his bolts of cloth and bags of merchandise, almost toppling the light frame which supported the canopy.

"You beast!" he spat contemptuously. "If I ever catch you laying one dirty finger—!"

Lifting his plow again to his shoulder, Jonathan stalked away through the crowd without a backward glance. Terrified and tearful, Lilah stumbled after him. But the Boy did not follow.

Bellowing with rage, the merchant extricated himself from the tangle and struggled back to his squatting position. By this time the young farmer was out of sight, and the ring of onlookers had tightened into an unsympathetic knot of townsmen united in defense of one of their number against an outsider. Jason contented himself with shaking his fist and muttering imprecations. Then suddenly he shouted in anger.

"The necklace! It's gone! Find that boy, he's the thief! By the great Zeus, I'll kill him! See, there he is now, running between those booths toward the grain bazaar!"

This was a commission more to the crowd's liking. Eager feet pursued the small darting figure. Eager hands pulled him, wriggling, from beneath a burlap tent erected by a grain huckster to protect his full baskets from the rains. They set him down, amid a great wagging of tongues, in the muddy lane before Jason's booth.

"*Ah hah*! It's that woman Mulcah's child!"

"Born to do evil as the sparks fly upward!"

But the child did not look like a thief to the Boy. He could not have been more than seven or eight, and his features still bore the pure delicacy of babyhood. Except that he had lost his head cloth, and his straight little tunic and short brown hair were powdered with grain dust, he was clean and well dressed. So unaccustomed was he to deception that he still clutched the necklace in his small palm, its jewels spilling into plain view like drops of molten sunlight.

The Boy stood by, distressed, listening with mounting dismay and apprehension, wishing he could do something to protect the child.

"What shall we do with him? Sneaky little thief!"

"Let him get away with it, and he'll soon be robbing all of us!"

"Punish him! We know what to do with thieves!"

"I'll loan my girdle for his flogging. It's good stout leather!"

"Flogging? Too good for the son of Mulcah. Pepper him with a volley of stones for his mother's sins!"

"What say, Jason? What shall we do with him?"

The merchant shrugged. "Flogging suits me," he agreed indifferently. "Give him one stroke of the lash for each jewel—twelve of them."

The Boy watched, quivering, while rough hands seized the small figure, stripped it to the waist, and swung it into the orbit of the coiled leather snake. With the first warning whine of the lash he could stand it no longer. Darting into the center of the group, he interposed himself between the child and his assailant just in time to receive the first stinging stroke across his own shoulders. It sent him stumbling to

34

his knees, but, concerned only with keeping the child's body covered, he managed to hold his smarting shoulders erect. The snake coiled again, hissed through a wide arc, fell slack. The stunned silence was broken by indignant protest.

"Young fool! Who—what—"

"It's the son of Joseph the carpenter."

"Out of the way, boy! What do you mean, obstructing justice?"

"It's not justice." Pulling himself upright, the Boy spoke with desperate earnestness. "He's only a child. He—he probably didn't even know what he was doing! Please—please don't punish him!"

"He's a thief," returned the administrant of justice doggedly, "and he's got bad blood in him. Out of the way, son of Joseph!"

"But," the Boy planted his feet stubbornly, "the Law says a person should be flogged in the presence of a judge and only after certain words have been pronounced." With more boldness than he felt, his eyes scanned the encircling faces. "Would you run the risk of becoming lawbreakers?"

Lips mumbled, eyes flashed with indignation, but feet shifted uncertainly. Like most Galileans, these Nazarenes were *amme ha-arez*, "people of the land," who respected but knew little of the ancient Law of their people, less even than those of their young sons who were subjected to its teachings in the synagogue each day. "Upstart! who is he to tell us—"

"It's dangerous business, boy, protecting thieves!"

"His father is one of the elders. Maybe he knows—"

"By the beard of Moses, I'd give both of them a flogging!"

But the zest for punishment was gone. Nobody knew enough to refute the Boy's claim, and none quite dared run the risk of lawbreaking by disregarding it. Sullenly the champion of punishment rewound his girdle. Jason, his property retrieved, had transferred his interest to more likely customers. The onlookers began drifting away. The flash of sunlight on a Roman helmet, as sure a symptom of trouble as a vulture of carrion, dissipated the remainder.

"Come," said the Boy, tucking the small quivering hand within his palm. "I'll take you home."

6

THE CHILD trotted willingly at his side. There was no need of inquiring the way. The location of the woman Mulcah's house had been impressed on the Boy as sternly as that of the tombs on the surrounding hillsides, their domes freshly whitewashed before each feast day as an added safeguard to all good Jews against pollution, and as rigidly to be avoided.

The big open space beneath the market place was as usual teeming with the life and color of far places. A caravan of Persian merchants was pitching camp in the cavelike shelters under the foundation arches of the inn, spreading their rich-hued, tattered carpets, shouting harsh gutturals as they eased towering packs from the backs of their kneeling camels. An old minstrel with a broken *kinnor* was singing in a quavering voice about the glories of the Maccabees, keeping a weather eye alert for the glitter of a Roman helmet that he might quickly change his plaint to a harmless love song. A pure-bred Arabian horse, black and glistening, impatiently pawed the ground while his master, a servant of King Herod Antipas, directed the loading of a hundred huge oil skins on a train of little donkeys.

But, alluring as these sights were, there could be no stopping now. The child must be gotten safely under his own roof and kept there until the resentful townsmen forgot his misdoing.

"Why did you take the necklace?" asked the Boy.

The small fingers were warm and trusting in his palm, " 'Cause it was so pretty," explained the child simply, "and would look good around my mummy's neck. And so she would stop crying when we're alone and would laugh and sing the way she does when other people give her pretty things."

"But it was wrong," said the Boy gently. "Your father must have told you it's wrong to steal—"

He stopped suddenly, remembering Nahor, the roistering adventurer who had appeared one day in Nazareth with a peddler's pack, a *kinnor*, and a beautiful wife named Mulcah. He had built himself a ramshackle house, filled it for a few months with laughter and dancing and strange foreign music, then, bequeathing to his cheerfull young wife a multiplicity of debts and a newborn child, had vanished as mysteriously as he had come. No, the child Daniel could hardly have learned the difference between right and wrong from his father.

Music and laughter were coming from the house now, audible even from the foot of the steep zigzag path where the Boy stopped short from sternly engendered habit. The respectable citizens of Nazareth, he knew, did not ascend that path—at least, by daylight. Once, returning from the well with his mother after dark, they had surprised Jered slipping out of the path between the thick cactus hedges. His mother had drawn him back quickly, pressing her finger to his lips, and afterward she had chattered gaily in an attempt to make him forget what he had seen, but he had not forgotten. Standing now in that same spot, he could still smell the heavy perfumes which had drifted from the flowing garments.

The small fingers tightened. "The son of Joseph will come with me?"

Accompany the child up that forbidden path? The Boy turned sick at the thought. All his instincts rebelled. But the child needed him. There was more than question, there was pleading in the bewildered brown eyes. And, if he did not go, who would tell the woman Mulcah what she must know to keep him out of danger?

"Yes," he said. "I'll go with you."

The path was matted and unkempt, like a beggar's hair. Spines of cactus, wet from the last rain, clutched at their coats as they made their way through them. From close vantage the little house looked even more ramshackle than from a distance, its stone walls ill-matched and sagging, only its door frame and roof beams, which had been Joseph's part in its construction, still as stout and true to plumb as on the day they had been put in place.

Following the child through the tiny courtyard into the single room, eyes still focused to daylight, the Boy sensed rather than saw that the cramped space was astir with people, their outlines barely distinguishable by the light of the high narrow windows and small oil lamps set in niches in the stone walls. The air was heavy with oil fumes and warm breath and that same sickly sweet mixture of perfumes which had clung that night to Jered's garments. A sudden impulse to flee possessed him, but the small fingers clasped his tightly.

As his eyes became accustomed to the dimness, they gratefully picked out a familiar face. He had often seen Gebal, the young merchant from the Phoenician coast, for the bright booth he set up occasionally in the market place was a favorite haunt of Nazareth children, and not only for the bright bits of glass and tattered silk he was always flinging to them, Gebal's wares seemed always a little more alluring than all other merchants, his brasses more gleaming, the gold and silver in his brocades more lustrous, perhaps because of the song and laughter he mingled with them.

The figure of the woman Mulcah needed no bright lights to reveal its grace and beauty. It was born to rhythmic motion, and the golden sheath of her gown, cut Egyptian style, followed each supple curve of her body. From one hand a tambourine showered silver notes. She had played the tambourine, the Boy remembered, when he came with his father to put up the roof timbers. And she had sung, too, soft lullabies to her newborn child, this same Daniel, in a low throaty voice like the cooing of a turtle dove.

"A song, Ishtar!" prompted a voice with a strong foreign accent. "It's said in Babylon you have the body and voice of the goddess. I'll grant the body. Now let's hear the voice!"

The Boy, Danny's little hand still in his, shrank against the wall.

She sang, to the foreigner's delight, a love song of his own people, accompanying it with soft strokes on the drum skin, her feet moving at first to a languid rhythm which barely set the anklet bells in motion, but slowly accelerating until even the hot little oil flames seemed to throb in quickened tempo.

" 'Thy love is as the scent of cedar trees, oh, my lord...' "

" 'Ah! How plenteous she is, how gleaming...' "

Then suddenly she broke into laughter, shattering the intense mood with a discordant jangle, and burst into a rowdy street song.

It was Gebal who spied the newcomers.

"Ho!" he cried gaily. "They're coming young these days! Look what we have here!"

The woman spun around and stared in the direction of the pointing finger, the high color of her cheeks flaming to rich crimson.

"No!" she murmured faintly. "Not—not *you*!"

"I came to bring Danny," explained the Boy simply. "He's in trouble."

She turned back with a swift expulsive gesture which included all the occupants in the room. "Get out!" she commanded sharply. "All of you!"

Even before they had gone, grumbling, cursing good-naturedly, she was down on her knees, pulling the child into her arms, cradling him against her breast. Her voice had not forgotten how to sing lullabies. It was one continuous melody of crooning tenderness.

"Poor lamb! You say they almost flogged him? You can't tell me about this town! I know how cruel it can be. Flogging my precious baby! Yes, yes, I understand. Of course I'll keep him in. I'll watch him every minute."

"But you don't understand." Patiently the Boy tried again to explain. "It was because he did wrong that they were going to flog him. He stole—"

"I know." She rose again to her full height, her soft brown eyes turning hard as agates. "He broke one of their precious laws, and they wanted to punish him, the way they'd like to punish me. Don't worry. I'll take care of him. He'll learn to conform to their ways if—if I have to die to make him. He's not going to be like me."

The eyes softened again. "Do you know why I was so—so frightened when I saw you standing there? Because ever since you came here with your father, I've wanted my son to grow up just like you. And—I couldn't bear to think you—you'd be coming to a place like this."

Turning abruptly, she crossed the room and, kneeling, fumbled hastily through an untidy pile of bright-hued garments. "Thank you for bringing him back. And—here, take this, son of the carpenter Joseph. I made it for a—a friend, but I haven't any better friend than you."

She held out a girdle of fine linen, embroidered with tiny gems and purple and gold threads. Then she thrust it into his hands as carelessly as if it had been a strip of goatskin.

The Boy accepted it with equal frankness and simplicity, fastening it over the one he already wore under his *simlah*. "It's beautiful," he said gravely, "just as you are beautiful."

His gaze lifted in appreciation from the delicate ankles with their little bells to the loveliness of her face as she watched her son.

"You're like a lily on a tall stem," he said simply, "whose raiment is finer even than King Solomon's."

The woman was used to compliments. Flushing, she searched his frankly admiring gaze for the usual sensual awareness. But she did not find it.

"I think God must have been extra pleased," continued the grave young voice, "when he made you. He must be sorry to know you're so unhappy."

She gave him a swift startled glance, then suddenly she was on her knees again, face pressed deep into the pile of garments, weeping. Words began pouring from her lips. She had been so lonely. She had wanted so much to make friends with the other women, but they would not have her. A stranger she had always been, an outsider, because she liked bright colors and danced and sang to strange tunes. After Nahor had gone, what was she to do, a lone woman with a child and no friends to help? She had known no trade—nothing but music and dancing and laughter. Heaven forgive her, it was for the child she had done everything!

The Boy stood by, not knowing what to do or say to express his sympathy, until finally the woman rose from her knees and, stooping, began nervously to fold the topmost garments on the untidy pile.

"But why should I be talking like this to you, a mere boy? I—I don't know what possessed me. It was just that—that you seem different, somehow, from most people. Even when you were here with your father, no bigger than my Danny... But you must go now." Dropping the folded garments in another untidy pile, she pushed the Boy toward the door. "And don't come back, do you hear? I—I don't want to have to remember that—that I've hurt you too."

Going down the path, the Boy heard her singing, no strange or rowdy tune this time, but a lullaby, in a low throaty voice that was like the cooing of a turtle dove.

7

AFTER the cloying closeness of the house the outdoor world seemed unbearably beautiful. The Boy drank long and deeply of the brisk mountain air, savoring each distinct aroma of new-washed earth and springing grass and leaf bud.

He decided to climb the hill by a circuitous path which circled the town rather than by the shorter route up through the winding lanes. For there must be no further interruptions. The sun was already close to the high rim of hills, and a little farther south, in the direction of the prevailing winter winds, there were rain clouds forming. He felt a fierce compulsion now to gain the solitude of the Hilltop.

The first sharp exultation of his birthday adventure was gone. He was troubled and restless and hungry, like the lonely kite drifting high over the village with the wind, turning its long pointed beak from side to side. Swiftly, with an urgency he had seldom known before, he climbed the ill-defined path, pushing through clumps of thorn and cactus instead of bothering to go around them. He must get to the Hilltop.

"Ta-a-a, ho-o-o! Ta-a-a-a, ho-o-o-o!"

Recognizing the shrill shepherd's call, he climbed up on a jutting rock and, spotting the toy figure, waved his hand vigorously, glad, however, that Old Simon was pasturing his flock on a hill too far away to permit even a brief exchange of words. The old shepherd would know who was waving. He had no other friends.

"Let him be *Cherem*!" The Boy shivered at the thought of the grim pronouncement which long ago had made Old Simon an outcast from his people. Devoted to destruction! To be like one dead, not permitted to live with others, to talk with others, to worship. To be avoided by all men forever as if he were a leper!

Had he done wrong in making friends with one whom the Law had declared *Cherem*, in going to his hut in the hills and talking long hours with his son Gad, in helping the old shepherd tend his sheep— even though he was always careful to keep the prescribed four cubits' distance from him? It surely had not seemed wrong, with Gad's face lighting up at his coming, and Old Simon showing him how to be a good shepherd! And yet, if he had not suspected it was wrong, why had he not told his father Joseph?

Troubled, the Boy slowed his pace and lowered his eyes from the Hilltop to the stony path.

"Jeshua!" cried a clear young voice. "Is it you, Jeshua?"

The Boy's heart sank. He should have known better than to take this short cut up the hill, passing so close to Deborah's house, built on the town's highest terrace. Of course Joel would have heard him coming, recognized his step. The child's ears were sharp enough to hear a lizard glide across an outcropping of limestone! Perhaps if he disregarded the voice, pretended he were someone else, and moved on as soundlessly as possible... *Ah hah*! Hot shame suffused his cheeks at the thought. This was Joel, his friend, calling.

"Stay where you are," he called cheerfully. "I'm coming."

But the child scrambled nimbly up the side of the terrace to meet him, barely touching the low hedge with the tips of his fingers as he followed the steep zigzag path. "I knew you'd come today, Jeshua. Something told me. And you came just in time!"

The Boy reached for the eager, groping fingers. Incredible that those wide eyes, as intense a blue as the sky to which they were almost constantly lifted, should be blind!

"In time for what, Joel?" he asked gently.

"To help my mother find something she has lost."

Casting a rueful glance over his shoulder at the fast-descending sun, the Boy followed Joel down the path to the tiny stone house, perched like a birds' eyrie on its high terrace within an encircling wall of cypress trees. Here on this familiar path the blind boy's feet were even surer and swifter than his friend's. He had no need of the staff with which he tapped and fumbled his way along the winding streets on the few occasions when his mother let him venture down into the town alone.

Entering the tiny courtyard, he moved with unerring precision, stepping over the round depressed stone mortar, expertly negotiating the narrow spaces between earthen jars and reed baskets and goatskin sacks. For the scrupulous neatness with which the widow Deborah kept her son's garments, decorating even his coarsest tunics with the fine embroidery, which was her one genuine skill, extended as little to her housekeeping as to her own person.

"Jeshua's here, Mother! He has sharp eyes. He'll find the coin for you."

The door swung open a reluctant crack. Deborah's thin body looked even more stooped, her brows more furrowed with worry than usual. Above the small lighted lamp cupped in the palm of her hand her eyes mingled the reflection of tie flickering flame with their own pale glitter of fear.

"Jeshua? Ah—Miriam's boy." The tense face relaxed in a smile. "One of the few in this town a person can trust. You wouldn't rob a poor widow of the few coins she can scrape together or of the fine embroidery which is her only source of food and shelter."

She opened the door a little wider, just far enough for the two boys to slip inside. "Sharp eyes you have, says my poor Joel. Ay, and sharp eyes it is we both need, he with his stone blind, and I with mine getting weaker and more bleary every day from bending in the dim light over my fine stitches. Peace to you, son of Joseph and Miriam."

Murmuring his polite greetings, the Boy's voice was guardedly sympathetic. No use reminding Deborah that there was no need of working in such dim light, that even in this cold rainy season she could have sat in the open doorway, getting the benefit of daylight! *Ah hah*! she would have protested in horror. Let every passerby see the fine work she was doing, so he could come back in the dead of night and steal it?

But today her fears were not for her embroideries. Indeed, she had none in the house, for only yesterday she had sold them, receiving in payment ten pieces of silver, just the amount needed to pay Jered the interest on his mortgage. And now, counting the coins this morning, she had found only nine. She must have lost one when she moved them last night from one place to another, trying to find a safe hiding place.

All day she had been hunting. Twice now she had refilled the lamp and moved it about while she swept the floor, shining it into all the corners. No use. The coin was gone. And there was none to take its place. Even the precious dowry coins which had hung from each side of her headdress in the good days when her husband Dathan was alive were all gone now. And Jered would foreclose the mortgage as he had threatened, and she and her poor blind Joel would be homeless. Always she had been afraid he would sometime have to beg for his living, and now the time was come, heaven pity them both!

Gently the Boy took the clay lamp from her trembling fingers. "In what places did you try to hide the money?" he inquired helpfully.

She told him, and with systematic thoroughness he searched each one of them. Finally, after he had shaken out the carelessly bundled sleeping mats, rerolling and restacking them in a neat pile, his eye caught a glint of silver in the dusty corner.

"Here it is! It must have rolled under the mats when you spread your beds."

Rubbing the thin disk on his sleeve until its Latin inscription boldly circled the laurel-wreathed features of Caesar Augustus, he placed the coin in Deborah's outstretched hand. The fingers, talon-slender, closed about it avidly.

"The God of Israel be thanked! You're a good boy, son of Joseph. May you always have thick walls to shelter you and a stout roof over your head!"

Fumbling for the other silver pieces in the pocket of her girdle, she held them close to her dimmed eyes while she counted. "Ten, praises be! If they were only gold instead of silver, all our worries would be over! Now when I pay them to Jered, I'll just have to start worrying about where the next ten are coining from."

With relief the Boy started toward the door. Fortunately the search had consumed only a few moments. Above the row of cypress trees he could still see light in the western sky.

"Are you going to the Hilltop?" asked Joel with the eagerness of a hungry beggar smelling fresh-baked loaves.

"If he is, you're not going with him." Deborah's voice was sharp with premonition. "It's too slippery on the rocks after the rain, and no knowing how many full cisterns you might fall into, to say nothing of the crevices."

"But I know my way on the hill, Mother. Even all alone, with my staff I'd be perfectly safe. And with Jeshua—"

"No. I'm sure the son of Joseph doesn't want you bothering him today."

In the wide sightless eyes the light died with the abruptness of the brief glow after sunset. The Boy hesitated, torn between relief over Deborah's prohibition and misery at his friend's disappointment. The woman would relent easily, he knew. She always made a great fuss about Joel's going anywhere.

But surely today he would be justified in taking her at her word. He could not—just *could not* surrender this little that remained of his precious treasure. Only two hours at the most! Share them with another, as he had felt compelled to share the other four? Give up this birthday tryst on the Hilltop with his Father? Perhaps never hear the Voice?

He looked again into the wide empty eyes.

"I'll be very careful of him," he said gently to Deborah. "I promise to bring him safely home."

8

JOEL'S HAPPINESS was irrepressible, his laughter cheerful and lilting. His slim body would accept no guiding hand. It was he who, staff in hand, led the way up the steep terraced slope, following the zigzag path with an uncanny sureness of step akin to animal instinct.

"*Watch out!*" the Boy called once. "That deep wine press is just to the left of the path. After the rains it's sure to have water in it."

Strange to be using such words with one who had no sight! "*Watch* out!" "*See* how green the grass is!" "*Look* here, the smoothest, roundest stone!" Yet it was usually Joel who perceived all these things first, the tip of his staff exploring a crevice while his feet were still picking their way through a tangle of branches; slender fingers fondling a tuft of new grass or reaching for a smooth stone unearthed by sensitive brown toes; ears cocked to the almost imperceptible dipping of wings.

Above the Hilltop the wind tore at the clouds. Wild, racing clouds they were, with rain in them. As the boys climbed out of the sheltered basin toward the stony summit, it rushed boisterously to meet them, lashing at their garments, clamping tight fingers about their throats. With dismay the Boy watched his thin headcloth sail gaily away like a bird, never stopping until it landed far below in the top of a pointed cypress. But he welcomed the rough coolness threading his hair, tingling along his scalp, its turbulence in some way akin to the unrest he felt mounting within himself.

Bracing his slim body, Joel laughed aloud and stretched his arms wide. It was Jeshua who had taught him to lift his face, unafraid, to the wind.

"Let's go to the highest place," he begged, "where it blows strongest!"

"Not that way," the Boy warned sharply, hurrying forward to seize Joel's arm. Facing full into the wind, the blind boy was heading straight for the western edge of the hill, where the rocks plunged with precipitous abruptness to the stony ledge below. "The crest of the hill is to your right."

They reached it after a brisk climb.

"You're sure," demanded Joel, almost with disappointment, "this is the highest place, the *tiptopmost* place, where the wind blows strongest?"

"Very sure," replied the Boy, puzzled by his friend's intensity.

The blind child stood on tiptoe, stretching, it seemed, to the limit of his meager stature, face lifted like an empty chalice to the pouring wind. Then, dissatisfied, he pulled off his headcloth and loosened his cloak, laying bare his throat. His wide, empty eyes, the color of the few bright patches of sky gleaming through the torn clouds, fairly strained from their sockets. Finally the fierce tension relaxed. He swayed a little, then, sinking to the ground, huddled, shivering, inside his cloak.

"No," he said in a small voice. "Not now. But I still think it might happen sometime."

"What might happen?" asked the Boy gently, holding the cold fingers in his own.

"The wind might blow away my blindness," replied Joel simply. "I'm sure it could if it would only blow hard enough. Just for a minute, I mean," he added almost apologetically. "Long enough to see what it looks like from here on our Hilltop. I really don't mind being blind most of the time. I can see so many things with my ears and fingers. But—if I could only see with my eyes the way you do, just once!"

For a moment the Boy also was blind, the salt of tears blurring his vision. But Joel's high voice, excited with a new idea, would allow no pity.

"You be my eyes, Jeshua. Tell me everything you see. Tell me all about the wonderful world our Father has made!"

The Boy crouched on the rough stone beside his friend. Was it a wonderful world? Until now he had always thought so. Even on a day like this, with earth lying dark and brooding and heaven all astir with unrest, he had felt sweet kinship with earth and wind and clouds. But not today. The elements had become suddenly antagonists instead of friends.

"Where shall we start?" he asked, trying to sound upbeat.

"With the sea," came the prompt reply. "The shining blue sea. I think I know what blue is, Jeshua. It—it's like the note of a shepherd's pipe. And red is like horses' hoofs and trumpets."

Pushing his hair back, the Boy turned his stinging eyes toward the west. "There isn't any sea today," he said. "Only gray clouds. And gray—"

"Like a pigeon's wing," supplied Joel happily. "You've told me before. But we can see the Plain, can't we?" he demanded eagerly.

The Boy turned south where, far below, beneath tattered veils of mist, the great Plain of Megiddo unrolled its huge scroll between the bulging handles of Carmel and Gilboa.

"Yes, we can see the Plain." As always the prospect quickened his pulses, as did the removing of the Sacred Rolls from their silk and linen wrappings. For this stretch of earth also was inscribed with holy writing, scored from end to end with the turbulent history of his people. "And there are caravans, more even than usual. Where the sun shines through you can see the gleam of the camels' trappings."

"Is the merchant there going to find the most precious pearl in the world?" inquired Joel eagerly. "The one you made up the story about?"

"Perhaps. He may be the one with the long string of camels away over toward the pass of Megiddo."

"And did he find the pearl?"

"No," replied the Boy slowly. "He has too many other things. If he had found the most precious pearl, he would have had to sell everything else, so he could buy it."

"Can we still see him?" asked Joel after a few moments of silence.

"No. He's gone. The clouds are thicker now. They're coming up through the mountain passes like marching armies."

Joel hugged his thin knees with the anticipatory delight of the story lover. "Whose armies?" he prompted. "The wicked Sisera's? And can we see the mighty Barak coming with his ten thousand men from Mount Tabor to smite him?"

The Boy stared at the restless, shifting shadows. "Whose, indeed?" Even as he stared, the dying sun burst through the clouds and glittered on a Roman helmet, then, tilting on the far rim of the hills, poured itself empty in a flood, which turned the valley's black soil crimson.

Joel's sightless eyes shone with fervor. "Or could they be the armies of—Messiah?" His lips intoned the word reverently. "He who is to come to deliver us from our enemies! How will he come, do you think, Jeshua? Riding a big horse, like a Roman captain, or in a chariot, like King Herod? Will he fight his big battle here on the Plain and kill all our enemies, the way Elijah did, until the River Kishon turns red like blood?"

The Boy sprang up. Today the Hilltop was not a place of high sweet adventure. He wanted to run with all the speed in his swift limbs, get as far away from it as possible. But—where?

His gaze turned northward toward Mount Hermon, serene and remote, its snows still triumphantly ablaze from the setting sun. If he could only have gone there today instead! Surely at last he would have heard the Voice speaking clearly! That must be the trouble. He had never gone high enough. Yet even as he watched, the shimmering radiance faded, and dark clouds drifted across the face of the mountain. Turning back toward Joel, he felt rain, cold and stinging, upon his face.

"Come," he said with inexplicable relief. "It's beginning to rain, and I promised your mother I would take care of you. We must go down."

It was raining hard before they reached the highest terrace of the town, so hard that, looking back, the Boy could not even see the outlines of the Hilltop. Drenched and shivering, he made his way down through the swiftly darkening streets of the town. His birthday was over.

9

"WHERE DID YOU GET that girdle?" demanded Joseph suddenly.

Following the direction of the blunt pointing finger, the Boy's gaze revealed as much surprise as his father's. It took him a moment to remember.

"It was a present," he replied slowly.

The woman exclaimed in delight, momentarily forgetting her concern over his exposure to cold and rain. Dropping his drenched cloak and the towel she had used to rub his streaming hair, her fingers traced the intricate embroidered pattern with an artist's appreciation.

"From Deborah, of course. She does the most beautiful work! Look, Joseph!" Unfastening the long silken strip tied over her own handiwork of stout homespun, she placed it in her husband's hands. "As many colors as a mountain slope in springtime! See how fine it is!"

"I see," replied Joseph, accepting it with gingerly reluctance. "Too fine for a carpenter's son."

The woman's eyes held a demure twinkle. "Even for one descended from the royal house of David?"

Joseph was only partially mollified. "He who displays a king s trappings without a crown and scepter," he asserted drily, "is a fool."

He regarded the unfamiliar object with increasing displeasure. "Deborah? Giving away expensive things like that? No wonder the woman is in debt!"

"Poor Deborah!" The woman's voice was as gentle as the fingers attempting to restore order to the damp, tangled hair. "Our son has been kind to her. She only wanted to show her gratitude."

"It wasn't Deborah who gave me the girdle," said the Boy quietly. "It was the woman Mulcah."

There was plenty of time to explain what had happened in the market place, for Joseph's amazement made him inarticulate. In horror he tried to rid himself of the despised object, but its delicate fabric clung to his calloused fingers like cobwebs. Then, lifting it, he attempted, like a pious man rending his garments in the presence of sacrilege, to tear the thing in two. But the fine silk was as tough as new linen. It writhed and strained and twisted, yet would not break.

So shocked and troubled was he that even when words came they possessed little coherence. A son of his—doing such a thing—letting himself be known as a friend of sinners—going into that woman's house! Cleanse his garments! Wash the scent of evil from his hair! Did his son not even know evil when he saw it? By the righteous bones of his ancestors, if he kept on doing such things as he had done today—!

The Boy listened anxiously even less distressed by his father's pained displeasure than by the silent agitation of the fingers in his hair. His mother, too, thought he had done wrong. It seemed that he was always making her unhappy these days.

"But what would you have had me do?" he inquired in bewilderment when his father had finished. "Should I have just stood there and let them beat little Daniel? Or let him go home un-protected?"

Joseph's deeply lined face grew even more troubled, and his bare feet shifted uneasily on the hard-packed earth floor. In the rigid performance of duty there were some necessities on which he always preferred to turn his back, like the slaying of a lamb for sacrifice. He turned it now.

"Who are you, a mere boy, to question the Law? It says such women are unclean, does it not? If they are apprehended in their sins, they must be stoned. Yes, and their children are sinners too. This son of the woman proves it. Didn't you yourself say he was a thief?"

Stooping, he lifted the pot of bubbling lentils from the rimmed lid of the clay stove and dropped the girdle on the glowing charcoal. The woman gave an anguished cry, but the Boy made no sound or gesture, only watched the fragile edges curl and shrivel, the rainbow yarns arch and glow like flaming script.

"What a pity!" moaned the woman softly. "She worked so hard!"

His duty completed, Joseph turned to the Boy with gruff kindness. "Enough!" His features crinkled into their usual good-natured creases. "It's your birthday, son, and your mother has made ready a feast. The Most High is just. He will pardon a sin that was not intentional. Let us forget the whole matter."

But the Boy could not forget. He performed the sacred washings which were the necessary preparations for the evening meal as if they had been a cleansing penance, concentrating upon each motion with feverish intensity. The repetition of the prayer, usually as joyous and intimate as a friendly greeting, became tonight a function of deadly seriousness.

"Blessed art thou, O Lord, our God, King of the universe! Thou who hast sanctified us through thy commandments…"

It was like talking to a stranger.

For his mother's sake he tried to make the meal a cheerful occasion, exclaiming over the rare treat of both salted fish and lentils, praising the fresh loaves cooked with honey and leaven. But every morsel of bread dipped in the savory dish tasted bitter on his tongue. He chattered merrily about the market place and the wind on the hill and the brown hawk hanging in the sky, and was rewarded finally by seeing her tense features relax, the color mount and glow again in her delicate cheeks.

10

HE COULD NOT sleep. Far into the night he lay on his mat staring into the dark and listening to the beating of rain on the stones of the courtyard.

His birthday was over. Not only had the Voice again failed to speak clearly, it had not spoken at all. The day was over, and it had brought nothing but disappointment No—worse. Disillusion. For he knew the truth now. It was not a good and beautiful and happy world which God the creator had made.

Falling finally into fitful sleep, he dreamed that he was climbing up the side of Mount Hermon. It must be Mount Hermon because it was so high and there was such a shining at the top, yet he could not tell whether it was the shining of snow or of dazzling white garments. He knew only that if he could reach them there would be someone there waiting to tell him everything he had to know. Moses? Elijah? They had climbed mountains and worn shining garments. God himself?

But he could make little headway climbing because of the voices. No sooner would he lay hold of a stout branch or jutting rock than one of them would speak. Then he would look down, and the stones would crumble or the branch slip through his fingers.

There were no forms or faces below, only darkness. Yet the voices were clear as the notes of a shepherd's pipe floating on a windless dusk.

"Ta-a-a, ho-o-o! Ta-a-a-a, ho-o-o-o!"

"Cold, Jeshua—cold tonight without my cloak—"

"Only because I like beautiful things so much!"

"For little Danny's sake—and because I was so lonely—"

"I'm afraid—no roof over our heads—"

"If only the wind would blow hard enough—so just once I could see—"

He awoke to a sudden consciousness of silence and profound awareness.

The beating of rain was stilled. There was no restless stirring of the goats or of the little donkey down below in the straw. Nor could he hear Joseph's heavy breathing and Miriam's uneasy sightings.

Slowly, to keep his straw-filled mat from rustling, the Boy drew himself upright. Because his cloak was still spread on the tall storing jar for drying, he wrapped himself in his goat's-hair coverlet, its scratchy texture an even more palpable assurance that he was no longer dreaming.

Feeling with his bare soles for the familiar depressions in the shallow stone steps, he descended to the lower level of the house where the animals were kept and Joseph did his work in rainy weather. He crossed its narrow space so soundlessly that even the goats, snug in their straw under the stone arches, did not stir.

The wet stones of the courtyard were a glimmer with stars.

The night air, crystal-clear and cold, swept all his senses clean, lifting his face to it; he saw the stone stairway leading to the housetop—no, not to the housetop. To heaven! And it was not a stairway, but a shining ladder, each glistening step rising a little higher toward the sky.

"Like Jacob's," he whispered soundlessly.

He mounted it with wondering reverence, bare feet bathed in each glimmering pool, cheeks brushed clean by the currents of chill night air. Reaching the housetop, he stood high on his toes and stretched his arms wide.

"Thank you, Father," he said simply.

Foolish he had been to think the Voice had not spoken! Why, it had been speaking all day, in a dozen different tones and accents!

"I understand." He still spoke aloud, with as easy an intimacy as if he had been talking to Joel or Jonathan. "I see what it is you want me to do. But—I still don't see how!"

The cold sponginess of the roof penetrated his bare soles and made him shiver. He perched on the stone parapet and drew his feet up under the goat's-hair coverlet, chafing them with equally cold fingers. He hunched his shoulders deep within its folds, but his bare head remained high-poised and alert.

He saw that, in spite of the deep gutters draining into the cisterns below, the scored clay surface of the housetop was spangled with untidy pools. It was hard to believe it would soon be bursting with green shoots; that after the rains it could be rolled hard and flat, be strewn with drying fruits and grains and humming looms, the center of joyous living! Or that the stark branches of the fig tree overhead would put forth glossy leaves to create a bower of shade! Yet he knew it would happen—knew what to do to make it happen. Put fresh layers of brush and reeds and grass and clay on the beams of the roof and roll them flat with the heavy stone roller. Prune the fig tree and loosen the soil around its roots and keep it free from stones.

But what could you do to bring new life to people?

He turned his face upward. Each star was a gold piece, and the sky an upturned velvet bag spilling them out.

Suppose—the Boy smiled to himself in the dark—they were real gold pieces and really being spilled! How quickly the town would waken and rush to its housetops! Especially Jason, sleeping uneasily on his bulging mat, with one eye opens for robbers. And how everybody would rush to empty their water pots and grain jars and clothes chests, so they could fill them with something more precious! Little Nazareth would become world-famous overnight. And—yes, it would solve so many people's problems! Like Jonathan's and Deborah's. Just one little bag!

A bag of gold pieces!

11

THE NEWS SPREAD through town like leaven in a pan of dough.

Jonathan, the son of Benjamin, had found treasure in his field!

When Miriam returned from the well, her eyes were brimming with excitement. Words spilled with breathless incoherence.

"He was out before daylight plowing—felt his share hit something—thought it was just an old broken jar until he looked inside—couldn't believe his eyes—real gold pieces—a handful, some said, others a whole omer—Jered was so angry—said the field belonged to *him*—but Jonathan went to him first thing and paid all his debts—Oh, Joseph, doesn't it sound impossible—and wonderful!"

Wonderful indeed, agreed Joseph, surveying with grim amusement the array of disabled plows which had been flowing into his shop since dawn. But not impossible. People often hid their treasure in a field. Remember how Shemuel, over at Cana, had found just such a jar of silver coins when working in a field as hired laborer and had covered it up and gone and sold everything he had in order to purchase the field? Oh, Jonathan had undoubtedly found something! The fact that his father was reported at the moment to be pushing a plow and his brothers to be industriously digging up the family patrimony with spade and mattock was proof enough of that! But as to the size of the treasure, whether gold or silver, handful or omer, Joseph would reserve his judgment until he heard the truth from Jonathan's own lips.

Before the day was over Jonathan appeared, a Jonathan with bright eye and determined step, broad shoulders upheld with confidence beneath his redeemed *simlah*, headcloth secured at a slightly jaunty angle.

"See!"

He displayed the marvels with his usual minimum of speech and emotion—the two broken pottery jars which he had found fitted together to form a clean and airtight chamber, a single gold coin which he removed with great care from a much-folded piece of cloth tucked in the pocket of his girdle.

"Twelve of them," he explained with simple candor. "Took five to pay Jered. Seven left. Enough to pay the rest of my bride's settlement and buy that old house of Nathan's next door to ours. I'll take Lilah there to live. Not so crowded. That's why I'm here. House needs a new door and roof timbers. Can see you're busy, both you and the boy." He looked around apologetically at the array of plows. "But if you could find time—"

Joseph took the coin and studied it, holding it high between thumb and forefinger, rubbing it on the end of his headcloth, looking at it hard again. The hands of the Boy, busily twisting a leather cord around the handle of an auger, became suddenly still.

"A Greek stater," commented the carpenter with interest. "Bears the head of some despicable conqueror, maybe Alexander, maybe Antiochus. Ben Arza could tell you which one. There are many of them about the country. Could have been there in the ground a long time, maybe a hundred years." He returned the coin to Jonathan's big careful fingers. "At least nobody can dispute your ownership. You found it in your own field."

"You can come soon and work on the house?" The habit of diffidence was strong. "I—I'll pay you as soon as the barley—that is, I hope—" Jonathan straightened his shoulders. "I can pay you immediately," he amended firmly. "And not with grain or oil. With money."

"We will come soon," said Joseph. "And not because you can pay money. The plows can wait."

Miriam curiously fingered one of the yellow-brown pottery fragments, tracing with the tip of her nail the design of dark concentric circles. "I had a jar just like that once. Remember, Joseph?"

The carpenter shrugged his broad shoulders. "They've been making that style in Nazareth for generations. Go out on the town dump and you'll find a hundred other broken pots just like it."

With deft speed the Boy finished twisting the leather cord about the handle, inserted the bit of the auger in the small hole marked at one end of a plowshare, and holding an end of the cord in either hand, spun it vigorously from side to side, driving the bit deep into the wood. Faster and faster his slim hands flew, until the whirling auger made a bright humming sound and the flying sawdust seemed like golden sparks in the sun.

12

SHAKEDH, the white almond, wakener of spring and symbol of new hope, burst into bloom overnight.

Never, the Boy thought, had spring come so early or been so beautiful.

Due perhaps to quickened zeal for plow and spade, every tiny plot was under cultivation, and the valley below the town, crisscrossed by little cactus hedges, was a tapestry of jade and emerald. On the high stone terraces oranges and apricots and pomegranates mingled their whites and pinks and scarlets. And, strewn thickly with the red and blue and yellow flowers of springtime, the fourteen rounded hills enclosing the valley looked more than ever like the petals of a full-blown rose.

Beautiful *shakedh*, bearing at the same time bud and blossom and fruit, in fulfillment of its own promise! This year, to the Boy's delight, it was the wakener of happiness as well as beauty. He took keen pleasure in rubbing Jonathan's new square doorposts of sycamore to such a fine finish that Lilah, stroking them, boasted they looked as fine as cedar.

It was a new, cheerful Lilah who came each day to inspect the progress of the house, laughingly helping to hoist the heavy roof timbers into place, pleased as a child when the layers of brush, reeds, grass, and clay had been rolled hard and smooth and she could trip up the narrow outer stairway to the housetop. There was no discontent in her sparkling eyes these days. No other bride of Nazareth this spring would be brought home to a house all her own—a small one, to be sure, no larger than a good-sized storeroom and with only the tiniest courtyard—but at least hers.

Though Jonathan said little, his strong, homely features glowed with happiness, and his big hands were never still. After working all day in the fields, he toiled late into the night on his new house, chinking the stone walls by lamplight, painstakingly fitting tiny chips of limestone into even patterns on the mud-plaster floor, patiently fashioning an oven out of alternating layers of clay and potsherds, pushing the stone roller over and over the housetop until its surface was hard and smooth as a threshing floor.

It was all for Lilah. His every look and motion proclaimed it.

But *shakedh* wakened others than Jonathan and Lilah to a springtime of fresh happiness.

On its high terrace behind the hedge of pointed cypresses the small tight house opened its doors wide to the sunlight. No longer did the widow Deborah bend over her fine embroidery by lamplight. She sat in her untidy courtyard, its door open to the street, and plied her needle on bordered robes and bodices and coverlets and girdles for all the world to see.

So sudden and amazing was the transformation that in the bubbling and spilling of gossip about the village well her name was heard almost as frequently as that of the lucky Jonathan.

"I couldn't believe it when she actually invited me inside!"

"She showed me just how she dyed her yarns and offered to loan me one of her patterns!"

"Is it true what they say?"…"That worthless brother of hers who ran away—" "—found gold in the mines down in Egypt—" "Not a brother, an uncle, I heard—" "Something must have happened, but what?"

Miriam could have told them, at least all that Deborah knew, for the latter came straight from Jered's house to Joseph's.

"God be praised! He has heard the cry of the widow and the fatherless in their distress! See, Miriam and Joseph, friends of my dead husband Dathan. Always now we shall have a roof over our heads!"

Wonderingly Miriam took the bit of parchment from the trembling fingers, "What—I'm so glad, Deborah, but—" she tried to make sense out of the scrawled markings—"I don't understand!"

"Let me see," said Joseph.

She surrendered the parchment gratefully, for she had always found business details confusing. Besides, she knew that it satisfied some deep need in her carpenter-husband to display his meager store of learning. Forced to leave school at an early age to care for his widowed mother and family, he had acquired such knowledge as he could through careful listening at the daily synagogue services and fierce concentration by lamplight on the two precious rolls of scripture which had been handed down in his family for generations.

Still it was a galling vexation to his sensitive spirit that his young wife, the daughter of a rabbi, could read and write better than himself!

"Yes, Joseph, tell us what it says. It looks like a business document, and you know how stupid I am about such things."

He studied the parchment, frowning, shaping each word slowly with his lips. "A receipt," he pronounced finally, "signed by Jered the elder. Stating that Deborah, widow of Dathan, has discharged all her debts."

"Yes." Tears of joy streamed from the weak eyes. "That's what he told me it said, only, not being able to read, I couldn't be sure. It's all paid. We're free now. We'll always have a roof over our heads. There's nothing more to be afraid of. Ever."

"Deborah, my dear!" Miriam hugged the thin, stooped shoulders. "I'm so happy for you. But I still don't understand. How—"

Deborah herself could hardly understand it. It had all happened so suddenly, this very day. A messenger had come to her house, said he was from a caravan camped down below in the valley and he had been told to bring her this bag—see, she had it right here—no, she must have left it at the booth of Jered—but, anyway, it was just a small goatskin bag such as anybody might carry in his girdle pocket.

At first she couldn't believe it when she looked inside. She thought it must be copper instead of gold. Not until she had taken it to Jered had she been sure. And there had been just enough of the beautiful shining sun-yellow coins to pay her debt, ten of them. The God of Israel be praised, was it not wonderful?

"Wonderful, indeed," agreed Miriam, her eyes shining. "But who—"

Ah, yes, who! Deborah had thought of that too. She had a brother, a wild sort of boy who had gone off to seek his fortune, in Egypt she had heard. And were there not gold mines down there somewhere? Or it might have come from an uncle, her father's brother, who had once lived beyond the Jordan but whom she supposed had died long ago. If she had only thought to ask the messenger where the caravan had come from—or even where it was going! But, then, it didn't really matter, did it? It was God who should be thanked for answering a poor widow's prayers.

Yes, agreed Miriam, smiling. It didn't really matter.

13

BUT IT WAS FOR the woman Mulcah that *shakedh*, the wakener, burst most whitely into bloom.

The town did not know exactly when it happened. It merely discovered suddenly that the sounds of music and dancing and laughter no longer drifted from the terrace overlooking the inn, that the small house at the top of the narrow winding path was by day wide-open to the sunlight and by night tight-closed and dark. And instead of slinking to the well before dawn and after dark, the woman Mulcah now came openly to draw water at the hours when the women of Nazareth were accustomed to gather.

It happened that the first evening she came the Boy was there also.

"Let me go with you, Mother?" When Miriam lifted her empty jar, he sprang up, shaking his coat clean of shavings.

She consented gratefully, yielding to him the heavy jar and taking a smaller one herself.

"I suppose I won't be able to go after I become a Son of the Law," he said ruefully, lifting the jar to the supporting coil of braided fibers he had placed on his head. "It wouldn't be considered proper for a man to be seen drawing water with the women!"

"Nor is it proper for a boy as tall as his mother to be doing woman's work," chided Miriam, her voice half teasing, half tender. "I don't know what people will say when they see you."

"They'll say," returned the Boy gaily as they fell easily into step, " 'What a wonderful mother that foolish Jeshua, the carpenter's son, must think he has!' "

"No," retorted the woman. "They'll say, 'Look at that foolish wife of Joseph. Acting like a queen with a slave instead of the poor carpenter's wife she is! But you can't blame her for looking so proud. With the most wonderful son any woman ever had!' " Then they fell silent, remembering the countless times they had traveled this familiar path together: slowly at first, the woman patiently adjusting her gait to toddling steps; then swiftly, breathlessly, in an attempt to keep pace with darting feet; slowly again while the lean little body and stubborn curly head learned to balance a small jar; then, as the years passed, bringing the two jars and the two heads nearer the same size and level, slowly or swiftly as mood or necessity might will.

Now it was the Boy who adjusted his longer pace to hers, carrying the heavy jar, turning to give her a supporting hand on the stony path. Discovering suddenly that she had to look up to meet his eyes, the woman felt a swift upsurge of nostalgia, almost of panic. Henceforth they would be growing, not closer together, but farther apart. Perhaps this was the last time they would ever come to the well together.

Seeing his face grow suddenly intent, she followed his glance to see who or what had caused it. Her step faltered, and she lifted her hand to steady the jar on her head.

The woman Mulcah stood at one side of the fountain apart from the others, obviously not from choice but because the chattering group huddled about the stone trough within the arched recess formed a tight knot designed to exclude her. She wore a plain robe of dark homespun, barren of embroidery or jewels. The oval of cheek visible beneath the drawn veil was devoid of artificial color. Only in the lustrous eyes did the fires of restless beauty remain unquenched.

The child Daniel ran to meet the newcomers.

"It's my friend! Look, Mother, my friend Jeshua!"

"*Shalom*, Danny!" The Boy laughed. So sudden was the assault of small arms about his moving limbs that the jar almost toppled. Steadying it with one hand, he patted the eagerly upturned head with the other. "Lucky this jar is coming instead of going! You might have had a bath."

The thread of chatter issuing from the knot about the well suddenly snapped. In the ensuing silence the childish treble was shrilly audible.

"Will you come to my house again soon, Jeshua? My mother said it was all right now to ask you."

Conscious of the eyes turned upon him, the Boy hesitated only a second. "Yes, of course I will, Danny."

So palpable was the silence that water could plainly be heard gurgling into the narrow mouth of a submerged and forgotten jug. In her swift movement forward the woman Mulcah did not break the silence but merely gave it form and substance. Never with all her artistry had she so claimed the awareness of these, her fellow townswomen. Eyes which had glanced fleetingly at bright imported silks stared, hypnotized, at homespun linen. Nostrils dilated in vain quest of exotic perfumes. Ears strained to catch the sound of tinkling anklets.

"We—we'd like to invite you all to come, my Danny and I." Her voice, too, higher than usual and nervously unrhythmic, had never so captured their attention with all its haunting and melodious sweetness. "I—I've been fixing up the house, and—I'd like so much for you to see it."

Less amazed than embarrassed, the women broke their tight knot but not their silence. Turning their backs again, they tried to act as if nothing had happened, instantly defeating their purpose by a spurious burst of activity, dipping their jars with such concerted haste and vigor that the water gushed from the trough into the overflow pool below.

"I—I want you to know that—things are different now." The woman's voice pursued them with desperate insistence. "My—my husband has sent us money so we can—can live the way we've always wanted to—"

Having filled their jugs, the women left the arched enclosure so hastily that elbows jostled, water was slopped, and one jar crashed to the stone pavement, its owner not even stopping to pick up the pieces. Only when they had reached the edge of the open space about the fountain did they drift together again into small knots, glancing back furtively, murmuring.

Stepping quickly forward, the Boy set down his jar and took the vessel from Mulcah's hands. "Come, Danny. Help me fill these. You take mine, and I'll take your mother's, and we'll see who gets his jar filled first. *Ah hah*, you can't reach the trough, can you! Here, I'll lift you up so you can kneel on the edge."

The child squealed with delight as his hands plunged into the cold pool and water gurgled into the round aperture. "I won, Jeshua! See, my—!"

The Boy rescued him just in time. "This isn't the time for taking baths," he teased, "nor the place. Come tomorrow morning, and your mother will give you and your clothes a good scrubbing in the overflow pool. Won't you, mother of Daniel?"

"I—I don't know—" The woman's voice was small, bleak, the gesture with which she reached for the jar clumsy.

Ignoring the gesture, the Boy lifted the brimming jar to her head. "Come early, when the sun is just peering over Mount Tabor," he advised cheerfully. "That's when my mother always comes to wash her clothes, and you can work together. You will be here then, won't you, Mother?"

Miriam's fingers tightened on the handles of the water jar so that the knuckles showed white. The color ebbed from her cheeks. In panic her glance fled toward the backs of the retreating women, then slowly returned to rest on the small figure of Daniel beside the overflow pool, balancing himself precariously on one bare foot while delightedly dangling the toes of the other. Exactly the way...

Without looking, she could sense the swift familiar tensing of the woman Mulcah, prepared to dash forward the instant the small body should sway a bit too far. But there was no need of worrying, she could have told her. You always expected your Little One to fall, yet he never did.

The color flowed back into her cheeks.

"Yes," she said. "I will be here."

14

IT HAD COME—the day of his long-awaited initiation into manhood.

Long before dawn he sprang awake, excitement tingling his flesh, the morning prayer of thanksgiving so singing-clear in his consciousness that it seemed the whole world must be shouting it.

" 'My God, the soul which thou hast given me is clean,' " his lips intoned silently. " 'Thou hast created it, formed it, and breathed it into me. While this soul lives in me, I thank thee, O Eternal One, my God, and the God of my fathers.' "

Then, because this sounded so distant and formal, like greeting some important visiting dignitary, he added simply, "Thank you, Father."

A fly buzzed against his forehead, and without thinking he almost lifted his hand to brush it away, but stopped, horrified, just in time. Suppose he had broken the Law the very first thing on this, of all days, touching his face with his hand before both had been properly cleansed from the defilement of sleep! The tingles of excitement turned to shivers of apprehension. It was a sobering, frightening thing, becoming a man. So many laws to keep! And after today he would be held responsible for every sin he committed!

He performed the morning ritual with a fevered intensity of concentration, moving no more than four steps from his mat before washing his hands and face and following the prescribed formula with nervous precision. Lifting the ewer, filled with clean water the night before, with his right hand and passing it into his left, he let the cool clear stream flow three times over his right hand, careful to keep its fingers open and pointing toward the ground...then repeated the process for his left. Once, twice, three times he washed his face, after which, joining the palms of his hands with thumbs and fingers outstretched, and facing southward toward Jerusalem, he mingled his voice with Joseph's in the morning prayers.

"Lift up your hands to the sanctuary, and praise the Lord!"

"Blessed art thou, O Lord our God! King of the universe!"

But once the door to the sunlit world outside had been unbolted, the mood of solemnity vanished.

It was a beautiful Sabbath, the tender spring day as full of new life and promise as a newborn lamb! A chorus of antiphonal psalms burst from a thousand feathered throats.

"You're sure," inquired Miriam anxiously for at least the tenth time as she adjusted the folds of his new prayer shawl, "you remember your Portion? And you won't forget to kiss the fringes at the proper times during the prayers?"

"He knows his Portion so well he could say it backward," Joseph assured her gruffly, his hands trembling as he checked again to make sure the new phylacteries were complete in all details. "And how can he make mistakes in the service with me sitting there beside him?"

It seemed strange accompanying his father and the other men straight through the main street of town, rather than going by back lanes with the women to keep from being seen. Stranger yet to enter the synagogue by the front door instead of the side entrance leading to the balcony behind the wooden grill.

Joseph was more nervous than his son when the time for presentation came. His hands trembled when he fastened on the new phylacteries, and, if the Boy had not whispered to him, he would have bound the wrong one about his son's head. But at last both were in place, the first, with its four tiny parchment compartments, fastened to his forehead exactly between the eyes; the second, bound to his left arm, its leather thongs wound seven times around the arm and three times around the middle finger.

Henceforth he would wear them every day of his life for morning prayers, except on Sabbaths such as this and holy days. The words written on the tiny rolls of leather had become part of his very flesh.

Hear, O Israel: the Lord our God is one Lord; and you shall love the Lord your God with all your heart, and with all your soul and with all your might...

Jered, the chief elder, looked oddly displeased during the presentation.

"He hasn't forgotten what I said in the market place," thought the Boy soberly, glad that after the ceremony he was bidden to sit by his father on the platform among the elders, where he need not look at Jered. Thankfully he fixed his gaze on the proud kindly face of the *chazzan*, Ben Arza, glowing like a florid sun in its halo of short gray locks.

"Steady, son." His teacher's mild eyes were warmly reassuring. So familiar were his every gesture and expression that the Boy could almost hear him speak the words. "There's nothing to fear. Have not you and I read together your Portion a hundred times in this very place? And you are not here today to be seen of men, but to be found acceptable in the sight of God."

Yet when the time came to recite his Portion and he faced the sea of upturned faces, the Boy was seized with panic. His hands trembled so that he almost dropped the roll delivered into them by Ben Arza. The familiar words blanked from his memory, and when he tried to find them on the scroll, the Hebrew characters swam together in blind confusion. He opened his lips, but no sound came.

Then slowly the waves of the sea parted, and features emerged, beloved, familiar features of friends. Jonathan, beaming with pride and satisfaction. Lemuel, their next door neighbor, whose yokes were left a little rough on the inside, but whose pockets always yielded generous doles of nuts and raisins. The brightly expectant eyes of the mild little man Hanan, who, having no relatives and no business of his own, managed somehow to relate himself to everybody else's business. Old Nathan, the vinedresser, eagerly leaning forward, hands cupped behind his deaf ears. Tubal, the burly innkeeper, become suddenly grim and pinched of feature since he had lost his only son.

The Boy's heart swelled almost to bursting. Afraid of these, his friends and neighbors? Why, they loved him as he loved them! Yes, and most of them were like Jonathan and Deborah and Gad and the woman Mulcah, needing something. So far he had been able to help such a few of them with his Gifts! But he would find a way, he must find it!

He delivered his Portion of the Law clearly, confidently, waiting after each sentence, as Ben Arza had so painstakingly taught him, for the interpreter to translate his Hebrew into Aramaic. When he had finished, the comments of the congregation, never slow to seek expression once the first devotional ritual of the service was completed, were loud and gratifying.

"I heard everything he said," this triumphantly from old Nathan, "even though I couldn't understand a word!"

"Well done, Joseph's son!" shouted another.

"A worthy Son of the Law you will be, like your father."

"A pleasing voice, clear as a ram's horn, yet sweet as with the drippings of honey!"

"Read to us more, son of Joseph! Let's see if you can do as well with something you have not memorized."

"Ay, you have recited from the Law. Now read to us from the Prophets!"

The Boy caught his breath. Again panic seized him. He turned helplessly to Ben Arza, who, hands clinging excitedly to each strand of his forked gray beard, was nodding proud but nervous encouragement.

"Whatever you say," the *chazzan* whispered. "Amos? Jeremiah? Isaiah?"

The Boy's senses slowly steadied. "Isaiah," he whispered back. "The second roll."

Ben Arza approached the recess at the back of the small enclosed platform, reverently drew aside the curtain, and with trembling fingers removed another of the Sacred Rolls. So excited was he that he could scarcely find the edges of the outer silk wrapping, and the inner ones of linen seemed to have no end.

Never had such a thing happened before to one of his pupils. It was the supreme compliment to his teaching, also its supreme test. There were stern critics of Hebrew among the elders. Some of them, Joseph the carpenter among them, had been suggesting of late that Ben Arza be replaced by a man of less liberal persuasion, preferably of the School of Shammai in Jerusalem, which taught the strictest observance of the Law. Ben Arza, being of the more liberal school of

Hillel, had never been too popular with these sterner believers, careful though he had always been not to commit himself too freely on controversial questions. Ay, he needed the prestige of a good pupil! And it was doubly satisfying that the honor could be shared with the most beloved of all his pupils, the son of Joseph!

The Boy accepted the scroll with steady fingers and purposefully unrolled it. Ben Arza began to breathe more easily. His pupil was not confused. He knew for what passage he was looking. Ah! The hands were motionless now, their slender fingers curled lovingly about the bulging ends. The rabbi again held his breath, waiting in an agony of suspense. Would he be able to find his place? And if he did find it, could he pronounce the words without halting? Would he—

The voice came, clear and confident.

> "The Spirit of the Lord God is upon me,
> because the Lord has anointed me
> to bring good tidings to the afflicted."

Of course! Ben Arza should have known he would choose that passage! It was his favorite. Only last week he had stayed after the school session and asked what it meant. And his recitation of the Hebrew had been flawless. To be sure, some of the questions he had asked about it had been baffling! But there would be no questions today. The rabbi drew a long breath of relief and, closing his eyes, swayed in ecstatic rhythm to the poetic cadence.

> "he has sent me to bind up the brokenhearted
> to proclaim liberty to the captives,
> and the opening of the prison to those who are bound;
> to proclaim—to proclaim—"

The voice faltered, and Ben Arza's eyes flew open. *Ah hah*! What was the matter? Had he forgotten how to pronounce the word? But he had spoken it faultlessly last week! Had he lost his place? But he wasn't even hunting for it! His eyes seemed to be lifted. He was looking over the scroll.

" 'The year,' " whispered the rabbi in Hebrew, adding with more audible desperation, " 'the year of the Lord's favor'!"

Ah hah! It was no use. The son of Joseph had disgraced both himself and his teacher. He had stumbled over the simplest of Hebrew words. Ben Arza clutched the two prongs of his beard in despair.

And now Jered was angry. He was standing up from his seat in the center of the elders. He was pointing an accusing finger...

"Out of here! Out of this synagogue!"

Ben Arza endured a thousand agonies until, sick with apprehension, he turned to face the congregation. Only then did he understand, with a mingling of relief and even greater horror, that it was not the son of Joseph at whom Jered, the chief elder, was pointing.

15

THE BOY stared unbelievingly.

It could not be Gad, the crippled son of Old Simon, coming slowly down the aisle between the two rows of pillars, stopping in the center of the room to look about him. And yet it was. No mistaking the grotesquely hunched body, the dragging foot, the harelip which distorted the face into a constant grimace.

But it was a Gad whom the Boy had never seen before. The usually clean tunic and coat of rough sheepskin were stained with blood, the headcloth awry, and in the outstretched arms—When he finally saw what it was that the son of Old Simon was holding, the Boy's head swam and his stomach turned suddenly sick. Hastily rerolling the parchment with cold fingers, he turned and thrust it into Ben Arza's hands.

"Out of here, I tell you!" repeated Jered in an outraged voice. "I command you to come not one step farther, *on penalty of death!"*

When the figure made no further motion, the chief elder angrily addressed the congregation. "Shame, men of Nazareth! Will you all sit like stones, your mouths gaping caves, and let the holy house of God be profaned? Take him away, someone! Get that—that infamous son of evil out of here!"

But he might as well have been commanding stones, for the congregation had become one staring, gaping mass, as incapable of action as Ben Arza, standing with hands frozen about the parchment roll. The first few moments only Jered broke the silence. Then behind the grill of the balcony a woman screamed. An old man laughed hysterically. The low buzzing of lips swelled to an excited murmur,

"Who…what's that he's holding…of Old Simon…cursed for his father's sins…what's he doing…come here to pollute us all… possessed of a devil…and carrying a burden on the Sabbath…a *lamb*…it can't be…a *dead* lamb, I tell you, freshly killed, can't you see, and it's still bleeding…anger of the Lord will smite us all… house of God made unclean…do what Jered says, get him out…"

But as the hunched figure bearing its strange burden moved down the aisle toward the elders' platform, no one moved to stop him.

Hands lifted in righteous horror, Jered retreated precipitately, and the other elders left their seats to huddle about him. With a sudden frenzy of agitation Ben Arza rewound the parchment roll in its voluminous wrappings and, thrusting it into the niche behind the curtain, spread his arms protectively across the sacred aperture. Of all the disturbed occupants on the platform, the Boy alone remained motionless.

But the son of Simon made no attempt to mount the steps. Extending his long arms with their gruesome burden, he burst into a torrent of sounds as distorted as his twisted lips.

Jered turned to the other elders helplessly. "Offspring of evil! By what sort of devil is he possessed? Can—can he neither understand speech nor make himself understood? Wh—what are we to do? Why doesn't somebody get him out of here!"

The Boy tore his horrified gaze from the lifeless object in the outstretched arms.

"I can tell you what Gad is saying," he told Jered reluctantly. "If you know him well enough, it's not difficult to understand him."

"You *can!*" The chief elder turned to him swiftly, eyes narrowing speculatively even in his relief and agitation. "You are saying that the son of Joseph—knows the son of Simon? Knows him—well?"

The Boy flushed. Beyond the bulky, silk-draped shoulder he caught a glimpse of his father's face, pale with shock and horror.

"Well enough to have talked with him sometimes when I've been walking in the hills," he explained carefully, "always taking heed, however, to observe the Law. Well enough to be able to tell you now what he is saying."

"So?" This time the warmth of genuine relief was in Jered's voice. "Then tell us, son of Joseph."

"He says," returned the Boy quietly, "that he killed the lamb just now with his own hands. It was a new lamb, just born, which his father had left in the house to keep warm while he went out to tend his sheep. Gad killed it and brought it here as an offering to God to atone for the sins of his father."

"He—what!" Though it was Jered's voice, the words seemed to spring from a dozen horrified throats.

Again the son of Old Simon burst into excited speech, and the Boy listened gravely, turning back to the elders when the outburst had ended.

"His father had told him about going to the temple in Jerusalem and offering a lamb for sacrifice to take away one's sins. Gad could not go to the temple, so he killed the lamb and brought it here, to God's house, so that his father might be happy again in the knowledge that his sin was pardoned."

At first there was an appalled silence, then a shocked buzzing of tongues, followed by the harsh tearing of cloth as one of the elders, convinced that he had witnessed sacrilege, dutifully rent his garments. Lifting his own jeweled fingers in the pious preparatory gesture, Jered himself desisted from the act just in time to prevent the destruction of his new, expensive tunic of imported silk. So loud and excited was the hubbub both on the platform and in the congregation that he had to shout to make himself heard. No need to consult his fellow elders as to the righteousness of his judgment! He had only to gather up their shocked articulations, weld them into the proper words and phrases, imbue them with the loud accents of authority.

Forgiveness for one who had been pronounced *Cherem*, devoted to destruction? Let the very stones of the synagogue echo their divine protest to such blasphemy! Did not the son bear evidence in his accursed body of his father's sin? And was not the house of God offended by his presence, to say nothing of his wanton Sabbath-breaking and defiance of the holy Law? Then let the righteous men of Nazareth arise and cleanse the sacred place of this abomination! Let them act...

They arose. They acted.

Frightened, confused, the Boy watched them come. Who were they? Not his friends, his beloved townspeople. He recognized none of them. That could not be Abner, the potter, lips curled over yellow teeth, crouched like a wild beast ready to spring. Nor the mild-mannered Hanan, his bright eyes sharpened into knife-points. It was

68

not Eben the silversmith, cursing and clawing the air like a vulture, even though it bore Eben's red-rimmed eyes and bony features. And surely that swift-moving giant with his teeth bared and his fists held high—not Jonathan! Quivering, the Boy braced himself.

But it was not he they wanted. They had forgotten him.

Swarming down the aisle between the columns, massing about the son of Old Simon, they bore him away, not by lifting him bodily—that would have been labor, forbidden by divine Law on the Sabbath—but as a wave might carry a bit of wreckage on its crest. Once outside the synagogue, however, there were those willing and ready to forget legal inhibitions. Stones and brickbats and clods of hard earth found their way into itching hands. Finding the motions of the cripple too slow, they hoisted him roughly to their shoulders, hustled him to the edge of town, then speeded him on his way with the aid of curses, jibes, and more substantial missiles.

Later at home, to the Boy's surprise and gratitude, Joseph did not chide him for his action in the synagogue.

"You read well, my son. And, though I confess you had me sorely troubled for a time, I must commend you for your contribution to the cause of justice. Without your help we would not have known the enormity of the offense committed, and the son of the accursed one might not have been properly punished. I—I am glad, however, that you made it plain to the elders that you transgressed no laws."

Miriam remained silent, her relief that Joseph was not angry deadened by the consciousness that the Boy's pleasure in this greatest of all days had been destroyed. Mechanically she folded the prayer shawls and laid them away in the chest, spread on the low table for the noonday meal the festive food prepared with such excited expectancy the day before—fresh bread, goat's milk cheese, salted fish, a kettle of boiled lentils kept warm with many wrappings, little cakes baked with honey.

Almost indifferently she noted that the small wine cask, its contents saved for just such occasions as this, had sprung a leak, and reached absent-mindedly for a bit of wax to seal the hole. Then she remembered just in time that such an act was forbidden on the Sabbath.

Trembling, she stood watching the crimson drops ooze from the hole like tiny beads of sweat, trickle down the side of the jar and disappear between the stones of the courtyard, not knowing why she trembled, whether because the precious wine was being lost or she had almost broken the Sabbath, or because the red drops might have been blood from a small lamb, freshly slain, held in outstretched arms.

16

THE BOY told no one where he was going. Hastening to the edge of town by back, unfrequented lanes, he followed a path which led up the hill for a short distance, then wound along a terrace between cactus hedges and vineyards, descending finally to the narrow pass through which ran the main-traveled road from the valley below Nazareth to Sepphoris. Following this road only a few steps, he turned aside again into another path, barely distinguishable amid the tumbling gray rocks and thick grass and thistles, for few people ever traveled this path. Today, however, it was easier to trace, for there were frequent red stains on the rocks and leaves and blades of grass.

"Like spring poppies," he thought miserably.

He had to know if Gad had gotten home safely and how badly he was hurt. The shepherd's hut was at the end of this long path which led over two more hills and halfway up another. If he hurried, he would be able to get there and back before Joseph wakened from his noon siesta.

He had reached the top of the first hill when suddenly he remembered. His feet stopped as if frozen, and his throat constricted. For a second time that day he had almost forgotten that it was the Sabbath!

Had he traveled more than the two thousand cubits, which were the limit of a Sabbath day's journey? Hastily he reckoned, relief flooding over him in hot waves when he assured himself that as yet the Law had not been broken.

Breathless both from exertion and emotion, he dropped down on a green patch of grass by an outcropping of limestone. Stretching himself full-length in this favorite position, toes dug into a soft hollow, slim body chin-deep in the warm earthy fragrance, he waited for the tumult within him to subside.

At least the Law said nothing about how far one's eyes could travel!

The intervening hill was too high to afford a view of Old Simon's hut, but the path leading over its stony top was devoid of life. Gad had presumably reached home, then, with his burden. And surely his father must be with him! As far as the eye could see, there was no sign of a shepherd with his flock, nor did his straining ears catch the faintest echo of whistle or clucking or long-drawn "Ta-a-a, ho-o-o-o!" Besides, if Old Simon had left a young lamb in his hut, he would not have stayed away this long.

"And he will have put oil on poor Gad's bruises," thought the Boy, suddenly relieved because the old shepherd, already a lawbreaker, would scorn the provision which forbade the application of soothing remedies on the Sabbath. Then he flushed guiltily, aghast at his own relief.

The day had turned hot and suffocating. Sunlight throbbed and quivered before his eyes like flecks of copper—no, like millions of round gold coins. There was mocking irony in their dancing. For, though a goatskin bag big as all Galilee were his and though it were full of gold coins, he could never buy with them new life and happiness for Old Simon and his son Gad. If there were only some way of making the old shepherd understand what God was really like!

The tender spring morning had been so sweet and full of promise, like—*like a newborn lamb.*

His hot cheeks sought cool solace in the grass, but even now, with spring barely come, it felt oven-crisp to his touch. A few handbreadths away, in the thin soil edging the rock outcropping, a tiny red anemone was fighting vainly to live, its stem growing limp and its petals already shriveling. The Boy stared at it in dismay. Born, like the lamb, in the very act of dying—and to what purpose?

Suddenly he was on his feet, digging at the sparse soil about the roots of the panting blossom. Carrying it tenderly, he hunted and hunted until he found a sheltered space between two rocks where the grass was thick and soft and the soil deep. Then he dug a hole with his fingers, set it inside and patted the earth firmly about it. At least this one bit of creation should not die so quickly.

It was only when he was on his feet, brushing the dirt from his hands, that he realized with horror what he had done. Performed labor on the Sabbath, both by plowing—breaking the ground—and cultivating! By attempting to give life he had disobeyed God, broken his holy Law. And on this first day of his manhood, when he had become responsible for his own sins! He must go home and do penance, perform the necessary washings to cleanse himself so the Most Holy One, the Lord God of Israel, would no longer be displeased.

Turning, he walked slowly back down the path, trying not to step on the stains which had once been red but were turning now into a dull, ugly brown.

"Like dead petals," he thought absently.

Though sweat stood on his forehead and ran down his limbs, he shivered.

If only he himself knew what God was really like!

FRANKINCENSE

ALL HIS LIFE the Boy had looked forward to his first visit to Jerusalem. Even the preparations for the pilgrimage, begun a full month before the Passover, were exciting. On all the hillsides tombs were freshly whitewashed. A labor levy, detailed to repair roads and bridges, preempted the inn for two uproarious nights, and for ten days an official money-changer from the Jerusalem temple occupied an imposing stall in the market place. The Boy went with his father to change the Roman denars commonly in use for the sacred half-shekel Hebrew coins required to pay the temple tax. Joseph left the booth grumbling.

"Thieves! Every year they demand a higher rate for the exchange!"

"Then why not wait until we get to Jerusalem?" inquired the Boy. "Ben Arza says there are money-changers in the porches of the Temple. They wouldn't dare cheat us there in God's house with all his priests watching."

Joseph gave his son a sharp glance. "Easier to do it here," he replied briefly.

On the morning of departure half of Nazareth assembled in the open space about the fountain, a confusion of heaped baggage, milling donkeys, stray dogs nosing at food packets, shouting and gesticulating men, mothers calling last-minute orders to children and their caretakers being left behind, bleating lambs, water-carriers, importunate peddlers. But at last order emerged. By sunrise the pilgrims were on the march, Jered riding at their head as chief elder, the bright yellow banner painted with the name of the town floating proudly in the spring breeze.

It was thrilling to be part of the curling lines of script scrawled across the great scroll of Esdraelon! As if he were helping to make the history of his people, exulted the Boy, not just reading it! That first day they passed over the dwindling streams of the Kishon, harmless ghosts of the torrent which had swept away Sisera; past Shunem, high on its slope, where Elisha had found sanctuary in an upper room; on toward the frowning battlements of Jezreel, from which a queen had been flung to her death; to the bold outthrust flanks of Gilboa.

There was no conflict in the valley today. Fields of green grass and golden grain bordered the road and stretched as far as eye could see. Larks soared low to mingle their songs with those of the rejoicing pilgrims.

Though many of the younger travelers ran ahead or embarked on adventurous side trips, the Boy did not join them. Time enough for wandering when his exuberant cousins, Jacob and Johanan, from Capernaum, joined the company! Today he walked with his father beside the two donkeys, their own Graylegs, on which his mother rode, and a lazy, stubborn little beast which Joseph had hired to carry the bulky packs containing food, clothing, and camping equipment.

The going was slow, for the good Roman road, though wide enough for ordinary traffic, was massed with pilgrims, all jealously vying for the foremost place. More than one such group, its banner proudly proclaiming another Galilean town, plowed a path through the fields and, with cheerful disregard of flattened grain and irate farmers, swept past the Nazareth delegation with good-natured taunts and triumphant wavings. Others turned off at the junction close to Jezreel, taking the road leading eastward toward the Jordan Valley. But the blue and crimson banner of Capernaum was not among them.

Miriam, who had looked forward for months to this reunion with her sister Salome, became more and more anxious.

"Suppose," she finally worried aloud, "the Capernaum caravan goes by the other route! We might never find each other! Are you sure, my husband, the message you received from Zebedee mentioned En-gannim?"

Joseph was sure. But Capernaum, he reminded her, was many hours beyond Nazareth, and the lake people were habitually slow in getting started. However, if they should change their plans and go by the Jordan road, he would not blame them. He had tried hard enough to persuade Jered and the other elders to do so. Safe though it might be, going through Samaria with a host like this, it was surely no way to prepare oneself for holy days, staining one's feet and garments with the dust of heathen soil. One might as well enter the cave of Panias and witness the despicable rites of the fertility gods as to have dealings with the ungodly Samaritans!

Samaritans! The mere name sent prickles down the Boy's spine. All his life he had been taught to fear and despise them, those mongrel interlopers wedged into the hill country between Galilee and Judea, their Hebrew inheritance diluted by centuries of compromise and intermarriage with foreigners. And now he was to pass through their country, perhaps even endure some of the injuries and insults they were said to perpetrate on their enemies of the true faith. He shivered at the prospect.

They camped that first night at En-gannim—Fountain of Gardens—on the border of Samaria. After helping to pitch the small goat's-hair tent and gather sticks for a fire, the Boy ran up the steep slope to one of the foothills of Mount Gilboa.

Strange, to be looking back across Esdraelon from the brown hills he had seen so often in the distance! He could still see the white stones of Nazareth pinned like a cluster of pearls on the bosom of the hills. Even as he watched, its luster faded, slipped into the gray folds of twilight. He knew with a sudden sense of both loss and anticipation that his childhood had gone with it. So quickly did night descend that he had to feel his way down toward the galaxy of little fires, his mountain-bred feet picking their way with the sure instinct of an animal.

"Jeshua! *Shalom! Shalom!*"

The two figures bounded from the circle of firelight and fell upon him joyously, their exuberant energy as all-pervasive as their smell of fish.

Jacob and Johanan, the sons of Zebedee, were hero-worshipers. But the object of their boyish adoration was no fabulous giant whose exploits were sung by wandering minstrels. It was a slim boy no older than themselves whose sole claim to superiority lay in his utter disclaim of any such assumption. During the remainder of the journey to Jerusalem they would scarcely let him out of their sight

"Look, Jeshua! There's a cave up on that hillside. If we run ahead of the caravan, we'll have time to explore it!"

It was Jacob, the older and sturdier of the two brothers, who was always planning such expeditions far afield; the slender and more thoughtful Johanan who wanted to linger curiously beside the road after the caravan had passed.

"Tell us again the names of all these flowers, Jeshua. Where did you ever learn them?"

"Are you going to be a Zealot when you grow up, Jeshua, and help drive out the Romans? If you join the party, then we shall too."

"Aunt Miriam says we may sleep in your tent tonight, Jeshua, if our mother says it's all right. Will you ask her?"

There was one subject, however, on which the two were quite agreed.

"*Ay yah!* Samaria! No more wandering now from the caravan!"

"Who taught you to sling stones so hard and straight, Jeshua? If these wicked Samaritans attack us, we'll stick close to you!"

The Boy ran and explored and jested and sang and romped with his cousins and, like all the other young members of the caravan, assisted them in consuming vast quantities of dates and melons and cucumbers. But often, as he looked from one to the other of the dark, intense faces or answered their questions, there was a sober, sometimes startled, awareness in his eyes.

"Nobody taught me the names of the flowers, Johanan. I suppose it's the same as with people. If you care enough about them, you want to find out their names.—A Zealot? I don't know, Jacob. I—never thought much about it. But I'm sure I shall be doing something. And of course I shall want you both to help me.—It was an old shepherd who taught me to sling stones. But what do you mean, 'these wicked Samaritans'? I haven't seen any."

He was surprised that it was so. The farmers whom they passed, plowing their fields, cultivating their fig yards and olive groves along the terraced slopes, looked exactly like the farmers of Galilee. A few waved to the passing caravans. Most continued their labors with a calm, and occasionally surly, indifference.

"They don't dare bother us," said Joseph when they stopped for a brief rest and refreshment in the shadow of the towering fortress of Geba. "There are too many of us. But don't let their indifference deceive you. From now on, boys, don't wander from the caravans. We're approaching their heathen strongholds. Accept nothing from them, especially not their hatred and contempt. Return each in measure full and running over."

They camped that night just beyond Shechem, close to the ancient Well of Jacob. Joseph pitched his tent eastward, away from the city, and was punctiliously careful to keep his back turned toward the offensive shrine of the Samaritans atop Mount Gerizim.

The Boy could not turn his back. Mount Gerizim was too beautiful. Strong and immovable it stood, its serene brow wearing the sunset like a halo.

"Is something the matter, dear?" Miriam's quick eye noted the puckered brow, the still fingers.

"I—I was just wondering—"

Carefully the woman removed the thick wrappings from an earthen vessel and with a pair of iron tongs lifted a flaming brand from the nest of live coals kept from the preceding fire. "Wondering what, son?"

"What makes one mountain holy and another—unclean. Why people can't worship God here on Mount Gerizim as well as on Mount Moriah in Jerusalem."

Joseph uttered an impatient exclamation. "You, a devout son of the Law, need to ask that? Is it not written that Jerusalem is the dwelling of the Most High?"

" 'The city which the Lord chose,' " quoted the Boy thoughtfully, " 'out of all the tribes of Israel, to put his name there.' "

"Exactly." Joseph's tone was approving. "You see? You could answer some of these foolish questions yourself if you'd only stop to think. Remember how some of these very Samaritans, in the time of their wicked Sanballat, plotted to keep the holy walls from rising?" He drove a wooden tent pin into the ground with sharp rhythmic strokes. "Yes, and they've been plotting against us ever since! Liars! Idolaters!"

While supper was cooking, the Boy slipped away along the path toward Jacob's Well. In spite of his nervousness he had to go. It might be his only chance to visit it alone, since his cousins would be coming to his tent after the evening meal. To his relief the stone-paved hollow within its ring of cypress trees was for the moment empty of occupants.

Seating himself on the low well curb, he peered down into the void, straining his eyes for some sign of ripple or reflection. Had Jacob sat here on these very stones? Jacob... Joseph... David... Elijah? Tenderly he stroked the worn and ancient stones, wondering how many other hands had touched them in just such loving memory.

The cracking of a twig in the cypresses brought him sharply upright, his pulses pounding. Light though it still was about the well, the surrounding spaces were thick with shadow. Another pilgrim? Not likely from that direction. The camps were all to the east or south. He sat taut with apprehension, remembering all the frightening tales he had heard of Samaritan treachery—arrows with poison tips, knife-thrusts in the dark. He would have run, but his feet seemed powerless to move. Then the sound came again, followed by a whisper of bare feet. His eyes caught a glimmer of red pottery and the flutter of a bright skirt. He almost laughed aloud. He had been afraid of a *girl*—and one even younger than himself! Relief made him suddenly bold.

"Come back," he called impulsively. "Don't go away without filling your jar."

The bare feet whispered again, briefly, on the stone pavement. "Come on," he encouraged. "Nobody is going to hurt you. See!" Rising from the well curb, he drew away. "I'll stand over here while you fill your jar."

A slender, frightened girl, clutching a scarf which hid all but her wary eyes, moved timidly across the open space and, poised rigidly for instant flight, lowered the vessel attached to the long coiled rope.

"It's deep, isn't it?" he ventured with reassuring casualness, for some reason wanting her to be as free from fear as he was himself. "I tried and tried, but I couldn't see to the bottom."

Her voice sounded almost as remote as the muted thud of the lowered vessel against the water. "When the sun's overhead, you can see water sparkle."

"But I can't wait for the sun to be overhead," replied the Boy regretfully. "We have to start before it even touches the top of your holy Mount Gerizim. You see, we are pilgrims going to Jerusalem."

The girl turned suddenly, her hands resting on the coil of braided hemp.

"You mean"—her eyes were wide and incredulous—"you knew I was a Samaritan—and yet you spoke to me?"

The Boy laughed. "*Ay yah!* And I was afraid of you! Silly, wasn't I? Why, you're just like the girls in Galilee, except you dress differently!"

The crouching figure straightened. Pulling with vigor on the rope, the girl hastily brought the brimming vessel to the top, swung it over the curb, and, holding it high, poured its contents in a silver arc straight into the neck of her red clay jar. Even the glistening coil of rope at her feet seemed charged with energy, like a thing alive.

"Wait here," she said breathlessly, lifting the full jar to her head. "I'll be back."

She disappeared into the shadows. Then the Boy saw her emerge and run swiftly up the nearby slope to a cluster of white houses almost hidden in another grove of cypresses. Watching curiously and with some anxiety, he presently saw her returning, slowly, but this time she was not alone. His muscles again drew taut, for behind her stalked a grimly reluctant youth, every line of his body stiff with hostility.

His first impulse was to run, but the approach of a group of pilgrims, two of them burly men, bolstered his confidence. By the time they had drawn water and gone, other emotions had become stronger than fear. The girl and her companion, he sensed, were hiding somewhere in the shadows. He couldn't give them the satisfaction of seeing him run away. Besides, if he never let himself get close to them, how could he ever find out what these terrible Samaritans were really like?

"There he is!" He could hear the girl's voice, cautiously muffled yet still breathless with excitement. "I tell you he did talk to me, and he's one of them! They don't all hate us! Maybe you'll see now why you shouldn't—"

The answer was a surly grumble, unintelligible but charged with such unfriendliness that the Boy shivered. Though he stood his ground, his limbs were tensed, ready to run. As the girl moved out of the shadows, alone, he saw that the object she was holding between her sheltering palms was a lighted lamp. Beckoning to him, she hurried to the well, placed the little clay saucer in the vessel attached to the rope, and prepared to let it down through the square stone opening.

He hesitated only a moment. Heart pounding, he moved slowly toward her across the pavement, expecting any moment to feel the stab of a stone against his flesh. But, arrived at the curb, he forgot his fear. Fascinated, he watched the tiny orb of light travel down into the black void, past row upon row of glistening stones which turned first silver, then gold, then shining black as basalt; down through a solid core of white limestone, neatly scored and striated, as if fitted, layer upon layer, by some master artisan; down...down...

Was there no ending? He stared, cold and motionless. If the light kept on going, he would be looking into that deep, dark underworld known as Sheol, cut off, so the Writings said, from the land of the living and from God. What would the tiny lamp discover as it journeyed down through the infinite darkness? His eyes burned with strain, and he could scarcely breathe.

The vessel hit the water with a faint thud. "Look sharply," said the girl. "Sometimes if you tip the jar a very little, you can see—Only you have to be careful, or the light goes out."

The Boy thought he glimpsed a faint rippling sheen, like the shimmer of olive leaves in starlight. Then the lamp was extinguished.

A brusque male voice broke the spell. "It's the deepest well in the whole world. Almost seventy cubits, they say." The Boy came sharply upright, fear again turning him cold as he remembered. But, though the youth towered above him, he did not look threatening. The grim hostility of his angular features was tempered by reluctant but unmistakable pride. Exactly the way Abel would look showing off his new slingshot to the despised six-year-olds! The Boy grinned suddenly. He couldn't help it.

"How do you suppose they ever dug it!" he marveled. "Straight down through the rock like that!"

The youth shrugged. "That! It's easy. My countrymen could do as well today. Better. If you know how, this soft limestone is as easy to cut as cheese—that is, before it lies in the air and hardens. If you want to see what we can do, go up to Sebaste and look at the city we Samaritans built for Herod."

"I know. We saw it as we passed." Looking back along the rugged horizon, the Boy's wide eyes kindled. "And Shechem too! I still can't believe I'm really looking at it—where our father Jacob came and pitched his tent, and Joshua assembled all the tribes!"

The youth pointed proudly. "See that big tree over there on the hill? No, not there, higher up—the one with the wide branches!" The Boy nodded. "That's an oak, the very oak where our father Abraham camped and built his altar! At least, some people say it is. If you ask me, an oak couldn't live that long."

The Boy gazed his fill. "Anyway, it could be," he marveled. "Imagine living close to such places, the way you do! Galilee is beautiful, but there's nothing there to remember. I—I almost envy you!"

The sullen eyes narrowed, searching the boyish features suspiciously.

"*You*—envy *me*! Ha! That's a good one!"

Startled, the Boy looked up, their gazes interlocking. He caught his breath sharply. He had actually forgotten that the youth was a Samaritan! He had been just another boy, a little older than himself, with the same heroes, the same wonders and enthusiasms. Now, dismayed, he saw the angular features tighten, the eagerly boasting lips freeze again into grim hostility. Suddenly it seemed a sad thing that the fragile bond forged so briefly between them should be severed. He had to do something.

"I—I'm thirsty," he said simply. "I wonder if you'd be willing to give me a drink."

The young Samaritan could not move fast enough. Seizing the rope in his big hands, he lowered the vessel with such haste that the rough hemp burned his palms, then hand over hand brought it up again, dripping full.

"Of course it's only cistern water," he explained with more pride than apology, "but I'll swear by the five holy books it's colder and clearer than any old fountain water you ever tasted!"

There was an earthen cup lying on the well curb, and he poured it full. "Here, stranger. Take and drink in memory of our father Jacob."

"The Lord requite you," the Boy made reply.

Gratefully he took it and started to drink, for he was really thirsty. But scarcely had the first cool drops touched his throat then a big hand shot forward and roughly snatched the cup from his hands, sending the water splashing in all directions.

"Son of disobedience! So this is the way you honor the Law and your father's commands!"

The Boy blinked the water from his eyes. "I—I didn't see you coming, Father."

"So it seems. And must a man keep his son within constant view to insure obedience? I told you to have nothing to do with these—these deceivers, these apostates, and here I find you begging their hospitality, even taking into your body defilement from their unclean hands!"

Joseph's features wavered, huge and distorted, filling the Boy's blurred vision. But he was more conscious of things he couldn't see—of the patter of frightened bare feet, of the silent figure frozen into immobility beside him. For his sake he must try somehow—

"But the food and drink of the Samaritans are not unclean, Father," he protested with desperate earnestness. "Many of the rabbis have said so. And besides"—he groped for words to make his meaning clear—"it—it's what comes out of a man that shows whether he's clean or unclean, not what goes into him!"

He stopped, aghast. What had he said! No uncleanness in what entered a man from outside? Then what use all the washings, the cooking in proper utensils, the—yes, even the long prayers before meals? These things were the very substance of his religion! A man who didn't believe in them was a heretic, a—a Gentile, worse even than a Samaritan! His head swam, and he held his breath, half expecting to hear a thunderclap of divine judgment.

A crash came, but it was not a thunderclap.

After flinging the earthen cup with all his might against the well stones, Joseph wiped his hands with righteous vigor on his coat

"Come," he said curtly. "Your mother has supper ready."

Turning his back, he strode toward the camp.

The Boy's gaze followed him with unbounded relief. His father had not sensed the implication of his words, probably in the heat of his anger had not heard them. Or—perhaps he himself had merely thought, not spoken, them.

He turned back toward the well, but the space surrounding the curbstone was empty. Swiftly his eyes swept the circle of cypresses, but darkness was falling, and the place was full of shadows. He opened his lips to cry out, then closed them. The young Samaritan was gone. No matter how fast he ran or how loud he called, he could not reach him. They had been close together, hands touching beneath a brimming cup. Now a gulf, deep as the Well of Jacob, lay between them.

HE THOUGHT at first they were hailstones.

Suddenly awake, he lay rigid beside his sleeping cousins and listened to the occasional dull thud on the taut canopy of goat's hair, waiting half subconsciously for the lightning flash and clap of thunder which this time of year were almost sure to follow.

"*Ay yah! Ay-ee-ya-ah*! In the name of the Lord and of Mount Gerizim!"

The shrill cry was the precursor of turmoil. A woman screamed, children began to wail. The night burst into a confusion of excited voices and pounding feet. The signal was followed by an increased volley of stones and shouted taunts.

"Come out, Jews! Face us if you dare!"

"We'll make you bend the knee at the true shrine of Jehovah!"

"Apostates, are we? Dogs? Amen, so be it! Mad dogs!"

"Come out in the name of our father Jacob!"

Joseph sprang from his mat, hands already flexed to the act of girding himself. "God help us! Just as I expected. The heathen deceivers are upon us."

Fumbling in the darkness, his fingers closed about the neck of a heavy goatskin. "At least we're ready for them. Thanks to Jered, they'll find the men of Nazareth prepared. Up, boys! Fill your girdles with a good supply of stones, and keep your slings in readiness."

"Joseph, no!" The darkness quivered with Miriam's sharp protest. "Not the boys! Let them stay here. This is a thing for men."

"Men, yes. For all true sons of the Law." There was a significant grimness in Joseph's voice. "It's time they learned to be defenders of the Faith."

"We're ready, Uncle Joseph. We're good with the sling, almost as good as young King David. If these Samaritans have a Goliath, we can hit him right between the eyes." It was Jacob's voice, deep with the new lustiness of manhood, but ending on a humiliating falsetto. "Can't we, Johanan?"

"*Ay yah!* Right between the eyes! At least Jeshua will." They sound, the Boy thought, as if they are about to play some exciting new game.

"Here's my girdle pocket, opened wide," proffered Jacob eagerly. "Fill it full of stones, Uncle Joseph."

The two sons of Zebedee overflowed the tiny tent with their abounding energy and excitement, absorbing the man's righteous zeal, the woman's apprehension, the Boy's dismay.

"Here you are. Fill your pockets, all of you," commanded Joseph curtly.

Silently, groping in the darkness for the bag's narrow neck, the Boy dutifully filled the folds of his girdle with handful after handful of the small missiles gathered at Jered's behest the night before. They had not been hard to find. Hostility and vengeance had been made easy in this stony land, which the God of Israel had chosen for his own.

"Come," ordered Joseph abruptly.

Outside, a full moon lit the scene. Following his father's example, the Boy dropped to his knees and, keeping his head lowered against the barrage of stones, crawled among ropes and pegs and baggage and tethered donkeys to the center of the Nazareth encampment, where a group of angry pilgrims, similarly armed, was hastily gathering.

Jered, eyes glittering in the glow of a hooded lamp, looked more excited than alarmed. "Only a handful of them," he assured them in a confident whisper. "They're hiding in the rocks on the edge of the encampment. I've had spies spotting them. I'm convinced they're only trying to frighten us, not counting on our being ready. Ungodly upstarts! This is our chance to show them! Let them use up their supply of stones, then wait till I give the signal. Let every man of you have his missiles ready!"

The shouts and jeers continued, punctuated by an equally taunting but not too ominous barrage of stones.

The Boy crouched in the silvered darkness, one hand clenched rigidly about a lump of jagged limestone, the other tightly clutching the folds of his cloak, drawn protectingly over his head. A stone, scarcely bigger than a pebble, smarted against his shoulder blade. Jered was right, he decided with relief. The Samaritans must be only trying to frighten them. Most of the missiles they were flinging would scarcely sting a rabbit. And they must be a small group. None of the other encampments seemed to have been aroused, only the Nazarenes. It was as if someone had a special reason for attacking them, and them alone!

"Wait till those wicked idolaters feel this stone!" breathed Jacob hotly in his ear. "It's sharp as Uncle Joseph's adze."

The Boy murmured an unintelligible reply. Unbidden, the features of the Samaritan youth drifted before his eyes, frozen, hostile. Fumbling in his girdle, he furtively exchanged the jagged lump for a smaller, smoother stone.

"Keep close to me," muttered Joseph, "and aim straight. Remember, it's for the one True God and his holy mountain in Jerusalem."

The steady rhythm of the barrage wavered. The taunting shouts became less frequent.

They're running out of stones," whispered Johanan excitedly. "How soon, Uncle Joseph?"

"Hist!"

There was a moment of silence when the night seemed to hold its breath. Then Jered's voice barked a command, followed by a harsh blast on a ram's horn.

"Forward, men of Nazareth!"

"In the name of the Lord and of Mount Zion!"

The Boy felt himself lifted, almost without his volition, and borne away, conscious more of propelling arms and pushing shoulders than of his own feet touching the ground. Then all at once there was a stony slope beneath his feet, and he was feeling with his toes, struggling to keep himself upright, climbing with a fierce sense of urgency and purpose. He heard a harsh cry issuing from someone's lips and discovered with sudden exultation that it came from his own.

"Death to the idolaters! In the name of the Lord and of Mount Zion!"

No longer was he afraid or hesitant. He was a son of Abraham crying out against the enemies of his people, treading in the path of all their mighty heroes—of Joshua and Gideon, of David and Jehu and the Maccabees—fighting for the freedom of Israel and her Promised Land. The enemy? For the moment it mattered little which it was, whether Philistine or Persian or hated Roman or despised Samaritan. Enough that it was someone who had dared defy the supremacy of the True God and of his chosen people!

Finding his cousins, more accustomed to the level seashore, too slow for him, he forged ahead up the slope. A face loomed close beside his own, its familiar features bold and vigorous in the moonlight and mirroring the impassioned eagerness he felt within himself.

"Come on, Jeshua!" Abel, the son of Jered, seized his arm. "You and I! Let's get there first. Let's show those idolaters what Nazarenes are made of!"

They charged up the slope together, pushing slower climbers out of the way, in a wild attempt to reach the front line of their attacking townsmen, crying out in triumphant excitement when they saw the dark shadows of the attackers skulking among the rocks. But they were not the first. Before they could lift their arms to fling, the first volley of stones was in the air, eliciting screams of pain and curses from above. The Samaritans, trapped and weaponless, were fleeing in panic, stumbling over rocks and hummocks and each other, frequently in the wrong direction.

"After them!" shouted Abel, choosing a likely target for his missile. He wound his arm, and the stone whined. "Hit him!" he cried. "There's one, Jeshua, coming right toward us! You can have him. I'm going after the others!" With a loud cry he disappeared into the darkness.

So bright was the moonlight that the Samaritan's pale features, less than a dozen arm's lengths away, furnished a perfect target. Clutching the stone tightly, the Boy lifted his arm, drew it back in a strong arc. But his hand remained upraised, his fingers locked about the stone, while his eyes stared at the pale, horror-stricken features. No, it was not the face of the youth whose cup he had shared at the well, but *it might have been*!

His hand dropped slowly to his side, weak and trembling. He closed his eyes. When he opened them again, the face was gone, and he was again caught up in the crowd of Nazarenes swarming up the slope.

"Here you are, son! What happened? Couldn't wait to wield your stones on the idolaters?" Joseph's voice was gruff with mingled pride and relief. "*Ay yah!* I commend your zeal. But in heaven's name, don't go running off from us again!"

Jacob and Johanan were half admiring, half reproachful.

"Did you hit many, Jeshua? *Ah hah!* You might have waited!"

The Boy made no reply, merely let himself be borne along with them in pursuit of the fleeing Samaritans. Again he moved almost without volition, as if his body were not his, but another's.

He was conscious of his cousins' excited mumblings, the speed of their fingers spinning missiles through the air. *Sons of thunder they are*, he thought with detached clarity. They would like to be called that. He must remember to tell them. But his own voice seemed frozen in his throat, his fingers, still holding the stone, useless at his sides.

The Nazarenes pursued their assailants to the ring of cypresses about the Well of Jacob. There, because the darkness offered too great concealment and their supply of stones was fast diminishing, they gave up the chase and, full of righteousness and satisfaction, returned to the encampment.

The two sons of Zebedee ostentatiously inverted the empty pockets of their girdles.

"*Ay yah*! I guess that will teach them!" Jacob disposed of the incident complacently.

"If the Samaritans are so wicked," puzzled the more thoughtful Johanan, "why doesn't God kill them the way he used to kill all his enemies? If I were he, I'd send down fire from heaven and destroy them."

"Maybe he will," answered Jacob, dusting off his hands, "when Messiah comes. Don't you remember how the rabbis told us Messiah will kill all our people's enemies and rule as king over the whole world?"

Painfully conscious of the unused stones bulging the pocket of his girdle, the Boy walked silently beside his father. What would his cousins say if they knew he had not flung a single missile? *Jeshua! Not you, a coward!* What would his father say?

Joseph waited until they had almost reached the tent and the sons of Zebedee charged ahead to apprise their Aunt Miriam of the victory before turning to his son.

"You see?" His voice was edged with triumph and satisfaction. "You wanted to know why a Jew should hate a Samaritan. *Ay yah!* The Most High has been patient enough to show you. It was that son of an infidel by the well who did this, of course. Probably planning it even while his deceiving hands were offering you a drink! Didn't you see the way he clenched his fists—the hatred in his ugly face?"

The Boy was silent.

3

WHEN THE faintly luminous triangle turned soft gray, the Boy eased himself noiselessly from his bed on the ground and crept through the low tent opening. The air was sweet as new wine, the dew-drenched grass soft as velvet. A few feet from where the tent was pitched was an old stone wall, and his bare feet groped until they found the hollowed path leading to it. The stones were hard and cold against his back, but a stooped old olive tree wedged among crumbling rocks reached down and brushed its soft leaves against his cheeks.

Jerusalem! The word sang and pounded through his veins with an almost unbearable ecstasy. The Holy City, into which no death, no impurity were allowed to enter—nothing but beauty and happiness and perfection!

Incredible good fortune that the Nazareth pilgrims should have found a camping place here, high on the northwest slope of the Mount of Olives, with the Temple just across the deep ravine of the Kidron! Last night in the sunset it had looked so shining, so splendid, he had only half believed it real. Now, with breathless eagerness he watched it being re-created, saw white walls spring up out of the gray mists, mount tier upon tier.

The Temple! Dwelling place of the Most High, shining embodiment of all the hopes and dreams of his people! Surely here within its walls he would find out at last what God was really like, surely here all his questions would be answered.

The camp was astir long before the dawn was proclaimed by a symphony of seven silver trumpets. When the topmost tier of marble and gold leaped into view, a shout of triumph seemed to burst from a thousand throats. Waiting for neither food nor drink, some even slighting the stern ritual of morning prayers and washings, pilgrims streamed down the hillside, choking the narrow bridge spanning the Kidron, and, if fortunate enough to emerge untrampled, swarmed up the steep slope toward the Golden Gate.

Joseph made no haste, performing the morning ritual with even more punctilious care than usual. Then, because it was the fourteenth of Nisan and the first day of Passover, he continued with scrupulous precision the preparations for the feast begun at sunset the night before: searching the camp again for any drop or crumb containing leaven, making sure that all the old metal vessels to be used had been properly cleansed and that the new clay dishes, bought for the occasion, had been dipped three times in running water.

"You're sure," he worried for at least the fifth time, "you can remember all the regulations? When you grind the grain for the unleavened cakes, you will make certain no dampness has come near it?"

"Yes, yes, of course." Miriam was almost in tears. "But—I'm not the only woman preparing the food to be eaten at your table. How can I make sure—"

"You must. Unless a few faithful are to be found who keep the Law, can there be hope for Israel? Look at our Galilean neighbors," Joseph complained bitterly, "rushing off to go sight-seeing without even washing their hands! Yes, and I'll wager your sister's Zebedee is among them. All the time talking about the fish market he hopes to start here in Jerusalem instead of the God he came to worship! And then we wonder why the Most High has not delivered us from our enemies!"

Last night, before the stars appeared, the Boy had gone with his father to the spring far down the Kidron Valley and watched intently while Joseph solemnly drew water into a cleansed vessel, covering it quickly and repeating, "This is the water for the unleavened bread." Now, cheeks flushed from the hot blaze kindled to destroy the fragments of leaven, he helped fill the iron mortar with red coals, feeding them into the black cavity until a thread of linen, bound around the outside, was burned to a crisp.

"Good!" pronounced Joseph with satisfaction, wiping the soot from his hands. "We have done all that the Law requires. Tonight we can eat our unleavened bread with a clear conscience, knowing that our prayers of thanksgiving will be acceptable to the Most High."

The Boy lifted a corner of his headcloth to wipe the sweat from his forehead, but, though he rubbed hard, two puzzled little lines remained between his eyes. Was it really so important to God that they shouldn't eat even the tiniest bit of leaven? Wasn't he interested instead in—in whether they felt thankful inside?

"Come now, son. We must wash and put on clean clothes and make ready to enter the Holy City. We go now to the House of the Most High."

The Boy drew a long breath. The time had come.

4

"KEEP CLOSE to me," warned Joseph as they climbed the steep eastern slope toward the city. If a boy got lost in these crowds, it might take days to find him!"

The Boy made no reply, and the man glanced at him sharply. What he saw softened his stem features, quickened his pulse. He had forgotten what one's first visit to the Temple could do to a true son of David. The rapt young face was uplifted, the wide eyes kindled with ecstasy. Smiling indulgently, he reached out a big hand, rescued the dangling headcloth, and tucked it, cord and all, into his girdle. The sunlit air lifted and threaded the fine soft hair.

For Joseph it was a day of fulfillment also. He carried, tucked away in the innermost fold of his girdle, the letter written by Ben Arza to the Rabbi Zadok, teacher in the school of Shammai, recommending Jeshua, son of Joseph of Nazareth, descendant of the house of David, as a pupil. Ben Arza had wished to direct the letter to another rabbi in the more liberal school of Hillel, but Joseph had demurred. If the Kingdom of David was ever to be restored, it could only be by the strictest observance of the Law.

But the Boy himself would be his own best recommendation. Surely anyone could tell, just by looking at him, that he was no ordinary lad. And if he could only be given a chance to display his keen mind and knowledge of the Law, provided he didn't take it into his head to ask some of his foolish questions! Perhaps the Boy should be warned—No, he had promised Miriam to keep their plan secret a little longer. She had some queer idea that the Boy should make up his own mind. As if any good son of David could possibly decide otherwise! What she really wanted, womanlike—Joseph smiled indulgently—was to keep everything unchanged as long as possible.

Well, let her have her way. He would make all the arrangements now, without the Boy's knowledge, entering him in the school of Shammai; then he would bring him back to Jerusalem in the autumn for the Feast of Tabernacles and leave him. Thanks to the three strangers and their Gifts, he could remain as many years as were required to train him for his heritage as a son of David. Nisan or Tishri, the Gifts would still be there, waiting.

Entering the city by the northern gate and passing under the high bridge spanning the long, descending Tyropean Valley, Joseph led his son up a steep stairway straight into the outer court of the Temple. The Boy gasped.

"*Ay yah!* I know," the man agreed with both sympathy and satisfaction. "It takes your breath away. Makes you realize how great a God is the Holy One of Israel. And how slow to anger," he added grimly, his glance shifting to the frowning fortress of Antonia bristling with Roman spears, towering above the northwest corner. "But his day of wrath will come. Who knows? Perhaps the Deliverer may even now be among us."

Joseph bore himself proudly, moving confidently through the throngs of pilgrims, as befitted a descendant of the royal house entering into his rightful inheritance.

"This is the Court of the Gentiles," he explained in a loud voice. "Anyone may enter here, even the uncircumcised. That space to the east beneath the double columns is called Solomon's Porch. We'll go to it later. Now we must enter the Royal Porch and make our purchases."

Because he walked confidently, men of wealth and importance made way for him to pass, many turning to look after the stocky, broad-shouldered figure with its wide-eyed companion, surprised and a bit disgruntled to find them wearers of homespun.

"Uncouth uplander! Who does he think he is?"

"A Galilean peasant! You can tell by his speech!"

Though the Boy walking close behind him was painfully conscious of their grumblings, Joseph heard none of them. Today he need take second place to no man in Israel—no, not even to Jered, moving in the crowd some distance away, conspicuous for his impressive manner and many layers of outer garments. For what greater honor could a man have at Passover than to be chosen by twenty of his fellow townsmen to purchase their lamb and offer it for sacrifice, and to preside later at their feast? This year for the first time Joseph was sharing this honor with Jered. The shekels contributed by each man in proportion to the size of his family were at this moment bulging his girdle.

As they approached the great portico at the southern end of the court, the confusion became so great that Joseph had to shout to make himself heard.

"We're entering the bazaars where the money-changers sit and the animals are sold for temple sacrifice. They call them the Booths of Annas because they're run by the high priest's family. Keep close to me."

A wave of elbowing pilgrims surged between them, and it was all he could do to force his way back to the Boy's side. Closing his big hand over the slender fingers, he was dismayed to find them cold as ice.

"Don't be frightened, son. See, your father is right here."

"Is he?"

Joseph gave his son a sharp glance, then at sight of the wide, troubled eyes his face softened. Fool, he was getting to suspect every casual word the Boy uttered, trying to put a double meaning on it! Giving the fingers a reassuring pressure, he closed them firmly about a hanging fold of homespun.

"Here! Keep tight hold of my sleeve. I won't let you get lost again."

Fortunately he need have no dealings today with the money-changers. Their rates were high enough upcountry, but here they were exorbitant. The air quivered with the noise of screams and curses and bitter wranglings.

As they passed the long line of chests with their crowds of shouting customers, they saw one angry Egyptian Jew boldly kick the wooden block from beneath the stout legs of a laden counter, sending it crashing to the stone floor with a great clatter of coins. But his triumph was short-lived. Before he could resume his harsh tirade, he was hustled away between two soldiers, and the fingers pouncing avidly on the scattered coins beat an even swifter retreat before pricking spear points.

"We'll do our business," muttered Joseph with distaste, "and get out."

Along the outer edge of the Royal Porch the cool shady spaces between the lofty columns were crammed solidly with booths of vendors. Here the confusion was even more bewildering, the discord of human voices augmented by the shrill chatter of pigeons, the stamping of oxen, the bleating of lambs.

Joseph looked about worriedly, not knowing which of the many vendors to approach. It was the first time he had been entrusted with such responsibility, and he did not want to fail his fellow townsmen. He had hopes even of returning some of the money contributed for the common purchase, so competent would he prove at bargaining. Of course he could follow abjectly at the heels of Jered, who was at the moment consummating his own purchase with noisy and condescending assurance, could even let the more experienced elder drive the bargain for him. But he would sooner crawl back to Nazareth on hands and knees.

Affecting far more confidence than he felt, he approached the only vendor who did not have a long line waiting, an old man whose half-closed eyes and gently smiling lips aroused a reassuring sense of pity.

"So? It's a lamb for you, Galilean?"

"A firstling, without spot or blemish," Joseph specified with dignity.

Seen closer, the smile became a leer, the half-shut eyes slits of shrewdness, "Without spot or blemish!" The insolent voice mocked his heavy Galilean accent. "I might have guessed, since that's the only kind we sell here. If it were a mere lamb you wanted, I dare say you'd have gone to the Sheep Gate and bought it for a paltry sum—say, ten shekels."

"Ten!" Joseph was sure he had not heard aright. "The top price for a lamb in Galilee is two."

"Ah, my friend, but that is Galilee."

Joseph began to sweat. He had just ten shekels in his girdle. The lamb was produced, a scrawny creature which any Nazareth shepherd would have been ashamed to put on the market. "Is this the best you have?"

"No. But the fatter the lamb, the fatter the price. I assumed," the narrowed eyes were contemptuously appraising, "my friend would not wish—"

Joseph wet his lips. "How much?"

"A mere four and twenty shekels."

"But that's robbery!"

The vendor shrugged. "Perhaps my friend would do better to purchase his lamb in the Sheep Gate, then bring it here for inspection. The *mumsheh* charges only a small fee, perhaps ten or twelve shekels. Of course there is always the chance that you might not have bought a perfect animal."

Cold sweat coursed down Joseph's limbs. He refused to look at his son, knowing that the wide eyes would be full of bewilderment and pity. Desperately he began to bargain, but, though the old man joined verbal battle with gusto, he suspected from the beginning that he was beaten, knew it when he heard Jered at the next booth closing his bargain after long and heated altercation.

"Seventeen!" The old man rolled the word on his tongue like a toothsome morsel.

"Eight—and two drachmas."

"Sixteen!"

"Nine!" Though the sweat streamed into his eyes and blinded him, Joseph dared not stop to wipe his forehead.

"Fifteen then. And may Annas forgive me for stealing from his coffers!"

"Ten!" Joseph barely whispered the word.

"Fifteen!" The note of finality was unmistakable.

"Ten—and—and six drachmas. And—and a good girdle of stout homespun linen thrown in!"

The gimlet eyes bored through the humble article in question. "Fifteen. But—since ten is all you have and you have become such a dear friend to me, like my own brother—I'll—" The old man lifted

THE AWAKENING OF JESUS

the lamb in his hands, his long talons of fingers completely spanning the pitifully lean midriff.

Joseph held his breath.

The curving lips opened in an ingratiating leer. "I'll hold the lamb for you while you raise the other five."

There was no alternative. "Wait here," he mumbled without meeting the Boy's eyes.

Spotting Jered's conspicuous turban of fine purple draped over a high skullcap, he pushed his way toward it. The humiliation was almost unbearable.

"What's this? You're asking me to loan you five shekels?"

"Only until we get back to camp," explained Joseph wretchedly. "I—collected only ten shekels. They told me that was what they paid last year. I had no idea—price of lambs so high—"

"How much did they charge you?" demanded Jered, his face still flaming from the indignity of his own transaction.

"Fifteen shekels." Pride once jeopardized, Joseph found relief in sharing his grievance. "And for a miserable beast that any Nazareth ewe would be ashamed to drop. Not nearly as big as yours," he added with reluctant but diplomatic surrender of his last vestige of pride.

Jered smiled and clucked sympathetically. It was almost worth having to pay fifteen shekels for a two-shekel lamb to see the stiff-necked son of Jacob come miching for a loan! Presumptuous offspring of a peasant, boasting he could trace his lineage to David! Not even for the sake of remembered kindness in his youth could he quite forgive the carpenter for this arrogance. And especially not when his meddlesome young son was present.

"My poor Joseph, I should have warned you. I forgot you were so unused to city ways. Not for worlds would I have let you suffer this humiliation. And your son with you, too, that clever, handsome son sprung like his father from the loins of David! What a pity he must spend his life on a carpenter's mat! Here, take the five shekels, my brother. I shan't miss them. See, I have a bag full."

They could leave the Royal Porch at last.

"Let me carry the lamb, Father."

Joseph relinquished his burden willingly. He had always been awkward at carrying any live thing, even his own children, though he could stroke a lamb's fleece or a baby's cheek with the lightness of a feather.

The sun had lost its luster. Even the tender spring day, quick to frown during these weeks of the latter rains, had filled with lowering clouds, turning the tiers of marble to lifeless gray. Or was the sudden dullness merely the draining of radiance from a boy's face?

Desperately Joseph tried to recapture the magic for both of them.

"Come, son! We'll go into the real Temple now, up those steps and through the Beautiful Gate. See that low lattice of marble? Read the inscription on it. Then put on your headcloth. Hold your shoulders high. There's not a king in the world who can pass through these portals!"

Wonderingly the Boy read aloud the inscription cut into a block of stone and blazoned with crimson, careful to choose of the three versions the Hebrew rather than the Greek, knowing that Joseph, ignorant of the latter, was sensitive about his little schooling. He himself could not have read the Latin.

" 'No non-Jew is permitted to pass beyond this boundary. He who does so will carry the guilt on himself, because death will follow.' " The wide eyes clouded. "Why should people be killed, Father, for wanting to go into God's house?"

Joseph looked about anxiously to make sure no one had heard the peculiar question. "Because," he explained patiently, "the Temple is holy. No unclean thing can pass into it. See, even that crippled beggar must remain outside the Beautiful Gate, for either he or his father must have broken the Law, or he would not be crippled. The Gentiles, being lawbreakers—"

But there was no time for more, for with no further warning than a spattering of fine drops, the heavens opened and let loose a deluge of rain. Screaming, jostling, improvising protections for their holiday finery, the crowds surged toward the porches. Joseph, caught in a confused eddy, found himself far from the Temple entrance, with the Boy nowhere to be seen. Propelling himself to one side by a determined use of stout elbows, he waited until the tide passed, then pushed his way back toward the steps. The Boy was still standing close to where he had left him. Sudden relief sharpened the father's voice and roughened the grasp of his hand.

"*Ah hah!* I thought I had lost you. God be thanked! Come, this way across the court to Solomon's Porch!"

They had reached the shelter of the huge double colonnade with its high, timbered ceiling before he gave the Boy more than a cursory glance. The headcloth was gone again. He might have expected that. But—

"Where's your cloak?" he demanded abruptly.

The Boy pushed back his streaming hair and blinked the water from his lashes. "I put it about that crippled beggar," he replied simply. "He couldn't move to get out of the rain. Don't worry," he added hastily, seeing the sudden tightening of Joseph's jaw, "it's not like that other time. I didn't give it to him. I'm going back to get it when the shower is over."

For a moment Joseph was speechless. For another he could only repeat the Boy's words, parrotlike. "So—you put it about that crippled beggar. And—and you're going back to get it—" Then the tension found release. Grasping the slender shoulders in both hands, he pressed the Boy backward into a tiny pool of privacy behind a marble pillar, prepared to give him the vigorous parental shaking he deserved.

"Please, Father, don't hurt the lamb!"

With a smothered exclamation the man loosened his grasp, fingers lingering in a sudden recoil of gentleness to separate the clinging strands of the Boy's hair from the sodden coat folds. The headcloth was not lost, after all, he discovered, but wrapped around the miserable little beast which was the chief cause of his seething irritation. With rough vigor, to hide the trembling of his hands, he rubbed the streaming hair with a dry corner of his coat sleeve.

"And I suppose you think the beggar will still be waiting, eager to relinquish a good garment that is his for the taking!" he scolded gruffly. "Sometimes I wonder whether it's a fool I have for a son—or if my son has a fool for a father," he finished helplessly.

They laughed together.

It was the sight of the venerable rabbi sitting cross-legged on a little platform, a circle of interested listeners squatting about him, which suddenly set Joseph's heart beating faster. He had forgotten that it was the custom for rabbis of the various schools to hold audience here in Solomon's Porch during feast days. Suppose it should just happen that this was Zadok, of the school of Shammai...

The Boy also spied the rabbi. "Could we listen to what he is saying?" he inquired eagerly. "Could we join the people sitting about him?"

"No," explained Joseph grimly, "it cost money to become part of such a group." But they could stand on the edge of the circle.

There were several such groups in view as they started walking through the huge, shadowy colonnade, and they did not stop at the first one. Joseph waited until he distinctly heard the word, *Shammai.*

"Who is this rabbi?" he murmured humbly in an ear half obscured by a richly striped *tallith.*

The man peered up from beneath a huge phylactery, noted the coarse country garb, and frowned disapprovingly. "Zadok," he muttered curtly.

Joseph's heart quickened. The very rabbi to whom the letter of Ben Arza was addressed! Surely the Most High had guided their steps. Just one further sign would prove it: if the Boy should in some way be brought to the attention of the great pupil of Shammai!

He glanced at the slender figure beside him to check the correctness, barring the missing cloak, of his appearance. He continued to stare wonderingly. Surely Miriam was right. There was something unusual about the Boy. It didn't take a dream, half remembered, out of the dim past to tell one that. Standing there sturdily, with his eyes wide and eager and that lamb in his arms, he actually looked like King David! The rain had passed, and a sunbeam slanting between the huge columns tangled in the ruffled hair and threaded its dark brown strands with gold. It was said that David had had just such hair, red-gold and lustrous. Joseph held his breath and prayed that Zadok's old eyes might be keener than they looked and that he would turn them in the right direction.

The group was discussing the coming of Messiah, wrangling, as usual, about when he should arrive and how, and in what manner he would destroy Israel's enemies. The discussion went on interminably, and Joseph, itching in his soggy garments, became more and more impatient. They should, he reminded himself guiltily, be out chasing that wretched beggar, who was doubtless by now clear across the Tyropean, gloating with his cronies about the easy mark he had found. But still he could not bring himself to leave.

And then suddenly it happened.

"*You* there! Yonder boy with the lamb! You look like a good Son of the Law. What do you know about the coming of Messiah? How will he appear?"

Joseph's heart missed a beat, then pounded swift hammer strokes. Would the Boy be frightened by the long, pointing finger, the silence, the stares of curious eyes? If so, then he was no true son of

David, and they might as well return to Nazareth for good and don their carpenters' aprons.

The clear gaze did not waver. "Sire, I know what the Scriptures say. It would seem that the Servant of God will be born and grow into manhood like other men, for it is written, 'There shall come forth a shoot from the stump of Jesse, and a branch shall grow out of his roots.' "

The rabbi fixed brooding eyes on the youth. "But do not the Scriptures also say," he demanded, " 'Behold, the Man came on the clouds of heaven, and wherever he turned his face and looked, all things trembled before him, and all that heard his voice melted like wax in the flame'?"

"In Esdras, yes," replied the Boy steadily. "The two accounts do not seem to agree. But Ben Arza and I prefer Isaiah."

"Ben Arza? The rabbi of Nazareth?" The brooding gaze quickened into interest. I know him. A good man, though not always in agreement with the school of Shammai. At least," the stern lips twitched, "something good once went into Nazareth, even though it is said that nothing good ever came out of it."

"Then we in Nazareth should consider ourselves fortunate," countered the Boy gravely, "that we do not lose all our goodness."

There was a ripple of amused approval, but Joseph endured a moment of anguish until the sardonic flicker of Zadok's lips flared into a smile.

"Well-said, pupil of Ben Arza. Who knows? You might be the one to refute the old saying. Is this your first visit to the Temple?"

"Yes, sire."

With a shaking finger Joseph stroked the parchment in his girdle. The relief, the exultation, were as unnerving as the previous suspense. The sign had been given. Zadok was obviously impressed. The upturned faces were agape with admiration. Whatever doubts he had entertained before, Joseph was sure now. His son was destined to be a leader in Israel, perhaps even—even…His head swam, causing the sunlight tangled in the Boy's hair to spin around in circles like a gold crown. The parchment crackled faintly against his trembling fingers, reminding him that his duty had barely begun. What should he do now? Return later today on some pretext and show Zadok the letter, completing the arrangements with all possible despatch? Or wait?

"What do you think of the Temple?" demanded the rabbi abruptly. "Does it come up to your expectations?"

"No," replied the Boy with simple candor. "I expected to find a house of prayer, and instead"—the clear voice made only the slightest pause—"instead I find a den of thieves."

The next few moments were a nightmare for Joseph. The sudden outraged silence...the gaping faces frozen in horror and furtive, malicious delight...Zadok's long accusing finger...the whiplash of his voice....

"Take care, young Galilean upstart! Let not cleverness of speech become the mother of arrogance. Who are you to set yourself in judgment over God's appointed servants?"

The crowds were kind. A man could plunge into them as into deep, dark waters and discover both escape and indifference. Joseph found himself at last in the great courtyard, his son beside him.

"I'm sorry, Father."

Just that, nothing more. The very words and tone he himself had often used in firm but kind refusal of some childish dream impossible of fulfillment. *I'm sorry, Little One.*

There were no words to release the frozen turbulence within him. "Let us go back to the encampment," he said with stolid absence of emotion. "You will have many chances to see the Temple later"

It seemed an endless journey back across the court. Joseph's feet dragged like lead on the glistening wet pavement. Sunlight smote the glittering gold overlay of the marble terraces and blinded his eyes. Only his fingers, thrust deep into the pocket of his girdle, found expression for his inner turbulence by creasing and crumpling the neatly inscribed parchment into a useless rag.

Joseph was too drained of hope and purpose to be angry. Too confused, also. For, mingled with the vast bitterness and disappointment were even more disturbing emotions. Humility. Fear. And, strangest of all, pride. For the Temple was a den of thieves. Since dawn ten thousand pilgrims, like himself, had mouthed the words silently, muttered them behind muffling fingers, whispered them behind closed doors. Only one—his son—had dared speak them aloud.

"If you'll wait here, Father," said the Boy when they reached the steps leading down into the valley, I'll go back and get my cloak."

He was gone through the crowd, and Joseph, staring after him, felt a wild desire to laugh. At least one person, the beggar, had garnered some harvest out of this mockery of a feast day! When he saw the slender figure returning, shoulders cloakless, his eyes gleamed. Here, at last, a tangible grievance on which to vent his anguish!

"Gullible young fool! How long will it take you to grow up to a practical knowledge of human beings? Expecting a worthless beggar—"

His mouth fell open.

"It's so hot," explained the Boy simply, balancing the lamb in the crook of his arm while he shook smooth the long striped folds draped over the other, "that I decided not to wear it."

Joseph stared incredulously. "You mean—the beggar was still—*waiting?*"

It was the Boy's turn to look surprised. "Of course. Didn't he tell me he would be?"

5

IN THE EARTHEN PIT under the roasting lamb the fire flared and hissed and sizzled, licking hungrily at the slowly browning meat. Its light ebbed and flowed over the circle of devout faces, diluting the ecstasy of religious fervor with less subtle emotions—nostrils dilating at the rare aroma of fresh meat, eyes glittering in jealous appraisal of the meager banquet ahead, lips still mumbling aggrievedly at the extra assessment.

"Take care!" Joseph issued grim warning to the Nazarene about to turn the small carcass on its pomegranate spit. "See that no meat comes in contact with a foreign substance. And if the fat drops back on any particle, make sure you cut it away promptly and let it fall into the fire."

The Boy sat hugging his knees and staring at the lamb, remembering the feeling of its soft body in the crook of his arm and its hard little head nuzzling his shoulder. Was it really so important that it should be roasted in just such a way and that not a single bone should be broken?

This should be the happiest night of his life. Today he had stood within the gates of the Temple. This afternoon he had climbed the shallow marble steps—fifteen of them by actual count—and entered through the splendid Gate Nicanor into the Court of Israel. There, though his feet had stood still, his eyes had kept on going, past the great altar in the Court of Priests, up the last broad stairway, through the golden doors.

There had been one exalted moment when it seemed his eyes had penetrated the embroidered curtain and entered the Holy Place, seen the golden altar of incense and the seven-branched candlestick. Another such breathless moment, and he might have gone still farther—placed his fingers on the blue and crimson folds of the last double curtain and passed into the Holy of Holies itself, that small dark room which no man except the high priest was permitted to enter, and he only once a year, on the Day of Atonement

The Boy shivered. So vivid had been the sensation that he actually *saw* the intricate patterns of crimson and purple and gold, shimmering in candlelight, felt the fine raised threads with the tips of his fingers. Suppose his bold eyes had carried him on, behind the curtain, what—*whom*—would he have found? He shivered again. What sort of Being would choose to live in darkness and emptiness, alone?

But there had been only the one moment. His eyes had dropped then to the scene around the altar in the Court of Priests, and after that he had been able to see and hear nothing else.

He relived the scene now in all its detail, sitting beside the pit and looking into the fire.

There they came again, marching out of the flames—the long lines of worshipers entering the court from the north gate, twenty at a time. Each placing his lamb carefully on the pavement, body pointing north and south but head facing the Temple. All lifting their knives. The white-robed priests passing the gold and silver bowls of blood from hand to hand, dashing it against the altar. The smell of burning fat. The creaking of ropes drawing buckets of water from the huge cisterns far below. The voices of the Levite singers chanting:

> "Praise the Lord! Praise,
> O servants of the Lord,
> praise the name of the Lord!"

More and more groups of twenty, each man carrying his lamb. Joseph in one of them, carrying his lamb.

More and more gold and silver vessels filled. Emptied. Filled again. Yet still the thirst of the great rock's bared veins remained unquenched.

More and more buckets of water, until it seemed the great sea below, which was said to hold two million gallons, must be drained dry. Yet still the stains on the altar were not washed away.

Louder and louder sang the chorus of Levites, so loud that the sound must be heard by the watchmen on the wall at Hebron and the Roman soldiers in their barracks at Jericho. Yet it could not drown the bleating of the lambs.

6

WAKING LONG BEFORE DAWN on the fourth day of the feast, the Boy lay tensed, listening.

It was the smell of fish clinging to his coverlet which reminded him that he was not in his own tent. Yesterday, after the waving of the first sheaves in the Temple, followed by lavish feasting, Jacob and Johanan had persuaded Miriam to let their cousin spend the night with them. It would be the last chance in Jerusalem, they had pleaded, for both the Capernaum and the Nazareth pilgrims had decided to leave for home early, on the seventeenth of Nisan, when the days became half holy and traveling was permitted.

Last night, before coming to their tent, the three boys had hovered on the edge of the firelit circle in front of Jered's tent and heard the elders of the two delegations, including both Joseph and Zebedee, making their plans. They would leave together soon after a hasty noonday meal; that had been easily decided, but the route of travel had been hotly debated.

"Samaria!" Jered had insisted, his fingers stroking the hilt of a new dagger he had bought that day in the Tyropean bazaar. "Those mongrel infidels must not be pampered in their terrorizing tactics."

But both Joseph and Zebedee, with others also startled by the dagger, had argued for the longer route through the Jordan Valley. The dispute had still been going on when the younger members of the delegations, heavy-eyed and heavier-bodied with much feasting, had stumbled toward their tents.

The Boy lay staring into the dark, sensing that it must be close to dawn. Even as he listened tensely, he heard very faint and far away the first throaty chirrup of a sparrow. The time had come, then. There were only a few hours left to do the thing he had known for many days he must do.

Noiselessly he eased himself from the sleeping mat, feeling with his bare toes for the spaces between his cousins' outflung legs and arms, stooping to balance himself by his hands and right foot while groping with his left for solid ground beyond the mountain of his Uncle Zebedee, Being a guest, he had been given the innermost place, farthest from all possible dangers.

It was not so dark outside as he had expected. The waning starlight silvered the olive leaves and shone on the dew-drenched grass between the black tents. It was easy to make his way through the encampment and descend the hill by the road leading to the bridge over the Kidron. All the way he could see the Temple shining like a luminous pearl.

The Golden Gate, high above the valley, was closed, but there was no hurry now. When Zebedee and his sons wakened, they would assume naturally that he had gone back to his father's tent. Joseph and Miriam would think he was still with his cousins. All would be so occupied through the morning with preparations for departure that he would not be missed.

Seating himself in an angle of the wall, his head finding a comfortable hollow between the bronze studs of the massive wooden door, he watched the sky arch into pale silver above the Mount of Olives. So still was the air that he was sure he could hear the whisper of feet on the marble pavements inside the wall, the pouring of water into brazen lavers, as priests and Levites and attendants made ready for the morning service.

The silver arch widened, quivered into pale yellow, and from within the Temple a voice rose in eager question.

"Has the light reached Hebron?"

"The light has reached Hebron," replied the watchman on the highest pinnacle.

Other voices sounded, ringing and imperative.

"Priests, to your ministry! Levites, to your places! Israelites, to your stations!"

The dawn was greeted by three blasts of silver trumpets, piercing sweet and clear, and the great gate swung open.

At last! His Father's House, just as he had always dreamed it! Nothing now to mar the beauty of dim porticoes and high-arched spaces and wide steps leading up and up to shining whiteness! Even the smoke of the morning sacrifice, haloed by the morning sun, became a pillar of light instead of darkness. And the fresh incense kindled in the Holy Place filled all the courts with such fragrance it must surely be mingled with the scent of balsam groves in Jericho!

If men had to build a house for God to live in, surely none more beautiful could be devised. Though why they should think he would keep himself shut up in a little, dark room when he could roam through lofty arches and lift his face to the blue sky—!

The Boy felt like stretching his arms wide and laughing aloud, as he often did when acutely conscious of the Presence on the Hilltop. It was such a relief to know that God was really here in his House and that he wasn't the sort who would stay brooding in the dark behind a musty curtain! It almost made one forget the cheating merchants, and the crippled beggars, and even the lambs.

Chilled by this reminder of why he had come, he turned reluctantly toward the Royal Porch, where the sellers of doves and lambs and goats and bullocks were setting up their booths. He was anxious to finish the unwelcome task as soon as possible and approached the nearest merchant, an old man squatting among an untidy array of cages, with a half dozen goats secured in a small pen on the marble floor behind him.

"You! A goat for sacrifice?" The good-natured, toothless grin was belied by small, suspicious eyes. "What for?" demanded the merchant impudently.

"For a sin offering," replied the Boy, flushing.

The grin widened to emit a loud cackle. "Sin offering! You? By my lousy beard! Hear that, comrades?" His lusty voice resounded thorough the lofty colonnades. "The babe from Galilee wants a goat for a sin offering!"

"How much?" demanded the Boy with tight lips.

"Huh! More than you can pay! A pair of turtle doves is more your style. Or how about a couple of baby sparrows?"

"A goat," came the firm reply. "A young goat without blemish, at least eight days and less than a year old. How much? I can pay you."

"Hm!" The lips clamped shut, forming a narrow line above the sparse, gray beard. "Maybe you're not as young and innocent as you look."

The old man reached a gnarled hand back into the pen, hesitating briefly before closing his fingers about a spindly shank.

"No," said the Boy. "The next one, please. I'd like the best you have."

The hand returned with the designated animal, grudging respect showing on the sharp, old features. "Thirty shekels," the merchant announced quizzically, still only half convinced he was not making a fool of himself even to discuss business with such an unlikely customer.

"It's far too much," came the prompt reply. "We paid fifteen for our Passover lamb, five times what it was worth. I'll give you ten shekels."

"Ha!" The thin lips exploded in mirth. The merchant's loud amusement had attracted a circle of his idle comrades, and he had no mind to risk ridicule by indulging in further bargaining. "If you have ten shekels cached away in that peasant homespun, I'll not only give you the goat in exchange but carry it into the Temple for you, like a slave, across my shoulders!"

"Hear, hear!" applauded the onlookers with relish, while one added maliciously, "I'd almost pay the ten shekels myself to see that sight."

Beaching into the pocket of his girdle, the Boy drew out a small packet of cloth. "I don't have ten shekels," he said gravely.

The old man smirked. "Aha! What did I tell you! I could see through this young beggar before he spoke a word. Upstarts all, these Galileans!"

The Boy unwrapped the parcel. "But I do have this piece of gold," he said simply.

The onlookers stared incredulously, then burst into howls of delight.

"Guess that will teach you, Absalom, you old son of avarice!"

"Thought you knew all about Galileans!"

"Twenty shekels he could have paid as easily as ten."

"Let us know when you start for the Temple with the goat on your shoulders!"

The old man's cheeks turned redder and redder. Baffled anger struggled with cupidity and suspicion in his small eyes. Then suddenly the spark of an idea appeared, igniting all three. His curling fingers closed over the gold piece.

"So it's a thief you are! No wonder you wanted to make a sin offering! Trying to get us all into trouble by making us accept stolen money! And, by the horns of the altar, if you'd picked a foolish man instead of a clever one, you'd have gotten away with it too!" The small eyes focused covetously on the girdle. "How many more of those stolen pieces have you hidden there?"

"No more." Pale and trembling, the Boy returned his gaze. "That's the last one. And it wasn't stolen. It was a Gift."

"Ha! Listen to the lying son of a peasant. A gift, he says. Whose gift?"

"I—I don't know exactly. A stranger he was, from a far country."

"Oho, a stranger! A king, perhaps?" The tone was scurrilously mocking.

"Perhaps. My mother said he looked like a king."

"Ho, better and better! And maybe you yourself are a prince! Prince of liars as well as thieves. Get along before I call a Roman soldier."

The Boy turned cold with dismay. "But—you haven't given me the goat—"

"Little fool! And do you think I'd sell a goat for stolen money?"

"Then give me back my gold piece."

"And encourage you further in your wickedness? Listen to the young reprobate!" The old man looked warily about him, testing the expressions on his comrades' faces. "Begging us to become accomplices in his crime! And in the courts of the holy Temple! A lucky escape for us, what, my brothers?"

Heads nodded, if somewhat doubtfully, for these were simple men. Each pair of eyes revealed only assent or bewilderment or stupefaction. Except one. The Boy's straight gaze was as fearlessly scathing as his voice.

"You'd better not judge others if you don't want to be judged yourself. You accuse me of being a thief, then steal my gold piece. While you're trying to—to take the splinter out of my eye, what about the big plank that's in your own?"

There was a burst of loud laughter and a resounding slapping of knees, for this was logic that even simple men could understand.

"That's right, Absalom, you old cheater!"

"How are you going to talk your way out of that one?"

"Boldly uttered, young Galilean!" spoke a clear voice approvingly. A tall young man stepped from the shadow of one of the marble columns. "Shame, Absalom! I have a mind to report you to the Temple authorities."

The old man crumpled into cringing respect. "By my white hair and ancient beard, I meant no harm, grandson of the Most Venerable." Hastily he delivered the goat into the Boy's arms. "I intended all the time to keep the bargain, only teaching the young renegade a lesson. See, here is his change, in good silver shekels."

"That's not all the bargain," reminded a comrade with malicious relish. "He promised, young sire, to carry the beast to the Temple, like a slave."

"No." The bewildered gratitude in the Boy's eyes gave place to amusement as they turned from the stranger to the unhappy merchant. "Your friend Absalom looks as if he needed a burden-bearer more than I do."

As they walked together through the Court of the Gentiles, he continued to study his benefactor with both gratitude and bewilderment. The young man was perhaps twice his age, tall and graceful of movement but with features too strongly defined to be deemed attractive. He wore a spotlessly white coat with a wide blue border. A prayer shawl covered his head, and phylacteries were bound on both his forehead and upper arm—but not over-large ones, the Boy noted approvingly, such as some of the strict Pharisees wore to make a show of their religion.

"Grandson of the Most Venerable," the man Absalom had called him. But who was "the Most Venerable"? Someone important surely, or the young man would not have spoken with such authority. The High Priest? It could not be, for Annas was not an old man and was just recently appointed to office. His mind whirled. For some reason the words sounded strangely familiar.

"So you did not steal the gold piece." The young man turned on him a pair of keen, dark eyes, their warmth almost hidden under bushy, protruding brows. "It was a gift. I believe you. I know an honest youth when I see one. I think I know a good one too. Why, then, must you make a sin offering?"

"Not for myself," explained the Boy simply. "For Old Simon. He did something very wicked, so wicked he was pronounced"—he shivered—"*Cherem!* I can't bear to see him so unhappy."

The bushy brows contracted into one straight line. "And why shouldn't he be unhappy? Isn't that the just penalty for his sin?"

"But he's sorry for what he did," replied the Boy earnestly, "whatever it was."

"Suppose he is." In spite of his intense gaze, the young man's voice sounded amused and indulgent, as if directed toward a child. "Don't you know that, even if this man were to make a thousand sin offerings, he would still be *Cherem* in the sight of the elders?"

"Yes," said the Boy gravely. "It's not the elders I'm doing it for. It's for Old Simon and his poor crippled son Gad."

"Gad." The tone was still amused. "And what has this Gad to do with it?"

The Boy explained how Old Simon's son had killed the lamb and brought it to the synagogue, not knowing the proper way an offering should be made. "So I want to do it for him," he finished, "even though Old Simon will still be *Cherem* and the elders will never know. Old Simon will know. And Gad will know. And, of course, God."

"God?" The young man looked faintly startled, as if surprised to hear the Deity spoken of in such casual and intimate terms, but after the first uneasy reaction he seemed more curious than shocked. "You sound as if you expected the Most Holy One of Israel to be more lenient than the elders!"

The Boy looked up at him soberly. "I hope he is," he replied.

"I'm not quite sure. I don't know him well enough yet. But Hosea thought so, didn't he?"

The young man stood suddenly still, the note of amused indulgence gone from his voice. "Yes," he replied thoughtfully. "So he did."

Thanks to his new friend, who went with him as far as the entrance to the Court of Priests, the Boy gained admittance easily and stood waiting his turn, pulses pounding, the fingers of each hand rigidly circling a bony foreleg.

The goat was an uneasy creature, rebelling against confinement with every knob and sinew of its stubborn little body. Perhaps that was why he had chosen it, knowing that it would not snuggle in his arms as the lamb had done. Nevertheless, he dreaded the moment when he must relinquish it.

When finally it came and the animal lay securely fastened to the ring in the stone floor at the north of the great altar, head unwillingly pointed toward the Temple entrance, his throat tightened and his hand trembled so that the bronze knife almost fell from his grasp. Then he remembered Old Simon, and Gad coming into the synagogue with his strange burden and exalted face. His hand steadied, and the knife descended.

> "Have mercy on me, O Lord!
> Listen to my voice as I cry unto thee!
> Let my transgressions be forgiven,
> Let my sin be covered!"

While his lips moved obediently, his every sense was acutely tuned to each small detail—the priest stirring the blood in the silver vessel to keep it from curdling, the crackling of wood on the altar, a trumpet note high and clear as the blue sky, the sharp stench of burning flesh. It was as if he must see and hear and feel everything twice as hard for Old Simon's sake.

When he came out of the Court of Priests, to his surprise the young man in the spotless white coat was still waiting.

"*Ah hah*, my young friend from Galilee!" The brooding eyes were gravely solicitous. "You look pale as death. Did you find it so hard, then, to take upon yourself the sins of another?"

The Boy made no reply, but when they had walked together through the Court of Women, he turned and looked back up the long marble steps leading through the Gate Beautiful.

"You're a strange lad," commented the young man almost with vexation. "I can't understand you. Perhaps that's why I couldn't go away. I can't bear to have my questions unanswered. Here you stand, gazing at a sight every Jew on earth would count himself in Paradise to see, and yet you look as unsatisfied as these hungry beggars pulling at our coats. Why?"

Before answering, the Boy turned and looked down at the thin hand clawing at his garments. "Because," he said, "the time is so short. I must leave for home in a few hours, and I have found out so few of the things I wanted to know."

The brooding eyes kindled. "What things?"

The Boy looked up at him, puzzled and distressed. "About life. And death." The words came haltingly. "And—God. Does—he really like that—that sort of thing—we did up there? Then why did he say to Hosea what he did, about sacrifice? Remember—"

"I remember," replied the young man promptly. " 'I desired mercy and not sacrifice, and the knowledge of God—' "

The Boy nodded eagerly. Once the questions had started, they came with a rush, like wine from a bursting skin. "And if the animals must be killed, why should the good meat be burned while beggars sitting right here in the gate go hungry? And why should a man have to suffer for his father's sins? And why—" He stopped, flushing in embarrassment. "But—I promised my father I wouldn't ask such questions. You're probably laughing—or angry."

The young man was not angry. Nor did he laugh. And when he spoke, it was no longer lightly, indulgently, as to a child.

"Come with me," he said abruptly.

Casting a swift glance at the sun to make sure the morning was still young, the Boy followed his new friend eastward across the great Court of the Gentiles. The tall white-clothed figure moved swiftly and with the assurance of authority. The crowds, gathered in festive spirit for the observance of this first half-holy day after the more rigid feast days, interrupted their fraternizing to let him pass. Important-looking people greeted him with respect, less assuming ones with groveling humility.

"Peace, grandson of the Most Venerable!"

"May heaven smile upon you, son of wisdom!"

"Behold your slave, young master. I take the dust from your feet."

The Boy's flush of embarrassment grew deeper. Who was this honored nobleman to whom he had dared speak the inmost thoughts of his being? Attempting to follow the long-striding figure through the closing crowds, he grew more and more self-conscious. The sun's barbs, dazzling sharp as the gold prongs surmounting the temple roof, stung his eyes and turned his coarse garments into clinging weights.

Nor did the cool shadows of the Porch of Solomon relieve his discomfort. The sight of the Rabbi Zadok haranguing his circle of eager listeners turned him cold with apprehension. Where was the young Pharisee taking him? Would he do something to bring distress and embarrassment to his new friend as he had to his father? But to his intense relief they passed on between the lofty columns, giving Zadok and his group a wide berth.

"See?" demanded his companion, turning suddenly and grasping his arm, eyes aglow with excitement. "See that old man with the big circle about him?"

"Old" was hardly the word to describe the rabbi indicated, for he seemed to possess a timeless quality to which no terms denoting age could do justice. Ancient he was, but as the cedars of Lebanon were ancient, hoary like Mount Hermon, constantly rejuvenated by its eternal snows. In spite of his extreme age he sat straight as a palm tree, disdaining the support of the pillar behind him, and, though his skin looked the color and texture of dry leaves, the eyes deep within their bony crevices were flame-bright with awareness. His voice, resonant as a ram's-horn blast, if a bit gusty, penetrated far beyond the circle of his intent listeners.

"You ask me to give you a summary of the Law, that you may tell it to a Gentile? Very well I repeat what I have often said. Go tell him this: 'What you would yourself dislike, never do to your neighbor. That is the whole Law. All else is only its application.'"

The Boy's pulses hammered. How could he have been so blind! A hundred times he had heard Ben Arza quote those very words, his wistful face alight with hero-worship! Yes, and those others, too, which had sounded so familiar.

Shammai says, my children, that such a man should be killed, but it is not the teaching of the Most Venerable...

If the Most Venerable were here, my sons, he would tell you...

How could he have failed to guess? Because the great teacher had always seemed more like a spirit, perhaps, than a person; an embodiment of truth instead of flesh-and-blood reality.

The Boy turned to his companion, speechless with eagerness.

"No wonder they call him the Most Venerable," murmured the young man with an affection akin to reverence. "And not just because of his age, though he stopped counting his years a generation ago, when he passed a hundred. If there is one on earth who can answer your questions, he is the one."

The Boy finally found his voice. "Hillel!" he whispered.

"Hillel, of course," replied the young man, adding with faint surprise, "Didn't you know? I am his grandson, Gamaliel."

7

THE BOY STARED, unable to believe his eyes.

So excited he must have been from the morning's adventure that he had turned off the wrong path from the road leading over the crest of the Mount of Olives. But, no, there was the pit where Joseph and his fellow townsmen had roasted their Passover lamb. He could tell it by the two rocks one on top of the other like grinding stones, against which he had leaned watching the meat turn on its spit. And just beyond were the two round spots of clipped grass where Graylegs and her lazy mate had been tethered, and beyond those the circle of flattened places where the tents had been pitched. Running to one of them, he found the earth still dark and moist about the tent-pin holes.

Bewildered, he ran back along the path and followed the road just over the brow of the hill to the field where the Capernaum pilgrims had been encamped. That too was empty. Slowly he retraced his steps to the fire pit.

"What's the matter, boy? Lost something?"

With unbounded relief he recognized the ill-natured landowner from whom the elders had rented their camping place, standing, arms akimbo, surveying the damage done to his property. The Boy ran to him eagerly. "Where are they? Where have they all gone?"

"Home," replied the man sourly. "Just my luck, renting to a crowd that stayed only three days instead of to the end of the feast!"

"But they didn't plan to go until afternoon!"

"Oh yes, they did! Made all their plans last night sitting around the fire. I heard every word. First it was afternoon, then that big mouth with the seven snakes hanging from his chin—"

"Jered," supplied the Boy, smiling in spite of his anxiety at this desecration of the sacred candelabra.

"Don't know his name. But he argued how he had to get back to tend to business. Might lose a few shekels. So they all agreed to start as soon after dawn as they could get packed."

The Boy stood silently, blaming himself for his stupidity. He had supposed the talk was all of the route they would take, not of the starting time. And instead of staying awake until Uncle Zebedee returned to learn the decision, he had taken it for granted! His parents would suppose that he was with Zebedee's section of the caravan, since he had stayed with them that night, and Zebedee would assume that he had risen early and returned to his father's tent. A natural enough mistake, and he had only himself to blame. But they could not have more than a few hours' start, and caravans moved slowly.

"Which way did they go?" he inquired eagerly.

The man shook his head. "How should I know? It's all I can do making sure they don't run away with any of my property. Thieves, these Galileans!"

"But didn't you hear them talking about the route last night?"

"Maybe I did. Maybe I didn't." The man shrugged his stooped shoulders. "At least I didn't hear what they decided." Lowering himself with a grunt to his knees and leaning over the fire pit, he laboriously lifted one of the blackened stones which had been used for a lining and, groaning with every movement, replaced it on a meticulously piled wall. "Can't even put back things they take apart!" he grumbled, panting.

"Here, I'll help you." Leaping into the pit, the Boy quickly lifted out all the rocks, then carried them one after the other to the wall. "You're right. We should have put them back. I'll lift them, then you can put them where they belong. It's such a beautiful wall I don't wonder you want every stone placed just right."

"Look out...don't...have a care...Uh..." To his surprise the man found there was nothing to complain about. After replacing the stones precisely in the desired pattern and with a minimum of discomfort, he grinned sheepishly. "I—I could have been wrong, about *all* Galileans."

"That's all right," the Boy assured him. "You're sure you can't remember which way they went when they started out?"

The man honestly tried to remember, but it was no use. He had been too busy, he confessed, making sure all his rentals were collected and nothing was missing, to bother about unimportant details. But there was nothing to worry about, he assured the Boy with grudging optimism. Children were always getting left behind in the holiday confusion. Sometimes parents never found them!

For hours the Boy went about the hill making inquiries among the throngs of pilgrims. Many knew individuals from Nazareth or Capernaum. Some had even watched them make preparations for departure. But none could tell which route they had taken. His anxiety increased to consternation. Suppose his parents were forced to return in order to find him! His mother would be frantic with worry, and his father more displeased than ever. He had caused him nothing but concern since they left Nazareth. First the episode at the Well of Jacob, then the encounter with Zadok, and now this.

Then all at once he stopped making inquiries. He found himself back in the empty field with the stone wall behind him, and the green grass sown with spring flowers at his feet, and a strong clean wind blowing in his face. Across the deep cleft of the Kidron the city clung to its stony hilltop, huddled about the glittering pile of the Temple as if seeking refuge from the dark storm clouds racing above it.

There was rain in the clouds as well as wind. Presently it fell, a fine mist at first, stinging his face; then a soft shower of gentle drops, flowing down his cheeks like tears. Tasting like tears, too, with the tang of salt when they reached his lips. No shame, surely, for a man to mingle his tears with those of heaven, to weep over his lost dream of a white and shining city.

Not only rain in the clouds. Thunder like the rumble of chariots, lightning sharp as swords! But—the Boy's eyes tried fiercely to penetrate the whirling shapes—what figures riding the chariots, wielding the swords? David, wresting the rocky stronghold from the Jebusites? Nebuchadnezzar, razing it to the ground? The bloody Herod? Pompey? Or men of violence as yet unborn? Even—the Boy shivered—Messiah? Would he too come riding, smiting, like the rest?

Wind tore at his garments and pushed him against the wall, pinning him there while rain lashed him and drenched him through and through. Yet still he kept his face lifted and his streaming eyes opened wide until the rumbling chariots passed and the swords were sheathed, until at long last the city emerged again into blue sky and sunlight, a new city white and golden and shining as an untarnished dream.

The storm passed and with it the Boy's anxiety. The mistake had been made and could not be undone. He knew suddenly that, in spite of the trouble he had caused, it was right, perhaps even important, that he should be here. His parents probably would not discover his absence until the caravan pitched camp tonight. It would take them until tomorrow evening to return to Jerusalem. And of course they would look for him first in the courts of the Temple.

Another whole day to sit at the feet of the wise Hillel! To learn the answers to some of his questions, perhaps even to discover more about what his work was to be and how he should prepare to do it! Swiftly his eyes measured the angle of the sun. Perhaps Hillel was still sitting in the Porch of Solomon. As he sprang eagerly to his feet, the folds of his drenched *simlah* weighing him down, in that moment he knew that he could not go now to Hillel. Even if he never discovered just what his work was to be.

He must go first to the bazaars and buy a cloak for the crippled beggar who was sitting outside the Beautiful Gate, wet and shivering from the rain.

When nighttime came, he found a shelter farther down the hill where an ancient olive tree spread its branches over an angle in a high stone wall. His sleep was uneasy, for there had been other beggars needing cloaks and many more needing bread, and there had not been nearly enough shekels in his girdle. He dreamed that it rained again, drenching his freshly dried garments, and he was trying to reach the shelter of the Porch of Solomon, but at every step he took hands reached out to stop him. He managed to escape them all until finally one, bigger than the rest but gentler, grasped him firmly by the shoulder.

"By my hair and beard," he wakened to hear a man's voice say wonderingly, "it's a boy! And wetter than a sheep's fleece that's been out in the rain! Until I heard you moan in your sleep, lad, I thought you were a bundle of rags thrown away by some pilgrim."

The face belonging with the hand was gentle, too, though seamed as an old olive trunk and sun-baked the color and toughness of leather. In the glow of the tiny lantern it shone with anxious solicitude.

"Come, lad. Come inside the gate. The rain is over now, but your clothes need drying. Besides, there are prowlers abroad on these feast nights. That's why the young master had me stay the night by his oil press. *Ah hah!* Still only half awake! What say I just lift you in my arms…there! We're inside. Now well close the gate."

The Boy rubbed his eyes. "Oil press?" he breathed. "It looks more like a garden!"

"Ay! *Gethsemane*—oil press. But it is a little like a garden, if I do say so whose job it is to keep it. The master likes to have it so. An eye for beauty as well as a taste for good olives has my master, the young Joseph of Arimathea."

As the Boy looked about the enclosed space inside the stone wall, he breathed a long sigh of delight, then felt an answering tremor, almost as if the garden too had been holding its breath, waiting for him. It was such a loved and loving place, with the old trees spreading their arms wide in invitation, their little gray leaves, silvered with rain and moonlight, aquiver with welcome! And wandering here and there among the shadows were white paths made of bits of stone lovingly fitted together and bordered with carefully tended beds of flowers.

"You're sure," he asked in a hushed voice, "your master wouldn't mind my being here? Perhaps you should ask him."

The keeper of the olive press added more fuel to the fire already glowing in the lee of a huge rock. As he turned again to the Boy, the fresh flames leaped high to illumine his kindly features.

"Mind? No, lad, he's a kind man, Joseph. And I couldn't ask him if I wanted to, for he lives in a big house beside another garden away on the other side of the city, in that new suburb just outside the wall. Maybe you know the place, not far from that ugly hill shaped like a skull?"

The Boy shook his head sleepily.

"No? Just as well," the voice chattered on cheerfully while the gentle hands removed the drenched cloak and spread it on the rock to dry. "Hope you never see it—the hill, I mean, not Joseph's garden. But if you're like me, you'll like this one better. More natural, less fuss. And you're welcome to come here whenever you please. I'll not forget you."

The Boy hugged the fire gratefully. So sleepy was he that he was only vaguely conscious of the kindly hands wrapping him in a warm dry cloak which smelled rankly of olives, laying him on a smooth flat shelf of the rock with a round stone for a pillow.

He dreamed that he was Jacob lying at the foot of a shining ladder, and that the gentle, ministering hands were those of angels, and that the big rock was the threshold of heaven.

8

"AT LEAST we know he's here somewhere in Jerusalem." Joseph's accents were as sharply incisive as the jabs of his knife into the willow sapling he held across his knees. "That cheating landlord described him well enough. 'A reed of a lad,' he said, 'with his headcloth half off.' "

Watching him from the shelter of the tent, the woman folded a square of damp homespun into one last neat triangle, smoothing and smoothing it as if her fingers could not get enough.

"It's his," she said. "He must have dropped it when he was lifting those stones from the fire pit."

"Another sure sign it was he," retorted Joseph, his knife severing a tiny twig cleanly at its joint. "Who else would help the scoundrel who cheated him make way with his loot? For the price that sour landlord charged us he should have had to cart the stones to Solomon's quarries!"

The woman's gaze clung fearfully to the willow stick. At last she could bear it no longer. "You—you're not going to punish him, Joseph?"

The blade ripped through a stubborn twig. "And why shouldn't he be punished? Causing us all this inconvenience, bringing us back a whole day's journey, making you nearly sick with worry!"

"You've been worried too," she reminded him quickly. "If I hadn't insisted on returning with you, you would have walked all night instead of sleeping in the camp and waiting until morning."

"Sleeping! You know neither of us slept!"

"You had no desire to punish him then." Her fingers, still stroking, moved ceaselessly. "Then why should you feel differently now that your worry is over and you know he is safe?"

"How do we know he's safe?" The knife dug a jagged gouge. "Just because that lying landlord said he saw him yesterday—"

"Tonight," corrected the woman with determined optimism. "He was almost sure he saw him earlier in the evening, hanging about the field, waiting. If we hadn't stopped so often on the way to make inquiries—"

"It wasn't the inquiries that made us late," objected Joseph angrily. "It was that lazy bundle of bones that disgraces the name of donkey. Stubborn as green olive wood! Still anchored like a stone a hundred feet away while I do his job as beast of burden. A curse on the miserable animal!"

"But we were late," insisted the woman gently, "and the landlord did say he thought he saw him."

"Then why isn't he here now?" demanded the man roughly. "Where is he?"

Fascinated, the woman watched him draw the supple stick along his sensitive, blunt finger tips, testing its smoothness, then start rubbing at an infinitesimal rough spot with the dull edge of his knife. *Oh, yes,* she almost cried out hysterically, *be sure and make it smooth!* But her voice when she spoke was firm and quiet. "In some warm, dry place, I hope, with someone to make sure that he's fed and well-covered. I—I believe God has been caring for him, Joseph."

He sprang up, the violence of his motion fanning the fire to a brighter flame. "And condoning him, do you think, in his disobedience? What would you have me do? Praise him for rushing off on some willful errand the very hour the caravan was due to leave?"

"But you changed your plans, Joseph. He may not have known.'

"He knew he was not supposed to leave the camp without permission."

"How did he know? Did you tell him?"

"Well—not in so many words. But by all that's holy, why shouldn't he have known! Cities are dangerous places!"

Patiently the woman kept smoothing the moist triangle, deriving strange comfort from feeling it grow warm and dry beneath her fingers. "He may have had important business, Joseph."

He snorted derisively. "Huh! What business could a twelve-year-old possibly have of more importance than his duty to his parents?"

The woman leaned forward suddenly, fingers still and eyes painfully intent. "I wish I knew, Joseph. *How I wish I knew!*"

"Asking more questions, perhaps!" Unheeding, the man continued with fresh bitterness. "As if he hadn't already done enough damage for one trip."

Her startled eyes warned him to silence. "What? Has he done something you haven't told me about, Joseph?"

"No, no, nothing." *Nothing*, he was tempted to add harshly, *but kill every dream I ever had for him!* "Nothing," he ended abruptly, "except disobey my wishes at almost every turn."

He gave vent to his frustration by whipping the stick sharply through the air. The woman winced as if she had been struck.

"Stubborn fool!" he muttered. I'll show him who is master!"

As he strode off into the darkness, the woman uttered a moaning cry and stumbled after him. "Joseph! Where are you going? What are you going to do with that whip?"

"Use it," he shouted back gruffly without turning. "Use it on that stupid donkey, of course. Why do you think I made it?"

She sank down weakly, not knowing whether to laugh or cry.

As soon as it was light enough to see, they began their search.

"The bazaars first," said Joseph, leading the way under the huge arches to the steeply descending Valley of the Tyropean. "It's the first place a boy would be likely to go to look for—for excitement." *For food* he had been about to say without thinking.

Miriam followed him silently, the folded headcloth clutched tightly under her long pointed sleeve. He hurried past the open stalls of merchants selling foreign silks and spices and jewels; cast only the most cursory of glances into the side streets where dyers and weavers, coppersmiths, brass-workers, and potters plied their trades; took a swift side trip through the Street of the Carpenters, peering into every open booth and shadowed alley; lingered a long time in the noisy mart where foods were sold. Here the smells of fresh bread and cakes, piled high on fiat trays and hoisted on the heads of screaming vendors, cruelly reminded Miriam that a boy had to eat. Fascinated and horrified she watched half naked urchins, some full-grown to manhood, snatch at the moldy crusts and bits of decayed fruit discarded from booth or basket. She almost hoped they wouldn't find him here.

"Come," said Joseph at last, and again she knew not whether to laugh with relief or cry with disappointment.

Down through the Valley they went, the heat growing more and more oppressive. The headcloth turned moist again beneath her fingers. As they descended, the streets grew narrower, the buildings more huddled and dingy.

She heard the voices long before she could distinguish words. Harsh and foreign they sounded, like those of the Romans who came sometimes with curt orders to the carpenter shop. Finally words became intelligible.

"Come now, what am I bid! Strong as an ox, can lift a block of limestone twice his weight and carry it twenty paces!"

She knew then where they were going, and her flesh turned cold.

So that was what Joseph feared—that the Boy had been kidnapped and disposed of to a slave merchant! He had not trusted the landlord's story about seeing the lad the night before. In all her dire images of rain and hunger and loneliness she had not thought of this!

There were children among the wares of the slave merchant, frightened lads with starved bodies, little girls shyly concealing their budding womanhood beneath straggling locks of hair or accentuating it with a bold swaggering of thin hips. But the Boy was not among them. An inspection of the other auction blocks in the slave market was equally reassuring. Yet Joseph did not seem to share her relief.

With mounting panic, she followed him about the mart while he made cautious inquiries and listened to what seemed endless conversations.

"It's all right." His grim lips relaxed into a smile. "No caravans carrying slaves as merchandise have left Jerusalem in the past three days."

But after that there was less purpose in his searching. Turning west at the south end of the Tyropean, he followed the narrow, winding street up its long flights of shallow steps until the towers of an imposing palace came into view, then stopped uncertainly.

"He wouldn't go there," he muttered. "Like every good Jew, he's been taught to hate the house of Herod."

Back to the Valley of the Cheesemongers, then deeper and deeper into the cleft between the two embracing hills. Smoke, sour and acrid, from the ever-burning refuse fires in the Valley of Hinnom stung Miriam's eyes and clogged her nostrils, making it hard to see and breathe. Huddled within the folds of her headcloth, she crept along aimlessly, seeing nothing except the striped border of Joseph's coat, the flapping soles of his sandals stirring little clouds of dust, the rows upon rows of stones beneath her feet

And then suddenly she stopped short. Her son down here? Searching for him in a deep, ill-smelling valley when there were hills to climb? Unwinding her headdress and flinging it back, she turned with such abruptness that a mule driver, plodding behind, just managed to swerve his loaded beast in time to avoid collision.

"Stupid she-donkey!" he bellowed.

But she did not notice.

Up, up her gaze traveled, along the valley's winding cleft, scaling the slope of David's ancient city, never stopping until it reached the shining pinnacle of the Temple crowning the hill high above.

She almost laughed aloud.

9

IT WAS THE WOMAN now who led the way, the man who followed.

Better to humor her, he thought, moving slowly and grimly after her through the swarms of pilgrims still, on this sixth day of the feast, thronging the Court of the Gentiles. Better than to tell her why they were unlikely to find the Boy here, where he had so disgraced himself in the presence of the great rabbi! Even now Joseph flushed at the possibility that someone who had been in the group might recognize him, and he walked with chin sunk in the folds of his headcloth.

The woman moved unerringly, turning instinctively from the Royal Porch where the merchants and money-changers still catered to a noisy but dwindling clientele. Occasionally he caught a glimpse of her face as she turned it expectantly from side to side, color ebbing and flowing beneath the arch of cheek visible above her veil, and, with each quick turn of her head, a little wider wing of shining hair appearing above the blue homespun.

How like they are! he thought, finding time for tenderness even in anxiety.

He knew she would stumble on the first step leading up to the Beautiful Gate—she always kept her gaze too high to be certain of her footing—but she was on her feet again long before he could reach her. Arriving in the court above, she turned and came swiftly toward him.

"I'll wait here while you look in the Court of Israel. Go quickly, please, Joseph. I can hardly wait to find him."

"But—" he began, then, closing his lips, departed to do her bidding. As well let her keep that look of confident expectancy as long as possible.

He searched slowly and thoroughly, yet knowing the answer no better at the end than at the beginning, returned even more slowly, reluctant to face her disappointment.

"Not there?" Her eyes were calm and steady above the line of veil. "I didn't expect him to be. But don't worry, my husband. We'll be finding him soon. There's still one place."

His lips set in an even grimmer line when he saw that she was leading him to the Porch of Solomon. No use to protest. Even if he told her the truth, she would still insist on looking, for women did not listen to arguments. They had to be shown. The coolness of the towering arches brought no relief to his perspiring agony.

When he saw that they were approaching the pillar where Zadok had been holding audience, he cowered more deeply into his headcloth. The rabbi was still there, he noted miserably out of a corner of his eye, the crowd of listeners even bigger than before, the old eyes just as penetrating.

"You there! You tall fellow from the country on the edge of the circle."

Slowly Joseph's heart resumed its beating. It was not at him but at some other luckless victim that the bony finger was leveled. The keen eyes had not noticed him. And Miriam, satisfied, turned away from the group gathered about the rabbi Zadok. His feet moved woodenly in her path.

Her cry of joy resounded through the huge portico like a *hallel*.

Joseph looked about him, dazed. She had been there but a moment ago. Now he found himself submerged in a sea of strange faces. Unable to face the direction of her cry, he floundered this way and that, finally spying the flutter of a blue veil far down between the central rows of columns.

"He's here, Joseph! I've found him! My son, my son!"

At first sight of the slender, familiar figure relief was his only emotion. He stood trembling, eyes drinking their fill, arms hanging awkwardly at his sides, envying his wife the abandonment of her affectionate embrace.

Then slowly other little barbs of emotion began pricking at his consciousness. Self-pity for the long hours of extra travel, the worry and expense; compunction for the anguish suffered by one equally dear; anger. But, strangely, it was the woman, not the Boy, who became their target.

"Daughter of weakness, have you nothing to give him but words of honey? Will you commend him for disobedience, reward him for all the trouble he has caused us? I tell you, reproofs are more in order than embraces!"

"But, Joseph—"

The woman looked up protestingly, saw not only the stubborn grimness of lips but the frustration of love in the hurt, bewildered eyes, and her own softened in quick understanding.

"Yes," she said. "I have been remiss in my duty." She turned back toward the Boy. "Son," her voice was firm but gentle, "why have you treated us so? All this time your father and I have been looking for you anxiously."

"I know." The reply was quick and contrite. "And I'm sorry. But how is it that you took so long searching? Didn't you know that I would be here in my Father's house?"

Joseph's temples throbbed with shock and premonition. Looking about cautiously to see if the audacious words had been overheard, he discovered to his horror that they were surrounded by a circle of intent faces, just such a group as they had joined about the Rabbi Zadok. Only this time they were not on its edge but at its center! And when the shocked denunciation came there would be no escape. Instinctively he thrust his body protectingly in front of his son, and found himself facing the keen thoughtful scrutiny of a very old man.

Hillel! He recognized the old man instantly, and his horror became even greater. Prince of all rabbis, a judge of such profound authority that his word might well determine life or death! And excommunication, the penalty for blasphemy, was worse than death. Joseph closed his eyes and waited.

"You heard what the boy just called it, this Temple of the Most High God?"

Gentle, the voice of Hillel, not like that of Zadok! Yet a blade was just as sharp when sheathed in velvet. The faces, Joseph sensed, were also tensed and waiting—clay in those frail hands which had been moulding the men of Israel for more than a century. Given the word, they would as soon frown as smile, snarl and tear to bits as fawn approval.

"The lad has been asking some—shall we say—searching questions. Perhaps in these simple words he propounds the hardest question of all."

Questions! Joseph groaned aloud. He might have known. Only one hope now. No more dreams of royalty or of divine calling! Nothing but to get his family back to Nazareth in safety, never to lift his aims again above the saw and adze and chisel.

"The nature of God," continued the ancient voice with amazing clearness. "Because we say, 'He is unnamable,' shall he then be nameless? Did not David say, 'Blessed be thou, Lord God of Israel, our *father*'? And Isaiah, 'But now, O Lord, thou art our *father*'? Tell me, is he who says, 'Thou Unknowable,' more reverent than he who says, 'I know thee'? I say to you, my children, he who has ears to hear, let him hear."

Joseph walked beside the Boy in a daze, occasionally casting a sidelong, wondering glance in which bewilderment, respect, and just a bit of awe were mingled. Twice he opened his lips to speak, twice closed them. The words were there, clamoring for release. If he kept the secret to himself much longer, it seemed he would burst, but whether from fear or elation, he could not tell.

You saw how the great Hillel called me back after we had left the circle? You would like to know what he said? "Your son is an unusual lad," he told me, those were his very words, an unusual lad, "With proper guidance he might become a leader of men, a rabbi, perhaps, remembered beyond his generation. Without it—without it—"

Here the words faltered, and, remembering, Joseph stumbled on the rocky path leading back to the encampment on the Mount of Olives.

"*Ah hah,* you hurt yourself, Father! Your toe is bleeding."

"Oh, no," he protested, too vehemently. "It's nothing."

Nothing, indeed. For, thanks to Hillel's promise, there would be the proper guidance. Again words clamored for release, and this time there was no fear, only elation.

The Most High has heard our prayers. He has listened to the voice of our supplication. For the great Hillel said to me, "Bring him back at the Feast of Tabernacles, and I myself will undertake his instruction. And when I am gone, he shall be the special charge of my grandson Gamaliel. Together we will mold his mind and spirit, and, I swear to you by the snows of my hair and beard, he shall become a leader in Israel."

Joseph trembled beneath the sweet burden of his secret. He wanted to shout it to all the world, yet for some reason he dared not even whisper it. Too much depended on its fulfillment. And the youth walking by his side was no longer the child who had left Nazareth. Something had happened to him during this journey to Jerusalem.

Again he cast him a sidelong glance, trying to decide what it was. Nothing that one could see. There were the same sharp boyish profile, firm arch of chin and throat, eagerly lifted eyes, slender fingers pushing back the tangled mass of fine, curling hair. The change, then, must be within.

"This way, son," he called sharply. "Can't you see the path turns—"

But apparently the Boy was not listening. Instead of heeding his father's warning, as he would surely have done a week ago, and following the path by its easier detour worn by centuries of plodding feet, he went straight up over the steep outcropping of limestone without a backward glance.

And suddenly Joseph had the answer to his question.

Elation turned again to fear as he remembered the final words of Hillel.

"Without it—without it I see him ending either on a rebel's throne or—on a Roman cross!"

10

IT WAS GOOD to be back home in Nazareth. After the stony starkness of Judea the green Plain of Esdraelon and richly verdured slopes of Galilee seemed like the Garden of Eden.

Thirstily the Boy drank his fill of familiar sights and sounds and odors—the gold of ripening barley and dusty threshing floors and curling shavings; the early morning rustling of goats in the straw below the arches, and the welcome grating of the grinding stones; the glad *shaloms* of neighbors; the smell of freshly planed cedar. It seemed he must have been gone as many weeks as just the few days one could count on one's fingers.

The morning after their return he took his place beside Joseph in the carpenter shop and, though no words were spoken, it was tacitly assumed by both of them that his formal education under Ben Arza was finished. Joseph opened his lips once to protest; then, seeing the mountain of unfinished work which had accumulated during their absence, closed them. After all, it was but a few months to autumn. Time enough then to face the raised eyebrows and quizzical jibes of these peasants who believed themselves to be his peers.

"What!" Still feeding your son the milk of infants when he should be eating the bread of manhood?"

"Careful, Joseph! Don't let his hands become so soft from fondling scrolls that they can't tell sycamore from cedar!"

"Who does the carpenter think he is! One of Herod's noblemen?"

Miriam, hoarding each precious moment like grain in time of famine, permitted herself no other emotion than gratitude for these extra hours of her son's presence. Rushing through her indoor tasks and foregoing even the briefest gossip at the fountain, she contrived to spend more and more time in the courtyard, until Joseph grumbled good-naturedly that when he reached for an adze he was more than likely to find himself holding a flail or pestle or distaff.

The Boy was content. For, while his slender fingers fashioned yokes and plows and threshing sleds, his mind was free to wander, and he had many things to think about. Now that his gold was gone, he had to find some other way to help bring new life to people, and the problem became more and more perplexing.

There were not just a few, he discovered, like Deborah and Mulcah and Old Simon, who needed help. Scarcely a person came into the carpenter shop but, if you looked closely enough, you could see was poor or hungry or sick or unhappy. Even the big, swaggering Roman captain who stopped by to impress Joseph's services for a month's labor on the new soldiers' barracks in Sepphoris had fine wrinkles of pain about his eyes and a nervous twitching of his lips. And Jered, the richest man in Nazareth, the Boy discovered to his amazement, suddenly seemed the unhappiest of all.

"A chest," he specified curtly, moving with restless impatience about the courtyard, his ringed fingers displacing neatly piled boards and probing into corners. "Finer, much finer than the one you made for my daughter's wedding. She—I must have the best there is. Spare no expense. The costliest Lebanon cedar, and inlaid with sandalwood. This piece might do…No, this!" As Joseph started helplessly to protest, "No matter whose it was, it's mine now. I tell you, I'll have this one and no other!"

As the Boy watched the nervous fingers stroking the cedar board, the fevered anxiety in the restless eyes, a sudden startled awareness came into his own. Strange! There was in Jered's eyes exactly the same look that had been in Jonathan's that day they walked through the market place, when his friend had been so afraid of losing his beloved Lilah!

The Boy did not go to the Hilltop these days. There was no time. In the brief interval before dark, after they had finished the day's work and the evening meal, there were more important things to do.

One night when they had finished later than usual, he climbed as far as the tiny stone house within its encircling wall of cypress trees. Even though it was already dark when he arrived, it did not matter, for Joel's slender fingers needed no light to inspect the treasures the Boy carried in the pocket of his girdle.

"Look, Mother! See what my friend brought me! The roundest, smoothest stones in the whole world, and they came from the Valley Kidron so close to the Temple that if you had a strong arm and could see, you could skim one right over the wall. Maybe King David was walking along the valley one day and picked this one up and held it in his hand!"

128

Deborah's narrow face swam toward them in a tiny pool of light, the tight seams of her forehead unraveling in swift relief. "Oh, it's you, Jeshua! Miriam's son. I might have known. Nobody else bothers to come near us—and I hope they don't, this time of night. The way that child rushes out into the dark!"

"See my stones, Mother? Hold them close to the lamp, and watch them shine. They're white, aren't they? The whitest white. I can tell by the feel of them."

The weak eyes filled with tears. "Listen to him! Doesn't it make your heart break? They say there's a wonderful pool in Jerusalem where an angel comes down every once in a while and stirs the water, and the first one in it afterward is cured of whatever ails him."

"Yes," said the Boy soberly. "I saw it."

"And were the waters stirred?" inquired Deborah eagerly.

"I guess so. There was a bubbling sound down in the rocks, and the water came rushing in."

"And was anybody cured?"

"I—wasn't sure. One man shouted and threw away his crutches—"

"There, now! What did I tell you!"

"—but after a little he came crawling back on his hands and knees and got them."

"Imagine!" The tearful eyes blinked enviously. "You, so strong and healthy, being able to stand right beside that pool while the waters were being stirred, and my poor blind boy here—"

"But we're not poor any longer, Mother, remember? We have a house all our own, a beautiful house, and all we need to eat and wear."

"I know." Deborah's thin fingers curled about the tiny lamp. "But if we only knew who sent us the money, whether it was my brother who went to Egypt or my uncle who lived beyond the Jordan, and how we could reach him—"

"But if he wanted us to thank him, Mother, he would have told us."

"I wasn't thinking only of thanking him," replied the woman pensively. "If he has so much, surely a little more—just enough to buy a donkey so we could make a journey to the pool in Jerusalem—"

The Boy went slowly back down the hill.

11

HE HAD BROUGHT other gifts with him from his trip to Jerusalem.

As he stood outside the low opening of the stout stone house, watching Jonathan and his bride come home after their day's work in the fields, joy filled and overflowed in him. Here, at least, his gift of gold had fulfilled its mission; indeed, had multiplied itself in abundance. Gold heaped high in the sheaves topping both their heads. Gold sifting in the dust about their bare feet. Gold gleaming in the arc of an upthrust arm, the curve of an uptilted profile. Beautiful, radiant gold, as splendid as youth and as prodigal of its wealth as sunlight!

Unwilling to break the enchantment, the Boy drew back into the tiny courtyard. Their vision impaired by their huge burdens as well as by their absorption in each other, they entered without seeing him.

"Minx! Don't look at me like that when we're in the street. Would you have me spill all this grain and—"

Teasingly Lilah eluded his lunging grasp, her graceful motions maintaining the load of sheaves in perfect balance. Jonathan was not so fortunate. His burden slipped, toppled, half burying both the courtyard and its visitor in a dusty golden flood. But he kept on undaunted.

"Jonathan—no! You'll make me spill—"

Laughing shamelessly, he pushed the bundle off her head and, heedless of her screaming protests, gathered her into his big arms, smothering her cries with eager lips. But in spite of his strength there was more of tenderness than roughness in his touch.

"Beautiful," he murmured. "You're as beautiful as—as—"

Pulling away, she looked up at him with sudden eagerness. "Yes, Jonathan? As what?"

"As"—he struggled with the helpless awkwardness of one slow of speech—"as the golden grain itself."

"Is that the best you can do?" Her voice sounded disappointed. "Grain! You should hear what some people used to call me!"

Jonathan's arms dropped. "You mean Jason?" he asked heavily.

She tossed her head. "Perhaps."

"What—what did he used to call you?"

He should cry out, thought the Boy in an agony of embarrassment, but some instinct forced him to silence. Better for a little wound to be opened up and cleansed, his mother often told him, than to be covered and allowed to fester.

Lifting a restless arm, Lilah pushed back her dusty headcloth, shaking free her black hair. Her eyes gleamed teasingly through her long lashes, a bit appraisingly, as if gauging the narrow boundary between provocation and displeasure.

"Oh—a golden topaz," she suggested hesitantly, "or—or gold brocade from Damascus." At the conjured images her restless eyes focused less and less on Jonathan. Her sharp voice softened. "Or a bowl of gleaming copper." There was no hesitation now. Words tumbled to keep pace with the images. "And silks and velvets and smooth pearls to hang about your neck and flowers of gold filigree the Egyptians make to twine in your hair."

Jonathan stood very still until she had finished. "Yes, you are like all those things," he said quietly. "You're like everything beautiful anywhere in the world. And I still think none of them is as lovely as wheat!" Somewhere, out of the urgency of his love, he found words. "New wheat, rippling in the wind like your hair. Ripe wheat kissed by the—the warmth of the sun like your skin. Golden, sifted wheat sweet with fulfillment, giving bread to hungry people, holding in its kernels the—the promise of new life, like—like—"

Again he was awkward and tongue-tied, but the words had been spoken. The girl gazed up at him, wide-eyed. Then suddenly she was close to him, face upturned, arms about his neck.

"Jonathan! I—I didn't know you could say such things. Oh, I want to be like the wheat, really I do! And I love you, I do love you. Don't"—her voice shrilled with earnestness—"don't ever let me stop loving you, Jonathan!"

The Boy suddenly sneezed.

Presenting himself to their astonished gaze, he began a stumbling explanation. But Jonathan, smiling broadly, did not let him finish.

"*Ah hah!* So this is the way I greet my friend, bury him under a load of wheat! *Shalom,* son of Joseph. May peace enter my house with you. It is well. Had you not taken us unawares, you would not know how happy we are. Look at her, Jeshua. Isn't she beautiful, my bride?"

The Boy's gaze followed Jonathan's proud, possessive gesture. Never had he seen Lilah look less prepossessing. Her face was sweat-streaked and smudged and sunburned, her shapeless outer garment, tucked high into her girdle, faded and bedraggled. There were lines of weariness about her eyes and lips. But the eyes were bright, the lips tender.

"Yes," he agreed gravely. "I've never seen her look so beautiful."

"And clever, too," boasted the young husband. "She reaps half as much again as any other woman."

The tone sharpened. "As your lazy brothers' wives, you mean," the girl interjected with some impatience. "Why should they work? Or your father and brothers? They know you'll do it for them."

Jonathan flushed. "Father hasn't been—feeling so well this spring," he countered defensively. "And my brothers have never been so strong as I."

"Strong? I wonder. Anyway they are wise—wise enough to know how to get something for nothing."

Stooping, Jonathan scooped a great bundle of the fallen sheaves into the circle of his big arms and hoisted it to his shoulder. "God has blessed us with an abundant harvest," he said simply. "Enough so neither the strong nor the weak need go hungry."

"Enough," corrected the girl swiftly, "so that, if you took the just return for your labors, you could sell some to the traders and have silver to buy the things we want and need. Some new wool to make you a *simlah*, for instance. Yours looks like a beggar's. And—and maybe a dress for me of crimson-dyed linen. You promised me one, you know, as soon as we could afford it."

Lifting a big hand, Jonathan smeared grain dust into the sweaty creases of his forehead. "I know. But—"

"Or some more furnishings for the house," continued the girl eagerly. "The daughter of Jered has a floor made of tiles instead of bits of limestone, and a stone couch on which to spread her sleeping mats. And—and she has a hand mirror of polished bronze and a net of gold threads to bind up her hair."

Her voice was more childishly petulant than angry. It pursued Jonathan and his burden up the narrow stone stairway to the housetop, mounting to a new excited pitch with every step.

Poor Lilah, thought the Boy. *She wants so many beautiful things, only she isn't sure yet just what they are.*

Jonathan descended the stairs heavily, brushing the golden dust from his big hands. "I want you to have all those things," he said anxiously, "everything you want. But I don't see how, this harvest, with my father so—so unwell and my brothers' children needing food. Perhaps when olive harvest comes—"

132

The girl stamped her small foot impatiently and flung back her head.

"Look!" cried the Boy suddenly, "Look at Lilah! She's wearing a net of golden threads!"

"When olive harvest comes, you say! I've heard that before. Will six months make you any less the dupe, or your brothers—What— what's that you say? A—a net?" Confused, she ran into the house and brought out a disk of battered copper in which she tried to see her reflection. "You're joking!"

"No, it's true. Stand here in the sun. See?"

Taking the copper disk from her fingers, the Boy held it high, so she had to tilt her head backward again, letting the long sunset rays glint through her hair, turning the clinging particles of grain to flecks of gold.

The girl laughed delightedly. "*Ay yah*! So I have! Look, Jonathan. See my net of golden threads?" Gaily she seized some of the wheat stalks from the sheaves on the floor and, knotting them swiftly into chains, slipped them about her neck and over the arches of her slender feet. "And I have a necklace of gold, too, and anklets. And—yes, a golden floor to dance on. Even the daughter of Jered doesn't have that. See, Jonathan?"

She danced toward him over the sheaves, and, joyful but bewildered, the young man opened his arms to receive her.

The Boy produced his present then—for Jonathan a handful of precious wheat seed grown by a prosperous farmer from the early-bearing Plain of Sharon, whose brimming baskets the Boy had admired one day in the Tyropean bazaar; for Lilah a bright peacock's feather.

"I saw it floating over a garden wall near the palace of Herod in Jerusalem," he told her, "and I said to myself, 'It is like the bride of Jonathan, lovelier than a string of jewels.'"

Exclaiming with pleasure, the girl stroked the soft prism of color, fondled it against her cheek; then, twining it in and out among the black strands of her hair, she hastened to view the effect in the battered disk of copper.

"It *is!*" she cried out in wonder. "More beautiful even than a string of jewels."

Cupping his hands, Jonathan let the golden seed spill slowly from one to the other.

"Precious," he said hesitantly. "More precious even than the treasure I found in the field. For the gold was—was a dead thing, and already it is gone. But this"—his slow mind fumbled—"this will—"

"Yes," said the Boy eagerly, "it will. It will go on and on, never stopping."

Jonathan closed his calloused palms on the shining particles. "A pity," he murmured, "that it must be put in the earth, must die, sort of, before it can—can—"

"Yes," agreed the Boy. He looked suddenly startled. "And yet," the words came slowly, his mind fumbling as awkwardly as had Jonathan's, "unless a grain of wheat does fall into the earth—and dies...unless it loses its life, how—how—can it give life to others?"

12

IT WAS NOT UNTIL the day his father went to fulfill his labor assignment at Sepphoris that he was able to perform his most important errand.

"No!" protested Joseph sharply when the Boy gathered together his leather apron and bag of tools. "You're staying here."

"But—"

"Enough for one son of David to defile himself building heathen atrocities for that usurper, Herod!" The carpenter's voice, though discreetly lowered, was harsh with accumulated bitterness. "I shall remain in Sepphoris until my days of impressed labor are completed—no, not even returning for the Sabbaths. More fitting that I crawl away into some cave and spend the holy days fasting in sackcloth and ashes. Then on my return I shall stop at a flowing spring and cleanse myself of defilement."

Bundling his oldest and dullest tools into a goatskin sack and providing himself with only such cooking vessels and laboring garments as could be burned or thrown away, Joseph reviewed for the last time the family's calendar of activities for every waking hour of the next thirty days; whereupon, head and shoulders rigidly erect, rebellion bristling in every fiber of his stocky body, he set off on his unwelcome assignment

Try as they would, mother and son could not maintain for long the mood of sympathetic gloom. At first they felt a little guilty, knowing Joseph's disapproval of mixing work and levity, but gradually the silence of his absence demanded to be filled with their bright chatter.

Since it was her day for taking her turn at the village oven, Miriam brought into the courtyard all her prerequisites for bread-making—grain from the clay bin, wooden mixing bowl, jug of fresh water, bit of dough reserved from the previous baking and carefully stored for fermentation in a napkin. The rubbing of the grinding stones and the kneading of supple hands kept rhythmic pace with the grating of saw and pounding of mallet. Laughter and cheerful words bubbled like the dough set under its wicker cover to rise in the warm sun.

"*Ay yah!* Listen to that old raven scolding us from the housetop! Know what he's saying, Mother?"

"No. What?"

"He's saying, 'Think I'm an ugly old thing, don't you, all you fine-feathered rollers and bulbuls and hoopoes? But have you seen how blue-black my wings shine in the sun? And God takes just as good care of me, I hope you notice. Gives me lots more to eat than he does you!'...Mother, do you remember how I wouldn't believe that tiny lump of sour dough could spread through a whole pan of meal?"

"Do I! So one day I left it out to prove it to you."

"*Ah hah!* And we ate hard flat loaves for a week!"

"There! My kneading is done. I'll let the leaven work for me now. What a great lady I must be to have such a powerful servant to do my bidding!"

"True. And since you're such a great lady, you must sit down for a while and fold your hands. *Shalom*, my lady! Here am I, another of your slaves, at your service. What now? Shall I bring a golden fan to cool your brow?"

"Tempter! You know very well I must go now and get my spinning."

"Not yet. Rest a little. See? Everything is resting all around us — birds, leaves, even the sun looks as if it were standing still! Let's you and I be like them, just for a little."

"But if I don't work hard and spin, we won't have any clothes to wear next winter!"

"So? I wonder. Look at those red tulips you planted in the earthen jar. They don't work hard or spin, yet our Father clothes them, doesn't he? Surely Solomon in all his fine robes was never dressed like one of them!"

To the Boy's surprise he completed the day's work prescribed by his father by mid-afternoon. All that remained was to deliver the ox yoke just finished to Elihu, the Nazareth farmer who was just now taking his turn at the village threshing floor. And if one kept on past the threshing floor to the main road through the valley and traveled just a little way up the narrow pass toward Sepphoris...

"Don't hurry back," said Miriam, as if in answer to his thought. "You've earned a few hours to yourself. And I shan't be lonely, for I shall be at the village oven baking our bread. Here! Take these loaves and olives and some of the fig cakes you like so well. If it were only tomorrow, you could have fresh bread!"

Gad, the crippled son of Old Simon, sat hunched in the shade of their stone hut. He did little but sit these days. Since the vicious beating he had received on the day he had interrupted the synagogue service, all power of balance seemed to have gone out of his limbs. Inside the hut he managed well enough, pulling himself along by hanging to the wall crevices, but out-of-doors he moved little and only by crawling on his hands and knees. As usual, his neatly parted hair was smoothly combed and oiled, his hands and face washed, and his tunic as spotlessly clean as the earth floor of the bare stone hut. For Old Simon stubbornly refused to extend the penalties of *Cherem*, demanding that a man let his hair grow wild and his body remain unbathed, to his son.

Gad's face lighted at sight of the Boy, and there burst from his twisted lips a volley of almost unintelligible sounds.

"*Shalom* yourself!" responded the Boy cheerfully, hiding the helpless distress he always felt at sight of the bewildered child-eyes in the man's distorted body. "*Ah hah!*" he lamented gently. "You've been giving away all your lunch again! I can see where the pigeons scratched in the dust for your parched corn, and where a coney dragged away at least half a loaf of bread. But no matter." He drew the linen napkin containing his own lunch from the scrip fastened to his girdle. "Here's some more food. And I'm going to stay right here and see that you eat it."

Pouring milk from the goat-skin left by Old Simon, he dipped into it morsels of the sweet, hard loaves and fed them gently through the ugly, gaping lips. The child-eyes shone delightedly at the taste of Miriam's honey-flavored fig cakes. Not until both scrip and bowl were empty and the hunched figure was comfortably settled in the wider shade on the east side of the hut did the Boy pursue the real purpose of his visit, to discover the whereabouts of Old Simon.

Leaving Gad playing contentedly with a little sheep he had carved for him out of a bit of seasoned olive wood, the Boy set off through the mountains. Following Gad's directions, it was easy enough to find the shepherd and his flock.

Lying flat on his stomach on a rocky ledge above the outlet of a swift mountain stream, the Boy watched them come, the shepherd leading, his thirsty sheep swarming eagerly behind. Most of them, that is. The Boy's lips twitched. Always there was at least one laggard of contrary mind. This time it was a lazy ewe, her huge tail dragging heavily on the steep path, which stubbornly refus to make the descent. Old Simon clucked reassuringly, whistled, ejected a harsh peremptory guttural, all to no avail. Then, placing a small stone in his sling, he landed it with a staccato ring and a shower of tiny pebbles within a handbreadth of the dragging appendage. Meekly the ewe descended.

The Boy chuckled aloud, almost giving away his hiding place.

Casually swinging his empty sling, Old Simon assured the chastened sheep with a soft, forgiving cluck and led the flock down toward the stream. Carefully he built a little dam of stones and earth to divert the swift waters into a quiet pool where the timid sheep would not hesitate to drink. When all had drunk their fill, he let them linger for a while and, passing through their midst, withdrew a little way up the path and seated himself on a rock. It was then that, although obviously still sensitive to every slightest motion of the flock, he ceased suddenly to be a shepherd and became a man.

An ugly man, dirty and unkempt in appearance, with hair and beard ragged and tangled like an animal's. A lonely and desperate man, crying out through the mournful monotones of a shepherd's pipe the wailing agony of a lost soul. The Boy listened with an acute mingling of emotions, ashamed to be a hidden witness to such naked anguish, yet eager to impart the exciting message which might dispel it.

As if the loneliness had become unbearable, the man rose abruptly and became again the shepherd. A flood of guttural sounds flowed from his lips. With soft croonings and duckings, like a mother hen gathering her chickens, he called certain trusted leaders of his sheep to him. One by one, as if called by name, they left the flock and went to him, and the Boy marveled. Just so, they would have answered had he called them amid a confusion of sounds and in a distant place. For he was their shepherd, and they knew his voice.

The Boy waited until the shepherd and his flock disappeared around a hillside path, then, scrambling down from the ledge, he made a wide circuit and came running down the path to meet them.

13

"SO," said Old Simon when they were seated overlooking the grazing flock on a high, stony slope, "you made a sin offering for me, on the holy altar in the Temple. Why?"

The Boy was so excited he was trembling. Suppose he said the wrong thing—instead of giving him a light to walk by, driving him still further into the dark!

"Because," he said slowly, "I couldn't bear to see you so—so lonely and unhappy. Like Gad. We both wanted you to—to feel free from your burden of—sin."

The old man sat silent, as if turned to the gray stone beneath him. And the Boy grew cold with waiting. It was an audacious thing he had done, knocking on the innermost door of a man's soul, almost like trying to enter the Holy of Holies! If only the Law didn't make him keep four cubits away, four times the length of a man's arm from his elbow to the end of his middle finger! Then he might get close enough to look into the craggy, sun-blackened face and see if the deep-set eyes were as stonelike as the body.

"*Cherem!*" The word, though scarcely audible, drifted over the gray rocks like a chill gust of wind. "What can you, a child—a good child, who finds favor with both God and man—what can you know of how it feels to be *Cherem!*"

The Boy shivered. Even the word had in it the power of cold and darkness. The sky looked less blue. The sun had lost its warmth. He did not need to look into Old Simon's eyes to know what he would find there.

"Tell me," he whispered.

Then suddenly the door to the secret place was flung open. It was Old Simon himself who bade him enter, quietly at first, almost with detachment.

"I wasn't always like this. I used to be like you, young, laughing, roaming these same hills and loving every fingerbreadth of rock, every blade of grass, as you do. In fact, I should have been even happier, for you are poor, while my father, being a wholesale dealer in wool, was wealthy. Almost like Jered, curse him!" The voice held its first hint of bitterness. "I went to the synagogue school, like you. My father was one of the elders. I tried to keep all the laws. We went to the feasts, three times a year, not just once, in Jerusalem. I—I can still remember it all. The songs we sang. The first glimpse of shining gold and whiteness. The sweetness which was like new almond blossoms and wind blowing over balsam groves and—and the breath of a fresh-born lamb."

"I know," The Boy scarcely breathed. It's the incense, which they burn in the Temple morning and evening. When you smell it, you can't help being sure God is somewhere near."

"Yes," said Old Simon. And again he sat quiet for a long time.

Twice the Boy opened his lips to speak and closed them. If one knocked on the doors within the secret place, he knew instinctively, the latchstrings would be pulled inside. One must wait patiently.

"She was beautiful." Quietly the voice led the way into a room of warmth and sunlight. "And kind and gentle. I have never seen another woman like her, except perhaps your mother Miriam. I loved her from the moment I saw her, when she was brought to our house as my bride. Perhaps I loved her too much. Perhaps that was the beginning of—of my sin. But I didn't know. Since God blessed me, I thought, he must be pleased with me. Our happiness was like springtime after the rains. It needed but one thing to make it complete. A son."

Another closed door, but this time no patient waiting. A harsh, abrupt flinging down of the last barrier. A sudden thrusting into darkness.

"She died when Gad was born. And I died too—if death is a black, cold pit with a stone over the opening. When I came up out of the pit and reached for a hand to hold, there were only pointing fingers, Jered's. All my old friends'. Yes—even your father's. 'How he must have sinned,' they all said, 'either he or his father, that God

139

should punish him so! His wife dead, his son an ugly cripple! Or perhaps it was his wife who sinned!' "

The chamber of darkness dropped suddenly to vast depths, peopled with frightening shapes. The darkness was no longer that of death, but of life in torment.

"Then I who was accursed began to curse. I cursed the sun for waking me again to sorrow and the stars for reminding me of brightness. I cursed my father who had begotten me and my mother who had given me birth, and the earth and the heavens, and the dark abode of my loved one beneath the earth. Until finally I cursed God himself. The sin of sins I had committed—blasphemy. And I had been overheard by two witnesses. One of them was Jered. They took me to the elders, who condemned me, then to the synagogue, and they pronounced me—*Cherem*."

The Boy closed his eyes. The shapes were gone now. He had reached the bottom of the secret place. And there was nothing there but cold and emptiness.

"You ask me—what is *Cherem*? It is day without sunlight. Night without stars. Life without living. Death without dying. A prayer, with no ear to listen. A sin offering—without God."

"No!" Desperately the Boy struggled up out of the pit of blackness. "God was there. I felt him. And he did accept the offering, I know he did."

The man turned his head then, and his eyes were not like stone but like gray ashes stirred into faint sparks. *"How do you know?"*

"Because—" The Boy hesitated, looked away for a moment to the far shining whiteness of Mount Hermon. "If Gad was angry at you," he said thoughtfully, "even if he—cursed you, but was sorry for it, would you forgive him?"

"Forgive Gad? Of course." Annoyed by the interruption, the shepherd spoke with even more than his usual harshness. I'm his father!"

An eagerness warm and bright as sunlight overspread the Boy's face. "Then—don't you see? God forgives you! Remember the psalm we sing?

> 'As a father pities his children,
>   so the Lord pities those who fear him'?

"I tell you, Simon, your sins are forgiven!"

140

The sparks flared. "If I could only believe it! Perhaps if I had been there with you—in the Temple—"

"Then come with me there," urged the Boy excitedly. "How shall we go? By the bridge over the Valley of the Kidron, then up the hill through the Golden Gate? That's the best way, because we can see the Temple all the time we are climbing, white and shining, like Mount Hermon up there. See? Here we are already in the great outer court, with the Beautiful Gate straight ahead! We'll go in through the marble lattice called Soreg and go up the steps, fourteen of them there are, let's count them as we go... only be sure and keep your eyes lifted, so you won't see the beggars. We must look only at the beautiful things today. One...two...three..."

Obediently the man moved his lips, body beginning to sway in rhythm, eyes fixed in desperate concentration on the shining crest of mountain.

"There! Now we'll cross the Court of Women and climb the fifteen steps leading through the Gate Nicanor. Isn't it beautiful, all overlaid with gold and silver? One...two...three... Shallow steps, aren't they, easy for tired feet to climb? Close your eyes for a minute, until I tell you to open them. Now we're in the Court of Israel, where only devout men of God can enter, but don't look yet. Wait until we're just a little farther... *Ah yah!* Now open them. See the Temple, all white and gold and shining? Now we're so close we can see the great golden door leading into the Holy Place and the gold grapevine carved on it with grapes as large as a man! Was that here when you came before, Simon?"

The shepherd sighed ecstatically. "No. It's finer now, much finer. All these years they've been building it. I've heard about the new things added since the despicable Herod's time."

"And now you're looking at them. See, there in the Court of Priests is the great altar where the smoke rises day and night. High it stands on the huge rock, the same rock where Abraham started to sacrifice Isaac and God wouldn't let him. See the smoke rising? It's the smoke of your offering, Simon, and God is pleased with it. Can't you feel him here, all around us, breathing his warmth on our cheeks, running his fingers through our hair? Yes, and if you listen hard, you can hear the choirs of Levites chanting and smell the incense the priests burned this morning in the Holy Place! Feel him, Simon? Feel his Holy Presence?"

Tense with eagerness he waited, lips parted and eyes fixed on the upraised face. For long moments Old Simon stared with burning eyes at the distant snow-capped crest. Then with a deep, shuddering breath he dropped his face in his hands.

"Almost—I thought for a minute—but—No, it's not the Temple. There isn't any Presence."

The Boy was bitterly disappointed. In his distress he almost forgot that the Law forbade him to go closer than two long paces.

He wanted so much to reach out and smooth back the confused tangle of hair, to pull away the grimy hands and compel the eyes again to look upward!

"But there is, Simon! He *is* here, I can feel him. Look up toward the shining mountain. Try once more—please!"

Obediently the shepherd tried, lowered his shaking hands, peered through his tangled hair. "*Ay yah!* The shining mountain—like the Temple—"

"See the smoke rising from the altar?"

"I—do seem to see a—cloud—"

"And hear the music? The chanting of the Levites?"

"Larks. It could be hymns they are singing. Yes, yes, I hear!"

"And smell the incense?" The clear voice held triumph now as well as eagerness. "The sweet fragrance all about us, like—like new almond blossoms and wind blowing over balsam groves?"

Again there was a long silence. "No." The shepherd shook his head. "Nothing. Perhaps—if I could have smelled just a little of the incense—"

It was then that the Boy knew what he must do.

14

WHEN HE CAME AGAIN to the hills, it was very early in the morning, and the stars were still shining. As he climbed the last hill, his heart beat with an almost suffocating excitement. Suppose Old Simon had risen earlier than usual to tend a sick sheep, or because Gad had cried out in his sleep. Or suppose just once the shepherd bad not brought his flock back to the cave, which he used for a sheepfold.

So much depended on every detail of his plan being carried out just right!

To his relief the hut was closed and silent, the night lamp shedding its flicker through the wall cracks a sure indication that Gad was safely asleep inside. The cave looked empty and lifeless, but one sensed vague stirrings in its depths. The sheep were beginning to waken. Old Simon, wrapped in his *simlah*, would be lying on the ground across the mouth of the cave, sling in readiness, the leather thong of his stout, nail-studded club bound securely about his hairy wrist. The slightest sound within a dozen cubits of his "blessed ones" and he would be instantly alert.

But the Boy made no sound. Lifting a moistened finger to ascertain the direction of the air currents, he chose what he considered the right spot and sat down to wait.

It was an audacious thing he was about to do, perhaps even a blasphemous thing. For all he knew, God might strike him down for it, as it was written he had done once long ago to a man named Achan. *Depending on what God was like.* He was taking a chance, betting his life, on God's being different from what other people thought him.

Good, at least, to have these moments of quiet to make ready for the thing he must do. Just as the priest, chosen this morning by lot in the Temple in Jerusalem to go into the Holy Place and spread the incense on the golden altar, would soon be making ready. For he, a twelve-year-old boy, in his incredible presumption, was about to make himself a priest, to turn a common, country hillside into a Holy Place.

Slowly the stars dimmed. He was reminded of the light of the golden candlestick kept burning before the entrance to the Holy of Holies. His heart beat faster and faster as he watched the outlines of the Temple take shape about him. Arches of hills and architraves of mountain ridges. Porches whose pillars were the trunks of oaks and cypresses and cedars. Cloud-gates of ivory and jasper and amethyst overlaid with gold. And, far to the north, emerging slowly out of the mists, a pinnacle of shining whiteness!

The time had come.

Swiftly he moved now, though still noiselessly. Searching the ground for a flat stone and dropping to his knees beside the earthen brazier he had brought with him, he scooped the protecting ashes from the live coals in the bottom, added a few lumps of charcoal from the bag tied to his girdle, blew gently until the coals were brightly glowing and the fresh fuel had begun to kindle. Then carefully he took into his hands the tall slender vessel of chased silver, and, removing the cover, with steady fingers broke the seal.

He would have liked time then, to breathe deeply of the exotic fragrance, to conjure visions of far-away spice groves and rustling palms and swaying camels; time most of all to wonder about the stranger who had come long ago bringing such a Gift to a carpenter's son, the one of the three who had been like quiet shadow, whose light had come from within, like a flame burning in a still place with no wind to touch it.

But there was no time. Already he could hear the tap-tapping of small hoofs on the stone floor of the cave, the clucking of the shepherd's soothing voice. Reverently, but with haste born of urgency, he tipped the vessel and, pouring some of the incense into his cupped hand, spread it generously and evenly over the glowing coals. Then, stretching himself flat in the cleft of a rock not far away, he settled himself to wait.

Frankincense! Sweetness of all the flowers that had ever bloomed, all the psalms that had been sung, all the prayers that had been uttered.

Old Simon stumbled drunkenly from the mouth of the cave, looking even wilder in the half light of dawn than in the glare of sunlight. Heavy nostrils dilating, eyes hotly blazing like the coals in the brazier, he advanced a few uncertain steps, then stood frozen, staring about in a frenzy of bewilderment and incredulity. Scarcely daring to breathe, the Boy watched from his hiding place, saw the bewilderment slowly give way to startled wonder, and then to child-like acceptance.

"It is!" he heard the shepherd mumble. "It can't be—but it is! The sweetness—just as it used to be—the Temple's whiteness—

The Boy trembled. So much depended on these next few moments! If only the eyes would remain lifted, fixed on that high pinnacle which was Mount Hermon, its snowy crests just touched by the first rays of dawn! Softly, but in a clear voice he began to sing.

> "Bless the Lord, O my soul,
> and all that is within me,
> bless his holy name!"

Old Simon did not turn his head, for the song was fashioned of the same dream fabric as the white vision and the fragrance. He must often have heard one of the Levites sing it in the New Year Temple service. True and unwavering, the voice soared to the psalm's triumphant climax.

> "As far as the east is from the west,
>   so far has he separated us from our sins.
> As a father pities his children,
>   so the Lord pities those who fear him!"

Weeping, swaying, beating his breast, Old Simon sank to his knees among the stones.

"My Lord!" he cried out in an agony of ecstasy. "My Lord and my God!"

He was like an empty vessel suddenly become full. Joy spilled from him. Springing to his feet, he flung his arms wide, tore off his headcloth, and waved it like a banner.

"*Ay yah!* Listen, you hills and valleys, you who have been partners in my loneliness! Can you hear me, my blessed ones? Rejoice with me in my freedom! 'As far as the east is from the west...!' Come out, Jeshua, son of Joseph. I know your voice, and I see you there in the rock. Gad, my poor son, can you hear? Your father has come back to you again. No longer *Cherem!* No matter what the elders say, no longer *Cherem!*"

But it was not enough, this miracle of freedom within his spirit. He must remove also the outer symbols of his bondage. While the Boy and his son looked on delightedly, he rummaged in the hut until he found an old bone comb. But his impatience was too great, the masses of his hair too hopelessly tangled. Finally, not to be thwarted, he severed the knotted ends with a shearing knife.

"Clean again!" he exulted, vigorously attempting to scrub from his arms and hands a quarter century of grime, then regarding the encrusted flesh ruefully. "Clean inside, at least. It happened all at once. The knowledge swept over me when I smelled the sweet fragrance."

"Did it smell the way you remembered it?" the Boy inquired eagerly, almost forgetting to keep the required four cubits' distance, "Like new almond blossoms and—and wind blowing over balsam groves?"

"Yes, yes. All that and more." Down on his knees on the rough stone platform before his hut, the shepherd splashed water from ewer to clay washbasin and, scooping up great handfuls, buried his features again and again in the cleansing coolness. "Like everything sweet and beautiful which God ever created. Like—" He lifted his streaked face to sniff the air. "It—it's gone!" he exclaimed in panic. "The fragrance! Suppose—suppose the Presence goes with it, and the old doubt returns!"

"It won't," returned the Boy confidently. "But if it does, you shall summon it again with your own hands. See!" He held out the gleaming silver vessel. It's yours. There's more incense inside. I used only a little. Bum it whenever you feel the need of it, and when the incense is gone, you can hold the lovely vessel in your hands, and the memory of fragrance will come back. Here, take it."

Only when the eager hands reached out to receive it did he remember and draw back, just in time. "I—I'll put it here, on the stones," he said hastily.

The streaks of lighter flesh were suddenly scored into harsh lines. "So, you tell me my sins are forgiven, yet you don't really believe it. You still think of me as—*Cherem!*"

"No, no! By all that's holy, I swear I don't—"

"Then why aren't you willing to touch me?"

The Boy stared at the old man, aghast. Why, indeed? Yet his feet were rooted to the ground. Never in all his life had he wittingly committed any act in violation of the holy Law. If, inadvertently, he had let even his clothing come in contact with an unclean animal, such as an owl or raven or lizard, or passed within four cubits of a leper, he had rushed home to remove and wash his garments and purify himself. In obedience to his mother's command he had taken a new, prized vessel in which a dead mouse had been discovered and without an instant's hesitation broken it in pieces. The keeping of the Law was the first desire of his life, inbred within his very blood and bones. But—whose Law? It was the elders who had pronounced Old Simon *Cherem,* and they had not changed their verdict. Then was he still *Cherem*—unclean, devoted to destruction—*even though God himself—?*

His head swam dizzily. Only one thing stood out clearly in his vision—the upturned face with its streaks of grime and cleanness, its ragged fringe of hair. No evading the question in those brutally searching eyes!

And suddenly the world righted itself. How stupid to be so confused, when it was all so very simple! Old Simon was what really mattered.

"But I *am* willing," he said simply. And, moving steadily forward, he put his arms about the bowed shoulders.

15

HE WALKED HOME through the dawn empty-handed.

"Ah, there you are!" cried the woman, her face filling with light at sight of him. "I missed you, even though I knew where you had gone. You've been up where it's high, haven't you? I can tell by your face. Though the sun hasn't reached here yet, you've been where you could see it shining."

"Yes," he replied. "That's where I've been. Up where it's high."

She made an excuse to touch him, pushing a stray curling lock under the headcloth, letting her fingers linger for a moment.

"But I've been looking up the hill for you ever since it was light enough to see!" Her tone was less curious than tenderly possessive. "And you were nowhere on the path. Did you find some new way leading to the Hilltop?"

The Boy lifted his face. "A new way...yes," he replied slowly. "But—I'm not sure yet—where it leads."

MYRRH

IT BEGAN like any other summer day in Nazareth—dewy, cool, and chaste as a maiden who has never known the heat of passion. There was no forewarning of the creatures of violence she was to bring forth before evening—except perhaps, the birds.

Joseph, going into the courtyard long before sunrise to repeat the *Shema* and his morning prayers, noticed whole flocks of them, moving from the Jordan Valley toward the northwest, silently and with scarcely a motion of their wings, as if carried on the wind. But there was no wind. Not for hours yet, when the heat would become well-nigh unbearable, would the refreshing currents begin to agitate the little olive leaves above the courtyard wall. And they would come from the west, please God, bearing on their breath the cool vigor of the sea to fan and to cleanse.

Hear, O Israel, the Eternal, our God, is one...

"A sign of storm"—his mind commented on the birds while his lips were praying—"even though the season of storms is long past." Then, appalled by his inattention to words being carefully audited by God and all his angels, he hastily lowered his head and repeated the *Shema* three more times, giving the heavenly beings ample time to respond joyfully after each one, "Happy the people whose God is Jehovah!"

The Boy saw them too as he went up to the housetop for an armful of nettles to kindle the morning fire. So busy was he watching them that he was less careful than usual, and the sharp hairs of the stacked dry weeds stung his fingers.

Birds migrating northward at this time of year? Or floating on the wind when there was no wind? He lowered his eyes to the horizon, half expecting to see bands of yellowing light over the southern rim of hills instead of to the north or east, above Mount Tabor. But no, the sun was still rising in the same place, and—he looked ruefully at his fingers—there were barbs in nettles! When he lifted his eyes to the sky again, the floating shapes were gone and he thought he must have dreamed them.

But that other shadow of impending evil, born of last night's darkness, had been no dream! The disturbing memory of what he had seen and heard seemed more uncomfortably real than the stinging sharpness of the nettles.

Holding them gingerly and moving as quietly as possible in order not to disturb his father's prayers, the Boy padded down the stairway and into the dark house, his bare feet slipping unerringly into the hollowed path across the earth floor and up the stone steps leading to the higher level.

Wordlessly Miriam took the prickly burden from his hands. As she bent over the stove, feeding the crackling weeds into the clay opening, her features sprang suddenly into bright relief, eyes darkly somber, lips drawn downward into tense, anxious lines. Almost instantly she smiled.

"Thank you, darling. Did you prick yourself too? If this is one of your days for getting rid of devils, how about starting on these thorns?"

But the Boy was not deceived by her forced gaiety. He had seen that same look on her face too many times lately. His heart sad, he watched her helplessly, unable to do more than mumble in reply. More disturbing even than what had happened last night was this sensing that for some reason his mother was unhappy! If only there were something he could do or say to bring the smile to her eyes as well as to her lips! Yes, if only he still had the flowers!

It had seemed like a miracle, finding them the evening before on the Hilltop, still white and perfect and fresh as in springtime, though all the other wild blossoms had long since shriveled in the hot sun. It was really Joel who had found them, leading him to their favorite stone grotto. It was like a cave, which must have a hidden spring, for the grass stayed green there longer than in any other spot around Nazareth.

"See, Jeshua? White, aren't they? I can tell by feeling them, they're so soft and smooth."

Remembering his mother's sadness, the Boy picked them, wrapping the stones in moist grass. After taking Joel home, he ran all the way back down the hill to surprise her with them before their freshness faded. But, instead of giving them to her at once as he intended, he hid them in an earthen pot of water by the courtyard wall. Why? Because on his way home he had seen an even sadder face, that of the woman Mulcah returning from the fountain in the twilight, looking so terribly lost and alone.

All during supper hour and evening prayers and preparations for the night, he had been unable to forget her, and later, after his mother and father were asleep, he had lain wakeful and tense with remembering, until finally he had risen from his mat and taken the flowers, traveled through the streets in the dark, groped his way up the narrow, untidy path toward the house on the terrace above the inn. So vivid was his memory of the night's occurrence that he could still feel the wet stems against his palms and the sharp prongs of the cactus hedge.

Though it was still early in the first watch, the houses of the town were dark, and most of the people asleep. But some of the arched spaces beneath the inn were aglow with lanterns and noisy with sounds of merriment. Recognizing one voice, higher pitched and more rollicking than the others, the Boy smiled to himself. Gebal, the young Phoenician merchant from the cities to the east on the Great Sea! Lights were always a little brighter, the merriment a little noisier, when Gebal was in town.

The woman Mulcah was not yet asleep. He could tell by the fingers of light probing the high slits of windows—not the faint steady glimmers of a night lamp, but uneasy flickers, as if someone were moving restlessly back and forth inside, constantly agitating the flame.

He knocked on the door.

There was a whisper of motion, a nervous flaring of the fingers, then silence. He knocked again.

"Mulcah," he called softly. "It's I, Jeshua. I can't come in, but I've brought you something. A present. Something beautiful, like you. I'll leave it here. If you'll open the door, you'll find it."

Loosening the moist fig leaf in which he had wrapped them, the Boy laid the flowers on the flat stone step, then drew back into the shadows and waited. Presently he saw the door open to reveal a narrow strip of light. A hand reached out to pick up the flowers. Just for an instant her face took shape in the lamplight—incredulous, delighted as a child's. Yes, he had done right to bring them. She needed them more than Miriam.

He was groping his way along the hedge to the path when the figure loomed suddenly in front of him, frighteningly big in the moonlight. His pulse hammering, he drew back just in time and dropped crouching into the shadow of the hedge while it went past him, so near that the folds of a long dark coat trailed over his head and shoulders. Linen it was, smooth and fine, that brushed his cheek, smelling of spices and perfumes. There was only one man he knew of in Nazareth who could afford to wear garments like that.

The hedge held the little house enclosed. There was no way out except by the path, and the Boy dared not risk discovery by venturing into its moonlit exposure. He crouched deeper into the tangled undergrowth, hoping its barbs were being kinder to his clothes than to his bare arms and legs. So close was he to the newcomer that he could hear the heavy breathing born of excitement and unaccustomed exertion, the nervous tapping of a sandal which preceded the hesitant knocking on the door.

"I—I've come back again. I—couldn't help it. I thought you— you might have changed your mind after all these weeks."

The hoarse whisper, issuing from lips pressed close to the small latch-opening, was plainly audible. It belonged to Jered, yes, but a Jered the Boy had never known existed—timid, humble, pleading as a beggar might plead for a crust of bread.

"I—know you're there—still awake. I saw you just now—open the door. If you'll—just open it again—I have a gift for you. It's something you—you'd have liked once, a necklace of real gold and pearls. And—you'll have to give nothing in return, I swear it. Just— just open the door—"

No response. The door remained tightly closed. Even the thin fingers of light betrayed no motion.

And then the voice was no longer a hoarse whisper.

"I—I'll do anything you say—go away from Nazareth—leave everything! I swear you're all that matters—everything I have—it's worth nothing without you! For the Almighty's sake, have pity!"

The Boy trembled. His cheeks burned, for he knew he had stumbled into another secret place, and this time without invitation. He burrowed deeper into the hedge, closed his eyes, tried to shut out the sound by putting his hands over his ears. But he could not.

Then he heard the woman's voice.

"No. I shan't open the door to you. Not ever again. No matter what you say or do. I told you before. I'm a different woman now."

The man made a harsh, tortured sound, akin to both weeping and laughter. "*You*—different! You lie. Can the zebra change his stripes or the leopard his spots?"

"Maybe not." There was a quaver now in the woman's voice, a desperation born of uncertainty. "But a person can change. I know, because I have. Go away. You must go away!"

His voice was all laughter now, dry and bitter. "Tell the congregation how you've changed, why don't you? See what they say! Try to enter with the other women of Nazareth into the synagogue! "How is it that you're never seen with them on the streets or at the well, if you're changed? *Ay yah!* Should a man laugh or curse? You—changed!"

"But I have!" The woman's voice mounted to a shrillness close to hysteria. "I'm different, I tell you, no matter what you say. He told me so. Just now. He—he said I was like them, like white flowers!"

"Who?" demanded Jered hoarsely. "Who said that?"

Even through the heavy door one could hear the woman's quick-drawn breath, sense the lifting of startled fingers as if to stifle the words her lips had uttered.

"Who?" The voice whipped, like a lash. "Is he in there with you now?"

"No, no! There's no one here—no one except Danny. I swear it!"

"But he was there. You said so. Tell me the man's name. Tell it to me, I say! Or I swear I'll find it out and—and kill you both!"

"But you don't understand!" The woman was weeping now. "It wasn't a man, he was just a boy—"

"*Who?*"

"The—the son of Joseph, the carpenter."

The man stumbled toward the path, cursing. As the smooth, scented linen brushed again over his hot cheeks, the Boy shivered.

2

EXCEPT FOR the flowers, the woman Mulcah must surely have opened the door that night. Not to Jered. For now she needed nothing that he had to give. But to the one who came after.

At first she put the flowers in a finely enameled brass vase, the gift of an old admirer from lands beyond the sunrise. Then she transferred them to a simple, brown earthen bowl. Their fragrance stole through the lamplit house like a benediction.

Beautiful they were and sweet, like the spirit of the boy who had cared enough to bring them. Almost enough to make one forget for a little the agony of loneliness. But not quite.

When the other knock came, later in the night, she trembled.

Months had passed since the stout door had resounded to that signal, an uneven, rollicking tattoo beaten with strong fingers to the rhythm of an old Phoenician street song.

"When you hear that," the lilting voice, so like another's, had once bidden, "put on your brightest colors, run for your tambourine, summon the gayest music to your throat and feet, for you'll know that Gebal is in town."

Gebal. So like Nahor, her boyish husband! The same light feet and slender rhythmic hands, never still, the same dark, smiling features. Even the same queer habit of beating time to her dancing with soft clicks of his tongue. Where Gebal was, there would always be music and dancing and laughter. Never loneliness.

The knocking continued, no louder, but with a gentle, playful insistence.

"*Shalom*, goddess of lights and music! Can you hear me?" The familiar voice breathed softly through the tiny latchstring aperture. "I know you're there. Haven't you learned yet that you don't belong all alone in the darkness? Let me in, and we'll dance together. I'll teach you new songs."

She lay on her mat with hands clenched, tongue clamped rigidly between her teeth.

"Listen to me, Ashtart, goddess of my people. Put on something bright and gay. Get your tambourine. Take off that old homespun robe. It doesn't become you. I saw you in it yesterday, going to the fountain, dragging your feet, you who were born for dancing in a flame-colored dress. Yes, and I saw the other women, too, turning their backs and leaving you alone."

Suddenly she was up and across the room, kneeling by the chest, opening it, burrowing with trembling excitement into the piles of colored garments, picking out the brightest one of all, scarlet like a flame, and—letting the rest fall in untidy heaps to the floor—slipping out of the coarse gray homespun. Even before the shimmering scarlet folds had fallen into place, her lips were humming softly, her feet tapping.

Light—brightness again! Little clay saucers of oil eagerly blazing on the two lampstands. The tambourine...where was it? In the deepest wall niche above the child's mat, she unearthed it, dislodging a handful of Danny's treasured collection of queer-shaped stones which Jeshua had helped him find. The child stirred as they pelted down on his coverlet but did not waken. For a long minute she stood looking down at him, hesitating. It was for his sake...But what good had this new life brought him? Friends? Her lips curled. A happy home? Was emptiness better than song and laughter?

Abruptly she reached for the tambourine, laughing softly. Her hand went to the door latch, to bid Life re-enter! The stage was set with all its old accoutrements of gaiety. Lights, music, color, perfumes...*Perfumes!* She turned back suddenly, her hand dropping from the latch. There was perfume, yes, but not—not the sort—

She stood looking down with sharp awareness at the flowers in the earthen bowl. White flowers. Fresh and clean as a child's outstretched fingers. As the face of a boy with smiling lips and fearless eyes.

Later, when the knocking had ceased and the lamps, all but one, had been extinguished, she took off the flame-colored dress and folded it with finality with the other garments. Then, picking it up again, she flung it to the floor with a sudden gesture of revulsion. She began flinging others from the pile, filling the room with bright color. But she could not rid herself of their clinging folds. They twined and tangled about her arms and knees and ankles, spun tight rainbow cobwebs...

And then she stopped trying. When day came it would be easy enough to get rid of them, A hot fire in the brazier...beggars...or even the poor wives of peasants who came each day to the well. Looking down at the rainbow pile, her eyes sharpened, grew bright with speculation. Suppose...After all, why not? Were they not women like herself? Had she not often detected wistfulness, even envy, in their resentful and contemptuous glances? Their grudging gratitude would be more endurable than resentment and contempt. Yes, it was worth trying.

But not the flame-colored dress. Not the tambourine. Nor the silver anklets with the tinkling bells. At least, not yet.

3

BIRDS. Traveling toward the northwest as if floating on the wind. There were others in Nazareth the next morning who saw the silent caravan and took warning.

In the market place vendors setting up their makeshift shelters of sticks and burlap anchored them more firmly to the ground. Farmers who had been using their flat housetops for threshing floors hastened to get the winnowed grain into storing pits and the rest of it under cover. In the courtyard of the inn the horse of one of Herod's soldiers sniffed and pawed the ground, and the Arab drivers of a caravan preparing to leave at dawn for Egypt postponed their departure.

Deborah was up earlier than usual in the cool dawn, glad when the first fingers of light probed the narrow slits, for she had been sleepless with excitement.

It was good to be able to throw open the door, to see the needle tips of cypresses pricking the gray shroud of the sky. Yet sometimes, in this hour of hovering between dark and light, she felt almost a recurrence of the old fear, shriveling her flesh and curling the bones of her fingers. She felt it now but would not yield to it, forcing herself to fold her sleeping mat with deliberate slowness, to stow it away in the corner with such quiet caution that the humped coverlet on the other mat showed not the slightest sign of agitation.

But a whisper of sound in the tiny courtyard sent her good intentions scuttling like a frightened rabbit. Suppose someone was hiding! In a fever of panic she was across the room, closing the door and bolting it, cupping the lamp in trembling fingers. Down on her knees beside the heavy chest, she fumbled in a wall niche and, drawing out a bundle wrapped in dirty, ragged cloth, set it on the floor close to the lamp while she worked nervously at the knot binding the four comers. When they fell away, disclosing a neat pile of heavily embroidered wools and linens, she dropped back on her heels, limp and trembling.

Safe! And not a soul in Nazareth knew her secret. Foolish neighbors, thinking the work she did in the sunlight for all eyes to see was her finest craftsmanship! All this time she had been fooling them, working quietly at least half the night by lamplight to make ready for this day. Even the wife of Joseph, whom she loved and trusted, did not know, believed that now the mortgage was paid her worries were all over. As if any mother could know a peaceful moment, with her poor son blind and people saying that in King Herod's court there was a physician—a sorcerer, some called him—who could cure all sorts of diseases just by selling magic potions!

One by one she took the pieces from the pile and, bending her weak eyes close to the lamp, wept with delight over the intricate patterns, the richly glowing colors. She would offer only one or two at first for the physician's services, keeping back the finest in case he proved a hard bargainer.

King Herod was in Sepphoris now with all his court. She had heard it only yesterday in the market place. If she started soon after sunrise, she could get there before the hours of greatest heat, maneuver her way into the palace and complete her business in time to return before evening. And, to make sure no thief would guess her secret, she would hide herself beneath garments as ragged and beggarly as the cloth which bound her bundle.

Replacing the chest in the niche and pushing it back into place, she became so excited that she kicked over the lamp, plunging the room into near darkness and herself into panic. Groping frantically for the door, she missed the direction and stumbled over the child's sleeping mat, falling forward on her outthrust hands. Her fingers sank deep into the coverlet.

"Joel!" she cried out in panic. Somehow she managed to find the door, slide its bolt, and move blindly across the dim courtyard. "Joel! *Where are you?*"

"Here, Mother. Up above you on the terrace."

"*Ay yah!*" Her voice was sharp-edged with relief, "You frightened me so! Why do you do such things? Getting up and going out in the dark!"

He laughed gently. "You forget. It's not dark to me. Think how lucky I am, being able to see just as well in the night as in the daylight!"

"Lucky!"

"And I can hear things better before people start making so much noise. Like the birds."

"What birds?"

"Didn't you hear them? Hundreds of them, so close you could feel the air from their wings! Yet they didn't seem to flying, just floating on the wind."

Her gaze strained past the spears of cypresses. "I see no birds."

"No. They're gone now." He waved his hand. 'That way."

She shook her head mournfully. As if birds migrated northward at this time of year! Or floated on the wind when there was no wind!

"Listen!" said the boy softly. "It's coming, isn't it?"

Deborah's skin prickled. "Who? What?"

"The dawn," he whispered, turning his face unerringly toward the east. "I can feel it coming. All the earth is so still. Can you see it, Mother?"

"Yes, of course I can see it I'm not bl—Oh, my darling, forgive me! What am I saying!"

"Then tell me what it looks like."

She stared bewilderedly at the dark line of familiar horizon with its arch of yellowing sky. "Why, like—like any dawn, I guess."

"I know. Jeshua has told me. The hills are black first, then blue, then purple. Have the hills turned purple yet, Mother?"

"I—I think so, a little."

"Purple is like the robe of a king. And the yellow bands that you see just above are his crown!"

Deborah could bear it no longer. "*Ah hah!* My poor blind child, accursed from the sins of nobody knows whom! Such beauty, and to think that you've never once seen it! How can you pretend to be so happy?" Suddenly she seized him by the shoulders, thrust her face close enough to glimpse the pale shimmer of his eyes. "What's the matter with you? Don't you care at all? Don't you wish you could see?"

She had her answer, in his swift-drawn breath, in the naked yearning with which he lifted his sightless eyes. But she did not tell him her secret, only that she was going to Sepphoris to try to sell some embroideries at a better price. Nor would she hear of his going with her. Hard enough it was to avoid being run down on the high road by Herod's terrifying horsemen without having the care of one blind and helpless. Besides, she wanted to surprise him. The sorcerer would give her the magic potion, perhaps a salve, and she would rub it on his eyes while he was asleep. Then she would take him outside and turn his face toward the dawn. Or perhaps his first blessed view of the world should be from the hilltop. At least, it would be she to whom he would turn in his first burst of gratitude, not the sorcerer— no, nor his idolized friend, the son of Joseph!

Before leaving, she made him promise that until her return he would neither go down into the town nor open the door of the house to any stranger. Enough worries she had already...

Lilah also awoke before dawn, not slowly and reluctantly as usual, closing her eyes as long as possible to the monotonous tasks of the day, but suddenly, every sense alert. Today she must make her decision.

Quietly she eased herself upright on the mat, sitting hunched and motionless until Jonathan, stirring restively at her slightest movement, subsided again into heavy slumber; then, reaching cautiously for her headcloth and wrapping it about her shoulders, she drew her feet slowly toward her beneath the thin coverlet and sat hugging her knees. It was good to enjoy these few moments of coolness before rising to the burdensome heat of another day! Even here on the housetop, with their mat spread wide to the sky, the night had until now brought little surcease from the heat.

But, breathing the cool, dew-cleansed air, her nose quickly wrinkled in distaste, as had Jason's only yesterday. For the garments of toil could not be laid aside even when one lay down to sleep.

"*Ah hah!* It's cassia and aloes you should be smelling of, you poor ghost of Hera, not wheat and olives and—must I say it?—the sweat of labor! But what can one expect—the wife of a Galilean peasant! I warned you...

She made an impatient gesture, and Jonathan once more stirred, murmuring her name and flinging out his arm to encircle the little hollow on the mat where her head had rested. Again she held herself motionless, fingers locked tightly about each wrist beneath the pointed sleeves of her dress, until his even breathing gave assurance that he had not wakened. Even then she could not relax, knowing that in another hour the weary round of labor would begin again—the endless grinding of the day's grain, the baking at the hot oven, the winnowing in the blinding sun, dust sifting into ones hair and throat and nostrils, grating into one's pores.

"A pity!" Jason had lamented, "So smooth your flesh used to be, and so golden! And your hair—!"

With relentless strokes she ran her hands up the length of her forearms, noting every trace of roughness, then lifted them for the same pitiless inspection of her hair. Not smooth and soft any more.

No time lately to brush and oil it. Until yesterday she had been unconscious of any change in her appearance, seeing herself only in the mirror of Jonathan's adoring gaze. But Jason's eyes also were mirrors, hard, polished ovals of bronze.

The meeting with the Greek merchant had been wholly accidental. She had not even known that Jason was in town. She had gone to the market place to buy a new earthen pot and had been unable to resist the temptation to loiter homeward through the brass and cloth bazaars. Resentment also had slowed her steps.

Galling it was that she must mix her dough in an earthen bowl when Hannah, wife of the ne'er-do-well Benjamin, was able to buy brass!

Still brooding over the thought, she had come suddenly face to face with Jason.

"Ah! Lilah is it, the beloved of the peasant Jonathan? Nay, if he really loved her, he would clothe her in silks and hang jewels about her neck. Even Jason, the poor Greek, takes better care of his treasures. Like this bowl of copper. Would I wrap it in sackcloth, do you think, or take it to the fields to fill it with earth and stones, so that its luster would be dulled and its surface scratched and scarred?"

Fascinated, she watched him unroll the silk wrapping, revealing the perfect hemisphere of gleaming metal. "Oh! Beautiful!"

"Ay, almost as beautiful as you yourself—once were."

"You mean—I am not so any longer? I—have become scratched and scarred?"

In spite of her dismay she found herself flushing under his intimately appraising gaze. "No. Not yet. Just a little less of luster, shall we say? Nothing that a little polishing could not efface."

One day. Just one day to decide. For Jason was leaving Nazareth for the coast at dawn tomorrow morning. He would wait for her until noon at the north of town close to where the road from Nazareth to Sepphoris joined the Way of the Sea.

She need only feign sickness when Jonathan went to the fields. He would be excited and tender, urging her to remain at home, probably wondering if at last his fond dream of a son was to be realized. Like the foolish women at the well. Always making sly inquiries, casting hopeful then disapproving glances at her meager girth. As if she wanted a son! Or did she? It would be sweet to circle one's arm about a small head with square sturdy features like Jonathan's.

In a rush of tenderness she turned toward the sleeping figure with its outflung arm, reaching one hand across the mat to balance herself. Instead of sinking into the pile of heaped straw her fingers encountered a round object. Puzzled, she pushed the straw bits aside. It took both hands to lift it, and she awaked Jonathan in the process. He sat up abruptly, yawning and rubbing his eyes.

"What—it hasn't even begun to grow light—Ha! So you found it already! And I thought it was such a safe hiding place. But no matter. Open it. I was going to give it to you in the morning."

Holding the bulky object in her lap, she excitedly pulled off the burlap wrappings. "Oh!"

Even in the gray half-light the brass bowl gleamed and shimmered as if reflecting some hidden hearthfire.

"Like it? The kind you wanted? Like my mother's?"

"Oh—yes! But I—thought you said—"

"You were right," said Jonathan gravely, continuing his slow fumbling for words. "I—haven't been fair to you. My family, they're—my problem, not yours. You're young and beautiful, and—I love you. It's a poor thing, I know, compared with all you should have—"

"But—I still don't see how—"

"No matter how," he returned gruffly, wishing he could dismiss the debt to Jered with the same abruptness. "It's yours. I'll get you the dress soon, too—somehow."

"You're too good to me, my husband. I—I don't deserve it."

Pressing her hot cheek against the cool brass, she was glad for the near darkness in which to hide her shame. Leave Jonathan, her beloved! How could she even have thought of it?

Palms cupped lovingly about the rounded surface, she stroked the outside of the vessel gently. Then her finger tips encountered rough spots in the metal, grooves which in the light of day must reveal themselves as unsightly scratches. A brass bowl, yes, but crudely cast for utility and not for beauty. As far removed from the velvet smoothness of polished copper as was this miserable, poverty-stricken existence from the one Jason had promised!

"Look!" said Jonathan suddenly, pointing upward. "Birds! Not flying, floating. And moving northwest—in the wrong direction. As if they couldn't help themselves!"

She stared silently, first with idle curiosity, then with a strange fascination. It was as Jonathan had said. Birds. Flying northwest, toward Tyre. Moving in the wrong direction. *As if they could not help themselves!*

Jered liked to do his business, as well as his praying, in public for all the world to see and hear. When secrecy was not imperative, he issued his commands in a loud voice, as in those hungry days of his boyhood harsh commands had been issued to him. Hence he gave audience to employees and menials in broad daylight on his platformed booth set prominently in the market place. That is, to all but one.

Hanan, as usual, came to Jered's own private apartment for his appointment, skulking by back lanes through the pre-dawn shadows. Even by daylight he was a nondescript figure, drifting aimlessly about town, managing always to be in the background. It was this talent for self-effacement which Jered found valuable for certain of his business projects, together with his three other assets: patience, sharp eyes, and a closed mouth.

There were times, however, when the latter seemed less an asset than a liability. It seemed so now.

"By the bones of my dead ancestors, why can't you tell me in so many words what happened? Must I pry it out of you as a builder pries stone from a quarry?"

"But was I not in the very act of telling my master—"

"Amen! Then so be it! I must pry." Swallowing his impatience with a big mouthful of the sour wine he kept always at his elbow, the chief elder tried again. "Suppose we review the whole matter. Last night, sometime about the beginning of the second watch, I summoned you, sent you out on a—a certain commission."

"Ay, master." For once the servant was disconcertingly communicative, "You sent me to watch that woman's houses, to bring you a report if anyone went near it, and if he went inside, to go and find a witness—"

"Enough!" Jered glanced around hastily. His wife, Leah, with the sharp ears, would not be far off. "And to preserve the utmost secrecy about the whole matter," he reminded curtly.

"Oh, yes, master." Hanan nodded his head eagerly. "The noble elder need have no fear. His servant understands. The utmost secrecy."

"You understand the reason why, I hope," continued Jered with dignity. "There have been complaints in the town of—of lawlessness. It is my business as chief elder to see that the reputation of Nazareth is kept high. That area about the inn—such places are always likely to be trouble spots—"

"The elder need not explain," Hanan assured him cheerfully. "As I said before, his servant understands. Perfectly," he added amiably.

Jered gave him a sharp glance, but the nondescript face was innocently blank. To control the trembling of his fingers, he tightened them about the silver goblet.

"You say you saw someone approach the—the house under discussion last night in the beginning of the third watch. Could you see his face?"

'Why not, most worthy patron? The moon was bright."

"Then what did he look like?"

"Like nothing and no one, master. Except, possibly—himself."

Jered choked, "You mean—you've known all the time who it was and haven't told me?"

"My master did not ask."

The elder made a hoarse exclamation. The half-swallowed wine scalded his throat. For a moment he could not speak. "Then I—I'm asking you now," he croaked finally. "*Who was it?*"

"It was Gebal, the young merchant from the coast."

"Gebal," muttered Jered. He remembered him well enough. Handsome. Fun-loving. One who sang and danced. He turned furiously on Hanan. "Go on!"

The little man retreated in a fright "My patron means—I am to go?"

"By the holy altar, no! Get on with your report. Tell me what happened."

"What happened when, master?"

"When Gebal, the merchant, went up to the house. Did—did she let him in?"

"*Ah hah!* Did I not tell my master that? I thought—"

"Did she let him in?"

"No, master."

Jered set down his goblet. In another instant his trembling fingers would have dropped it. Belief turned him weak as water, knowing that others beside himself were refused admittance. Except for this final indignity of weakness, this humiliating proof of his eternal servitude, he might still have been able to forgive her.

"Enough. You are dismissed now, Hanan. Until tonight—the same commission."

To escape from the stifling prison of his inner apartment, Jered went up to the housetop. But he found no relief. Whichever way he paced, he confronted the devil within.

It was then that, looking up, he saw the birds. Stopping his futile pacing, he watched them grimly. It wasn't time yet for birds to be flying north. Trying to escape from something, were they? Storm? A desert fire? Famine?

At least they knew better than to fly around in circles. And once they had chosen their course, they moved with silent and relentless purpose, letting nothing turn them aside.

He also had chosen his course. Had he not vowed long ago, in his boyhood, that no one who ever rejected him should remain unpunished?

He moved resolutely toward the stairway.

4

MIRIAM NO LONGER enjoyed her daily trips to the village fountain. She was too afraid of meeting the woman Mulcah. Whenever possible, she went early in the morning, when it was scarcely light enough to see, washing her clothes and filling her jugs with almost frantic haste, returning home by an out-of-the-way route which afforded not even a glimpse of the shabby stone house overlooking the village inn.

She had kept her promise to the Boy. She had gone that morning, months before, to the fountain and washed her clothes side by side with the woman Mulcah, brushed elbows and shoulders with her, even though her body had shrunk from the contact. She had even forced her dry lips to utter pleasantries, hear thoughts all the while rebelling, seeking escape.

"The child is small for his age, isn't he? Seven, you say?" *Ah hah! What would Joseph say? Suppose someone tells him!*

"Yes, I have lived here in Nazareth all my life, except for a few months twelve years ago." *The Law says such women shall be stoned!*

"My son? Yes, he is different from most boys his age. As you say, more thoughtful, kinder to his—friend!" *Too kind, too thoughtful, if such as she can call him friend! Heaven help us, why does he do such things?*

She had endured the drawn skirts of the women, their disapproving glances, their whispers. Then Leah, the wife of Jered, had come, her habitually sullen features twisting into fury at sight of the woman Mulcah, and not bothering to mute her comments to a whisper.

"So! A good pair they make, don't they? No wonder the son makes such friends, with his mother to set the example! Did you know he was actually seen going into the woman's house?"

Blindly Miriam gathered together her dripping clothes, thrust them into her basket, and fled. It was the last time she exchanged even a glance with the woman Mulcah.

Today she was even later than usual at the fountain, for Joseph and the Boy had gone to the neighboring village of Japhia to build the frame of a house and she had had to pack a lunch for them. Anxiety hastened her steps, for she knew Mulcah often waited until the other women left before going to the well. The prospect of meeting her alone, of having to make the choice between polite conversation and deliberate rebuff, appalled her.

But she need not have worried. The women were still there, a tight knot of them, gathered some distance away from the fountain and talking excitedly. It was not the casual gossip enjoyed by loiterers postponing the day's further labors as long as possible. These women had not yet been to the well. The water jars poised carelessly on shoulders or hanging from lax fingers by the handles were empty. Yet the morning was already advanced, well past sunrise.

Fresh alarm hastened her steps. What had happened? Could the eternal fountain have ceased to flow? Yesterday, she recalled, its stream had been thin and slow, yet she had thought nothing of it. Trembling with apprehension, yet not knowing why, she descended the last steep slope of the path, bringing into view the little walled enclosure about the well. Then she understood.

The woman Mulcah sat alone within the arched stone space, beside her an empty water jar and a large bundle tied in a linen cloth. Seemingly indifferent to the group of indignant women, she made no motion either to open the bundle or to fill the jar, only sat quietly, watching the child Danny splash happily in the small trickles from the overflow pool.

Miriam moved toward the tightly knotted circle.

"She hasn't even filled her jug."

"We ought to be able to do something!"

"Brazen hussy! If she thinks we're going to fill our jars—"

"I think we should go and tell the elders!"

"No!" The decisive voice of Leah silenced them all. "We don't need the elders to tell us what to do to such women. We'll soon get her out of there!"

Stooping with difficulty, for she was a woman of wide girth, the wife of Jered balanced her jug with one large hand while she gathered together three good-sized stones with the other. After a moment's hesitation several others followed her example.

"*Ay yah!* Come with me now, and do just what I tell you."

Horrified, Miriam opened her mouth to protest, but her voice choked in her throat. Memory of the one time when she had tried to befriend the woman warned her to silence. For the Boy's sake she must not identify the household of Joseph with the unfortunate Mulcah more intimately than he had done already. Denying the impulse to flee, she forced her trembling limbs to follow with the other women in the wake of the threatening Leah. Some like herself, she noted gratefully, moved empty-handed and with reluctance. Close beside her was Lilah, the wife of Jonathan, so pale she looked almost sick.

"They—they aren't going to hurt her, are they?" she whispered.

"I don't know," replied Miriam with stiff lips.

"Can't they—can't they understand just a little how she feels?"

Miriam clamped tense fingers about the girl's arm as the tightening circle drew closer to the well. "Look! Oh, heaven help us!"

For, instead of being intimidated by their approach, the woman Mulcah seemed actually to welcome it. Could she be unaware of the angry, threatening faces—the stones? Rising from her seat, she came forward a few steps to meet them, smiling and with both hands outstretched. Before the wife of Jered could open her lips, she had greeted them with as simple and genuine hospitality as if she had been standing on the threshold of her own shabby cottage.

"*Shalom*, sisters of Nazareth! I have been waiting for you. See! I have brought gifts for you all."

Swiftly unknotting the four corners of the linen cloth, she displayed its contents and, while the women stared spellbound, held up one object after another for all to see: silver necklaces, bracelets and anklets, gossamer scarves spangled with gems or fretted with gold and silver threads, embroidered girdles, soft sandals of porpoise skin, robes of every color and weave and texture.

Miriam felt the girl Lilah draw a deep sharp breath.

"For you," Mulcah continued swiftly. "I want you all to have these. Perhaps then you'll believe that I've really changed, that I no longer have use for such things. Here, take them!"

Arms overflowing, she descended the steps and, before the stupefied women could even exchange wondering glances, was distributing her treasures with a lavish and impartial hand. Not carelessly, however, but taking time with the disposal of each gift for deliberate choosing.

"No, no! Not such heavy bracelets for those slender arms! Try these light bangles. Good!"

"Pearls for that pretty throat, not silver."

"Ah, Leah the wife of Jered! Purple for you, of course, and a heavy chain of silver for your neck."

"And blue for Miriam the wife of Joseph. You should always wear blue. And a scarf with gold threads."

"And for you, Lilah, the bride of Jonathan—Ah, how beautiful you are! A robe of crimson silk, and this chain of copper disks to match the gold of your skin...

The speechless wonderment dissolved into "oh's" and "ah's" as calloused fingers fumbled the smooth metals and tangled in the soft fabrics. Jars remained empty, ignored. Bursting into noisy chatter, the women tied the embroidered girdles about substantial waists, peered at each other excitedly through the wisps of scarves, draped the bright folds of silk and brocade and linen over robes of drab homespun.

"Heaven be praised!" exulted Miriam silently. "She's going to make them her friends. I shall never have to be unkind to her again."

"Beautiful," murmured Lilah, as she hugged the precious bundle to her breast *Ay yah!* What more of happiness could this day possibly bring! First the brass bowl, and now the crimson robe and copper chain. And to think that this morning she had even remotely considered—!

"Beautiful indeed," responded Miriam with an understanding smile.

Folding the blue robe neatly, she laid it over her forearm, the wisp of a scarf glinting brightly above it. Of course she would never wear them. They were far too fine for a carpenter's wife, even one who traced his lineage to David—*especially* one who traced his lineage to David, she thought whimsically, picturing Joseph's outrage at seeing his wife garbed in a robe he himself was unable to purchase. But surely there would be no harm in keeping it in the bottom of the chest, in taking it out sometimes in the gray cold of winter, just to remind one of the clear deep blue of a summer sky.

Still smiling, she waited for the exclamations of delight to subside into murmurs of gratitude. The women would be awkward and hesitant about expressing their thanks. Enough if today they made only the barest gestures of friendliness. Time would take care of the rest.

Her smile faded. A determined figure elbowed through the circle and approached the well stones where Mulcah knelt filling her arms a second time from the bundle. Tightly clutching an end of the embroidered girdle which had accompanied the purple robe, the wife of Jered lashed it with stinging vigor across the woman Mulcah's face.

"You accursed sinner!" she cried hysterically. "Would you buy the favor of good women with the same despicable coinage for which you sold your own? Well, you can't, do you hear?"

Mulcah, on her knees, made no effort to resist. Except for the streak of crimson left on her cheek by the lashing, her features might have been chiseled from stone. Her only movement was to protect the whimpering child Daniel by a quick backward thrust of her arm which placed him behind her and covered his frightened face with the long folds of her sleeve.

Loosing the girdle with one final stroke, Leah grasped the purple gown in both hands and tried with all her might to tear it, but it was of stout weave and would not yield. Then she flung it on the ground and spat and stamped upon it.

"So may it be done to all workers of iniquity!" cried Leah shrilly. "Let them be trampled under the feet of the righteous!" Her sharp black eyes swept the silent circle. "Come, sisters of Nazareth. What's the matter with you? Has none of you the courage to defy evil? Must the wife of your chief elder do it alone?"

Following her lead, but reluctantly, a few of Leah's friends removed the newly acquired ornaments and tossed them halfheartedly on the well stones. Others, remembering debts to Jered, followed suit.

"Shame to you!" With desperate determination Leah taunted them to action. "Will you let her make dupes of you? Take off those bribes of iniquity. Fling them in her face!" When they still hesitated, her black eyes narrowed as anger gave place to shrewdness. "Have you thought what your husbands will say when they see their wives wearing the baubles and dresses of a loose woman? Do you want me to tell them?"

"No, no!" This time gasps of horror were genuine, their revulsion complete and devastating. If they must part with such treasures, better that it be done violently. Easier to tear a silken scarf to shreds than lay it regretfully aside! They tore. They spat. They shouted. They stamped upon.

"No, no—please! Have pity—she meant no harm—can't you see—"

They had not even heard her voice. Miriam closed her eyes and tried to shut out the noise by putting her hands over her ears. But the motion brought the folded blue robe close to her face, filled her nostrils with such strange and disquieting perfumes that for a moment her senses reeled. Revulsion seized her. What was she doing with this symbol of an evil woman's shame?

Aghast, she bundled the soft folds into a tight wad, and, eyes still closed, flung it away from her with all her strength, then sank shuddering to her knees, covering her burning face with her hands. But the perfume still clung to her fingers, to the flesh of her arm and the sleeve of her dress. Even when she pulled her head scarf tight about her nose and mouth, she could not quite shut out the cloying fragrance.

When she lifted her face again, the woman Mulcah was gone.

"Well done, my Nazareth sisters." Now that her purpose was achieved, Leah cheerfully disclaimed any personal interest or emotion. "I'm glad you saw your duty and did it. That should show her once and for all what virtuous women think of those who do evil. Be sure the Righteous One of Israel is pleased with you." The black eyes veered from piety to practical appraisal. "We'll sell the unclean stuff to some merchant and—and buy bread with it to give to the poor. I myself will attend to the matter."

Already the mood of violence had passed. Hands lingered on the bright fabrics, regretfully rubbing away marks of soil, piecing torn edges together, and relinquishing with more and more reluctance. Some, in spite of Leah's vigilance, failed to relinquish, slipped instead, surreptitiously, into wide sleeves or the pockets of girdles, even into the narrow mouths of water jars.

Miriam filled her vessel hastily at the end of the fountain farthest from the wife of Jered and, keeping as close to the outer walls as possible, slipped back down the broad stone steps. As she started to climb the hillside path leading up from the spring, something bright caught her eye.

There it hung, where she must have flung it, impaled on a thorn bush growing on the stony hillside high above the arched enclosure. For some reason she was glad it was there instead of on the dirty disordered pile down below. Perhaps by nightfall some beggar would be wearing it over her rags, believing she had wrapped herself in a little bit of heaven.

5

AS THE SUN climbed higher its heat overspread the clean freshness of the sky with a hard lacquer of bronze. Enclosed within the furnace of its blaze, the parched hills seemed to crack and shrivel, and the little town with its yellowed limestone houses looked like an oven full of loaves slowly browning to a crisp. Animals and old men and children crept into the narrow ribbons of shade. Women crouching in open doorways over handmills or baking troughs wiped the sweat from their eyes and watched hopefully for the first fluttering of fig or olive leaves. And on housetops and threshing floors men sat idle beside their winnowing forks and waited for the strong refreshing wind, which should come from the sea to fan and to cleanse.

"He will be here soon," they assured each other confidently when the shadow cast by a man's body was as long as he was tall. "He must have reached the coast long since."

"He's late in coming," they murmured uneasily, when the shadow had shrunk to but half a man's actual size.

But when the shadow had become a mere dwarf of a thing huddled at a man's feet, they said nothing at all.

He did not come.

Joseph also, laboring hard in spite of the heat on the framework of the new house in Japhia, kept careful watch of the sky. Each time he stopped to wipe the sweat from his eyes, which was often, he lifted them. Not toward the northeast, however, out of which the prevailing summer winds should come, but toward the southeast, where the rolling hills of Samaria and Gilead melted into golden haze. And when at noon he and the Boy stopped to eat their lunch of bread and oil and goat's milk, he sat with face turned in the same direction, heedless of the sunlight quivering against his eyes.

By the time they finished eating, the golden haze had crept upward until half the sky was tinged yellow, and with his last mouthful of bread Joseph ground tiny particles of grit between his teeth. Once more wiping the sweat from his face, he found the end of his headcloth earth-stained, not dark like the soil of Galilee but pale like the sands of the desert. Without a word he returned to the house and swiftly assembled his tools.

"But we haven't finished, Father, and it's only noon."

"Home," replied Joseph briefly.

"But why?"

"*Sherkiyeh*," came the curt reply.

The Boy turned a startled face toward the coppery outlines of hills to the southeast. "But—it can't be. It's summer, not springtime. And the wind isn't even blowing!" "He will come," answered Joseph. "And we must hurry " He came—*Sherkiyeh*, the dread East Wind, with the desert's scorching heat on his breath and fine mists of sand in his throat. Before they reached the edge of Japhia the sun swam in a gray mist, and dust mounted in swirls as high as the housetops. Scarcely had they begun the long climb up the path into the Nazareth hills when the fury of wind and dry heat and dust was upon them, blinding their eyes, clogging their throats, snatching at their heavy garments wound closely about them for protection.

"I should have known"—Joseph muttered once into his tightly bound headcloth—"when I saw birds—"

But after that he saved his breath, imparting only the briefest of directions. "Head low…you first…don't miss the path…turn aside for nothing…"

Leaving to the younger eyes the task of watching the path, Joseph placed his stocky body between the Boy and the force of the wind and pushed with grim doggedness up the steep slope. Better perhaps to have remained in Japhia until tomorrow, for *Sherkiyeh* seldom lingered in one place more than part of a day. But he could not have borne the thought of Miriam alone.

The sun faded into a pale floating disk, like the moon in daytime, then disappeared. Gradually the wind increased until it was difficult to stand upright. Bodies bent almost to the ground, they worked their way slowly up the steep incline. Joseph issued no more commands. His breathing became slow and labored, his eyes stung and streamed as if he had thrust them into a bed of nettles.

It was the Boy now who assumed direction of the long, laborious climb.

"Take care, Father, there's a tree across the path... Don't try to open your eyes, hold fast to my girdle...stop here in the lea of this rock, get our breath...almost to the top of the hill, not so bad on the other side... Father—just over there—Nazareth! See the outlines of houses?... Just a little farther, we're almost there... Here, let me take your fingers—touch the blessed *mezuzah*..."

Miriam wept with relief when they stumbled into the courtyard.

All that afternoon and evening *Sherkiyeh* raged, a brutal giant mercilessly wielding thong and lash, prototype of that divine judgment foretold centuries ago by the prophet: *a dry wind of the high places in the wilderness, toward the daughter of my people, neither to fan nor to cleanse.*

The town retreated, cowering, behind tightly barred doors and let him have his way. Fields and streets and market place were deserted, booths soundly shuttered, and shelters of goat's hair or burlap lashed firmly to the ground. But there was no escaping the thoroughness of his cruelty, even in retreat He tore loose shutters and anchoring vines, bored cracks and sifted needles through the thickest walls... played havoc with housetops and hedges and threshing floors, stripped vines and olive branches clean of their swelling fruits.

6

YET in spite of the storm, never had Lilah been so happy.

The sweltering little house, tight and snug in its newness, resisted the wind sturdily. Bluster as he would, raging *Sherkiyeh* could not probe a single crack. But he made full atonement for his frustration on the tiny housetop. Whipping the well-anchored burlap covers from the pile of threshed and winnowed grain, he strewed the golden stalks far and wide over neighboring housetops, then, returning, vigorously swept the flat surface clean of both chaff and ripened kernels, depositing in their place a miserable and useless litter.

"You might have moved some of it," reproached Jonathan with more sorrow than anger, attempting to wipe the dust from his reddened eyes, "or at least put some heavier stones on the edges of the burlap."

"So might your good-for-nothing brothers," she retorted. "They're the ones who will suffer most from its loss, since our grain jars are already full. But I did try," she added contritely. "I couldn't see for the dust in my eyes, and I was frightened."

"I know." His swift response was comforting. "Don't blame yourself, beloved. We—we'll manage somehow."

She was not in the mood for bitterness. Bringing a ewer of water and a cloth and basin, she tenderly washed the caked dust from his cheeks and lips and enflamed eyelids. "All the other men came from the fields long ago. I was worried when you didn't come! Where have you been?"

"In the olive grove," he replied wearily, "saving what I could."

She drew back in dismay. "You mean—the crop—"

With a silence more eloquent than words Jonathan reached for a basket, opened the overlapping folds of his coat pouched above his girdle, and poured out its contents. The hard green ovals, scarcely bigger than full-sized olive pits, only half filled the basket.

"Gone," he commented tonelessly when he had shaken out the last pellet. "Stripped clean. We may find more later lying on the ground. Maybe a few on the trees. I couldn't hunt any longer—so much dust in my eyes."

Lilah wordlessly lifted a handful of the hard green berries. Misfortune indeed! No ripe black olives to savor on one's tongue through the dull winter months? No rich golden oil to sweeten bread, to give light to the lamps, to make smooth one's hair?

But even this prospect of future poverty could not spoil her mood. "We'll find more of them," she promised. "I'll go out with you as soon as *Sherkiyeh* has passed. And this green fruit doesn't make such bad eating. I'll bruise every one, even the smallest, before putting it in the pickling brine, so the pulp won't taste so bitter."

Slowly, persuasively, she nursed him into sharing her mood of gaiety, even silenced his protests when she set three tiny clay lamps burning instead of one to dispel the midday gloom of the tightly closed little house.

"But—with the oil so near gone and no more—"

"Just this once!" she pleaded. "Forget about the wind, forget about winter—and poverty—and hunger—everything except that today is beautiful, and we're here together!"

"A day of *Sherkiyeh*—beautiful?" But his words voiced wonder rather than protest. While she ministered to him as a dutiful wife, pouring water over his hands and feet, bringing a clean coat to replace his dust-caked working garments, his gaze clung to her every motion with incredulous delight.

All the rest of that day, while the wind raged, she kept her precious secret, revealing her excitement only in the heightened color of her cheeks, the shining of her eyes. Once she passed close to the water jars standing on their clay platform beside the door. Jonathan's back was turned and she thrust her hands deep into the mouth of one of them, its every nerve tingling at the contact with silken softness.

They made a banquet of the evening meal, pretending that they were a nobleman and his wife being served by slaves, that the boiled lentils were wild rice cooked with bits of veal and pheasant, the coarse bread tender white loaves baked in the shape of stars and lotus flowers, the earthen cups of water silver goblets of wine sweetened with honey. Jonathan gladly let her have her way, his plodding wits stumbling awkwardly in the wake of her nimble imagination.

"Though I'd as soon have it the way it is," he protested mildly.

"At least we don't have to pretend about one thing." Lilah's fingers lovingly stroked the curves of the new brass bowl. "Isn't it beautiful? See how it catches the flame of the lamp, like—like a queen's crown of gold?"

"More like your eyes," amended Jonathan humbly.

When the meal was finished she waited, her excitement mounting, while he repeated the prayers and made the necessary washings.

"Now," she continued demurely, still playing the role of nobleman's wife, "if my lord pleases, I have a surprise for him. No fitting after dinner spectacle, to be sure, for one of such noble station, but if he will just close his eyes—"

Reluctantly, for he desired no other spectacle than the loveliness of her slender body and glowing face, Jonathan obeyed. Lilah plunged her hand into the clay water jar and with trembling fingers drew out the robe of crimson silk.

It was even more beautiful than she had remembered. With quivering haste she slipped off her garments of homespun, all but the straight tunic, and draped it over her shoulders, letting its softness flow down and over her limbs. Then the sandals of porpoise skin, soft as new lamb's wool, encased her small narrow feet.

"Now!" she breathed. "*Ay yah!* Look at me, Jonathan!"

Smiling indulgently, Jonathan opened his eyes. He stared up at her, the smile fading. Then, still staring, he rose slowly to his feet.

As the girl gazed back into his grim features, the color and eagerness ebbed from her own. "D-doesn't my lord like his—his humble slave?"

Still he did not speak, only stood staring at her with cold rigidity, his silence all the more terrifying as it seemed to magnify the howling wind outside.

Then with a great flood of relief she understood. "I didn't buy it," she assured him with shrill eagerness. "It will cost you nothing, Jonathan, I promise you. It—it was a gift!"

The words faltered before the explosive vehemence of his anger. One instant he was standing across the room, the dining cloth and serving dishes on the floor between them. The next he was towering above her, eyes blazing, hands raised.

"Jason!" he hissed between clenched teeth. "He gave it to you!"

"No, no, not Jason! I swear it!"

"It was a crimson gown you wanted!"

"Yes, but—"

"And you said Jason had one, only yesterday."

"But it wasn't Jason. By the God of Israel, I swear it!"

The big fingers clamped shut, not about her neck but over her slender shoulders. "Then *who*—"

"It—it was—the woman Mulcah—" Again her voice faltered. Even to her own ears the truth sounded too preposterous. "It was at the well this morning. She—she gave them to all the women."

She felt as if the bones of her shoulders were being crushed slowly into pulp. When she thought she must surely cry out with pain, strength seemed suddenly to pass out of his fingers. Abruptly he dropped his hands.

"You're lying," he said quietly. "It was Jason, of course. And he would not give you such a present for—nothing."

"No, no!" But even while she sobbed out the story, leaving out not a single detail, not even her hiding of the treasures in her water jar while the other women were shouting and slinging them back, she knew it was no use.

"Take it off," he said abruptly when she had finished.

Wordlessly she removed the clinging folds of crimson, letting them fall to the floor in a shimmering heap, then with a smothered cry groped her way to a dark corner and sank, sobbing, to her knees.

The harsh ripping of cloth blended in her ears with the screaming of the wind. The big fingers, which could be so gentle, tore and tore, until it seemed they must have torn the beautiful garment into shreds, and with each rending she winced with pain.

Later, much later, she crept out of the corner.

The wind was still blowing, harder even than before, but she knew *Sherkiyeh* had passed, for it was coldness now instead of hot dust, which seeped through the cracks of the walls. So sharp was the contrast after the day's intense heat that, instead of bringing surcease, the new wind seemed to bear the chill of winter on its breath.

Shivering, she made her way noiselessly to the water jars, fumbled about until she found the old homespun robe, and wrapped it around her. But it was still clammily moist from the sweat and grime of the day, and she felt colder than before. A few coals glowed red in the pit of the clay stove, and she huddled over it, chafing her hands. All but one of the bright little lamps had gone out, and that one was flickering low.

Wearied by his long day of back-breaking labor, Jonathan had fallen asleep on the floor without spreading the mat. She could hear his heavy breathing and see the dark bulk of him in the dim lamplight, lying face downward as he always did when worried or overtired. But it was an uneasy sleep.

"Lilah!" he muttered, reaching out his arm to find her.

But she did not hear him. On the floor, she gathered the tattered remains of red silk into her arms and hugged it to her breast. So beautiful it had been! Even in the dark she could feel its brightness. Creeping to the little stove, she held it close to the few glowing coals, as if their warmth and light might have power to restore wholeness. One of the tattered ends hung too close and burst into crimson flame.

Suddenly, with fierce urgency, she began feeding the sorry tatters into the fire pit, watching fascinated, while one after the other leaped and danced in a frenzy of gold and crimson, turning the little room bright. But when the brief brightness had passed, shrinking to curling black ribbons, the glowing coals died with it, leaving her crouched, shivering, in even deeper darkness than before.

She awoke, chilled and cramped. The wind had died, and the two small windows showed faint light, like eyes slowly opening from sleep. A bulky shadow loomed above her.

"*Ah hah!* Sorry I—tore it," murmured Jonathan humbly. "I should have been glad he gave it—you wanted it so much. Just couldn't bear the thought of you and Jason. I should have known you wouldn't—wouldn't—" His big hand fondled her hair clumsily. "I'll buy you another, I promise—perhaps when the olive—when the wheat harvest comes."

"It's all right," she said, rising heavily. Pain darted through her cramped limbs. "It doesn't matter."

Preparing his lunch in the dark, because oil was now so precious, she added a few fresh figs to the hard bread and cheese. There were still ten round flat loaves in the earthen jar, she noted with relief, enough to last until the day after the Sabbath, when his mother would take her turn at the oven. She must remember to borrow some live coals to start the fire, get it to burn brightly and bank it well. Then she would lay out one of Jonathan's clean coats and headcloths, for he never remembered where to look for them. And she would place some loaves and fresh milk where he could easily find them.

The eyes of windows turned from charcoal gray to pearl. She was glad to turn her back on them when she slipped the little packet of lunch into the pocket of Jonathan's girdle.

"*Ah hah!* When I said I would help with the gathering of the olives, I didn't know... What a pity! I—I don't feel so well—"

The conflict of dismay and hope left him almost inarticulate.

"And I treated you so—C-could it be—Has the most Holy One b-blessed us—?"

"No, no—that is, I—" Why did she find it so hard to deceive him, knowing those eyes were watching? Almost in panic she evaded the eager solicitous clumsiness of his caress. "It's nothing, just that I—feel like staying home from the fields. But you must go now. It's beginning to be light."

He did not move. Even in the dimness she could see the troubled shining of his eyes. "But I can't leave you alone. I'll fetch my mother."

"No!" In spite of her effort to appear calm her voice grew shrill, adding fuel to his anxiety. "I—I want to be alone!"

"Then I will return at midday. I'll leave my lunch here and eat it with you." He took the packet from his girdle.

"No, no! Promise me you won't come back, swear it by—by—" She stopped suddenly, letting the waves of panic subside. Then, deliberately she went to him, took the packet from his hand and tucked it into his girdle. "Can't you see, my husband?" Her lips pouting, she smiled up at him. "A woman likes to be alone, at first, with her—her secret. And if—if the Most Holy One *has* blessed us, you must work even harder than before. Now do you understand why you must promise not to come back until evening?"

When he had gone, tender and reluctant to the last, Lilah sank to her knees, weeping, lifting her hands to shut out the steadily brightening light entering through the slits of windows.

"Don't! Don't look at me like that!" She sobbed aloud. "Can't you see why I—I have to do it, have to go away? It isn't just for myself, because—because I want beautiful things so much and can't be happy without them. It's for his sake as much as mine. I can't be the kind of wife he wants, and I shall make him unhappy. He'll be better off without me. Can't you see? It's for his sake too, I tell you!"

Lifting her face, she looked straight up at the two windows, defiantly, then uttered a stifled sound, halfway between a laugh and a sob. Eyes? What could possibly have given her the idea that they were eyes—young eyes, wide and grave and clear—those empty slits in the wall!

7

THE BOY KNEW when the wind changed. It was as if the night outside suddenly relaxed, stopped gritting its teeth and bracing itself. He could no longer remain on his mat.

Out in the courtyard the new wind caught him full in the face, cool and cleansing, almost taking his breath away. For a little he just stood still, letting himself be swept clean of *Sherkiyeh's* heat and grime and sand, as the world was being swept clean. Even the stars looked freshly polished.

Climbing the stairs to the housetop, he had to keep close to the wall to maintain his balance. His body seemed a heavy thing, unwieldy, like a stone tied to the feet of a flying bird. But once on the housetop the dragging burden fell away. He became one with the wind and the night and the stars.

Indeed, he seemed to have no body. It was as if he had left it behind, earth-bound, trying to climb the stairs. Up here he was *Ruach*—Spirit—as the wind was *Ruach*. No one knew where the wind came from or where it was going. It had no beginning and no end. Lake God. God was *Ruach*, and so was the wind, and so was he, Jeshua, the son of Joseph. He felt as if he were being born all over again.

He could not go back to his mat again that night. Rolling himself in his cloak, he lay down in the center of the housetop and dreamed that he was standing with his feet in the snow on top of Mount Hermon, plucking stars out of the sky.

Wakened by a sudden sound, he thought at first it must have been the crowing of a cock. But the sky over his head had not even begun to pale. And the sound came again.

"*Ah hah! Ah hah!* God help me!"

The wind had died, and he could hear the words plainly. He was on his feet and down the stairs leading to the courtyard when the beating started at the door.

Seizing the long wooden key from its peg on the wall, he fumbled for the hole of the crossbolt. His fingers seemed all thumbs.

"I'm here, Deborah," he called soothingly. "Just be patient. I'll have the door opened in the twinkling of an eye."

"Joseph—"

"Not Joseph. Jeshua. But my father will be here soon. I can hear him—talking." *Grumbling* would have been the better word.

The key slipped into the groove, and the Boy quickly drew it out with the bolt's crosspiece. As the door swung in its socket, Deborah almost fell inside.

"God have pity on me! Let me never behold the light of another day! Let me—"

"Hush!" The Boy guided her gently but firmly across the courtyard and into the house. The shrill hysteria subsided to a thin wail. "What's all this noise?" demanded Joseph gruffly. "It's Deborah, Father," explained the Boy quickly. "She couldn't help it. She's in trouble." Joseph was only half awake. "Deborah's always in tr—"

"Joseph!" Soft fingers muted his lips as Miriam brushed past him down the shallow steps. "It's all right now, Deborah," she assured her quietly, her arms reaching out to the shaking figure. *"Ah hah!* You're so covered with dust I can hardly see your face. Come! Up the steps now, while Joseph holds the lamp high. A stool, please, Jeshua. Now just sit quietly while you catch your breath, then tell us. Is it Joel?"

The mere name provoked further hysteria. Certain words could be distinguished through the shrill wails...gone...sins of his father...soon as I could...wicked *Sherkiyeh*...buried somewhere in a heap of sand..."

But finally Deborah became calm enough to sob out the story. She had gone to Sepphoris early that morning before it was light, with some precious embroideries she had saved, because she had heard there was a worker of magic in Herod's court who claimed he could cure people of every ill, even blindness. The king being a great patron of magicians—

"Ay, we know," interjected Joseph bitterly. "He'd go a mile to see a man swallow a sword, but not one step to help him swallow a morsel of bread."

After a long time and many difficulties she had gained audience with the magician, and, praise God, he had been willing to give her a magic potion in exchange for all her embroideries! With trembling fingers she removed a tiny packet from the cleft of her thin breasts, opened it, and held it out for their inspection. Joseph touched the tip of a blunt finger to the little heap of powder and applied it gingerly to his tongue.

"Dust is cheap," he muttered glumly into his beard.

"Hush!" warned Miriam in a whisper.

But just as Deborah had started home, *Sherkiyeh* had come, and she had been forced to remain in Sepphoris all day, crouching in the shelter of a wall. Finally the day had passed and most of the night, and when the wind changed, she had come home, keeping to the road somehow with the stars so bright, only to find the house empty and *Joel gone!* Tears flowed afresh.

With a cool cloth Miriam gently wiped the caked dust from the quivering features. "He cannot have gone far," she soothed. "It's likely he went into a neighbor's house when the storm overtook him."

"And if he *is* lost," Joseph reminded with gruff sympathy, "we can't do anything about it until morning. But of course we know he isn't."

He lay down on his mat and turned his face to the wall and tried to sleep, while Miriam comforted and assured Deborah, and the Boy made himself as useful as possible, filling the basin again with water, shaking clouds of dust from Deborah's coat. Watching the waning stars, he wondered anxiously about Joel.

Finally the cocks began to crow, and the town slowly awakened. Joel was in none of the neighbors' houses. By sunup half of Nazareth knew that he was missing, and by the third hour the town had been so thoroughly searched that an insect would have found concealment difficult. He was not in the market place, nor in the stone recess of the fountain, nor in more unlikely places where excited women took time to peer, such as grain pits and earthen jars and inside the small domed cavern of the village oven. Little work was begun in courtyard or in field or in bazaar booth, for the blind boy was a favorite with all the townspeople.

The Boy took no part in searching the town. As soon as he was sure Joel was not in a neighbor's house, he went straight to the Hilltop. The child had promised, according to Deborah, not to go down into the town or to open the door to any stranger until her return, and Joel was not the sort to break his word. But he had not promised he would not go up on the Hilltop! Sure-footed though he was, he might easily have fallen into a hole and twisted his foot or even broken a leg.

"Joel!" Cupping his hands and moving in a slow circle, the Boy sent the cry ringing through the still morning air. "Joel! Jo-o-o-el!"

When no answer came, his confidence remained unwavering. Joel was somewhere on the Hilltop, asleep perhaps, or too weak or weary to answer.

Patiently he began his search, first in the child's favorite spots: a cleft between two rocks with sheer, smooth sides, a grassy hollow where anemones grew in springtime as thick as a Damascus carpet, the cave-grotto where he had picked the flowers and where there could be found, Joel once said, the roundest, smoothest stones in the whole world. And, of course, the tiptopmost place, where the wind blew the strongest. But Joel was in none of these places.

At the top of the hill, the Boy lay down, flat on his stomach, on a bare outcropping of limestone. Pushing back his headcloth, he let the first fresh stirrings of air from the sea fan his hot cheeks and ruffle his hair.

"*Ay yah!* a voice shouted. "Look, there he is! There on the rock!"

Raising his head, the Boy saw a group of neighbors, hot and panting, running toward him.

"*Ah hah!* Not the blind one!"

"It's Jeshua, the son of Joseph!"

Cheated out of their expected triumph of discovery, the group eyed him with disappointment mixed with irritation.

"*Shalom*, son of the carpenter! What are you doing here?"

"Looking for Joel," he replied simply.

"Queer way to hunt," one of them grumbled, "lying on a rock!"

"Good way to get out of a morning's work," another chided good-naturedly.

But they were too busy to bother long with him. Leaving him as abruptly as they had come, they fanned out over the Hilltop and began their search, exhibiting far more zeal than thoroughness.

Though he lay motionless on the rock, the Boy was also searching—searching his memory for some knowledge of the child Joel which might shed light on the path he had taken. What could have enticed him from the little house on a day when all the rest of mankind was seeking shelter? Nothing that could be seen, of course. Something that could be smelled, or heard, or—*felt*. Something that Joel loved, like the smell of almond blossoms, or the song of a lark, or a smooth round stone, or wind...

Wind! The Boy tensed, then slowly relaxed.

No, Joel would not have ventured to the Hilltop yesterday. It was clean fresh wind he loved, not the brutal harshness of *Sherkiyeh*, wind such as had blown last night, with the *Ruach* of God on his breath.

Wind such as had blown last night!

The Boy got slowly to his feet. He turned his face westward toward the sea from which already the wind of God was breathing.

Let's go to the highest place, Joel had begged, *the tiptopmost place, where it blows the strongest.*

He had brought the child here, to the tiptopmost place.

If only the wind could blow hard enough, it might blow my blindness away. Just for a minute—long enough to see what it looks like from here on our Hilltop...If I could only see with my eyes the way you do, just once!

Memory beat against the Boy's temples in agonizing rhythm. Just here Joel had stood. On tiptoe, arms stretched wide open to the pouring wind, muscles taut and empty eyes fairly straining from their sockets. And—he had tried to walk straight into the wind. If the Boy had not stopped him...

His anguished cry brought the searchers running.

Warily they approached the edge of the sheer precipice dropping from the western flank of the hill, not daring to stand upright but dropping to their hands and knees and creeping, some even worming their way forward on their bellies. Reluctant, terrified, yet with that strange fascination born of horror, they peered over the edge.

"God have mercy! Look below!"

"Him, all right! Wearing that striped coat his mother made him—know it anywhere"

"—always thought somebody would fall over there—"

They stood staring at each other stupidly, strong men grown suddenly helpless, unsure of what to do next.

"I suppose we have to go down," one muttered finally, "though there's no need to hurry now."

"God pity his poor mother!" groaned another. "And the one who has to tell her!"

"I say, where's the carpenter's son? He was here—"

"God have mercy! *He too*—"

"No. We'd have seen him."

"What is he—a magician? Just vanished into thin air!"

But the Boy had used no magic.

He had found the path long ago, wedging himself between two rocks which from a little distance looked like a solid wall. Perhaps some shepherd had carved it to reach a fallen sheep on the ledges below. He had often followed it during his childhood, but never with this desperate haste. So cold and stiff were his hands that he had difficulty clinging to the ledges of rock, the sparse bushes, and grass tufts. He was not just crawling down a steep slope. He was descending into a pit, into Sheol, the place of the mystery of Death.

He reached the rocky ledge at last.

It wasn't Joel lying there. Only the eyes were Joel's—wide, sightless as they had always been. Had the wind blown hard enough? Had there been just one moment, perhaps, when the glory of the stars had burst upon him? God—*Ruach*—had been in the wind. The Boy had felt him on the housetop. Surely he who created the sun and the moon and the stars had cared enough to allow Joel one glimpse of his creation.

But the sightless eyes gave no sign.

The Boy did not linger. There was nothing he could do now for Joel. Soon the crowd of neighbors would appear, panting and stumbling, around the western edge of the hill, a look of horrified helplessness in their eyes. They would straighten the twisted limbs, wipe away the stains, close the sightless eyes, and start the loud wailing which would continue until the burial rites, shortened to a few hours on these hot summer days, were completed. But they would be doing none of these things for Joel. Nobody would be doing anything for Joel. Not ever again.

Hearing a faint chit-chit of sound, he stooped and, reaching into the space between the child's body and the sheer wall of rock, gently lifted in his hands a ball of down and feathers. It was a tiny sparrow whose nest, dislodged by the storm or by Joel's fall, was still miraculously alive!

The Boy regarded the little creature with wonder tinged with resentment. What right had it to possess the strange mystery of life when Joel lay dead? But before starting back up the path, he tucked the quivering ball into the pocket of his coat, close to the warmth of his breast, and during the long ascent soothed it with soft chit-chits such as a mother sparrow might make.

Out of the pit of death he climbed, toward a sky as wide and blue and empty as sightless eyes. Before he had reached the top, the wailing had begun. As he listened, the Boy's eyes grew more and more bleak and puzzled. He need not go back to the village now. Fortunately Joseph would not expect him. Out of respect for Joel's father no work would be done in the courtyard of any Nazareth carpenter today. Nor in any other courtyard, for that matter. For a few brief hours the little town would beat as one heart, move as one grief-stricken body.

Where or how long he wandered the Boy could not have told. He could not have left the Hilltop, for every now and then he kept coming back to one of the places Joel had known and loved.

Feel, Jeshua! Did you ever see rocks so straight and smooth?

Strange, thought the Boy, to be able to hear him speak so plainly when there was no voice except the wind!

Our little hollow, Jeshua—remember? Where we found the anemones growing last spring? Too bad the grass has to be so brown and dead! But it will be green again!

Here we are, on the tiptopmost place! Feel the wind, Jeshua? Lip your arms to it—wide! Stand high on your toes!

Come, Jeshua, hurry! I can smell the green grass already! Isn't it cool here in the grotto? And, look, the roundest, smoothest stones! Let's see who can find the most!

Obediently, as if in response to the voice of Joel, the Boy knelt in the cool grass and plunged his hand into the pool. The blind child had always beaten him at this game, for it was a skill of feeling, not of seeing.

What—only four! Poor Jeshua! Here, I'll give you one of mine, then we'll have five apiece. Put them safe in your girdle, but be careful. Don't hurt the little sparrow!

The Boy tacked the five smooth round stones into his girdle, carefully. Queer, he had almost forgotten about the bird, might easily have crushed it if Joel had not reminded...if Joel—

Startled, he raised his face toward the wind.

A gentle wind it was, not like *Sherkiyeh* but one that cared what happened to a little sparrow. It danced and spun gaily with the long sunbeams in the mouth of the grotto, like a child so happy it could not stay still.

Perhaps it was the wind's voice he had heard, since it could not have been Joel's. Wind—*Ruach*—Spirit. You didn't know where it came from or where it was going. You couldn't see it, yet you knew it was there. Lake—like *life*!

So suddenly did he spring up from the ground that the bird fluttered in fright against his breast, and in spite of his excitement he had to stop and soothe it.

"*Ah hah!* I'm sorry, little sparrow. It was just that it came to me all at once—and really no mystery at all! You're important too, did you know it? You can't even fall to the ground without our Father s knowing and caring. Just be patient a little longer, and I'll find you another nest."

It was when he turned to leave the grotto that he heard the sound of laughter, bright and lilting like a bubbling spring that would never run dry.

8

HE COULD NOT WAIT for another day. He had to tell Deborah.

It was sunset when he came down the hill, and the burial was finished. The procession of musicians, wailing women, friends and neighbors who had accompanied the wicker bier to the burial place had long since disbanded, but the seven days of mourning had barely begun. Outside the little stone house in its circle of cypresses sat the hired mourners, black-clad and shaven, swaying and beating their breasts, each trying to outwail the other.

"Alas! The hero has fallen! The noble lion is no more!"

The tiny courtyard was also filled with women, neighbors most of them, still loyally lamenting but, as the day waned, with more detachment. Facing their sudden silence and curious stares, the Boy almost turned and ran.

"Deborah?" he inquired timidly. "I—I brought her something."

"In the house," replied Hannah, the mother of Jonathan, with her usual efficiency for managing other households than her own. "But if it's food your mother has sent, I can promise she won't eat it. Not one morsel has she taken since they brought him back, and I don't know how long before. And if she'll let you in, Jeshua ben Joseph, you'll do better than we have."

Knocking on the inner door, he received no answer, but, finding it unbolted, he swung it open a little way and, entering, closed it behind him. The single room was dark and hot and airless.

"I see you, son of Joseph and Miriam. Come to mock me, have you, with your big strong body, your bright eyes, while my poor son lies dead?"

The Boy moved quietly into the dimness. He could see better now, picking out of the untidy confusion the figure squatting on the floor, thin shoulders hunched beneath the heavy garment of black goat's hair. The pinched features seemed grayer than the ash-strewn hair above them. He dropped to his knees beside her.

"But that's what I came to tell you, Deborah. Joel's not dead—that is, not really. He's alive!"

She stared at him with dull hostility. "*Ah hah!* Come to mock me!"

"No, no!"

"Alive, you call it?" Her voice was caustic with the bitterness of ashes. "Didn't I lay out his poor body with my own hands, cut his hair and nails, anoint and bind him in my best embroidered cloths, and put salt upon him? God forgive your lying tongue!"

"Not his body, Deborah. *Joel himself!* The Boy spoke with a fierce earnestness, yet hesitantly, trying to find words for what he himself scarcely understood. "He—he didn't need eyes, did he, before, to see? Neither does he need a body now to—to live. He—

188

he's more alive now than when he had one. Can't—can't you see, Deborah?"

Deborah could not see. The very word caused her grief to pour forth afresh. She rocked and swayed and wrung her hands. "God pity me, my poor blind child! And just when I had the magic potion so he wouldn't have to be blind any more!" Drawing the little packet from her breast, she held it so close to her weak eyes that some of her tears fell on the small heap of dust. " 'Mix it with water,' the magician told me, 'which has been boiled with swines' teeth and poppy seeds and lay it as a poultice on his eyes when he lies down to sleep.' *Ah hah!* Why didn't I mix it and put it on his eyes when he lay there on the bier? Then perhaps he wouldn't have to wander around blind in that terrible, dark Sheol."

"But"—the Boy was trembling now—"he's not in any terrible, dark place. That's what he's been telling me, all day, up on the Hilltop."

Deborah's eyes flared, two live coals amid gray ashes. She gripped his arm. "You—*you've seen him?*"

"Not the way you mean," the Boy replied patiently. "Not with my eyes."

"But you said he talked to you!"

"He did. He always will, every time I see something beautiful. Joel so loves beautiful things."

"You heard him?" persisted the woman incredulously. "With your ears?"

"Yes. He used to have just one voice, but now he has thousands. The wind singing through the mouth of the grotto, the spring bubbling, the grass whispering—"

"Stop!" She pushed him away with a cry of anguish. "You're just trying to torture me. As if there could be any beauty left now that he is dead!"

"But, Deborah, he isn't—" He stopped, miserably aware of the pain he was causing her. "I'm sorry. I didn't mean to hurt you."

Her only answer was a groan.

He stood awkwardly on one bare foot, rubbing the toes of the other up and down the hard calf of his leg. What to do next? He was always making mistakes, it seemed. Even his gift of gold had not brought Deborah happiness. She had been just as worried about things afterward as she had been before. And now, unless he could find some way to make her understand, she would never be happy again.

He had to try once more.

"I—I brought you something, Deborah." Taking the five perfect little stones from his girdle, he held them out in his hand. So white were they that even in the dim light they seemed to quiver and glow. "Joel would want you to have them. They're the kind he likes best. We—we found them today when we were up on the hill together—"

His voice trailed off into anguished silence before the ashen horror, which distorted her features. "Take them away! How can you torture me so? Don't you suppose I know my son is dead? Get away from me, son of Joseph! It's hard enough just to look at you, to see you young and strong and—and alive! For God's sake get away—and stay away!"

As the Boy entered the courtyard, Joseph looked up from his work, first with relief, then with a slow knitting of his heavy brows.

"*Ay yah!* About time! We were beginning to worry, your mother and I. We looked for you in the funeral procession," he continued with mild reproof. "Surely a good son of the Law knows it is deemed irreverent not to follow the dead to his last resting place!"

Miriam appeared in the door so swiftly that the long wooden spoon she was holding still breathed steam from the kettle of lentils.

"I'm glad he wasn't there. He loved Joel, and it would have caused him unnecessary pain. Death is always hard for a child to understand."

"For a man too," replied Joseph. "But a man," he emphasized the word with dignity, "does not turn his back upon it."

"Then a child," returned the woman with equal emphasis, "may be wiser than a man. I wish"—she shivered suddenly, and her face, framed in the dark doorway, became pallid as an inlay of ivory—"I wish I had had the courage not to go myself. It—it was as if I were Deborah and—it was my son—" She turned back into the house.

"But Mother!"

Eagerly the Boy started to follow, then stopped. He had tried to tell Deborah, too, about his wonderful discovery. Perhaps—he stood suddenly very still—perhaps there were some things that you couldn't make people understand by telling them. Perhaps—you had to find some way to—to show them.

At the far end of the courtyard, he climbed to the top of a tall, earthen storing jar from which he was able to reach a deep wedge in the stone wall. Uttering gentle "chit-chits," he reached into his pocket for the sparrow. He had made such a pet of her that at his touch she barely ruffled her wings.

"What are you doing?" asked Joseph, eyeing him curiously.

"Putting a sparrow in this nest," replied the Boy. "One that I found when—when I was trying to find Joel."

Joseph grunted impatiently. "Too many sparrows in the world already," he commented brusquely. "Two full-grown ones are worth no more than a penny. Who cares whether one lives or dies?"

"But—" again the Boy opened his lips eagerly, closed them.

"But if you must waste your time on such foolishness," continued the carpenter more mildly, "better make sure the creature does live while you're about it. Take a handful of that new wheat from the jar under your feet and toss it in the nest."

9

THERE WERE OTHERS in Nazareth who did not walk in the funeral procession.

"You say"—so cool and even was Jered's voice that it gave no indication of the tumult within—"you saw him just now, coming out of the woman's house?"

Hanan nodded. So out of breath was he with running and so paralyzed with fear that his usual slow speech was reduced to halting phrases. He had come just now. The shortest way. Even though it was still dark, he had had the master wakened.

"And you're sure it was the young merchant Gebal?" demanded Jered in the same cool voice. "You could swear to it?"

This time the nod was more vigorous. Perhaps Jered was not going to be angry with him, decided Hanan hopefully, for failing to make his report earlier. Perhaps he would not even ask the question—

"Then why," pursued Jered softly, "didn't you see him when he went into the house and go find another witness, as I told you?"

Hanan gulped. No word came from his mouth.

"I can tell you why. You went to sleep, didn't you?"

Hanan drew back, terrified. "I couldn't help it, master—the wind almost blew me over—crawled under hedge—No, no, for the Almighty's sake, don't—"

His gushing explanations were choked into silence as determined fingers dug into his throat.

"I send you on a commission! I pay you good money! Then when the one hour comes I was waiting for—*you fall asleep?*"

The sudden consciousness of bulging eyes and of a rattling gurgle brought Jered to his senses. Aghast, he released his grip, and Hanan retreated swiftly into a corner, where he sat straining painfully and eyeing his employer with mingled emotions, not all of them related to fear. Now that the danger had passed, there were values to be derived from the barely averted tragedy. He stroked the throbbing throat tenderly.

"Surprise people—" he wheezed aggrievedly—"when I show—red fingermarks—tell them—noble chief elder—and especially when I tell them *why*—"

Without a word Jered reached into his girdle, drew out a leather pouch and, taking from it a small gold coin, flung it, together with a glance of deep disgust, into the corner. It fell noiselessly to the carpeted floor, and Hanan crawled toward it with agility.

"But of course I shall not tell them," he amended cheerfully.

Now that the angry tumult had found release in action, Jered felt weak and humiliated. The hands which retied the pouch trembled. Fumbling for one of the seven curled strands of beard, he found the locks hopelessly intermingled by the night's unrest

It was as if the whole carefully wrought pattern of his adult years had fallen into like confusion.

"Shall I go back tonight?" asked Hanan with new-found boldness. "I'll wager this gold denarius my vigilance will be repaid. Any man who gained admittance once at that door would surely enter it again. At least," he dared slyly, "like some others I could mention, he would *attempt* it."

Jered flushed dangerously. Had he had his hands about Hanan's bobbing neck at that moment, he would surely have strangled him. But fortunately there was half the distance of the room between them.

"Come back later," he said curtly, "and I'll give you your orders. But let one word of this be whispered in the town and—"

"Heaven forbid!" the menial assured him hastily. "My master should know by this time that the lips of Hanan are a tomb."

"Then woe to Hanan if he lets the tomb be robbed," warned the elder with grim finality.

Jered slept no more that night. He had forgotten that the sweetness of revenge must be mingled with the bitterness of his own rejection. Even the miserable Hanan had openly mocked his humiliation. And if Hanan knew, then perhaps others in the town had discovered his carefully guarded secret. Unless he acted with the utmost caution, not only his hard-won self-esteem but even his position as chief elder might be in jeopardy. Not for years had such helplessness of fury possessed him, not since he was a boy, smarting under the slights and jeers of his fellow townsmen.

"My husband is restless," remarked Leah a little later as he paced nervously within the inner courtyard. "He has heard something, perhaps, which disturbs him? Something which may have happened yesterday?"

"I know of nothing which happened yesterday," he replied tersely, "except a storm."

Leah thrust a bone needle into rose-colored linen, her fingers unduly vehement to hide their agitation. "There are storms," she remarked, "and storms."

Jered watched her with baffled annoyance. "If you're not careful," he admonished sulkily, "you'll tear that expensive garment to shreds."

She lifted her face then, her dark, moody eyes looking straight into his. "It wouldn't be the first time I tore a garment," she replied with grim satisfaction.

When the news came of Joel's disappearance, Jered, who shared with others a genuine fondness for the boy, was ashamed to feel his first concern swiftly tempered with relief. There would be little business transacted in Nazareth until the child was found, and he would not be expected to occupy his booth in the bazaar. Nor would he be missed among the searchers, especially if he spared some of his servants to the task.

No need of measuring words, probing familiar faces, wondering if people knew. Besides, he needed time to plan. The punishment he had first devised for her—a mere reprimanding by the elders, perhaps a flogging—was not enough. For only him, Jered, to know of his rejection was one thing, but for the town to know, to smile furtively, to whisper to each other of his humiliation...An idea had begun to shape itself, one that to succeed would require all the wit even a clever man could summon.

10

JONATHAN WALKED to his olive orchard with Isaac, the young son of a neighboring farmer, an energetic lad whose limbs and tongue were in constant motion.

He was still not quite clear what had happened. Pride in the possibility that he might have a son, remorse for his anger, hurt bewilderment that Lilah could have deceived him, jealousy of Jason—all were so jumbled in his mind that he scarcely knew which was which. He wished he were alone so his slow mind could untangle its confusion. It was all he could do to follow Isaac's trail through the town without stumbling, much less through the maze of his chatter.

"Worst wind since young Herod took the throne, my father says. Imagine calling *him* young! Looks old to me, but I suppose it's because he remembers the other one, the Great they used to call him. And he was worse even than this one. Killed all his relatives, even his wife and sons! Ever hear that before, did you?"

"Yes," replied Jonathan breathlessly.

"Inn looks dark, not a soul stirring. Must be an hour yet to sunrise. Can't be many guests. Not many camels in the courtyard, are there?"

"No," replied Jonathan breathlessly.

"Light up in that woman's house! Haven't seen that for a long time. Used to be a lot of light and music. I never went there myself, but I could name some people in this town that have, especially one, only I wouldn't dare. Ever go there yourself, did you?"

"No," replied Jonathan with more firmness.

"Ha, we aren't the only ones up this early. Look, plenty of life around the fountain! Beggars! They always get there before light. Yet they don't look like beggars, do they? Look—I say, *look!*"

Both the swift motion and the chatter ceased abruptly as Isaac and Jonathan paused to stare. Even in the faint light there was no mistaking the strange assortment of colors and fabrics bedecking the usually sober and ragged brigade. Purples and crimsons, silks and linens and velvets were mingled in careless and violent combinations.

Isaac burst into laughter.

"Ho, I see now! Remember what happened here at the fountain yesterday? It was all over town. That woman Mulcah gave away all her fine clothes. Then what did the women do—"

"What's that?" Jonathan's fingers dug into Isaac's arm. "You—you say the woman Mulcah—"

"Ow! Let go my arm! By my sprouting beard, what a grip! You don't mean you hadn't heard!"

"Tell me!"

"All *right!* Just wait till I make sure my arm isn't broken!" Rubbing his arm gingerly, the young farmer launched eagerly into the story, embellishing it with such wealth of detail that it consumed all the rest of their journey to the orchards. Jonathan did not once open his lips.

He did his work that morning with grim desperation. The night's heavy wind had completed the damage done by *Sherkiyeh*. The ground was covered with the hard, green olive berries, and it took much time and patience to gather them. While his fingers moved with wooden detachment, his mind circled dumbly, like a blind ox about an oil press.

"She told me the truth, and I didn't believe her. The woman Mulcah did give it to her and I thought it was Jason. It was the lovely thing she had always wanted, and I tore it, tore it! She told me the truth, and I didn't..."

When the news came about Joel's being lost, Jonathan did not comprehend it, though he was one of those who loved Joel deeply. He was scarcely conscious of being left alone in the terraced orchards. He knew only that he must finish his task and get back to Lilah and beg her to forgive him and try all the rest of his life to make amends.

Going back through the town, the heavy basket poised on his head and shutting out most of his view, he did not notice the emptiness of the streets. It was when he passed the narrow lane leading to the bazaar that the idea came to him. A spark of hope was born in him. If only...But of course it was impossible, more so now than yesterday when the olives were still ripening on the trees. There would be only one way. At the mere thought his whole body quivered with revulsion. No, not even for Lilah. *For Lilah!* He bowed his head beneath the burden. *Ay yah!* For Lilah he would lie down on the ground and let Jered make of him a mat to wipe his feet.

The booth where the moneylender usually did business was shuttered tightly. Without pausing to look about and taking the shortest route to Jered's house, he knocked on the chief elder's door. A harassed looking menial named Eben admitted him with reluctance.

"The master is here, yes, but"—he dropped his voice to a whisper—"if it's a loan you want, he's in no mood, and he likely won't even see you."

"I'll wait," said Jonathan firmly. Even the sight of Eben, who had attained his menial status through borrowing too frequently, did not dissuade him from his purpose.

He waited. An hour passed and he shifted his squatting position on the stone floor of the courtyard. The enclosing walls quivered behind heat waves, and the paving stones became so hot one could have baked bread upon them.

Eben wrung his hands. "I told you! When he's in this mood—Something must have displeased him. Better to go back home."

"No," said Jonathan. "Tell him again that I'm here. I'll wait."

And then suddenly all was changed.

"Master will see you!" Eben blinked in bewilderment "Says to hurry. Asked me why I didn't tell him it was Jonathan the son of his dear friend Benjamin. As if I didn't tell him a dozen times!"

Jonathan entered a cool inner court sheltered from the sun by the giant leaves of an overspreading fig tree. He might have been an honored guest. Water was brought for his feet, a cup of wine thrust into his hand, a cushion laid for him on the paved floor. The reception rendered him far more speechless than the contemptuous hostility he had expected. But words, it appeared, were not necessary.

"Ah, *shalom*, peace to you, my dear son of Benjamin! It's a loan you want, I suppose. How much this time? Ten denarii? Then here are twenty. The usual terms—and no security. Are we not both good sons of the Law? The word of a young Israelite should be enough. *The word—yes.*" Jered repeated the phrase with satisfaction. "The word of a respected young Israelite. And that my dear son of Benjamin, is all I am asking from you in return."

Jonathan could not believe his good fortune. No more than ten would he have dared ask for, yet here were twenty, stacked in two neat piles, within reach of his hand. And such a little thing he must promise to do, in place of giving security—nothing any good loyal Israelite should not count a privilege!

Nazareth was becoming a more and more lawless community, Jered explained with flattering candor, especially during the night hours and in the vicinity of the inn. It wasn't good for the town's reputation, which was already bad enough. As chief elder, Jered was anxious to improve conditions, but the testimony of casual witnesses was frequently not of sufficient weight to convict the offenders. They were men whose word was not respected —not solid citizens like Jonathan. If tonight, for instance, he would be willing to patrol the terraces about the inn with one of Jered's hirelings, then merely report to the elders and the congregation what he had seen with his own eyes, he, Jered, would be most gratified. And just to make it all legal, knowing Jonathan was waiting outside, Jered had prepared this simple agreement.

Jonathan was willing. With eager haste, before Jered could change his mind, he signed his name on the piece of papyrus beneath the scrawled ink markings which were not yet dry. He left the house trembling, with the twenty hard silver coins tucked into his girdle, and hastened to the market place.

To his dismay he found the stall usually occupied by Jason as tightly shuttered as Jered's.

"Looking for the Greek?" inquired a garrulous mule driver. "Gone. Went off bag and baggage this morning before sunup. Didn't say where to."

Disappointed, Jonathan wandered through the bazaar, still hardly noticing its unusual emptiness. It had not occurred to him that the merchant might be gone. News which yesterday would have set him rejoicing today seemed dire misfortune. For Jason had in his possession the coveted treasure. Without Jason to advise him, how could Jonathan even tell the difference between silk and linen? And yet—just last night he had held silk in his hands and torn it to shreds.

With sudden excitement he made his way to the booth of another merchant, a Phoenician named Gebal, well known in Nazareth for his irrepressible jollity. Here, Jonathan sensed with relief, was one of the few foreigners a man could trust. If Gebal said a piece of cloth was silk, it was silk.

"Ho, farmer!" The black eyes shone teasingly. "What today? A few measures of Tyrian purple, or a girdle studded with gems?"

"A robe of silk," said Jonathan tensely. "Crimson silk."

He knew it was a mistake the instant the words were uttered. He should have appeared indifferent, asked to look at different kinds and colors of cloth, pretended crimson silk was the one thing he least desired.

The black eyes widened in amazed appraisal.

"Ha! Silk. Sure you don't mean homespun?"

"Silk," repeated Jonathan.

He knew when he saw it. It felt the same in his fingers as the stuff he had torn. Crimson it was like drops of fresh blood quivering in sunlight.

"Enough for a woman's garment," he said hoarsely. "How much?"

The shrewdness in the merchant's eyes was mingled with both pity and contempt "Silk, my dear Galilean peasant, is worth its weight in gold. And this is double-dyed, which makes it even more costly. But fortunately silk is light. I could sell you enough to make a woman a decent coat for—two gold aurei."

Jonathan wet his lips. "How—how much in silver?"

"Fifty denarii," replied Gebal, turning away his eyes.

Jonathan felt sick. It was no use, he knew. These foreign merchants were hard bargainers. Most of them weren't even honest.

"I—I'll give you ten," he offered desperately.

The merchant turned toward him again. He looked strange without the little laughter lines crinkling the corners of his mouth. His eyes were soft once more.

"I know," he said soberly. "I've seen her here in the bazaar. Beautiful. I used to have a wife who looked like her. Died while I was on a trip. How much have you?" he asked abruptly.

"Twenty denarii," said Jonathan. "I—I just borrowed them from Jered."

"Let's see them."

With trembling fingers Jonathan spilled them on the faded carpet. For an agonizing moment he thought he had lost one, but it had slipped along the fold of his girdle nearly to his hip bone. With stiff fingers he laid it beside the others.

"*Ay yah!* said Gebal, smiling again and reaching to pat Jonathan's arm almost in sympathy, "it's enough."

Jonathan's brown sandaled feet moved on air. The packet of crimson silk was soft and weightless within the overlapping folds of his coat, but with each breath he drew he could feel the rise and fall of it against his breast. Even the laden basket on his head was no burden. He was glad for its wide protecting rim, hiding from curious passers-by the triumph in his eyes.

But, oddly enough, there were no passers-by. The back lanes through which he hastened were strangely empty.

There was a crowd moving in the main street; a funeral procession it sounded like, for he could hear women's voices chanting to the wail of flutes and the clatter of cymbals. The demented old grandfather of Abner the potter, perhaps. He had been near death for days. Jonathan felt only a momentary qualm for failing in his obligation to the dead, for he had scarcely known the old man. And to his mood of the moment the sounds of mourning seemed as remote as if coming from another world.

When should he surprise her? Tonight, after the lamps had been lighted and the door shut and barred? No, it would be all he could do to wait until his hands could lower the basket, his awkward fingers untie the packet.

"Lilah!" he cried out eagerly even before setting foot in the courtyard.

The silence seemed louder than the sound of his voice.

She had gone with the other women, of course, to chant and wail in the funeral procession, walking in front of the wicker bier as was the custom in Galilee because, so the rabbis said, it was women who had introduced death into the world. She would be back soon, setting the heavy basket on the floor of the courtyard, which, considering Lilah's dislike of housekeeping, looked strangely neat. She will be here, he kept telling himself as he slipped off his sandals, wiped his dripping face on an end of his headcloth, and went into the house.

But he knew it was not so. Even before he felt the clean-swept emptiness. Even before he saw the carefully banked fire, the clean coat and headcloth laid neatly on the pile of bed rolls, the low table spread with a clean cloth and set for one person with a dish of small flat loaves and a bowl of fresh milk.

11

NAZARETH WAS LIKE a sea after storm. Though the fierce winds had died, tides of emotion still ran high. Afterward, those who felt shame for the act committed on that second day after the wind made this their excuse.

"It was *Sherkiyeh*," they muttered. "It put heat into a man's blood, made him do things…"

Or, "Seeing that blind child lying there so innocent in the wicker basket, it did something to you. Made you want—to punish somebody!"

Or, "It was for Jonathan we did it, I guess. The look on his face when he stood there!"

If the town had gone back to work on that morning after the storm, the tide would slowly and naturally have subsided. But scarcely had the potter begun to wedge and knead his wet clay or the goldsmith to liven his fire with his goat-skin bellows than the new excitement was noised abroad. Women on their way to the fountain turned back, jars still empty. Farmers bound for field or orchard or vineyard heard the news and hastened to change their courses. Tongues were the only tools that did not remain idle.

"What's that? Jered has called the elders together, you say?"

"But why on the steps of the synagogue? Why not on the elders' platform?"

"A grievous offense it must be, one that merits dire punishment, perhaps even *Cherem!*"

"Murder? Perhaps someone saw the blind boy pushed—!"

"They say Jonathan's wife could not be found last night. Suppose—"

"Has anyone heard who—"

"Ay, that's the question! Who—"

Who!

The word set rhythm to their pace, like a drumbeat, as the entire town with few exceptions moved toward the synagogue.

One exception was Deborah, who, when the women had left her courtyard at dawn, shut and bolted the outer door behind them, then, retreating again into the dim airless room, closed and locked the inner door also, pushing the crossbolt into the socket of the doorpost with the energy born of hopeless grief.

Another was Miriam.

"You look pale," Joseph said worriedly as he made ready to obey Jered's summons. "And no wonder, after these two days! When you come from the fountain, return home and remain here. A court of judgment is no place for a woman."

Her relieved eyes thanked him. "Or for a boy?" she queried hopefully.

His lips tightened. "A man, a son of the Law, is always present to do his duty in the congregation."

Another exception was a Roman mercenary, the sole representative for the moment of a small detachment of soldiers stationed to keep order in the town. His comrades had been summoned to the neighboring capital to augment the king's personal guard during the visit of a foreign dignitary. Having employed the unaccustomed liberty in late night dissipation, the soldier was late in rising. Roused from his mat on the barracks housetop by the noise, he stumbled to the parapet and stared down.

Gods of his native Phrygia, not another parade! After a dust storm and a funeral this should be a day of quiet and hard labor. The captain, counting on it, had left him to keep order alone. But he should have known! You couldn't depend on these excitable Jews for anything, least of all quiet! Get them moving in a crowd like this, and anything might happen!

"Jove blast them with his thunderbolt!" he swore expressively, in imitation of his captain.

What to do? Ride to Sepphoris for reinforcements? And get himself berated, likely, for making an incipient riot out of a simple morning trip to the synagogue! No, it was only a short ride to the capital. Better to wait and watch developments from this vantage point. Or, better yet, to shut himself up in the barracks with a tray of fresh dates and a flagon of wine, as far from the infernal noise as possible!

Who! What!—

The questions beat an accompaniment to the Boy's thudding feet. Somebody must have committed a grave offense indeed, for the elders to be summoned to pass judgment at the synagogue. Only once in his memory had there been a similar occurrence, when a farmer named Malluch had been accused of secretly digging a grain pit in his house, lining it with stones, and filling it with newly threshed wheat, all on the Sabbath. Malluch had been pronounced *Niddui*, had been banned from the synagogue for thirty days, and his humiliation had been so great that he had left town soon after, never to return.

It was impossible to get near the synagogue. Tall though he was, the Boy felt submerged in the crowd. Whichever way he tried to move, he encountered an impenetrable blockade of beards and stout backs and rough coat sleeves and dangling headcloths. The air was so hot and fetid he could scarcely breathe.

"Ho, son of Joseph!" It was Tubal, the innkeeper, his round face almost on a level with the Boy's own. "Can't see a thing, can you? Neither can I. What say we get together? I'll be the platform, and you be the eyes."

Dropping to all fours amid indignant protests, the innkeeper made of himself a substantial hillock, and the Boy climbed nimbly upon it, steadying himself by a nearby shoulder. He took several deep breaths and a long look about before stepping down. Grunting, the hillock righted itself.

"Well? Did you see who?"

The Boy shook his head soberly. "Just the elders," he replied. "Ten of them, sitting on the broad stone step in front of the synagogue."

"Ten. Good." The round face lengthened into grim lines. "It takes ten to pronounce a person *Cherem*. But if it's something to do with that blind boy dying, somebody who pushed him, maybe, *Cherem* isn't enough. I know what it is to lose a son. I'd kill the scoundrel!"

The Boy's eyes were wide. "But nobody pushed Joel. He fell."

"Maybe he did. Maybe he didn't. There've been queer things going on in this town the last two days, and somebody ought to suffer for them. Nobody ever paid the price for my son's death," the innkeeper added grimly.

Instinctively the Boy drew away and, when an opening appeared in the crowd, slipped through it. There was something vaguely frightening in Tubal's face, like leaves turned inside out before a rising wind.

"Jonathan—"

He looked about eagerly for his friend. Jonathan, at least, would be his usual dependable self, no matter what winds might blow. But the words were being spoken of the son of Benjamin, not to him.

"Gone. Vanished like the morning dew. He came back sometime between noon and sunset and found the house empty. Clean too. Sure sign she had it all planned beforehand."

"I'm not surprised. The daughter of Abner had roving eyes."

"—heard that Greek peddler was gone too."

"Ha! That explains it. He always had an eye for the daughter of Abner."

"By the holy altar, if I were Jonathan, I'd have his blood!"

"*His!* What about *hers?* By the Law of Moses, if it were my woman—!"

The Boy felt sick. Somehow he wormed and twisted his way out of the crowd until he was at the far edge of the bare sloping space surrounding the synagogue. He wanted to get away as far as possible from the cruel tongues, the curious, gloating faces. But he could not escape. He came face to face with a stone wall.

Leaning his shoulders and the back of his head against it, he closed his eyes and tried to shut out the blur of shifting faces, the discordant voices, but he could not escape knowledge of what was happening. The ripple of excitement told him when the chief elder rose from his seat, the startled gasp when the accused was brought before the platform, the expectant hush when the two witnesses appeared to present their evidence. And even though he was too far away to hear the charges, the news of them came swelling to the edges of the crowd like ripples from a stone cast into a pool.

"By heavens, it's the woman!...See her, all dressed up like a painted Jezebel?...Caught in the very act, so that Hanan says, though I wouldn't trust his word...Not just Hanan, Jonathan is the other witness!...Jonathan, you say? There's justice for you!...I'd take Jonathan's word, no matter what he said, he wouldn't lie...*Ay yah!* No wonder he wants to see her punished!...See him there, right of the platform? Face like a mask of stone...Hist! Let's hear what the elders say."

Flattening his slim body against the wall and using his lowered head as a wedge, the Boy managed to work his way along the edge of the crowd until he reached a narrow lane between two houses. He hastened through it and into another to a dead end, then jumped for the low-hanging branch of an olive tree and pulled himself up to the next higher level. Then, following a maze of little alleys, he scaled walls and stairs and housetops leading from terrace to terrace up the steep hillside. Accustomed though he was to climbing, his throat swelled painfully and his breath came in short gasps.

Ay yah! Here he was at last, on the high ledge of limestone overlooking the synagogue area. Worming his way out to the rim of the ledge, he could see all that was happening in the open space below. He had lain here often beside one of his schoolmates and chuckled to see their mystified comrades hunting for them in a game of hide-and-seek. But he was not chuckling now. His eyes sought out the figure crouched in the open space before the platform.

Not Lilah! The tension of his body melted in relief, then froze again. Not Lilah—*Mulcah!* The sight of her kneeling there on the ground, apart from the crowd, was like a stabbing pain. She looked so beautiful in her shimmering gown, like the bright flame of a candle—and so alone!

He could hear now what was being said, as Jered, rising again from the chief elder's seat, raised his voice to surmount the excited murmurings.

"The elders have heard the evidence and are ready to pass judgment. But, lest there should be doubt in the congregation of the defendant's guilt, let the second witness repeat his story. Hear, men of Nazareth, the testimony of Jonathan, the son of Benjamin."

The Boy stared unbelievingly as Jonathan, his face grim and tortured, rose slowly from his seat at the right of the platform. He opened his lips, then closed them, cast his eyes once, desperately, about the tight-enclosing circle, as if searching for a means of escape. When finally he began speaking, the words seemed torn from him, against his will. He—he had been walking last night, late, on the path overlooking the inn, and—

"How late?" demanded Jered bluntly.

Jonathan turned to stare at him, hostility blazing in his eyes, his hands clenching at his sides. A choking sound burst from his lips.

"How late?" repeated Jered. "Surely the son of Benjamin *has not forgotten*—"

As suddenly as it had blazed into being, the flame of hostility died. To the Boy's incredulous dismay he saw his friend's features harden, become cold and impassive as a stone. When Jonathan spoke again, it was with slow precision, like a man in a stupor.

How late? He did not know. The town had been asleep. It might have been midnight—or even early morning. *Ah hah!* Here emotion briefly flared again. How could a man know when he had been walking—walking—

Heads nodded, and tongues clicked in ready sympathy. Easy to understand, that, a man in Jonathan's plight walking and walking.

"Go on," said Jered with satisfaction.

Lapsing into the strange stupor again, Jonathan continued. The houses of the town had been dark, even the inn. All but one. In that one, high above the inn, a light had burned. Music had sounded. He had seen a dark figure creeping up the path, entering. Anger had stirred him. It was such lawlessness which gave Nazareth a bad reputation. He had seen another man walking. Hanan. They had entered the house. They had found the two there, together. In the confusion the woman's companion had fled. But the woman they had brought here, to expose her sin to the elders and the congregation that—that she might be punished—

Jonathan's voice broke on the word. But there was no need for him to finish. Again heads nodded, and tongues buzzed approvingly. Easier still to understand how a man betrayed by one woman should seek vengeance on another. Yes, and by all their combined heads and beards, they would help him get it! The buzzing swelled to excited babbling, the babbling to an insistent clamor.

"*Ay yah!* Punish the daughter of iniquity!"

"Show her what the righteous do to sinners!"

"We know how to punish. We don't need the elders to tell us!"

The Boy stared and listened in agony and bewilderment. Was there nobody in all the crowd to speak one word for Mulcah, to tell how lonely she had been and how hard she had tried to make friends, to explain *why?* Jonathan? Joseph? But Jonathan, her accuser, was still standing as if turned to stone. And Joseph was sitting in his place among the elders, frowning and impatiently drumming his blunt fingers on his knee, obviously anxious to get the matter over with and return to his carpentering.

"Listen!" the Boy cried out suddenly. "listen to me—*please*—"

But his voice might have been a reed pipe blowing into a high wind.

Even Jered found it difficult to make himself heard. "Hear, men of Nazareth! Silence, I tell you!" Finally he lost patience. "Quiet, fools!" he shouted. "Listen to your elders' verdict. Let the woman be given forty strokes of the lash, then let her be driven from the town and banished from it forever, even as Hagar—"

But he also might have been speaking to the wind—not the gentle, predictable cleanser from the west, but *Sherkiyeh*, blowing hot and harsh from the desert of their ancestors. Tomorrow the fever would pass and they would become again like the west wind, mild, docile, obedient. But today...

"We know the Law of Moses," someone shouted hoarsely. "Let her be stoned with stones until she is dead!"

The storm quickened to fury.

"Ay! It's Moses we follow, not the elders!"

"Stone her, stone her!"

Jered gazed with horror into the unfamiliar faces. It was he who would be held responsible for the administration of justice. To a certain limit the towns of Galilee were permitted to render and enforce their own judgments, according to their religious codes. Flogging, excommunication, banishment, even mutilation—all were within the elders' prerogatives to administer. But not death! A stoning might well cost him his position as chief elder. In fact, he had had trouble explaining to the snooping captain that incident of the son of Old Simon last spring, when only a few stones had been flung.

In a panic he cast his eyes about, searching for the flash of sunlight on a Roman spear or helmet. Heaven knew there were usually plenty of the hated symbols! But today the only glittering blades were thrusts of the morning sun against white limestone. He tried again.

"Men of Nazareth! Fools! Have you lost your senses? In the name of our fathers, listen!"

The men of Nazareth listened, and in the name of their fathers, but not to Jered. The voices they heard belonged to men whose flesh, bitten by desert sands, had never felt soft garments, who had worn no rings on their fingers.

She shall be stoned with stones, her blood shall be upon her!

So shall you purge the evil from the midst of you!

I shall judge you as women who break wedlock. They shall bring up a host against you, they shall stone you and cut you to pieces with their swords.

Helpless, the chief elder stood and watched a wave of the crowd surge forward, engulf the kneeling figure, sweep it away on its crest.

He could no more have stopped them than he could have stopped *Sherkiyeh* the day before.

The Phrygian mercenary looked up stupidly at the serving boy refilling his flagon with wine and his ears with the latest gossip. His wits, always a bit slow and now further dulled by wine, stumbled in wake of the boy's chatter.

"So," he grinned hazily, "the whole town is parading to the burial place outside of town, and a woman is being stoned to death. Listen, slavey, you're only one day behind the times. It was yesterday we had the funeral parade, and it was a boy, not a woman, and he fell on the stones, not—" the fog cleared slowly. "What's that you say? A woman—!"

Jumping from his seat so hastily that he tipped over the freshly filled flagon, the soldier rushed into the courtyard, cleared the stairs to the housetop two steps at a time. The barracks, built at one end of the inn and projecting far out over its roof, commanded a clear view of the lower town and its burial ground. What he saw brought pallor to his florid face and sent him stumbling back down the stairs to the courtyard of the inn, where he mounted a horse and went clattering down the road leading through the hills to Sepphoris.

12

THE BOY dug his fingers so hard into the jutting shelf of rock that flakes of whiteness appeared beneath his palms—bits, not of limestone, but of his own nails. Warmth trickled from his tight lips through his clenched teeth.

For a long time he lay still, unable to move.

Then he was on his hands and knees, crawling back along the ledge of rock; on his feet again, he flew along the path edging the high terrace, downward through the maze of housetops and stairs and alleys, dropping finally by the branch of the olive tree into the narrow dead-end lane. But now he found the adjoining alley choked with people, all like himself seeking a short cut through the town to the slope of the hill below. To his dismay he found himself caught in the sluggish stream, unable to move except at a snail's pace, a wall on one side of him and townsmen before and behind.

"*Ah hah!* Just my luck!" Benjamin's voice, always a little tired and peevish. "Think you have a bright idea, and somebody else gets it first! We'd be there now if we'd taken the main street."

"But think how much energy you're saving," his neighbor Eliah said good-naturedly. "And surely that lameness in your arms you're always complaining about would never let you fling a stone!"

"My father should have a chance to fling stones if anyone should," retorted one of Benjamin's sons hotly. "Don't forget what another woman just did to my brother."

"At least Jonathan won't be cheated of his rights," threw in Tubal grimly. "It's the duty of the accuser to fling the first stone!"

In spite of the little tunnel's stagnant heat, the stones of the wall felt cold to the Boy's fingers. The stream flowed with agonizing slowness. If he could not somehow move faster, he would be too late. Spying an opening below a white-draped elbow, he slipped into it, leaving his headcloth dangling from a metal inkhorn projecting from its owners girdle.

"Here, boy, you lost something. Ah! It's you, Jeshua, my dear pupil. Why so fast, lad? Are you so zealous for the Law that you can't wait to help them fling their stones?"

The Boy looked up into the gentle face of his teacher, Ben Arza. The usually florid cheeks haloed by the short gray locks and forked beard looked drawn and pale, the eyes above them as bewildered and concerned as his own.

"Oh, no, sire," he protested eagerly. "I don't want to help them. I—I want to stop them."

The rabbi smiled sadly. "Stop them! *You?*"

The Boy flushed. "I—I didn't mean I thought I *could* stop them, sire. I just thought somebody ought to—to try—" An inspiration suddenly came to him. He seized his teacher's coat sleeve, looking up eagerly into his face. "But surely you could stop them, master! You're the rabbi. They would listen to you!"

He saw color mount into the pale cheeks, felt the muscles of the white-draped arm grow tense beneath his fingers.

"Yes, son, I—suppose they would. But it probably would do no good. If—if I only had the courage—"

The Boy's heart thudded. "I'll stay beside you," he blurted excitedly. "I know I wouldn't be much help but no matter what happens, I promise not to run away." Suddenly, looking into the anguished eyes, he knew that it was not only for Mulcah's salvation he was pleading, but for Ben Arza's. "Couldn't—couldn't we just try?"

Dismayed, he felt the tensed muscles slowly relax. The rabbi shook his head.

"The elders tried," he said regretfully. "And—who knows? Perhaps the crowd is wiser than the elders. After all, it is the Law of Moses."

"But"—the Boy's eyes continued to plead—"it's Mulcah I'm thinking about, not the Law. She may be killed!"

"Suppose she is," returned Ben Arza gently. "She has sinned, you know, and who are we to pass judgment? Men wiser than you and I wrote the Law." Turning his troubled gaze on his pupil, the rabbi laid his sensitive hand on the uncovered head. "Don't look so concerned, lad. You've always been too—anxious about some things, too much for your own good. When—if—you live to be as old as I, you'll have learned long since that the crowd usually knows best. At least, the wise man lets it have its way."

The Boy's tortured eyes looked straight into his. "Isaiah didn't think so," he reminded him soberly. "Nor Amos."

The rabbi turned away his gaze. "Ah," he said, "so they didn't. But—they didn't live to be as old as I."

The tunnel spewed its human flood into bright sunlight. Just below, on the stony hillside, was the burial ground, its rock tombs streaked with whitewash from the spring festival, on one edge of it the bare, circular space still known after generations of disuse as "the stoning place."

The crowd took one look and burst into an angry confusion of sound.

"*Ah hah!* They're there ahead of us!"

"Beard of Joshua, look at the stones fly!"

"Accursed woman! A pity it couldn't be a Roman!"

"Come on! Still plenty of stones…"

"*Ay yah!* In the name of Jehovah and of his servant Moses!"

They streamed down the hill, stooping to gather stones as they went, fitting them to their palms with an ease half forgotten through the centuries, shouting slogans hoarsely reminiscent of desert sands and smoking mountains.

The Boy stood and watched them, all the warmth draining slowly from his body. A hand touched his shoulder.

"Put on your headcloth, lad," said Ben Arza gently. "You can't see too far without it."

13

"WHERE are we going?" asked the child anxiously. "To the end of the earth?"

The Boy squeezed the small hand reassuringly. "No, Danny, just over this hill and down again. We're almost there now."

"Why did you pack my clothes in a bundle, Jeshua?"

"Because you may be needing them. Don't you remember what I told you—that your mother had to go away on a long journey, so suddenly that she had no time to tell you? She—she wanted me to take care of you."

"And am I going with her on her long journey?"

"No, little one. Sometime perhaps, but not now."

"Did you see her go, Jeshua?"

"Yes, Danny. I—I saw her."

"And was she wearing her pretty red dress when she went away?"

"Yes, little one."

"She was wearing it last night, and she looked happy again, all laughing instead of crying. Was she happy when she went away, Jeshua?"

"I—I'm afraid not. It was hard for her, having to leave you. But I hope she's happy now."

"I wish she'd waked me up before she went, and kissed me good-by, and—and sung me one more song!"

"Listen to me, Danny." The Boy was on his knees beside the small figure, smoothing back the fluff of short hair, wiping away the tears. "Lift up your face—this way—to the sun. Feel how warm it is on your cheeks and lips, just like your mother's kiss?"

There was a long silence, as the tight-closed eyes and quivering lips strained upward. Then the small head nodded.

"And now listen. Listen hard, little one. Hear that lark up there?" Doesn't it sound sweet, like your mother's voice, singing a lullaby?"

The brown eyes shone through their tears. "Yes, Jeshua, yes, I hear her!"

"You see?" said the Boy. "She's not far away. She couldn't go far because"—he lifted his own eyes with startled awareness—"because she loved you too much."

They went on to the top of the hill and down the other side.

Gad, hunched in his strip of shade against the west wall of the stone hut, watched them come. His old-young features, usually alight at sight of his one friend, remained expressionless, eyes fixed with hostile fascination on the child Daniel. This was a Gad whom the Boy had never seen before, neither man nor child, but animal, wary and defensive, crouched ready to spring. One big hand, man-size, moved out to encircle the neck of an earthen water jar beside a basket of loaves and a bowl of milk.

The Boy caught his breath in dismay. It had not occurred to him that the cripple might resent the child's presence. Dropping Danny's hand and tensing himself to leap in front of him at the slightest hostile motion, the Boy crept cautiously forward until his body was between the child and the cripple.

"*Shalom*, Gad," he spoke soothingly. "See, it's your friend Jeshua."

But the son of Old Simon was not to be diverted. Giving his friend a cursory grunt of welcome, he peered around him at the new visitor, muttering ominous sounds and clutching the water jar.

Yet, strangely enough, Danny was not frightened. Before the Boy knew what was happening, the child was close beside the cripple, squatting on all fours and peering into the neck of the jug.

"Water?" he guessed hopefully. "Danny's thirsty."

The Boy endured a moment of agonized suspense. His first impulse was to snatch the child away. Instead he stood waiting, nerves strained to an aching tautness. Slowly the big hand unknotted, reached out, stroked the short brown hair with a clumsy tenderness; the wary eyes softened, then quickened with intelligence; the twisted lips burst into a delighted grimace.

"Whee ighugh angh," they babbled.

The Boy drew a long breath. "Yes," he said gently. "He is, isn't he? 'Sweet little lamb.' But better even than a lamb, Gad. A little brother. One who needs you to take care of him."

211

The big hands carefully poured water from the jug into a gourd and held it with steady fingers for the child to drink; then, tearing off bits of bread from one of the round, flat loaves and dipping them in the bowl of milk, he fed them with the utmost gentleness into the small mouth.

"Gad's little brother," the Boy heard him repeat again and again.

He watched with wide-eyed wonder. Dropping awkwardly to all fours and lifting himself to an upright position by thrusting his fingers into the wall crevices, Gad balanced himself precariously for a moment, then walked unsteadily but without support around the corner of the house. The Boy started forward to keep him from falling, for the cripple had not walked without assistance since being driven from the synagogue. But he checked the impulse. Presently Gad reappeared, still on his feet, hands filled with some tiny wooden sheep, which the Boy had once carved for him, and with eager garbled sounds proffered them to the child.

Danny laughed delightedly. "Lambs!" he exclaimed. "I know now what you're saying, Gad. 'Sweet little lambs.' "

Side by side they squatted on the ground, the old-young man and the young-old child, the big fingers skillfully creating a sheep-fold out of stones and earth, assisting the small ones with infinite patience to lower the tiny rod to just the right level as each member of the flock entered, that it might be counted; to hold the bit of a shepherd's crook at just the right place under a little wooden belly so that the sheep might be pulled out of a hole or helped over a rough place.

It's because he cares so much, thought the Boy wonderingly. Already he loves Danny so much that he's forgotten about himself. That's what made him walk.

His pulses suddenly began to hammer. Suppose—suppose he was to care that way about Gad, so much that he forgot all about himself? His head swam. To share with that poor hunched body some of his own straightness, to reshape those twisted lips! For a moment it seemed possible.

The moment passed, leaving him empty and shaken, staring helplessly at Gad, still hunched and twisted, squatting on the ground. And yet, perhaps, *if one could only care enough...*

Leaving the child with Gad, the Boy went in search of Old Simon.

212

When he found him, the shepherd's back was toward him. The older man was sitting on a rock half-way down the slope, his flock scattered over the hillside like bits of wool lint blown on the brisk sea wind.

The Boy went on down the hill, wondering how near he could approach before the keen shepherd ears would become alerted, amazed to find himself within a half dozen steps of the motionless figure. He could see now the uplifted hands, knotted, grimy, clamped rigidly about the slender silver vase, the closed eyes and gaunt profile half hidden in a gray tangle of hair and beard. Dismayed, he drew back noiselessly, retraced his steps up the slope until he was a long stone's throw away.

"*Shalom!*" he called. "Simon! I'm here again. *Shalom!*"

As he approached, noisily this time, the old shepherd barely changed his position, merely turned his head just far enough to let his gaze clear the concealing folds of headcloth.

"Stop!" he cried hoarsely when the Boy was just a little over four cubits away. "Don't come any closer!"

"But"—though he obeyed, the Boy looked puzzled and distressed—"why? Don't you remember? That doesn't matter to us any more. Now that we know God has forgiven you."

"We don't know it. Not any longer." The reply was harsh. "Don't come any nearer, I tell you!"

Miserably the Boy dropped to his knees a little farther down the hill, where he could peer up into the shepherd's face. "But—the frankincense—don't you remember? When we burned it, how the Presence was all about?"

"Yes, yes, of course I remember. I thought God was there, and my sins were forgiven."

"Not there, Simon. *Here*. Can't you feel him?"

"I thought I could—when I smelled the fragrance."

"Then burn it again, Simon! You promised you would if the doubts came."

"I have burned it!" cried the shepherd despairingly. "Again and again. It's all gone!"

"Gone?" For a moment the Boy was speechless, then his thoughts found words. "But the Presence isn't gone. He's here, Simon. Can't you feel him—in the cooling wind—the healing sun?"

The old man shuddered. "The sun doesn't heal. It shrivels and scorches. And the wind—cooling? With the sands of *Sherkiyeh* still gritting in my teeth?" Letting the slender vessel slip through his palms, he closed grimy fingers about the coiling handles. "I—did feel it—once. I thought perhaps it might come again—if I held this in my hands."

"It will come, Simon. Try just once more."

"I have tried." Abruptly the grimed hands extended the vase. "Here. It's yours. I have no further use for it. Take it."

"No." The wide eyes were dark with misery. "You keep it. Maybe—maybe if you take it outdoors some morning, early, and sit very still with the birds singing and the smell of sweet earth all around you—"

They lapsed into silence, the old man motionless on the bare rock and the Boy crouched beneath in the parched grass, and for a while it was so still that they could hear the faint tapping of hoofs against earth and stones, the munching of patient jaws, even the swish-swash of a fat tail being dragged over dry leaves and pebbles.

The Boy suddenly exclaimed and sat up straight. He had forgotten all about little Daniel! Hastily he recounted to Old Simon the story of the day's happenings, all except his visit to the stone hut. The old shepherd listened grimly.

"Ha! Kinder they were this time, weren't they? A stoning is soon over, while *Cherem* is for life. Yes, the people of Nazareth are becoming more tenderhearted every day. Maybe the time will come when they'll really show mercy to their victims, merely thrust them into a furnace or throw them over a cliff... What's that you say? You've brought the woman's child here?"

"There was no one to take care of him," explained the Boy with desperate earnestness. "I couldn't take him home."

"Hardly!" grunted Old Simon with a twist of his lips. "The son of a harlot in the house of the righteous Joseph? So you brought the little outcast here, hoping he could find shelter with another outcast."

"No!" The Boy's voice rang out in swift protest. "Hoping he could be loved here and be happy. Hoping"—his tone softened—"the lamb might have a shepherd to take care of him."

Old Simon rose abruptly. "Let's see him."

It was not far back to the hut, and the shepherd decided that for once it would be safe to leave the sheep. Calling the flock together into a grassy hollow on the stony slope, he issued a sharp staccato command to the leaders.

Danny had fallen asleep in the thin shade edging one side of the hut, a spindly arm thrust out into the hot sun to encircle the flock of wooden sheep. Close beside him in the sun crouched Gad, head lowered and big arms spread wide apart, eying the approach of the Boy and his father with the watchful belligerence of a mother protecting its young. Old Simon looked from one to the other with eyes suddenly aglow.

"So that's the way it is."

He stood looking down at the child for a long moment, then gently lifted the thin arm and moved it into the shade.

"Guess I can't do any harm, touching *him*," he murmured gruffly.

The movement caused the child to stir, and he sat up rubbing his eyes and looking frightened. The Boy quickly reassured him.

"See, little one. This is Simon the shepherd. Remember, I told you about him? He takes care of real sheep, not toy ones."

"You like sheep, son?" asked the old man softly.

"Oh yes, sir." The thin face lighted. "Better than anything, almost, except my mother, and Jeshua."

"Listen, son." The grimy hand smoothed back a drift of brown hair. "How would you like to have a lamb of your own?"

The huge eyes were incredulous. "My own?"

"Your very own. Yours to name, yours to take care of, not just once in a while, but every day. If you're going to live with Old Simon and Gad—that is, while your mother is away—you'll have to learn to be a shepherd. What say? Shall we go down to the flock and pick one out?"

The child put his hand in Old Simon's and the two started off together.

When they had gone a few steps, a sound of helpless frustration burst from Gad's throat. With fascination, the Boy watched the crouching figure hunch awkwardly along the ground for a few arm's lengths, hoist itself unsteadily, then stand shakily for a few breathless moments before starting off with lumbering but determined steps in their wake.

"Wait!" he called excitedly. "Gad is coming too!"

Old Simon turned, stared incredulously, then stumbled back toward his son, arms outstretched.

As the Boy returned to Nazareth along the terrace path, he felt a deep happiness he could not entirely explain.

14

JUST TWO MORE THINGS he must do before going home.

The little house still smelled of newness. All Jonathan's rubbing with oil and polishing with handfuls of raw wool could not wipe the fragrance of fresh wood from the stout cypress doors and crossbeams. And the reeds and branches and thistles forming the roof foundation still smelled like reeds and branches and thistles.

After they had been soaked by their first rains, the smell would be that of musty straw.

In the courtyard the Boy heard the sounds first—shuddering sobs which bore no more kinship to weeping than deep ocean currents to little lapping waves. Then, as his eyes became used to the dimness of the inner room, he saw the figure hunched in one corner, face buried in its outflung arms, half kneeling, half sprawled on the pile of neatly rolled sleeping mats. For a long time he hesitated; then, crossing the room, he gently touched one of the heaving shoulders.

Jonathan lifted a haggard face, his eyes dry as tinder. For a moment they held no recognition.

"Let me alone—don't touch—for God's sake, go! Ah! It's you, Jeshua. I should have known. Who else in this town would care? Yes, you too—go away and leave me. You're too young for—this. A man should not take a boy with him into hell. Go away, I tell you!"

The Boy did not go away. Neither did he speak, merely stood quietly with his hand on the hunched shoulder. And presently the shuddering subsided a little. He could feel the rigid shoulder relax a little.

"I can't go away," he said at last, "when my friend is unhappy."

The agony of the tensed lips finally found release in words.

"My fault. All mine." Jonathan wielded the short phrases like strokes of a lash. "I drove her away. She told me the truth. I didn't believe her. I tore the beautiful thing she wanted. Trampled on it. Burned it. And that's not the worst. I helped to kill that other. Like doing it to my own beloved. God have mercy on us all!"

He choked out the story, and the Boy listened silently, distress tempered by relief when he learned that his friend had not willingly testified against the woman Mulcah but had been forced to do so under the terms of his agreement with Jered.

"I had no idea that was what he meant," explained the young farmer miserably. "I was to walk about the inn—watch for lawbreakers—one of his servants with me. I just walked—and walked. Then Hanan came and said I was to go with him, he had found something that looked suspicious. He took me to—to her house. I didn't want to go in, but he said I must. Jered's orders. After we had—had found them there and that fellow Gebal had escaped and—and the servant had taken her away, we went to Jered's house. He said I'd have to witness. My duty as a good Israelite. But I knew what he meant. Part of our agreement. He had it all planned. But—not the stoning! I swear to that! She was just to be flogged—run out of town—" Fire flared suddenly in his eyes. "By the holy altar, I swear I didn't know!"

The Boy wiped the drops of sweat from his friend's forehead. "Of course you didn't."

Jonathan shivered as if he had a chill. "They—made me throw the first stone—put it in my hand! I can feel it now. Round at one end, sharp at the other. I—threw it hard but—too far. Much too far. I swear it didn't hit—"

There was little more the Boy could do. But he saw the clean coat and headcloth, laid out carefully on the cedar chest, and, bringing a basin of water from the brimming jars near the door, he washed the haggard face, the grimed hands and feet, and, like a mother dressing a helpless child, managed to get the soiled garments removed and the clean ones in place. He found the ten loaves wrapped in a napkin in the earthen jar, and some fresh dates, and a pat of goat's-milk cheese in a covered wooden bowl, fresh as if made only that morning. Finally he persuaded Jonathan to eat a few mouthfuls. And all at once he knew that there was something else he could give his friend.

"She was thinking of you," he said, "even while she was getting ready to go away. See? She made sure there were coals in the stove and banked them carefully. She must have gone to the well for you, all the jars are full of water. And she put out a clean coat and headcloth, and wrapped the bread in a napkin so it would stay fresh longer."

Then it was that the flames raging through the tinder of Jonathan's eyes were extinguished by a flood of tears.

***

Just one more errand now.

When he came to the stoning place and found it looking just as usual, rocks strewn helter-skelter over the barren hillside, so great was the Boy's relief that he sank down on the ground, trembling. Just what he had expected to find he had not admitted even to himself. He had known only that he must come.

A Roman captain was pacing the ground not far away, closely followed by a swarthy young mercenary. The former was talking in loud angry tones, and, though he spoke in Greek, the Boy understood most of what was said.

"I should have your head for this! Getting us away over here from Sepphoris—making us miss the king's parade! A stoning indeed!"

"But there *was*, sir, I swear it! I saw it from the barracks roof. Half the town was out here flinging stones. Yes, and I could see the woman too. She wore a dress of the color of fire—"

"Idiot! If you saw fire, it was in your own wine cups."

"No, no sir. I saw her being stoned. By my life I swear it!"

The captain spat. "At the moment your life isn't worth swearing by." He prodded among the stones with the point of his spear. "But there is blood spattered about on the rocks, I'll have to admit. Fresh blood. Though how you can prove it's a woman's and not a sheep's?"

"It was a woman, sir! Ask any of these accursed Nazarenes. There, ask him, ask the boy!" The mercenary raised his voice and gestured curtly. "Come here!"

The Boy rose slowly to his feet. He felt cold all over. They were going to ask him what he knew about the stoning. If he told them, he would get the whole town in trouble. Yet if he spoke an untruth, he would be violating one of Joseph's and Ben Arza's sternest precepts. Better, perhaps, if he pretended ignorance of Greek and said nothing. Yet he had already revealed some knowledge of it by heeding the mercenary's command.

"Hurry, you snail, or I'll prick your heels with my spear!" The soldier took pleasure in venting his own humiliation on another. "There now! Can you speak Greek?"

"A little, sir."

"Then tell the captain all you know about the stoning."

"I'm sorry, sir. I saw no stoning."

"B-but"—the swarthy face turned angry crimson—"you must have! You can't tell me a red-blooded boy like you would have stayed away! By that insufferable god of yours, if you're lying—"

"I am not lying, sir. If there was a stoning here, I did not see it."

"What did they do with the body?" demanded the captain abruptly.

The Boy's pulses quickened. This man was keener of eye, swifter of intellect. But he dared not hesitate to think. "I do not know, sir," he said frankly.

"Ah! But you do know there was a body? And a stoning?"

The Boy regarded the captain steadily. "Can one really know, sir," he inquired gravely, "that anything has happened unless one has seen it? And I saw no stoning. I saw no body."

The captain threw back his head and laughed. "Shades of mighty Cicero! You should go to Rome, boy, and study to be a lawyer. With that honest face and that quick tongue, you could confound the devils themselves! Come on, soldier. We'll get no information out of him."

The crestfallen mercenary was loath to leave. "Impudent dog!" he grumbled. "I could get it out of him quick enough with the point of a spear!"

"No." The captain was curt. "Spears are for cowards. Let the boy alone."

The stoning place seemed even emptier after they had gone. The sun, too, had vanished behind the hill, leaving the earth as devoid of light and life as the streaked and faded tombs. The Boy shivered.

It was then that he saw the torn scrap of flame-colored silk caught in a crevice between two rocks. In the same moment the wind seized it and bore it away across the stony hillside, like a thing alive.

15

SUMMER, ALWAYS DREADED for its merciless heat and choking dust, had never flown so quickly. Miriam grudged the passing of each day, each hour.

Working in the courtyard on the new coat and cloak, girdles and headcloths, which the Boy would be taking with him to Jerusalem, she memorized anew each line of the young features bent over adze or saw or chisel, each ripple of hair, incising them on her heart with an even sharper needle than she used for her painstaking embroidery.

"But you can't be doing that for me!" the Boy exclaimed once, fingering a blue and crimson border. "It looks more like a *meil*—a festive robe—than a poor man's *simlah*. I'm just a small town carpenter!"

Joseph lifted his head from his work then and seemed about to speak, and the woman's heart almost stopped beating. *Not yet!* she prayed silently. *Let it be as it has always been just a little longer!* He must have seen her face, for his lips closed, and he bent again to his planing, shaking his head with grave indulgence.

The last late crops of wheat and millet were gathered and the threshing floors swept clean. The gold of the fields in the valley below faded to pale yellow, almost to silver. And then the first early grapes were being gathered, the wine presses on the terraced hillsides alive with music and laughter and agile feet. Children went past the house with their hands and mouths stained crimson, the songs of the vintage bubbling like new wine from their lips. Instead of bundled wheat and flax, the high-poised heads of laborers bore wineskins and baskets of red grapes or figs. At night the surrounding hillsides blossomed into light as lamps were kindled one by one in vineyard watchtowers. Once again the tombs gleamed with fresh whitewash, for another holiday was close at hand, the Feast of Tabernacles.

And then one day Miriam looked up from her work to watch Joseph and the Boy lift a new chest of cedar across the courtyard. Many times before she had watched them lift things together, smiling tenderly to see the man's hands slip surreptitiously along the boards to bear the brunt of the load without hurting the sensitive, boyish pride. Today she noticed that it was the Boy's hands which slipped a little closer to the center, lifting easily, apparently without effort. And when they stood upright, side by side, in the path of the slanting sun, the shadow of the one on the floor of the courtyard was almost as long as the shadow of the other.

She knew then, even more than by the flowing in the winepresses and the kindling of the lamps and the whitewashing of the tombs that the time had come.

"Tomorrow," said Joseph suddenly, when the Boy had gone to the house of Lemuel, their next door neighbor, to borrow a hand cart, "we must tell him."

"Not tomorrow," she replied quietly. "Today."

It was the man now who looked startled, reluctant "Today? *Ay yah!* So be it. But not until we have taken the chest to the house of Obed, the goldsmith. I—would not want to make Lemuel wait for the return of his cart."

She watched them load the chest on the rough two-wheeled conveyance and tie it securely with lengths of soft, torn cloth, which could not mar the smooth surface. Fastening the ropes of twisted hemp about their bodies below the armpits, they guided the cart up the stony lane. Then swiftly she went through the courtyard and into the house.

The stone manger was on the lower level against the farther wall. As the woman bent over it the fragrance of hay filled her nostrils, stabbing at her memory. There had been fresh hay in that other manger long ago.

With trembling hands she pushed the hay aside, fumbled for the edges of the loose stone in the wall and pried it loose. She had to kneel to reach into the opening, for it was low, just the right height for a small child to reach. She remembered the day he had found the stone, grunting and sweating as he tried to pry it loose. She had helped him finally. Crawling into the manger, he had thrust his head and shoulders fearlessly into the hole, laughing excitedly, then laughing again at the hollow sound of his own laughter. Such a small hole, really, and how little he must have been!

"See, Mother, how deep it is! A place to hide all my treasures!"

Trembling now with fear, she reached in her hands and drew out the little cedar chest.

Just so she had held it in her hands on that day weeks before when she had first begun to wonder, the day she had heard those fragments of gossip at the well: "...said he saw that old reprobate Simon sitting on the hillside, and the son of Joseph not more than four paces. He swore there was a strange smell, as if something was burning, like incense."

She had not dreamed it. The little chest was much lighter than it should be. She had lifted the Gifts of the three strangers too many times to forget how heavy they were,

A *thief!* she had conjectured at first, wildly—hopefully. And for many nights following, with Joseph away at Sepphoris and the Boy sleeping soundly, she had lain wide-awake, taut with listening, fingers closed rigidly about the handle of a stone hammer hidden under her mat. But she had known even then that it was not a thief.

Are they really mine, Mother, to do with just as I please?
Why—yes, dear. Yes, of course.

She laid the little chest in the manger, and the hay rustled faintly—just as it had done when the three strangers had laid their Gifts in that other manger, as if murmuring a gentle sigh of surprise and pleasure. But there was no pleasure for her in the sound now, only a dry harshness of foreboding.

Suddenly she caught her breath. Her troubled eyes narrowed. Her fingers reached out and touched the tiny bolt. It slid back easily, having been thrust in not quite far enough to engage the pins. The chest was unlocked!

Hot blood pounded against her temples. With feverish haste she slid the bolt free, inserted her fingernails into the crack between base and cover, felt the lid move upward. Now at least she would know...

Then as suddenly she paused. The feverish haste left her fingers. Carefully she replaced the lid and with a firm gesture thrust the bolt hard into its groove, until she heard the tiny pins of the lock drop into place.

No. She had never pried into the secret recesses of his spirit. Not when he was a baby. Nor when he was a child. Nor when he was a boy. And she would not begin now, when he had become a man.

She replaced the little chest in its niche and after it the loose stone. Then, just before turning away, she rested her hand caressingly, in a fleeting farewell gesture, on the hay in the empty manger.

16

"A SON OF DAVID," thought Joseph with shame and bitterness, "should not have to draw a cart."

He approached the galling task doggedly, proud head subdued, nose to the ground, a war stallion demoted to the duties of a pack ass. Not for himself did he resent the humiliation, but for the noble tradition into which he had been born. It was an insult, he felt, to King David himself.

Clumping along the street, he derived ironic satisfaction from making his heavy sandals sound as much like hoofs as possible. And he looked neither to right nor left, as if by refusing to see he insured himself against being seen.

It was the Boy who had to keep eyes alert, weaving in and out through the tangle of traffic, swerving to avoid hucksters' trays and pushcarts and little mules buried beneath mountainous packs, and pedestrians with towering bundles on their heads, hastily pushing or dragging his father and the loaded cart against a wall to get out of the way of a Roman soldier clattering through town on horseback. Then, indeed, Joseph not only lowered his face but covered it with his headcloth. That the hated usurper should look down from his high horse and see a descendant of the royal house of Israel in a donkey's harness was beyond enduring.

The Boy's cheerful acceptance of the demeaning role was almost as galling as the humiliation itself. He seemed actually to enjoy this enforced kinship with beasts of burden and made it the occasion for accosting every casual acquaintance that he chanced to see.

"*Shalom*, Eben! A good day for pulling stout loads, what say?"

He raised his voice to greet Nathan the vinedresser, bearing a fat skin of new wine atop his head; inquired cheerfully after the health of Hadassah's ailing little one; even urged the slow-moving and garrulous wife of Benjamin to walk beside them and rest her heavy basket on the cart.

But once the chest had been delivered, Joseph straightened himself to his full stature, loosened his headcloth, and again faced the world with pride and dignity. He paid one of Obed's sons two copper coins to take the cart home to Lemuel.

"Come," he said to his son with satisfaction. "What say we go home the long way around, through the market place?"

Joseph felt suddenly expansive, almost exuberant. The long-awaited day had come at last. Overindulgent he had been in pampering his wife's whim for postponing it. Now he would savor his triumph to the full. It was all he could do to keep from breaking the news now, so that the Boy might share his excitement. But, no, that would not be fair to Miriam. She had a right to enjoy those first moments of his wonderment, see the incredulous lighting of his eyes. As he led the way through the market place, Joseph held his shoulders at a proud and rigid angle. Already he could hear the comments that would soon be following them.

"See! That man there, with the tall youth behind him? Joseph, the carpenter. His son is a student in the school of the great Hillel, in Jerusalem."

"Carpenter, you say? I wouldn't have thought it."

"*Ay yah!* Look like a pair of princes, don't they? And no wonder! With the blood of King David himself flowing in their veins!"

The sight of the slender figure standing motionless gazing at the unloading place of a new caravan brought Joseph out of his reverie. He saw that the Boy's eyes were wide with distress.

"Father, look! See what they're doing? They're selling people!"

Joseph followed the Boy s stricken gaze to a confused huddle of camels, donkeys, carts, and noisy bargainers. In the center of the group a stout, well-dressed merchant, whip in hand, was loudly declaiming the assets of his human commodity.

"Naturally," replied Joseph. "They're slave merchants. Why shouldn't they be selling people? You act as if you'd never seen such a sight before!"

"I haven't," returned the Boy miserably.

The man glanced at him sharply. It might be so, at that. Slaves were not a profitable commodity in Nazareth, and the Boy had been only once to Jerusalem. "Don't let it upset you," he said more gently. "They aren't Israelites, you know, that are being sold. Not our people."

"Not—our people?" echoed the Boy faintly.

"No. That ugly fellow on the block right now is an Idumean. Strong as an ox, by the looks, and as dumb. Hide so thick he can't feel the whip. Those blacks are Ethiopians. And I'd wager my best adze the bundle of skin and bones tied to the cart wheel yonder is a Samaritan. Look at him. Muttering like a mad dog! No wonder they have to keep him tied. I wouldn't be surprised to see him gnaw those ropes in two."

"He's so young," murmured the Boy through tight lips. "Not much older than I am. And he looks so—so hot!'

Irritated by the Boy's naiveté, Joseph turned gruffly away to end the conversation. Then turning back, he said, "We've wasted enough time. Let's go."

The Boy was nowhere to be seen. He was not in the narrow lane leading through the brass bazaar, nor on the lower terrace of the market place. With mounting vexation Joseph's gaze swept the arched stables of the inn. Finally he spied the Boy emerging from the fountain stairway, coming slowly along the terrace, a gourd of water held carefully in both hands. He uttered an exclamation. Of all times to choose for going to the well!

The Boy went straight to the scowling young slave tied to the cart wheel and, kneeling beside him, held the gourd to his swollen lips. Then, slipping off his headcloth, he dipped an end of it in the remaining water and began washing the emaciated body. As he bent over, he seemed to be whispering to the slave.

Joseph lunged toward him, his first instinct to drag his son away to safety. But he stopped himself just in time. Better not call attention to the Boy's foolishness. The burly merchant looked quite capable of wielding his whip on both slave and meddler alike. Joseph stood and sweated and prayed that the loud voice would continue its bombast without digression.

"By Isis and Osiris, what's the matter with you Nazarenes! Don't you know a bargain when you see one? Look at those arms, those shoulders, those thighs!" The whip smartly designated each asset of the huge, stolid body. "If you're a goldsmith, he can wield your bellows. With those lungs and chest, you won't need one! If you're a farmer—" The monotonous chant exploded in a roar. *"You there! What are you doing to my slave?"*

Joseph's hands clenched, and he braced himself to intervene.

"Just cooling him and giving him a drink," replied the Boy calmly. "You shouldn't leave him lying in the hot sun. He's half dead from thirst."

The whip whined and cracked as Joseph lurched forward, but the long lash coiled harmlessly about the rim of the wheel. The merchant was too much the opportunist to resent any gratuitous improvement of his property. "Fool Nazarene!" he grumbled. "No wonder your townsmen are too poor to own slaves! Get along with you. That's a bad one you picked to play nursemaid to. Tried to run away. Deserves to burn in the sun. Accursed Samaritan! By that ass-headed god of yours, I won't have him pampered!"

When they were out of the market place and in the lane leading up the hill to the Street of the Carpenters, Joseph was so relieved he could find no words of rebuke. And, after all, the Boy had committed no sin. The Law commended mercy, even to one's enemies. Soon, thank God, he need have no more worries! It would be Hillel's task to answer his troublesome questions and call him to account for his strange actions.

He must have imagined it, thought Joseph, that fleeting impression he had gotten while the Boy was bending over the slave—a sudden brightness, like the brief flashing of sunlight against steel.

17

THE BOY'S FACE shone like all the eight candles of Hanukkah.

"You mean—I am to stay in Jerusalem when we go to the Feast of Tabernacles? I am to—to sit every day at—at the feet of the Venerable One?"

Joseph tried to appear nonchalant. He squinted along the edge of a cedar board, frowned when he discovered it too warped to suit his purpose, and, moving leisurely to the pile in the far corner of the courtyard, exchanged it for another. But he was so excited that he chose one of ash instead of cedar.

"Would you like that, Son?" he asked, smiling.

"Oh—yes! Perhaps Hillel can help me—Father, it was this one you meant to take, wasn't it?" The Boy extracted another board from farther down in the pile, carefully inserting chips of a similar thickness to hold the others flat in their places. He laughed. "Wouldn't it look funny to see a piece of ash in the middle of a cedar table?"

Joseph looked a bit shamefaced. "Ay! Sun must have been in my eyes." Examining the new board from all angles, he could find no fault with it. "Perhaps Hillel can help you do what, my son?"

The Boy laid the ash board back in its place on the pile. "Help me find out how—how to do the work I have to do," he replied slowly.

Joseph shot a look of triumph at Miriam, who sat embroidering on the lowest of the stone steps leading up to the housetop. "Ah! Then you think you have some work to do? Something more important than carpentering?"

"Yes," said the Boy. He turned toward them, his face troubled. "I've—felt it often—inside me. Only—I'm not sure yet—"

"Some special task, perhaps," pursued Joseph eagerly, "to which you feel called as a descendant of the royal house of David? Perhaps"—his hand did tremble now, so that, although he had taken up the saw, he dared not use it—"perhaps even—deliverance for our people?"

The woman cried out sharply. "No, Joseph! Please!"

The man's fingers closed firmly about the saw handle. Tucking his tunic deeper into his girdle, he anchored the cedar board with a stout knee, grasped it firmly with his left hand, and started sawing. The flint teeth bit raspingly into the hard wood. "Amen! So be it! Your mother has always had a queer idea you should be left alone to think things out for yourself. Not my way of thinking. Not the way you train a boy to be a carpenter. But as long as she's got the idea across to you that you have some special!"—he groped for the word—"some special job to do, maybe that's all that matters. We can leave the rest to Hillel and"—he accented each significant word with a firm upward rasping of his saw—"to your duty as a son of David."

The Boy looked even more troubled. He crossed the courtyard slowly. "Don't you want me to go to Jerusalem, Mother? If you don't—"

"Of course I want you to go, my son. It's what your father and I have always planned for you. I only wanted to be sure it was—was what you wanted." She managed a bright smile. "Why did you think I was making you all these fine embroidered clothes? If my son is going to follow in the footsteps of the venerable Hillel and become a great rabbi—"

"Unh unh!" grumbled Joseph. "Now who's trying to make up his mind for him?"

They laughed together, and for a little all movement and sound in the courtyard seemed melded into harmony. The needle flashed in and out of the homespun cloth in rhythm with the cheerful buzzing of the saw. Squatting cross-legged beside the half-finished table, a rubbing stone in his palm, the Boy polished the new surface with long smooth strokes. Behind him the little leaves of the olive tree above the courtyard wall moved gently in the slight breeze.

Only to the woman's ears was there discord in the harmony. Her flying fingers felt cold and stiff. The agitation of the olive leaves seemed born not of ecstasy but of fear. As she lifted her eyes, her apprehension seemed to take shape in a face—thin features, tense, anxious—peering over the wall through the branches. She did not cry out, believing it a figment of her own creation, and almost instantly it disappeared.

There was a sudden pause in the rhythmic grating of the rubbing stone. "But—it costs money to live in Jerusalem, Father. Much money. And didn't you say that we're poorer now than ever before? How—"

The saw severed the board with one decisive upward stroke. Bright dust rose in a haze about the curling gray hair.

"Your mother and I have that all planned, my son. It will be left to you, as I promised her, to make the decision, but I'm sure you'll agree. What other desire could a true son of the Commandment have than to learn more of God's holy Law and to do it?"

"None, Father. None, of course."

"Then bring me the box."

"The—box, Father?"

The woman was unaware of the swift darting of pain as the bone needle jabbed into her finger.

"The little cedar chest I made for your birthday. Remember—you put it in your secret hiding place behind the manger? Bring it to me."

Without a word the Boy rose, crossed the courtyard, and went into the house. The courtyard seemed to hold its breath. The woman sat motionless as stone, heedless of the drop of blood from her finger mingling with the crimson threads of the embroidery pattern. The little leaves had ceased their quivering. Even Joseph, having laid the new cedar board in place on the table top, stood still, regarding the perfect fit of it with satisfaction. Then quietly the Boy returned, the little chest held in his hands.

"*Ay yah!* Good! Put it on the table. Now…is the key still around your neck?"

"Yes, Father."

"Then open it."

Suddenly the woman was beside them, her hand gripped tensely about the man's arm. "Remember, Joseph—the Gifts—they are his, not ours!"

"Ay, of course they're his." He shook off her hand impatiently. "Isn't it for him they're going to be used? What else—"

She knew the moment had come when she heard the thrust of the tiny key, the creak of the lid being raised…then felt the sudden stiffening of his hands and the abrupt dropping of her own. There was no need of looking to see the horror his gaze held. Eyes closed tightly, she stood tensed and waiting.

The silence was even more frightening than the expected outburst. It was like the silence before *Sherkiyeh*. Finally she could bear it no longer. She opened her eyes and looked at him.

He was not angry. Not yet. Before anger could come, there must be comprehension, and as yet only his eyes had discovered the emptiness. And his hands. He stood holding the soft leather bag, fumbling in it with three of his big fingers—all he could get through the narrow opening—finally tipping it upside down and shaking it over the palm of his hand. Even then he did not quite comprehend.

"It's—gone," he muttered huskily, almost without a movement of his lips. "The gold—where—"

The Boy's wide eyes revealed full, agonized comprehension.

"I'm sorry, Father. Truly I am, I—I didn't know—"

"Where—?"

The Boy shifted his weight miserably from one bare foot to the other.

"I—used it, Father. I—I had to. There were so many people in Nazareth who—who needed it, like Deborah—"

"Ah! Deborah!" The wind was rising now, filling the void with comprehension, but as yet there was no fury in it, only a dry harshness. "I—see. So—you were the brother away in Egypt—or the uncle beyond Jordan. And—Jonathan too, of course! That treasure he found in his field! What fools we all were to believe—! And—who knows how many others, probably even less deserving—!" He turned on the woman with mounting bitterness. "*Ah yah!* You've had your way. I always thought he had too much freedom, but you never wanted him curbed. Oh, no! He should be left alone to make up his own mind! Heaven help us, I hope now you're satisfied!"

The Boys lips quivered. He turned from one to the other in growing bewilderment and distress. "You mean I shouldn't have used it?"

Miriam returned slowly to the stairway and, dropping down on the stone step, covered her face with her hands. "Oh, my darling, how—how could you!"

"But—I thought you said it was mine, Mother, to do with just as I chose."

She groaned. "Oh, I did! And it was. But I didn't suppose you would use it for anything like this!"

"But"—the Boy's eyes pleaded with them desperately—"what else could I do? There were people needing it!"

Joseph turned on him with sudden, furious intensity. *"What did you do with the frankincense?"*

The woman moaned softly. It was here now, the moment she had really been dreading.

"We—burned it, Father."

"Burned it!" The man's cry was harsh with incredulity.

The Boy turned to his mother, eagerness momentarily in his eyes. "It did smell like the incense in the Temple, Mother! And like balsam, just as you said it would."

She smiled wanly. "Did it, dear?"

"I thought of you while it was burning, wishing you could smell it."

"So—" there was sand in the teeth of the wind now—"you burned it. You took incense that was worth nobody knows how many shekels an ounce and—burned it. Just to see how it would smell."

"Oh, no, it wasn't for me, Father. It was for Old Simon."

Miriam uttered a little, strangled sound.

"Simon!" Joseph drew his adze from his girdle. "You—say you—burned this incense for—*Old Simon!*"

"Yes, Father. Let me tell you about it, may I? I'll try to make you understand. You see, Old Simon was so unhappy—"

"Of course he was unhappy. Why shouldn't he be?" Joseph's fingers fumbled with the handle of his adze, then closed hard about it. "Is it the purpose of God's judgment to make a man rejoice or to punish him for his evil-doing?"

"I—" The Boy spoke timidly, his eyes very wide and earnest. "I should think it would be to make him good again."

"Good? A man who has been pronounced *Cherem?*" Joseph shuddered. "May the Most Holy One requite him in full for all his sins!"

"Oh, but that's just it!" cried the Boy eagerly. "He hasn't any more sins. That's what I was trying to make him understand when I told him his sins were forgiven."

Joseph looked more stunned than shocked. "You told him— *what?*"

"That his sins were forgiven," repeated the Boy simply.

Closing her eyes, Miriam leaned her head back against the stone wall of the house and clenched her hands tightly over her breasts. Even she, a woman, knew the enormity of the words the Boy had uttered. Nothing he had ever said, no questions he had asked, had compared with this. It was near to blasphemy.

Surely the violence of the storm would break now! She even hoped it would. The waiting was becoming unbearable.

But Joseph's voice when it came was incredibly calm.

"Careful, son. Only God can forgive sins."

"Of course," replied the Boy promptly. 'That's what I meant."

"And you dare to stand there and tell me that God has forgiven the sins of a man whom the elders have pronounced *Cherem?*"

"Yes, Father. I'm sure he has."

Miriam opened her eyes, and there was the face again, peering through the olive branches. This time in the brief moment before it disappeared its eyes met hers, wild and suspicious, the embodiment of her own uncertainty and horror. She shivered. God have mercy! Was it devils she was conjuring now instead of angels?

Then, lowering her eyes, she saw Joseph's face, gaunt, distorted, not with anger as she had expected, but with fear even greater than her own. He was staring at the Boy as if he thought he might be mad or—she shivered again—possessed of a devil!

"You say you know Old Simon's sins have been forgiven. How do you know? Who—who told you?"

"You did, Father," returned the Boy simply.

"I!" Joseph lifted his hands, adze and all, in a gesture of horror.

"Yes. You forgive me when I make mistakes, don't you? You'd forgive me no matter what I did. And you're just an earthly father. You can't be better than God, can you?"

Joseph uttered a cry which was half groan, half curse. "*Ay yah!* God help me! Isn't it enough you're killing every dream I ever had for you? Must you also shame me before the congregation and bring the wrath of the Most Holy One upon your head? In heaven's name—out of my sight before you speak words so blasphemous that even a father must report them to the elders! Is it my son—or a devil within him who speaks? Out of my sight, I say!"

The woman's heart was torn between the two of them: the Boy, huddled miserably just inside the outer doorway, uncertain whether to follow his father's injunction or to attempt somehow to make amends; the man, crouched over his half finished table, head and shoulders bowed to an angle which, for the proud descendant of the royal house of David, betokened utter abasement.

Rising, she slowly crossed the courtyard and, standing between them, stretched her hands to both. "My poor loved ones," she murmured ruefully. "It's because you love so much that you can hurt so much."

"I'm sorry," whispered the Boy, his eyes bright with misery. "I didn't mean to."

"If he could only have gone to Jerusalem!" muttered Joseph, gouging deeply into the new board of cedar. "Hillel is wise. He might have known how to get this—this devil out of him."

Stooping, the woman picked from the little chest all that remained of its contents, the box of sandalwood wrapped in a white napkin. Unwinding its cover and rubbing it gently with an end of her sleeve, she lifted it to her face, then closed her eyes, letting the awakened fragrance of it plunge her deeply into memory. The warmth and duskiness of a peasant's house with fire and candles glowing...the softness of a featherlight burden against her breast...the face of the third stranger looking up out of the shadows, framed by hair the color of goat's milk and seamed and wrinkled as the wilderness lands which encircle the Sea of Death, a face young in hope and old in pain... She opened her eyes.

"There is still the myrrh," she told Joseph quietly.

He raised his head, eyes sharpening. "That's so. The—myrrh." He held out his hand, took the box, sniffed it as she had done, and lifted the lid.

"The box is full," she continued, eagerness stirring as she saw the shrewd speculation in his eyes, "and they say myrrh is precious. Don't you suppose—" She paused, breathless with excitement, watching the bowed shoulders slowly straighten, the grim face light with a small hope. Why—*why* did it always take him so long!

"You're right. The myrrh can be sold—not worth a great deal— but it would pay for a few months in Hillel's school. The rabbi seemed to be interested in him. Perhaps if the Boy once got started, the Venerable One could find him some rich patron—or even take him for a protégé himself! Yes, it's still possible—"

"Do you hear that, darling?" Miriam turned eagerly, to include the Boy in her sudden blessedness of relief. Your father thinks you can still go to Jerusalem. Come here, son, listen—"

But the Boy was gone. It was another figure which she saw, crouched and cowering, just inside the courtyard entrance. Hastily Joseph rewrapped the box in its napkin and returned it to the chest.

"Deborah!" cried Miriam, running to her, all her being one swift outflowing of pity. "Welcome! It's been so long, and I've tried so many times to come to you, but always the door was tight shut."

Eagerly she reached out her arms, but the thin figure only shrank more deeply into the protecting shell of its drab dress and veil.

"Don't touch me! I don't want anybody—touching me. It's the first time I've been out of the house—gone anywhere—since—"

Nor had she left the house this time because she wanted to, Deborah continued, kneading her thin hands, only because after the men had come and it was all over, she had been so frightened.

Miriam pushed a low stool into the shade of the house wall and placed a cushion on it. "It's all right now," she assured her gently. "Whatever it was that frightened you, you're safe with us. Sit here and tell us about it."

The story was confused. Deborah had been sitting in her house alone, as usual, with the door bolted, when she heard sounds outside, loud knocking and men's voices. Open the door, they told her in the name of some strange god, and if she didn't open it they would break it down. Terrified, she had finally obeyed, and they swarmed into the courtyard, then, heaven help her, into the house, turning everything upside down, looking for him, as if they expected to find him in her house just because they found the door locked and somebody thought they had seen him running up the hill...

Patiently Miriam waited for the hysterical tide to subside. "Whom were the men looking for?"

Ah hah! Hadn't Deborah told her that? It was the slave, of course, the runaway slave from the caravan, one so murderous they had to keep him tied. A Samaritan he was, and if he wasn't found by nightfall, it was likely they would all be murdered!

Joseph's smooth-flowing adze missed its rhythm, bit deep into the wood. "A slave escaped, you say? A—*Samaritan?*"

But Deborah had told her story, and the hardness within her suddenly melted. She lay in Miriam's arms, crying.

"Hush! It's all right now. You're safe here with us. There's nothing more to fear, I tell you."

But even while her voice soothed and her hands smoothed gently, the woman's eyes fled fearfully to the spot between the olive branches above the courtyard wall where she had seen the face.

18

"COME," said the Boy. "There's no need to be afraid. No one will hurt you here."

His arm about the naked bony shoulders, he drew the cringing figure into the courtyard.

Deborah screamed. "Heaven help us! There he is—that murderer!"

Miriam's eyes darkened with horror. So she had not conjured the face out of her fears! There it was, wild, suspicious, malignant, just as she had seen it peering through the olive branches.

For once Joseph needed no time to weigh his decision. "Stop!" he roared angrily. "This house is going to be no asylum for runaway slaves, especially Samaritans."

"But please, Father—"

"I know what you did. I saw you. I heard you whispering together. Had it all planned, didn't you, told him just where he was to come! If I'd had the sense to look around, I'd probably have seen him skulking after us. Where have you hidden him all this time?"

"Nowhere, Father. That is, I didn't know he was there. I just saw him a little while ago. He had climbed up in the olive tree overhanging our wall. If I can just take him inside the house—"

"Heaven forbid! I won't have you harboring criminals."

"Don't bring him any closer!" wailed Deborah hysterically. "And to think I came down here to get away from him!"

"But he's not a criminal, Father," pleaded the Boy. "He didn't do anything wrong. He was sold as a slave because his father couldn't pay his debts. He told me about it."

"And you believed him?" demanded Joseph harshly. "Haven't you learned yet never to trust the word of a Samaritan? Lying dogs!"

Quivering with rage, the little slave drew his body to its full height and clenched his puny fists. The skin stretched over the rack of his protruding bones looked ready to burst "We're not lying dogs!" he spat furiously. "And I wouldn't stay here in your accursed house if—if—"

Escaping under the Boy's protecting arm, he darted for the door and disappeared. But he was back immediately, terror distorting his grimy features. "He's—coming!" he gasped. "Up the street—my

234

master—he'll beat me—put a brand on my forehead—*stigma*! Please save me!"

Miriam's eyes widened in horror. A branding iron put to the tender flesh of a boy—even a Samaritan? Her sensitive spirit recoiled at the very thought. "Here!" she cried suddenly, pointing to the inner doorway. "In there—quick! Into the straw, under the arches! Help him, son!"

Gratefully the Boy seized the slave by the hand and pushed him under one of the arches where the animals slept, covering him with a few armfuls of loose straw. Hardly had he returned to the courtyard to face an angry Joseph when the outer entrance was darkened by a broad shadow. It was the Egyptian merchant, with two of his Nubian camel drivers.

"You there, carpenter," he accosted Joseph brusquely. "Seen anything of a young ruffian slave, a Samaritan? I've lost one. Bad boy, murderous looking. Somebody saw him run this way."

Before Joseph could reply the Boy was between them. "No, sir," he replied boldly. "We've seen no bad boy around here. Certainly none that was murderous looking."

The merchant's eyes narrowed. "I've seen you before," he commented, scowling. "Where—" Light broke. "You're the young Jew who gave that same slave a drink of water. By your ass-headed god, I wouldn't put it past you to have—" He turned to the two Nubians. "Search this house. Look in every grain jar and wine cask. Take the stones out of the walls if necessary. By the breasts of Hathor, if he's here, well find him!"

"If he's here, it's no doing of mine," disclaimed Joseph with righteous dignity. "I am a law-abiding Jew, and I give no succor to another man's slave, especially a Samaritan."

But to the Boy's infinite relief, he divulged no further information. Turning his back deliberately, he plied his adze with stubborn vigor, the stiffness of his upheld head announcing to his family in no uncertain terms, "So be it! You got yourselves into this, you two. Now get yourselves out of it."

The two Nubians combed the courtyard thoroughly, looking behind and into earthen casks, overturning a neat pile of lumber, contemptuously and with deliberate intent upsetting two full water jars to look behind them. Then they went into the house. The Boy waited in an agony of suspense, not daring to look at his mother, who stood pale and silent, tensed to every sound of violent upheaval.

Finally they reappeared, shrugging their huge, black shoulders and erupting streams of foreign gibberish.

"All right," the merchant admitted grudgingly. "If he's not here, he's not here." He eyed Jeshua speculatively. "But you keep away from my caravan, young one!"

He had almost reached the door when Deborah's voice pursued him, quavering and hysterical. "No! Don't leave him here to kill us! He's there—under the arches—hiding in the straw!"

The Nubians dragged him out, cowering, and flung him to his knees before their gratified employer.

"Ha! I thought so." Seizing the cringing figure by the iron ring about its neck, the merchant shook the slave viciously. "Thought you could outwit your betters, did you, you dregs in a bowl of sour wine! Then, by the eye of Horus, I'll show you what we do to runaways!" He struck him a sharp blow across the cheek, then two more in quick succession.

The Boy could not help himself. One instant he was standing, stricken, every nerve quivering. The next he was across the courtyard, pulling on the long, embroidered coat sleeve, thrusting his slender body into the path of the blows.

"Don't do that, sir!" he cried out in anguish. "Please! You have no right to strike him!"

Out of sheer surprise the merchant stopped, one hand still poised in the air. "Who says I haven't the right?" he demanded with bluster.

"God does," replied the Boy steadily. "He who made every human being in his own image."

The merchant's mouth fell open. "Well, by the beard of Osiris!"

Joseph moved forward hastily. "I beg of you, pardon my son's boldness. He doesn't know what he's saying. We know this is your slave, sir, and you have every right to do with him as you wish. We pray you, take him and leave us in peace."

The slave twisted about until he could reach an end of the Boy's tunic. "Don't—let him—" he gasped, clinging to it.

The merchant gave him a contemptuous kick. "Bah! Sniveling coward! You're not worth the denarii I paid for you. Made in the image of a god, are you? I'll agree to that. The Jews' ass-headed god! But I'll make a decent slave out of you or kill you in the attempt! Out of my way, young upstart!"

But the Boy stood staunchly between them. "Even animals shouldn't be treated like that," he protested stoutly. "And he's worth more than any number of animals."

"Hush, son!" warned Joseph grimly.

"Hush yourself, Jew," retorted the Egyptian. "The boy's impudence is worth twice your long-bearded caution." Spreading his feet wide and folding his fleshy arms, he appraised the slender figure from head to ankles, his shrewd eyes registering approval. "By Horus, what a slave you'd make! Put your spirit in that miserable carcass yonder, and he'd be worth twice the twenty silver pieces I'll get for him."

The Boy's head turned quickly from slave to master. "Is that his price? he asked in a small startled voice. "Twenty pieces?"

The merchant chewed his lips. "Did I say twenty? If I did, it was a mistake. Thirty was what I should have said. Even a weak-livered slave like this should be worth thirty pieces of silver."

The Boy cast a swift sideward glance at the little chest on the table, its lid still raised, the white napkin humped carelessly to hide the square outlines of the sandalwood box. His warmth of excitement changed as suddenly to coldness. No, he could not. It might mean that he would never find out what his work was to be—or how to do it. With the contents of this box he must secure new life somehow, not just for one—the Samaritan—but for many.

"Take your slave and leave us in peace," demanded Joseph with harsh finality. Abruptly he returned to his work.

The merchant gave a brisk command to one of the Nubians, who seized the slave roughly and dragged him toward the door. But with one of his clawlike hands the youth managed to cling to the Boy's tunic. His face, upturned, was desperate with fear and pleading.

"Don't let him! You said I'd be safe!"

"Wait, sir," said the Boy suddenly. "Suppose—suppose a person didn't have the money but had something else that was worth just as much. Would you take it?"

The merchant turned, an amused smile on his lips but the glint of the crafty bargainer in his eyes.

"Well, Jew, that would depend on what he had to offer. But I'm sure a Galilean peasant—"

The Boy ran to the table and, removing the little box from its wrappings, thrust it into the merchant's hands, "This," he said simply.

Miriam made a slight movement toward him, then stopped as if frozen.

Before Joseph, intent on his work, had even sensed what was happening, the merchant had the box open, was staring into it with eyes widening in amazement.

"Myrrh!" he exclaimed wonderingly. "Where did you get this, boy? Steal it? By Horus, this is worth fifty—" His lips clamped shut. "I'm not sure what this would bring in the market," he continued warily. "Spices are plentiful right now, there isn't much demand. But"—he shrugged—"I'm willing to risk it."

"You, mean," said the Boy, "you will take it in exchange for the slave?"

"It's a bargain," assented the Egyptian. "The slave is yours." Gesturing to the two Nubians, he backed hastily toward the door.

The adze fell to the floor with a clatter. "Give me that box!" shouted Joseph as he lunged forward.

But the merchant was already in the doorway, the two Nubians covering his retreat with their stolid black bodies. "That slave has given me plenty of trouble," he responded cheerfully. "Whether I've struck a good bargain or not, I'm well rid of him."

"Thief! Swindler! Can't you see my son doesn't know what he's doing? I may be only a carpenter, but I'm an elder in this town, and I can make trouble for you. If you don't give me back that box—"

Joseph charged forward, his big fists clenched, and the Nubians, more brawn than courage, shrank before him. He had reached the Egyptian when a slim figure stood in his way.

"Father, please! Don't try to stop him. I have to do it."

Joseph's hands clamped about the slender shoulders. "Are you mad?" he demanded hoarsely. "That myrrh is all we have left. Without it you may never be anything except a—carpenter!" The Boy nodded miserably. "You'd give up all our plans for your future—for a dirty heathen slave? A Samaritan?"

"Look at him, Father," the Boy pleaded. "Can't you see he's more important than a box of myrrh?"

"I can see—my son—possessed—" muttered Joseph.

Lifting the Boy bodily by his shoulders, he thrust him forcibly to one side. The two Nubians fell back before the fury in his face. "Now, you son of the serpent Nile, *give me that box!*"

The merchant hesitated. He was in a strange town, and he had no appetite for trouble. Neither was he minded to relinquish a good bargain. He uttered a sharp curt order in a foreign tongue. But it was not the two burly Nubians who arrested the grim Nazarene's onslaught. It was the touch of another hand on his arm.

"No, my husband. Let him go."

Joseph stared down at her. "You, too!"

"The Gifts are his, Joseph," she reminded him, her eyes calm. "I told him long ago they were his, to do with just as he wished."

His anger exploded. You mean I'm to stand here and let my son make a fool of himself—drive a worthless bargain—jeopardize his whole future?"

"He's very sure of himself, Joseph," she answered quietly.

"But"—he sputtered helplessly—"it's absurd! He—he's only a child. He doesn't know what he's doing!"

"It was you who insisted on calling him a man," she persisted. "And the Gifts are his, not ours."

Joseph groaned aloud. He lifted his clenched hands and beat them against his forehead. "*Ah hah!* How much can a man be expected to endure? First his son possessed—then his wife! God pity me! I who thought myself blessed in my son above all other men! Instead—accursed—"

The merchant chuckled. "Oh, come now, Jew! Maybe your boy has more sense than you give him credit for. Slaves bring good money these days. Who knows? He may become a trader instead of just a carpenter."

With a cheerful wave of his hand, the Egyptian made his exit with his two Nubians at his heels. Out in the street he stopped and opened the box again, just to make sure he had not been fooled; then, smiling, he thrust it into the folds of his coat. The box of carved sandalwood alone was worth the price of the slave. Queer, finding it in such a place! It was the sort of thing you would expect to find in a king's palace, instead of in the hovel of a carpenter!

19

WHAT HAD SHE DONE!

Miriam's stricken gaze picked out the occupants of the courtyard one by one. Deborah, huddled on the stool against the wall. The slave, crouched on the stones. The Boy bending over him, working at the tight knots of rope which bound his wrists. And Joseph, poor Joseph!

He had gone back to his mat and taken up his adze again. But he handled it awkwardly, as if his fingers were unskilled in its use, and he bent low over his work, like a man tired with much labor.

"He will always be like that," she thought with dull pain. "He will never lift his head proudly, like an uncrowned king, again." Somehow she had failed. But how? When? Her thoughts raced agonizingly—if only I hadn't tried to stop him when he was trying to get back the little box! If I hadn't helped the slave to hide! Oh, Joseph was right, I must have been possessed, an ungodly Samaritan in my house! If I hadn't told the Boy the Gifts were his—yet they were, God knows they were! *If only I hadn't trusted him!*

The Boy untangled the last knot and jumped to his feet, pulling the slave with him.

"There! Doesn't it seem good to get those ropes off? I'll get some oil for your wrists, and my mother will get you something to eat. But, first, stretch your arms out wide, like this!"

Rising high on his toes, the Boy flung back his head and threw out his arms as far as his fingertips could reach, seeming to gather into his embrace all the bright sunlight streaming into the little courtyard. Timidly, the slave tried to follow his example.

"No, no!" The Boy could not help laughing at his attempt. "You think you're still wearing ropes. You're not going to be wearing them, ever again. And as soon as we can find a file, well get that iron ring off your neck. You're *free!*"

"Free!" The voice was scarcely more than a croak.

Patiently the Boy began again. "Come, stand here in the sun with me. Don't be afraid. Lift your head and stretch your arms to it. Let it fill you with warmth."

Miriam held her breath. So close was her bond with the Boy that even now, in her confusion, she knew the agony of his desire. In spite of herself she felt her own nerves tingling, the muscles of her arms and shoulders straining in sympathy with the slave's attempt.

"Feel it?"

"Yes," replied the slave breathlessly. "I feel it."

"Yes, yes," uttered the woman silently.

"Then say it over after me," urged the Boy joyously. "I'm free!"

"I'm free! I'm free!"

"Free!" echoed the woman, lifting her face to the sunlight That was what she had given him—freedom to grow as he would. Anything else would have been like taking a white almond tree out of the sun and rain and wind and planting it in an earthen pot!

Joseph cleared his throat. "*Ay yah!* Now that you've got him and given him his freedom," he said acidly, "what are you going to do with him?"

The Boy's arms slowly dropped. "What—I—I don't understand—"

"Where is he going to sleep tonight?"

"Where—"

"Ah!" Joseph contemplated the Boy's dismay with grim satisfaction. "You hadn't thought of that, had you?"

"He—he can have my bed."

"Oh no!" protested Miriam in swift horror.

"You see?" Joseph's voice was bitter with triumph. "Even your tenderhearted mother can't endure the thought. No! They may have been your Gifts, but this is my house, and, the God of Abraham bear witness, no Samaritan sleeps under its roof, no, nor breaks bread here! Heathen devils! Give them a crust, and they'll knife you in the back!"

The Boy turned to his mother in incredulous dismay. "You mean you wouldn't—"

Miriam shivered. She took another swift look at the slave. He seemed to shrink visibly into his cowering servility, staring back at her with sullen hatred. "Keep him here in this house? Sleeping in our beds?" Try as she would, she could not keep the horror out of her voice. "I—I'm sorry for him, son. I'd be glad to do something for him—give him something to eat—but—can't we help him without having him here in the house?"

The Boy's eyes were wide with hurt. In desperation they scanned the courtyard, lighting eagerly on its only other occupant.

"Deborah! You're all alone in your house. You need somebody. Couldn't you—"

She screamed in outraged protest. "*I!* Take that murderous Samaritan home with me? Let him sleep in my Joel's bed? Heaven forbid! Keep him away from me. Don't let him come one step nearer!"

"*Amen!* So be it!" assented Joseph heartily. "Perhaps you'll believe me now. There isn't a house in Nazareth that would take him in."

The slave tried to slink unnoticed toward the doorway. With a cry of dismay the Boy ran and put his arms about him.

"What they say doesn't matter." he cried with desperate earnestness. "Nothing matters—if you keep your freedom inside you where no one can touch it. I tell you, you're free!"

"Free—" The echo was filled with bitter irony.

"Please help me," the Boy pleaded, turning to the others. "He almost had it, and—and you're letting him lose it again." Meeting only hostility and pity and horror, he turned back desperately to the slave. "Listen to me. Don't mind what they say. You were alive a little while ago—free. Don't let them—don't let them—kill you!"

The cringing figure became suddenly imbued with vigor, but it was the vigor of anger and not that of hope.

"I don't want your freedom," he cried with harsh bitterness. "I— I'd rather be beaten and hungry than despised. I'd rather be a slave again."

Fiercely he struggled to free himself from the restraining arms, but the Boy held him. "Where—"

The slave was sobbing now. "I don t know. Maybe back there— to the caravan! To my master! At least I'm worth something to him!"

With a final desperate effort he twisted himself free and ran for the door. "Curse you!" he quavered shrilly. "The God of Abraham curse you all!"

"Wait!" cried the Boy, starting after him.

But Miriam managed to reach him in time. "No, darling." Her hand on his arm was gentle but restraining.

His eyes pleaded. "But I must, Mother. He needs me."

"No, son. Can't you see? There's nothing at all that you can do."

"Nothing—" He stared at her uncomprehendingly.

"It's just the way things are," she continued gently, her heart aching for his bewilderment and anguish. "We're Jews, and he's a Samaritan. Did you really think you could make people love their enemies?"

Feeling the urgency of purpose go out of him, she relaxed her grasp. The Boy moved slowly to the door and stood looking out, searching vainly for some sign of the slave, but he made no attempt to follow.

"That—that despicable merchant!" complained Joseph bitterly. "Now he has both the slave and the myrrh. I wonder—if I went after him—" He laughed harshly. "Ha! Even I am not such a fool as that, though I do have a fool for a son. The Egyptian would laugh in my face."

It was then that Deborah suddenly remembered she'd left her house open. "What if that—that murderer doesn't go back to his master, but goes on up the hill!" She sprang up wringing her hands. "Heaven help me, how shall I dare to go in alone!"

"The Boy will go with you," soothed Miriam. "Won't you, dear?" He turned, a little dazed. "Go? Yes, of course." His face lighted. He could show Deborah some of the places Joel loved best, the smoothest rocks, the little grotto. Then the smile died. He had tried before but she hadn't understood.

Miriam stood in the door and watched them go. From the courtyard behind her came the slow scraping of the adze. No smooth rhythm in its sound now, or spicy fragrance…no sunlight of bright, curling shavings. It bit into the wood with a harsh and grim finality.

20

IT WAS two months later. The Boy lay on his mat and watched the flickering of the Sabbath lamp on the walls.

Only a few hours ago he had helped to kindle it, bringing it from its wall niche and placing it on the stand, making sure that there was enough oil in the deep clay bowl to last until well after sunrise. He had helped his father put away all the tools and his mother store the hot food in the clay oven lined with hot stones and covered with many thicknesses of heavy cloth.

Once these had been joyous as well as sober duties, the prayers accompanied by singing and laughter and excited sniffing of the extra-special, Sabbath day food. But not tonight or any night since he had closed and locked the little cedar chest and put it away empty.

He lay with eyes wide and staring, watching the lights and the shadows. Perhaps he had slept and wakened. Perhaps he had not yet fallen asleep. It made little difference these days where he was or what he did. There were always the lights and shadows…thought flickering helplessly against blank walls.

His Gifts were gone. And the world was just as unhappy as it had been before. More so, if anything. Deborah was even more frightened,

Jonathan more despairing. The slave was still a slave, Old Simon a lonely outcast. All the gold in the world, all the precious spices, couldn't have bought them happiness. And the beggars were just as poor and hungry. It wasn't going to be enough, just to love people. *He had to find some way to help them love each other.*

When he first heard the sound, he thought he was dreaming. It couldn't be, not here, not in the middle of the night! Or was it the middle? Perhaps it was only the beginning—or the end. Then it came again.

Joseph was breathing heavily, and on the mat beyond him Miriam was lying quietly. Stepping over the two of them, he tiptoed down the stairs, slid the bolt of the door, and stepped into the courtyard.

The sound came again, and he gave a low, almost inaudible whistle in answer. "I'm coming," he wanted to call. "Please, Gad! You don't need to cry out again."

The lantern was hanging on its hook close to the outer door. He had almost lifted its leather handle from the hook when he remembered. One could not carry a lantern on the Sabbath. So close had he come to breaking the holy Law that he stood still for a moment, trembling. But there was no time for either compunction or relief. Hastily he unlocked the outer door and slipped outside. Gad's ears were keen. He had heard the whistle and was waiting for him.

"Hush!" Checking the flow of garbled sounds by a swift pressure of his fingers, the Boy put his arm about the hunched shoulders and drew the cripple into the narrow alley between their courtyard and the wall of Lemuel's house, where they were less likely to be heard.

"Now tell me," he whispered with sharp urgency, knowing that only the direst of needs would have prompted such a journey, marveling also how the crippled body, so lately helpless, could have dragged itself over the long mountain path.

Excitement and anxiety made Gad even more incoherent than usual.

"*Ah hah!* Tell me again," whispered the Boy in bewilderment.

He understood finally. When Old Simon had brought his flock back to the cave two sunsets ago, he had found one sheep was missing. Leaving Gad to guard the cave, he had set out at once to find it. The night had passed, and he had not returned. Another day and Gad had become frantic. His father had made him promise never to go into the hills alone, no matter what happened. But when another sunset came, he had decided. There was only one person in all the world who would help him and that was Jeshua. He could follow the path to town even in the dark. He hadn't wanted to leave Danny alone—"Gad's little lamb" —but what else could he do? Someone must watch the sheep to see that they stayed in the cave and did not panic.

"You did right to come to me, Gad," whispered the Boy. "Wait here while I go into the house and get what we need. We'll have to hurry."

He ran out of the alley and along the wall of the house as noiselessly as the shadow he made in the moonlight. Briefly, without thought, he touched his hand to the *mezuzah* and raised it for the kiss of reverence. Then, as awareness stabbed his senses, his fingers turned cold against his lips.

He could not go with Gad into the hills to find Old Simon. It was the Sabbath. Even to the stone hut alone the journey would be three times the two thousand cubits the Law permitted one to travel!

His legs froze. He felt numb all over. At first he could not even think. Then slowly, painfully, thought began to stir, but without getting anywhere, like a blindfolded beast on a treadmill.

It was lawful, the rabbis said, to save life on the Sabbath, if Old Simon was actually in danger. But even if he was, the elders would say the life of one *Cherem* was of no value! Yet he had heard there were ways people devised of traveling more than the prescribed distance. If one went to a spot two thousand cubits away from home before sunset on Friday and left food there, or even if one just sighted a landmark—say, a tree or a hilltop—and said in the presence of witnesses, "That is my dwelling place," one could go to that spot on the Sabbath and start one's journey from there. But it was already the Sabbath, and in the darkness how could one see a tree or a hilltop? And, anyway, both his father and Ben Arza had taught him to scorn such devises.

"He thinks he can fool God," Joseph had once scoffed grimly when Jered had practiced such a stratagem.

No, it was no use. Like the ox on the treadmill, at the end he was right where he had started. He could not go with Gad.

And yet, what about Old Simon? He might be lying somewhere suffering, maybe with a leg broken, or dying. By the time the Sabbath was over, it would be too late.

And suddenly the treadmill was gone from beneath his feet, the blindfold from his eyes. *Old Simon needed him. He had to go.* It was as simple as that.

Re-entering the courtyard, he worked quickly. Fastening an empty goat-skin bag to his girdle, he put into it all the things he could think of which he might need: a length of stout braided hemp, a hammer and chisel, an old headcloth he might use for a bandage, a knife his father had given him. He put on his sandals. Lucky, he thought, it was his leather sandals he had left by the outer door and not his wooden ones, which it was forbidden to wear on the Sabbath…before he remembered. As if it mattered now!

He took down the lantern from its hook.

The moon, well into its second quarter, was still high overhead, so he knew the night had barely begun. The town slept soundly. In the streets, they encountered no life, animal or human. But when they left the town behind and were circling the hill by the stony terrace edging one of Jered's vineyards, a shadow drifted across their path.

Heart pounding and throat constricting, the Boy lifted his lantern. "Who is it?" he inquired boldly, forcing his hand to remain steady. If he let himself become frightened here, on the outskirts of town, how could he bring himself to face the threatening darkness of the hills?

The thin rays of light probed into the shadows of a hedge, picking out a lean bearded face with curious eyes.

"Oh, it's you, Hanan!" he exclaimed in relief. "*Shalom!* I couldn't think who it could be—here—at this hour."

The nondescript figure detached itself from the hedge.

"Ah! The son of Joseph. As you say—I couldn't think who—here—at this hour. I just happened to be passing. I couldn't sleep," Hanan muttered apologetically while his curious eyes darted nervously about, from lantern to goatskin bag, on to the accompanying figure with its hunched shoulders and dragging foot. "But don't let me stop you if you're—going somewhere?" As if inadvertently, the hesitant words shaped themselves into a question.

Swiftly the Boy explained about Old Simon, and Hanan clucked sympathetically. "*Ah hah!* Poor Simon—what could have happened to him! I never did believe he was so bad. By the beard of Moses, I'd go with you if I didn't have—other business. But I'll be thinking of you, son of Joseph. Tch! Tch! What a pity! Such a long way—and on the Sabbath, too!"

Two thousand cubits. The Boy tried to count them, reckoning that each one of the slow, dragging steps must be the distance from a man's elbow to the end of his middle finger.

"Now," he thought when they had finally traversed them, "with every step I am breaking the holy Law."

But it did not seem to matter. All that mattered was that they should get to the cave before something happened to frighten little Danny, that he should find Old Simon before—before... The thought, like the narrow path along which they crept, had no ending. Always there was just the thin blade of light marking the next few steps they must take, nothing beyond it or around it but darkness.

They reached the stone hut at last and found it dark and silent; then went on along the side of the steep hill toward the cave. Already they could hear uneasy sounds, the pounding of small hoofs, anxious bleatings. In his agony of uncertainty the Boy broke away from Gad and hurried on ahead, yet not daring to run for fear of spilling the oil in his lantern.

"Danny!" he called anxiously. "Are you there? Are you all right?"

No answer. The thin beam from his lantern barely pinpointed the yawning blackness, which must be the cave's mouth. He played it frantically about, picked up a quivering nose, a black woolly stripe, the bulk of a tail, finally the heaped rocks flanking the entrance on either side. His fingers turned so weak with relief that they almost dropped the lantern.

"It's all right," he called to Gad. "Danny's still here."

The child was lying fast asleep, wrapped in his little cloak, hand tightly clutching a miniature shepherd's crook which Old Simon had carved for him out of wood. If the sheep had been driven into panic and had taken it into their foolish heads to stampede, they would have run straight over him.

Quickly the boy turned to Gad. "How can we quiet them so they'll stay safely in the cave while I am gone to find your father?"

Gad uttered a nasal sound.

"Fire—" The Boy stared at him stupidly, but not because he did not understand. Of course—fire. They must kindle a fire in front of the cave. Even though it was the Sabbath, when no flame might be lighted or extinguished, a fire must be kindled. A worse sin even than the bearing of a burden or the taking of a journey, the lighting of a fire. But Gad could do it. All days were alike to Gad.

"You—have live coals in the hut?" he asked hopefully.

The cripple shook his head. In the flare of the lantern his eyes reflected dumb misery and guilt.

"No matter," the Boy assured him quickly. "You had reason to forget to keep the fire alive. We can manage."

Hastily he gathered handfuls of dried grass and twigs and placed them in the circle of blackened stones on the limestone shelf in front of the cave, arranged above them a pyramid of larger sticks taken from the pile of dried wood Old Simon kept close to the cave's entrance. Then, kneeling, he opened the cover of the lantern and carefully removed the lamp, holding it close to his breast to shelter the flame from the currents of night air. Such a small, thin flame it was, and so much depended on his keeping it alive!

He held it to the little pile of grass with steady fingers.

21

THE HILLS were not, after all, a place of death. Life, or the threat of it, lurked around every turn in the path, peered watchfully from every crevice. Outside the thin beam of lantern light the darkness was astir with slinking shapes. Rocks and bushes crouched like animals. Silence was but the hush concealing stealthy footsteps.

"Ta-a ho-o!" called the Boy again and again bravely, in a high piercing treble. "Simon! Ta-a-a ho-o-o!"

He followed the path blindly. While on one side the lantern beam picked out clumps of dried grass or tangles of scrub, on the other it probed timid fingers into emptiness. Once the whole path slipped away beneath him, and he had just time to set his lantern on solid ground before sliding downward. His fall was stopped short by a rocky ledge but with an impact which shook his whole body. Cautiously, he crawled back up the slope. After that he moved more slowly, keeping his eyes on the path instead of on the lurking shadows. Except for the smarting of his hands, he seemed none the worse for his fall. Not until he stooped to remove the grit from under his sandal thongs did he discover that his feet as well as his hands were bleeding.

He knew that he was moving north, away from Nazareth, because, climbing, the path was silvered with moonlight, while, descending, it plunged into shadows. Up into the shimmering hope of light. Down into the certainty of darkness.

> "Though I walk through the valley of the shadow of death, I will fear no evil…"

But the ancient psalmist had not walked alone through his valley. A Presence had gone with him. Here there was no Presence. Deliverance from evil was for those who kept the Law, not for those who broke it

"Ta-a ho-o-o! Simon! Ta-a-a ho-o-o-o!"

Sometimes there was a response to his cry—the distant, mournful laughter of a jackal or the baying of a wolf, and once a low growl so close that his flesh froze. He waited a long moment then crept again along the path. No animal sprang out of the shadows; he breathed more easily.

He had not known there were so many hills between Nazareth and Sepphoris. There was no way of measuring distance except by counting footsteps, or time except by the moon's progress.

"Simon! Ta-a-aho-o-o!"

"Ta-aho-o-o!"

He thought at first the faint answer was an echo. But when it came again, after a silence, he trembled.

It was over at last. He stood close to the edge of something—pit, crevice, precipice—looking off into a shadowy depth. "Are you there, Simon?"

"*Ay yah!* So it's you, son of Joseph! I might have known. Who else would care? Look out! Don't come too close to the edge. Might start another landslide!"

The Boy dropped to the ground, face down, and wriggled forward. It was a precipice, as he had feared. Beyond the pale strip of limestone ledge a half dozen yards below there was nothing but yawning blackness.

"Are you hurt badly?" he inquired anxiously.

The shepherd grunted. "I can tell better when I get this ass's load of rubbish off my legs. Could have moved it myself if this left arm hadn't been pinned down. Ass's load is right!" he muttered bitterly.

"Only an ass would have tied a rope to a loose prong of limestone. I deserved to get myself buried."

Fumbling in the goat-skin bag, the Boy drew out the length of rope, then searched frantically for a stout object of anchorage. Finally he slipped a noose over a long jagged stone, pulled it tight, and wedged the stone into a narrow rock crevice. Then, clinging to the rope with both hands and gritting his teeth, he carefully let himself down to the narrow ledge.

As he bent over, a face lifted itself, and a quivering nose nuzzled his cheek.

"So you found the sheep!" he exclaimed joyfully.

"Ay. Foolishest one in the whole flock," the old man grumbled, "and the most disobedient. It would have served her right to let her lie here. Running off by herself and falling over a precipice!"

"But you went out in the night after her!" the Boy marveled.

Old Simon snorted. "Any shepherd would have. I couldn't have rested, knowing that one of my sheep was out wandering in the hills."

"Even if that one were the worst sinner in the whole flock?"

"The worst—" The eyes peering from the wild tangle of hair and beard looked startled and a little suspicious. "Humph! Trying to be clever again! I suppose next thing you'll be telling me that somebody once tried to make God into a shepherd."

"But he is, isn't he?" returned the Boy simply. "Remember—"

"I know what the old psalm says. You needn't tell me. *Ay yah!* So the Lord is a shepherd. I haven't seen him doing any hunting around these parts for any lost sheep."

The prong of rock pinning Old Simon's left arm was too heavy to lift, and it took more than an hour of patient hacking with the hammer and chisel to break it. The sky was graying and their bodies were drenched with sweat when finally the shepherd was able to work his shoulder free. But the pain which distorted his features was blessedly that of awakening life. The rock had been tipped at such an angle that the arm was badly bruised but neither crushed nor broken.

"God be thanked!" gasped the Boy.

"I'll thank the son of Joseph," retorted Old Simon caustically.

They worked together then, wasting no words, lifting the earth and stones from the imprisoned legs and feet, handful after handful. The Boy found it hard to breathe. The tightness about his throat was like clamping fingers. Slowly, he knew, dawn was breaking and form was shaping itself out of the void below, but he dared not look. He plunged his tortured hands into the sharp rubble again and again, fighting off dizziness.

"Your hands are bleeding," said Old Simon suddenly. "And your feet."

"Your's too," answered the Boy. "Rocks. Thorns. Shepherds—have bleeding hands—and feet."

Wincing with pain, Simon flexed his stiffened limbs, chafed the life back into his numbed feet, finally stood erect.

"You first." He pointed to the rope abruptly. "Then the sheep."

Hand over hand, the rough fibers cutting into his raw palms, bare toes straining desperately to find a foothold in the sheer limestone, the Boy worked his way back to the top of the cliff and threw himself trembling on the ground. But there was no time yet to rest. Crawling to the edge on his stomach, he watched Old Simon tie the end of the rope into a noose and slip it under the sheep's shoulders.

"*Ay yah!* Ready? I'll lift her high as I can."

He pulled himself slowly to his feet. "Ready," he replied.

No darkness now to hide the yawning depth. He must keep his eyes open to maintain his balance. His arms seemed to tear from their sockets. But he managed to dig in with his feet and pull the rope slowly upward. Then the sheep was in his arms, his fingers groping deep into the wool to release the strangling noose. No time yet to still her terrified bleating! Down went the rope again. He braced himself behind a rock as Old Simon made his way up the sheer incline. Pain from his bruised hands and feet washed over him in dark waves. He was afraid for a little that he was going to be swept away before...Then suddenly the weight on the rope slackened. The waves burst in one last rushing fury of foam, and he sank into them.

"*Ah hah!* A pity! Such tender young hands to know the tearing of stones and thorns! And all for such a miserable and worthless sinner! Would God I could have spared them!"

His flesh felt the soothing coolness of oil even before his ears heard the voice, very faint and far away, as if issuing from a vast height.

"No!" Even though the flood still enveloped him, making it hard to move, he tried to protest. "Not today—don't put on oil—medicine—mustn't try to heal—on Sabbath—"

"You say—*this is the Sabbath!*" The voice moved suddenly close, like a bird swooping down to plunge beneath the waves. "You did all this for me on the Sabbath?"

"I've already—broken so many laws—" Battling his way to the surface of the waves, he tried hard to make himself heard. "Had to—save Simon—more important than laws—walked too far—made fire—carried—"

It was no use. The waves were insistent, comforting, warm as a thick woolen *simlah* and smelling like a sheepfold, yet as cooling to one's burning flesh as the oil in the cruse which always hung from the girdle of a good shepherd

Thou anointest my head with oil—yes and my hands and my feet.

Then there was light where a little while before there had been darkness. He opened his eyes. A fire was burning on the ledge beside him. It flickered against the whiteness of the limestone, and, as he turned toward it, he could feel its warmth on his cheek. Yet the light did not come from the fire. The sun had risen. It was morning.

It was then that he turned his head and saw Old Simon's face.

A clean face it was, as clean as the contents of his shepherd's waterskin could make it. And he had managed somehow to tame the wildness of his hair and beard. The hands, too, except for their ugly scratches, were as clean as those which at this very moment Joseph was no doubt lifting in similar homage of thanksgiving, palms joined and fingers outstretched to hail the new day's restoration of life.

"Blessed art thou, O Lord our God! King of the universe..."

But the words Simon was speaking had never passed the lips of Joseph.

"Is that you, O Lord my shepherd? *Ay yah!* I know you now. I understand. Forgive me for being such a foolish, stubborn sheep. Forgive me, not for the sin you forgave long ago, but for doubting your forgiveness. Forgive me for believing that you weren't even as good a shepherd as I am myself. Forgive me most of all for having to be shown by a mere lad what you are like! But thank you—thank you—*for coming to show me!*"

The Boy closed his eyes. No, the light he felt hadn't come from the fire, or from the sunrise. Nor had it come from Old Simon's radiant face. Even now, with his eyes closed, he could feel it growing brighter and brighter, like—like the bush which had once been on fire with a Presence, yet had not been consumed.

He knew then that the light must be within himself.

22.

HE THOUGHT AT FIRST it was a bush or a stump; then, as he came closer, that it was a bundle of rags tossed beside the road by some caravan. Not until he had almost passed by did it occur to him that it might be a person.

It was a woman. As he approached, she drew the end of a tattered veil over the lower part of her face. Above it her dark eyes peered up at him through a tangle of hair. He noted that the hand clutching the veil was gracefully long and slender.

"*Shalom!*" he greeted gently. "May peace attend your coming, stranger. You must have traveled a long way."

"Yes." The natural sharpness of the voice was muted by the folds of her veil. "A very long way."

"There's a town just a little farther along the road," said the Boy. "It's called Nazareth. You go over this next hill and down in a valley—"

"Yes," said the woman. "I know."

"You do?" The Boy looked surprised. "You've been there?"

"Yes. I've been there. A—a long time ago, it seems."

"You have friends there, perhaps?" he inquired helpfully.

"No." Even the veil could not muffle the high, clipped sharpness of her voice. "No friends. Not there or anywhere."

The Boy stood looking down at her, puzzled and distressed. She had obviously traveled a long distance, for the soles of her sandals, dainty scraps of soft leather bound about slender ankles by frayed lengths of silk ribbon, were completely worn through. Her other garments also, though of fine, soft weave, were torn and travel-stained. In spite of her uncouth appearance she did not look like a beggar. For some reason her voice, muffled though it was, sounded hauntingly familiar.

"You don't know me, do you, son of Joseph?" she said suddenly, letting the veil fall from her face.

The Boy gasped. "Lilah!" he whispered.

Impossible that such a few months, less than the number of fingers on one hand, could have wrought such changes! A gray pallor, only partially dust, overspread the bloom of her cheeks, which, like the lovely smooth forehead, were scored now with tiny lines. The full lips, usually gently parted halfway between pout and smile, were tightly compressed. Only the gesture of the slender hand, lifted to push back the dull tangle of hair, was graceful as it had always been.

"You have come a long way," he said gently.

"Yes," she said wearily. "Farther than from Tyre, where I started walking." She shuddered. "Much farther."

"I'm sorry," said the Boy with simple honesty. "You wanted so very much to be happy. Jonathan will be sorry too."

"Jonathan—!" She choked on the word. "Sorry to see me like this? After what I did to him? You poor innocent child, you don't know men! Go and tell him what you've seen, and you'll find out whether he's sorry or not. Tell him I got the silk garments I wanted and that they turned out to be nothing but rags. Tell him you found me begging beside the road, not for sweet cakes such as he couldn't give me, but for a crust of bread. Tell him —yes, tell him I know now what it's like to—to have someone scorn you and—and cast you aside for another. *Ay yah!* Go and tell him, son of Joseph. I owe him that much satisfaction."

"Why don't you go and tell him yourself?" asked the Boy simply.

"I—go to Jonathan?" The dark eyes were wide with horror. "Isn't it enough to have to know that he despises and hates me without—without having to see it in his face? And after what I've done to him, he—he might kill me. Not that it would matter—"

"Then why did you come back to Nazareth?"

"Because—" She shivered convulsively, then buried her face in her hands. "Oh, heaven help me, I—I don't know why. I—I just came, that's all. I have no other place to go. Maybe I thought I might get a glimpse of him again—going to the fields or somewhere! Maybe— Oh, I don't know, I don't know!"

The Boy stood looking down at her, his face troubled and pitying. "Come," he said suddenly. "You mustn't sit here by the road. Come up the path with me toward the village. I know a place where you can rest without being seen. You're hungry. I'll go and find you some bread."

She went with him willingly enough, and he left her in a warm grassy spot where rocks hid her from view. Once out of her sight, in spite of his stiff limbs and sore feet he began running, following the path until it brought him almost to the edge of town, then leaving it for another less traveled path which led along a higher terrace and ended close to Jonathan's small house.

The narrow street was deserted. He remembered that it was the hour of the Sabbath service, and Jonathan would be with the rest of the town in the synagogue. Judging by the sun, he decided that the service must be nearly over, but the worshipers would not hasten back to their homes, as they had gone, in joyous anticipation. They would return slowly, as was fitting, reluctant to leave the divine Presence.

Thinking how his parents must be worrying, he was filled with compunction. Why must he always do things to hurt them? Miriam would believe he had risen early to go to the Hilltop—until he failed to return for the synagogue service. Never before had he missed it. She would be distressed, and Joseph angry. And their distress and anger would be even greater when he returned to explain! And even now he must make them wait a little longer.

To his relief Jonathan was in the courtyard of the little house. When he entered, the young farmer was removing his *tallith*, changing his best Sabbath cloak for the one he wore every day. He regarded the Boy with mingled relief and anxiety.

"So it's true what they're saying in town!" His eyes took sharp, swift inventory of torn garments, disheveled hair, bruised hands and feet. "You have been out in the hills with Old Simon, breaking the Sabbath. I couldn't believe it at first. You—*breaking the Sabbath.*"

"I had to do it," the Boy replied miserably. Swiftly he explained to his friend all that bad happened. "Can't you see, Jonathan? I had to do it."

The square features remained unsmiling, the dark eyes brooding. "Yes," the young man said at last, slowly. "I guess you did. Being you, you had to do it. But I'm afraid you're going to be sorry."

"I expect to be punished for breaking the Law," the Boy told him eagerly. "I want to be. I planned all the time to go right to the elders and tell them."

Jonathan groaned. "You won't need to do that. They know already. That miserable Hanan told them. He saw you—followed you—must have broken the Sabbath himself, but nobody thinks of that! Even watched you light the fire! And he took a witness along with him, too. They're waiting for you like a flock of vultures! I was getting ready to go and try to find you—warn you—"

"It's all right," the Boy assured him. "I'm here now. And I'll go to the elders right away. Only there's something I must do first, Jonathan, and—and I need you to help me."

The young farmer was reluctant. It was no time to be worrying about beggars, he muttered, and especially a strange beggar sitting by the road. Weren't there plenty of beggars right here in Nazareth? And weren't they always hungry? Surely one more or less didn't matter. Better to worry about what he was going to tell the elders! But, of course, if the son of Joseph thought it was really important—Yes, he would go next door and get a loaf of bread from his mother's jar...

As they turned out of Jonathan's street into the little path, they could hear behind them the voices of worshipers returning from the synagogue—voices buzzing with agitation, charged with special excitement. Jonathan looked anxiously back to make sure they were out of sight, then looked worriedly at his companion.

But the Boy was unaware both of the voices and of his friend's anxiety. He was too busy wondering what was about to happen. Had he made a mistake? Had Lilah been right in believing that Jonathan was like most other men?

"Is that your beggar? That bundle of rags down among the rocks? By the horns of the altar, it looks like a woman!"

"It is a woman," replied the Boy simply. "She's traveled a long way, and she's tired and hungry. Will you take the bread down to her, Jonathan?"

The young man turned in dismay. "I—a man—accost a strange woman? It's bad enough for you, a boy! But you've already talked to her. Why don't you do it?"

The Boy avoided his gaze. His feet lagged on the path. "I—should be going back to find the elders."

"Ay, that you should! Then let us not bother with the beggar. If I'd known she was a woman, as well as a stranger—"

"But she's—"

"I know." Jonathan threw up his hands in grim resignation. "She's traveled a long way, and she's tired and hungry. So be it! We'll have no peace until I go and feed her."

"Wait, Jonathan!"

He turned. "What is it now?"

"Be kind to her, won't you, Jonathan?"

"And why shouldn't I be kind?" The grim lips twisted. "Do you think because one woman wronged me I should hate all women? It's

256

the elders you should be worrying about now, I tell you! Then home to your mother to have those bruised hands bound. Forget the beggar."

The Boy retraced his steps a little way, stopping in the shelter of a cactus hedge where he could not see the path but could look down on the grassy place among the rocks where the woman sat. Urgent though it was to allay his parents' anxiety and then make his explanations to the elders, he had to wait and see what happened. It was not just the happiness of his two beloved friends which was at stake. It was somehow everything he hoped to do and be. Jonathan was the kindest and most loving person he knew. He had loved Lilah the way—the way God must love people. But he was just and honest, and he had been deeply wronged. Was love really stronger than hate? Stronger even than justice? Before you staked your life on something, you had to be absolutely sure.

He saw the stocky figure approach the grassy place with slow, diffident steps and take the loaf of bread, wrapped in its napkin, from the pocket of the homespun girdle. The Boy's fingers closed spasmodically about a spike of cactus, and his heart almost stopped beating.

Jonathan was drawing closer now. He was holding out the bread. But the woman seemed turned to stone. She did not even stretch out her hand. Suppose—suppose she kept her face covered, spoke no word. Would he recognize her by her eyes? Would some instinct tell him—? The knot in the Boy's throat tightened until he could scarcely breathe.

Something fell. The loaf? The hand which held it? Both. It was Jonathan now who seemed turned to stone. The woman was suddenly on her knees, hands outstretched. Then she had flung herself, face down, on the ground. Weeping? Were words of contrition pouring from her lips? Was she crying out for mercy, like Old Simon? A flock of crows swooped low over the hillside, beating the air noisily, their raucous babel drowning out all other sounds.

The Boy's fingers tightened about the cactus spike, but, though its barbs dug into his bruised flesh, he did not feel the pain. The crows passed over, and there was sudden stillness, as if time had stopped, and the whole world were holding its breath. A gull hung motionless in the blue void overhead. Even the caravan moving to the north along the distant Way of the Sea stood still like a string of painted toys.

And then suddenly everything was changed. A cry of joy tore the stillness apart as Jonathan stepped forward, stooped, and lifted the prostrate figure from the ground. He stood there rocking her, as a mother might rock a child, against his breast. The caravan swung gaily into a pass between the hills. And the white gull mounted straight up into the sky on a golden path of sunlight.

As the Boy's hand released the spike of cactus, pain flooded his body. He welcomed it, exulted in it, for it was the blessed token of reawakening life. Turning his eyes from the precious intimacy of the two figures merged into one, he made his way back along the path. He moved swiftly, without hesitation, taking the shortest way into Nazareth.

23

SURELY it must be a bad dream from which he would soon awaken!

Could this be Nazareth, his own town, its stone houses glaring cruelly in the mounting sun, its mien that of hostility?

He looked about the circle of dark, intent faces, every one of them familiar from his childhood. They had smiled at him, teased, frowned good-naturedly at his blunders, chuckled over his awkwardness, worried over his bumps and bruises, ever since he could remember.

There was old Abner, who had let him sit between his knees and kick his bare feet against the potter's wheel, who had praised the lopsided bowl he produced and waited patiently until his back was turned before reducing it again to a moist lump of clay...Eben the silversmith, who, before starting to go blind, had made him a little ring just big enough to circle a child's finger...Nathan the vinedresser, never too busy to let awkward little hands help in whitewashing stones and piling them up for jackal scares... Tubal, the jolly innkeeper, with his bottomless reservoir of adventurous, ribald stories...

These were his friends, his neighbors, his own people. They loved him. Surely they couldn't have changed, just overnight. Yet as he scanned their faces, he encountered curiosity, shock, virtuous indignation, outrage. Some, meeting his gaze, looked away. But nowhere did his eyes meet a glance of concern or pity, a smile of understanding.

Nowhere? Yes, there was one face. He could not bear to look at it, so full was it of love and concern and pity, if not understanding. If they had only let him go to her first to explain! But a little group of them had been waiting for him on the path beyond Jered's vineyard, had greeted him with silence and shocked faces and brought him straight here to the open space before the synagogue, where other shocked and silent townsmen quickly gathered.

They were not silent now. The excited murmuring which had accompanied the swift assembling of the elders had swelled first to an angry burr, then, following the formal accusation by Hanan, to a loud buzzing, shrill and harsh, like the rasping of a saw against metal.

Jered clapped his hands. "Quiet, men of Nazareth! Must your leaders seek the aid of Roman spears to make themselves heard?"

Other louder voices seconded his appeal, their very fervor defeating their purpose.

"Quiet, fools! Don't you want to hear what's being said?"

"Down there in front! You're shutting out our view!"

"Show us the lawbreaker! Put the son of Joseph where we can see him!"

The Boy felt himself hoisted by urgent and none too gentle hands to one of the broad, shallow steps leading to the stone platform, then shoved forward by an abrupt push which sent him stumbling to his knees. Picking himself up, he found that he was looking straight up into the face of Joseph, so ravaged by shock and grief as to be barely recognizable. The eyes, bleak and tortured, looked down blindly into his. He saw the thin line of lips twist and break open, like the gash of a deep wound, and then heard the anguished words.

"Not—not the son of Joseph!"

"You have heard the accusation," said Jered in such hushed and solemn tones that the crowd had to be silent in order to hear, "which our good and respected neighbor Hanan brings against the son of— whom shall I say?" He cast a swift, sidelong glance at Joseph. "Since my worthy brother-elder does not wish to claim the accused as his offspring, suppose we say—the *son of David*. At least the illustrious king, being dead, cannot rise up to disown him."

If Joseph heard the malicious jibe, his tormented features gave no indication.

"The son of David," continued Jered, "is accused by Hanan of traveling farther than the two thousand cubits permitted on the Sabbath. Much farther. And by deliberate intent. Hanan declares that he met the accused in a path on the edge of town close to the end of the first watch, *carrying a lantern*. He further states that the accused boldly announced his intention of breaking the holy Sabbath Law. And for what purpose? To save the life of a devout Israelite? Or even of an animal? No! To give succor to one whom the divine Law as interpreted by the servants of the Most High has pronounced—*Cherem*!"

The murmuring swelled again, but quickly subsided when the chief elder held up his hand for silence.

"So what did Hanan, being a loyal Israelite and one zealous for the Law, do then? In order that he might not accuse any wrongfully, without full evidence, he followed this son of David. More, he took a witness with him. The elders have heard the testimony both of Hanan and of this witness. They followed the accused to the hut of this outcast far beyond the prescribed two thousand cubits. They watched to see if he stopped at any time to partake of food previously deposited in some spot, which might thus have been established as his legal residence. He did not do so. He went straight to the hut of the outcast, and there, outside the cave which the condemned one uses for a sheepfold, they saw the accused break another law. He kindled a fire!"

The crowd dutifully gasped. But the keen edge of pious horror inspired by this further revelation was blunted by a drawling voice.

"*Ay yah!* Then isn't Hanan a lawbreaker too? He went too far on the Sabbath, didn't he? Why isn't he up there before the elders?"

Eben the silversmith! the Boy thought gratefully. He hoped that the voice was not as easily recognized by Jered, to whom the old artisan was heavily indebted. But at least he had one friend.

Not just one. Many. The half-curious, half-frightened tension of the crowd snapped like a taut thread. Horror dissolved into laughter. Even the elders, Jered and Joseph excepted, seemed relieved. Seated cross-legged on his mat at one end of the stone platform, the rabbi Ben Arza lifted an end of white coat sleeve to wipe the sweat from his florid face. Other voices picked up the drawled inquiry eagerly.

"By the beard of Abraham, it's the truth!"

"Why is Joseph's son any worse than Hanan?"

"Why pick on a mere boy when you have a man?"

Jered's face flamed red. He waved his arms, shouted, rose finally to his feet before he could succeed in restoring a measure of order.

"Silence, fools! Who are you that you should presume to interpret the Law for the elders of Israel? How many of you have paid all your tithes to the treasury? Or washed your hands always before partaking of food? Or sacrificed your first fruits if the firstling happened to be a fatter beast or sheaf? You see? The guilt is written on your faces. No wonder they hold us Galileans in contempt. If we elders had no mercy, we could impose penalties on every one of you!"

His gaze swept the crowd in grim challenge before turning upon Ben Arza. "Tell me, rabbi. Is it lawful or is it not lawful for the priests to perform such labor on the Sabbath as may be necessary for the defense and observance of the Holy Law?"

Ben Arza's hand trembled and he hesitated a long moment before speaking.

"It is lawful," he murmured unhappily.

Poor Ben Arza, thought the Boy miserably. I've disappointed him so terribly, just as I have my father! And he has to tell the truth, even though he's afraid of hurting me. If I could only make them both understand that it doesn't really matter!

"Exactly," continued Jered with swift triumph. "And when Hanan followed the accused into the hills, was he not acting in defense of the Holy Law? Who then in this congregation will dare to come forward and accuse this defender of the Faith of Sabbath-breaking?"

No one dared. Though few understood the logic of Jered's reasoning, all understood the risk involved in incurring his displeasure.

The chief elder resumed his seat and, before proceeding with the inquiry, cast a wary glance at Joseph. The carpenter's profile was enigmatic in its grim stoniness of outline, but the bowed head and slumped shoulders presented no enigma.

"It is well," declared Jered, resuming the tone of hushed solemnity. "The elders have listened to the evidence. All that remains is to give the accused an opportunity to speak in his defense. Then we shall decide upon his punishment. Have you heard the accusations against you, young Jeshua?"

The Boy closed his eyes. He was so tired that he could scarcely stand upright. His hands and feet throbbed with pain. The noon sun beating against his lids and temples made it almost impossible to think. Yet he must think. He must try somehow to make them understand.

"I have heard, sire," he said faintly.

"You admit they are true?" Jered's voice sharpened. "You did walk farther than a Sabbath day's journey? You did carry a burden and kindle a fire? You did give aid and succor to one whom the elders had pronounced *Cherem*? And all in defiance of the holy Law of God?"

The Boy opened his eyes. "I did all of these things, yes," he replied. "But I don't believe I broke God's holy Law by doing them."

Even the humblest, most ignorant member of the congregation gasped, and at least one of the elders lifted his hands to his breast preparatory to the tearing of his garments. Ben Arza stopped wiping has forehead on his sleeve and leaned forward with sudden alertness. Only Joseph remained apparently unmoved, as if his dulled senses had become incapable of further shock

Except for the sudden gleam in his eyes Jered as yet revealed no evidence of triumph. Slowly his finger relinquished one perfectly twisted, glossy strand of beard and curled about another.

"So," he prodded carefully, "the accused admits that he broke the Sabbath on three counts. Yet he claims not to have broken the divine Law. Why?"

"Because," returned the Boy simply, "Old Simon needed me. He had fallen on a ledge, with a heavy stone on top of him. He couldn't move. He might have died if I hadn't gone to him."

"And suppose he had died." The chief elder's voice was quiet, assured. "Would that have mattered? A man outcast from the congregation?"

"But you yourself, sire, just called him a man," returned the Boy steadily, "and don't the Scriptures say that man was made in God's own image? Doesn't that mean that God thinks he's important? More important than anything else he created? Even than—the Sabbath?"

"You mean," demanded Jered sharply, "you think the Sabbath belongs to man rather than to God?"

The Boy looked troubled. It was hard to put into words things which had as yet barely become thoughts. "I think," he said slowly, "God must have made the Sabbath for man and not man for the Sabbath."

"*You* think!" At last Jered permitted himself the luxury of triumph. "You hear that, men of Nazareth? Do you need further evidence, my fellow elders? The son of a carpenter, a mere boy whose beard has not yet sprouted, presumes to make himself an authority above the rabbinical wisdom of the centuries! Perhaps this noble son of David thinks also that we should no longer obey the Ten Words of the Law of Moses, especially that sacred word which commands, 'Remember the Sabbath day to keep it holy'!"

"No, no," protested the Boy earnestly. "The honored elder knows I do not mean that. The God of our fathers bear witness, I've always tried to keep the Sabbath until today!"

"Then you admit you did break it?"

"Yes, I—I suppose I did. Unless—unless God thinks it's more holy to do good than evil on the Sabbath."

The Boy sank down wearily on the step. He had known he could not make them understand. In fact, he did not really understand yet himself.

Somewhere in the distance he could hear the murmuring of the crowd and the voices of the elders arguing his case and trying to decide what should be done. Jered was doing much of the talking, and he sounded very sure of himself. Occasionally words, phrases broke through the barrier of weariness.

"You have heard the evidence...next thing to blasphemy... should be excommunicated...if he weren't too young to know what he was doing...the son of one of our honored elders...recommend leniency...severe enough penalty to teach him a lesson...always seemed like a good boy, though a bit outspoken...must not condone lawbreaking...old enough to suffer the penalty of his sins..."

Then suddenly he heard a new voice speaking, as familiar to his senses as the smell of ancient parchments or the ruffling of papyrus leaves. Timid at first but gaining in confidence, it was Rabbi Ben Arza's voice.

"Is it possible that the son of—of David is not so—so far wrong as one might think? After all, it is considered permissible by the rabbis of all schools to save life on the Sabbath. If your ox or donkey fell into a pit, would you not pull him out? If a wall fell, and you thought there might be a—a man under it, would you not break every law to try to find him? I even recall that one of the great rabbis once said, 'The Sabbath is for you, but you are not for the Sabbath.'"

"Ay, ay!" Others of the elders seized on the mitigating arguments with relief. "The rabbi speaks wisely!" "Let us rebuke the carpenter's son and let him go." "Too young to realize—"

"A few strokes of the lash, perhaps, and a sharp reproof—"

The Boy opened his eyes. So blinded were they with tears of gratitude that he could hardly see. Ben Arza, his beloved teacher, still believed in him. He had risked the anger of his fellow townsmen and a none-too-secure position for his sake!

The crowd-face too had grown kinder. It swam toward him through the blur of his tears, a confused composite of features, half strange and half familiar, as ready to smile as to frown.

"They're like sheep," thought the Boy pityingly, "without any shepherd."

But Jered was anxious and willing to be their shepherd. His voice rang out warningly, sharp with the urgency of possible defeat.

"Take care! Let us not act hastily, men of Nazareth. Is it possible that in the *chazzan's* seat itself sits one who would tear down the very foundations on which our Faith is built? Could it be that the accused derived these strange and almost blasphemous ideas he has voiced from the lips of his teacher Ben Arza?"

The excited ripple was followed by a moment of shocked silence.

"It could be," said the rabbi quietly.

The crowd-face wavered, blurred. The tears filling the Boy's eyes were of remorse now as well as gratitude. Yet of exultation also. For he knew that Ben Arza would never speak timidly again.

Jered turned to the other elders with grim triumph. "*Ay yah!* What are we waiting for, my honored colleagues? It's two we should be accusing instead of one. No wonder we have lawbreaking in Galilee with rabbis who condone it, who even teach it to their pupils! But at least we can make an example of the one." His voice sharpened. "Don't tell me you are still in doubt! Then you are not good sons of Moses!"

But to the chief elder's obvious chagrin his colleagues were still disposed toward leniency. They respected Ben Arza. They had known and loved the son of Joseph almost from his babyhood. For once they were tacitly agreed to forget the debts they owed to Jered. One by one and with increasing confidence they voiced the courage of their convictions.

"As Ben Arza says, if a life is actually in danger—"

"And is not mercy as much an attribute of God as justice?"

"Ay! For the sake of his youth, let us rebuke him and send him away."

"Ay, ay! And for the sake of his father Joseph."

"*No!*" The voice rasped like the harsh edge of a carpenter's saw. "It shall not be. God help me, if I must be accursed by having a lawbreaker as my son, I shall yet perform a father's duty. He is a son of the Commandment, a man in the sight of the Law. He knew he was breaking the Sabbath, and he did it deliberately. Let—let him pay the full penalty for his sin according to the Law. Let heaven bear witness! I, his father Joseph and an elder in Israel, have spoken it."

The sheep had found their shepherd. So complete and noisy was their capitulation that the woman's cry, one single despairing note, was quite drowned in the sound of stampede. Of course the young lawbreaker should be punished. Had they not said so from the beginning? Come to think of it, had there not always been something a little strange about him, not quite like other boys? Remember, there had once been talk…some queer stories at the time he was born…

The elders quickly conferred, and Jered rose to announce their decision. There was nothing now to threaten his hour of triumph. This young upstart who had twice dared cross him, who, according to a woman's testimony, had been more than a little responsible for his humiliating rejection, should at last be punished. He should know something of the contempt and derision he himself had experienced in his unhappy youth. The knowledge muted the triumph of Jered's voice almost to gentleness.

"Let the accused stand forth."

Wearily the Boy drew himself to his feet. Opening his eyes, he fixed them steadily on the curling strands of beard, which glowed and glistened in the sun like the seven branches of a candlestick.

"Listen to the decision of the elders, son of Joseph. Because this day you have broken the Sabbath Law and have brought shame to the house of your father and the name of Israel, I therefore declare that from the hour of sunset you shall be *Niddui—thrust out*. Since you have chosen outcasts as your companions, then go and make your home with them. For thirty days you shall be to your brethren in Israel as one dead. Let no blade put its edge to your hair. Let no oil or water remove the soil from your body. Let no righteous man come closer to you than the distance of four cubits. Like a leper shall you be unto men. If you die within that time, you shall be given no honored burial. Stones shall be cast on your coffin. I, Jered, chief of the elders of the city of Nazareth, have spoken it."

24

THE SUN was close to setting. Already there was a hint of purple in the deep blue canopy above the courtyard, and the shadow of the olive tree above the west wall had crept to the top of the stairs leading to the housetop. The reddening sun reached long warning fingers into the room where the woman crouched beside the sleeping figure. Finally she dared wait no longer.

"It's time, my darling," she murmured, touching his shoulder gently.

The Boy woke, smiled up at her, saw her stricken face, and remembered. His eyes darkened with pity.

"I'm sorry," he whispered. "I didn't want to hurt you. If—if I could only make you understand that—that it doesn't matter about me!"

She brushed his bruised hands with her lips. "It matters," she whispered back miserably, "that because it's the Sabbath I can't apply any remedies to heal your hurts."

He regarded her thoughtfully. "Yes," he returned slowly. "So it does."

"And that when the Sabbath is over you'll be too far away for me to even—kiss them."

"You can put some herbs in the package of food you bring to the cave tomorrow," he comforted, still in the muted voice that would not carry to the courtyard.

She shivered. "I—I can't bear to think of you all alone—up there on the Hilltop."

His eyes were very wide and bright. "I shan't be alone," he said simply.

With her help he made his preparations in silence, but they were few, since the carrying of even the smallest burden was forbidden on the Sabbath, even to the weight of a dried fig. He adjusted his clothes, then, after performing the proper washings, ate the food, still deliciously warm, she brought to him, for not once during the day had the storing oven been opened. Finally she brought him the cloak she had woven from new, strong wool and carefully embroidered with fine stitches for his going to Jerusalem.

"It's warmer than the other," she whispered, "and you won't have any live coals to make a fire until I can bring them to you tomorrow." She regarded him anxiously. "Do—do you think it would be unlawful if you wore two coats—one over the other? I—I'd feel so much less worried."

He smiled at her. "No," he said gently. "I'm sure God wouldn't mind."

As she helped him put it on, unconsciously her woman's senses appraised it, proudly, critically. The most even stripes and the finest embroidery she had ever done. Even Deborah would have been proud of it. An excellent fit, too, though already it was a bit short. She could not have guessed how he would grow in these months of its making. All in all, a garment of which no youth need be ashamed, even in the fashionable circles of Jerusalem...Then full consciousness and pain stabbed her.

Her hands trembled as they lifted the shoulder-length hair to slip the cloak under it, lingered under the pretext of setting free the short fine hairs springing from the hollows of the youthful neck, crept about the slim throat, cupping the firm chin for a moment before coming to rest against the familiar contours of cheeks and temples. Thirty days would pass before she touched him again.

"We'll be able to see each other every day," whispered the Boy comfortingly. "And four cubits aren't really much, no more than two good, long paces."

As they went out through the courtyard, the man sitting stooped and silent on his mat, all implements of labor stored carefully away out of reach, made no motion, did not even raise his eyes. At the door the Boy turned and looked at him, shifting his weight unhappily from one foot to the other.

"I—I'm sorry, Father."

But the man gave no sign of having heard, and the Boy did not try again.

The woman stood in the doorway and watched him go, her eyes straining upward and into the sunset

"Has he gone?" the man asked tonelessly.

"Yes," she replied.

"I did what I had to do." He spoke heavily, seemingly with no other emotion than a stubborn hopelessness. "When a man's sure of a thing, he has to do it. No matter what it costs him. He had broken the Law. There was no other way. You blame me for what I did?"

"No. I don't blame you."

"You mean you—understand?"

"Yes. Yes, I—I think I understand." There was a sudden note of wonder and relief in her voice. "There was no other way, was there? Being you, you had to do it."

There was silence for a little. Then, "Is it nearly sunset?" the man inquired.

"Almost. The sun looks but an arm's length from the Hilltop."

'Tell me when it drops below. The instant the Sabbath is over I must begin to make ready."

"Make ready?" She was only half listening. "For what?"

"To go after him. Make preparations for our spending a comfortable night in the cave. Many nights. Pack coals for a fire, mats for bedding. Two mats, in order that I may keep the prescribed four cubits' distance."

As she turned toward him, the radiance of the sunset seemed to have transferred itself to her face. "You mean, you're going with him?"

"Of course." His voice was gruff. "You didn't think I could let him spend the nights up there alone, did you? Naturally I shall have to return home each day. With the rainy season coming, and everybody bringing their plows, and only one pair of hands to do the work, with the Boy gone—"

"He'll be back." The woman's voice was suddenly confident, her eyes once more serene as she turned again to the doorway. Her gaze had to climb higher now. He had left the village lane and turned into the narrow path which led straight up the steep slope of limestone to the Hilltop. "Thirty days aren't long. Almost before the rains are here, he'll be coming back to us, Joseph."

"*Ah hah!* Yes. He'll be coming back," the man agreed, not bitterly, not angrily, but with a vast weariness. "And to what? All our hopes and dreams for him—where are they? Gone! All gone! Like the Gifts of the three strangers. He'll never make any real difference in the world now. He'll always be—just a carpenter."

The woman kept lifting her gaze to follow the slender figure climbing. She saw the last golden arms of sunlight reach down to enfold him as he went up and up toward the Hilltop.

"I wonder," she murmured thoughtfully.

25

THERE WAS no sound of young laughter in the little grotto now. The wind had died with the sun, leaving it a place not only of shadows but of silence.

Even the grass, which stayed green here longer than in any other spot around Nazareth, was pale and dead, for the spring had long since dried up. Thankful for something to do, the Boy gathered some of it to make himself a bed, piling it in the far end of the cave, then spreading the new cloak upon it.

Already, though the sun was not long set, it was night within the grotto. He had slept in the darkness of a cave before, on trips to Capernaum and once when caught in a storm on the way home from Sepphoris. Yet always before his father had been with him, and it had seemed a warm and friendly place, safe and sheltered from the danger and loneliness outside. Tonight he was outside. Wherever he went in the next thirty days, he would be outside. For he was *Niddui*, thrust out, despised and rejected of men.

Shivering, he lay down on the heap of grass and wrapped himself in the new cloak, covering even his face to shut out the empty darkness. But the cloak smelled of fresh bread and cedar shavings and of the sweet oils his mother brushed into her hair, and in a rush of homesick emotion he thrust it away. There was nothing then between him and the night.

Finally in a panic of fear and loneliness he sprang up and ran from the cave, not stopping until he had climbed up over the jutting rocks to an open space close to the hill's crest. There, lying face downward in another familiar stony hollow, he felt himself relax, the tension drain slowly from his body.

It was still daylight here. Earth hung suspended in that hushed, clear moment between day and night. The Great Plain seemed a nearby courtyard, Mount Hermon but a stairway leading to a higher housetop.

The Boy too became still. He held his breath, and his heart seemed almost to stop beating. Perhaps it was here now, the moment for which all his life he had been waiting, when he could see farther than he had ever seen before, when he would hear the Voice speaking clearly, telling him just what he was to do and how he was to do it.

But, though his eyes ached and strained to pass the barrier of the far horizons, he saw only the familiar line of hills changing from purple to blue to gray, the yellow shimmer which was the Great Sea growing fainter and fainter. And though he stopped even the gentle noise of his own breathing the better to listen, the twilight hush remained unbroken.

He buried his aching head in the outflung circle of his arms.

Maybe he would never hear the Voice, nor be able to see very far. Perhaps he would always be as he had been last night, trying to find his way through the dark by the thin beam of a lantern. It lighted up the path just a little way ahead, scarcely more than a few steps. But at least it was something, being sure you were on the right path.

He had not been sure at first. He had wandered all around, like somebody trying to get to the top of a mountain by walking around it in circles at the bottom. He had thought he could give life to people just by giving them his Gifts—things he could see and smell and touch, things he hadn't worked or paid or suffered for—when all the time it was so very simple! *He had to give himself.*

It wasn't the darkness which would make the coming nights so long. It was the silence. He broke it now.

"Father!" The cry, together with the words of an old psalm, sprang unbidden to his lips. "My God and Father! Why hast thou forsaken me?"

Even before the words were out, he knew the answer. God, his Father, would not forsake him. God would forgive him, yes, if he had done wrong in breaking the Law, as He had forgiven Old Simon; as Jonathan had forgiven Lilah; even as Joseph would sometime learn to forgive him. Always he had looked for the Presence outside. Now he knew to look within himself.

And then the Voice came.

"Son! *Ay yah!* I'm here!"

Wondering, incredulous, the Boy lifted his face.

"*Ay-ee ya-a-ah!* My son, where are you?"

In a blaze of joyous understanding, he knew that his Father was with him.

ABOUT THE AUTHOR

Dorothy Clarke Wilson (1904-2003) was an amazingly prolific American author and playwright, who published more than 25 books and over 70 plays, as well as writing numerous essays, poems, and other literary works. Dorothy was a biblical scholar and social activist specializing primarily in biographies and religious subjects with themes running to faith, altruism, and fortitude.

Her historical fiction focused on the lives of Jesus, Moses, and other biblical figures. Prince of Egypt, perhaps her best-known novel depicted the early life of Moses, was published in 1952, and won a prize for the best religious novel of the year. More than 500,000 copies were sold and it became the primary source for Cecil B. DeMille's famous 1956 film, The Ten Commandments, starring Charlton Heston and Yul Brynner.

Ms. Wilson's biographies were mostly about women who overcame the prejudices of their time to make a difference in the world. Martha Washington, Dolley Madison, and Alice and Edith Roosevelt, as well as groundbreaking doctors and reformers such as Elizabeth Blackwell, Mary Verghese, Clara Swain, and Dorothea Dix were all topics.

Other works tackled ordinary people living under extraordinary circumstances such as Hilary Pole, a British woman with a rare, degenerative disorder. She also put pen to paper about life in rural Maine. Books on India and its people included a travelogue and a novel whose subjects were missionaries and doctors treating the "untouchables."

Dorothy Wright Clarke was born in Gardiner, Maine in 1904, the daughter of a Baptist minister and his wife. She excelled throughout school, was valedictorian of her high school graduating class and began attending Bates College at seventeen. In her senior year at Bates, Dorothy won an essay contest for "Arbitration Instead of War." This experience began her lifelong interest in activism for peace and social justice.

After graduating Phi Beta Kappa in 1925, Dorothy married a college classmate, Elwin Leander Wilson, who went on to attend Princeton Theological Seminary and the School of Theology at

Boston University. After Elwin completed his graduate studies, he and Dorothy returned to Westbrook, Maine where he became a minister and she began her long and distinguished literary career.

She traveled extensively (Palestine, India, Egypt, Mexico, and England) always conducting thorough research in order to capture the authenticity of her subjects and settings. Over her lifetime, Dorothy Clarke Wilson presented over one thousand illustrated lectures, and received numerous honors—including Doctor of Letters from Bates College (1948) and the University of Maine (1984). She was the recipient of the Maryann Hartman Award from the University of Maine in 1988 and the Deborah Morton Award from Westbrook College in Portland in 1989. Other honors include the New England United Methodist Award for Excellence in Social Justice Ministry (1975); the Woman of Distinction Award of Alpha Delta Kappa (1971); the Award for Distinguished Achievement from the University of Maine at Augusta (1977); and the Achievement Award from the American Association of University Women, Maine Division (1988).

Today, deserving students attending Orono High School and the University of Maine are presented with the Dorothy Clarke Wilson Peace Award. The Maine Christian Association Board named one of its buildings, The Wilson Center, honoring her support of their organization.

Dorothy Clarke Wilson's papers (including many unpublished works) can be found in the Edmund S. Muskie Archives and in the Special Collections Library at Bates College. Ms. Wilson's work has been translated into dozens of languages and condensed into guides and digests for readers worldwide. Collectively, she is the author of 213 works in 473 publications in 17 languages with 16,154 library holdings.

Elwin, her husband, died in 1992; and her only son, Harold, died in 1977. Dorothy's own death occurred in 2003 in Orono, Maine after a brief illness.

www.ingramcontent.com/pod-product-compliance
Lightning Source LLC
Chambersburg PA
CBHW061558170626
46811CB00001B/246